A Land Without Wolveſ

Daniel Wade
MMXXI

Temple Dark Bookſ

A Land Without Wolves
First Edition Paperback
Copyright © Daniel Wade 2021

Cover art by Gaia, AKA Bekka Björke
www.thebekkaffect.com

Cover design & Typesetting by Temple Dark Books
Temple Dark Publications Ltd.
www.templedarkbooks.com

The Author asserts the moral right to
be identified as the author of this work

ISBN (E-book): 978-1-8382594-3-3
ISBN (Paperback): 978-1-8382594-2-6

'Everything seemed to find definition that spring—a congruence, a miraculous matching of hope and past and present and possibility. Striding across the fresh, green land. The rhythms of perception heightened. The whole enterprise of consciousness accelerated.'
Brian Friel, Translations

'It is oppression which has armed the people of Ireland - by justice only you can disarm them.'
Arthur O'Connor, United Irishman, 1798

'I leave to the admirers of that era to vent flowing declamations on its theoretical advantages, and its visionary glories; it is a fine subject, and peculiarly flattering to my countrymen; many of whom were actors, and almost all spectators of it. Be mine the unpleasing task to strip it of its plumage and its tinsel, and shew the naked figure. The operation will be severe; but if properly attended to, may give us a strong and striking lesson of caution and of wisdom.'
Theobald Wolfe Tone, Argument on Behalf of the Catholics of Ireland

'...or those who, like me, have seen their houses in ashes, their property destroyed, and their nearest and dearest dead at their feet; though they must forgive, they can never forget.'
Jane Barber, Diary

Acknowledgementſ

I am hugely indebted to The Gatekeeper and everyone at Temple Dark Books for their patience, encouragement, and editorial astuteness, all of which ensured this book became far better than it initially was; to my parents, Paul Wade and Julie O' Brien, and my sister Layla Wade for their (often heavily-taxed) belief in me in seeing this through; my uncle Brian O'Brien for setting several passages of the book to music and for introducing me to Wexford; to Katie O'Donovan, whose creative writing class allowed this story its inception; to Yvonne Cullen, whose writing retreat in Inishbofin saw it initially get underway; Sam Comerford, Sam McGovern, Justin McCann, Rachel McCarren, Liam Douglas, Graeme Coughlan, Peter O'Neill, Gary Grace, Rosa Kearns, Shane Collins, Frankie Gaffney, Marc Di Saverio, Kevin Wade, Frank Armstrong, Ilsa Carter, Rob Buchanan, and Karl Parkinson, for being available for chats, laughs, pints, Zoom calls, practical support, and all the basic essentials we've had to remember are sorely needed in the grip of a pandemic. It's been a rough and surreal time to be alive, but we've managed to get through it.

Part I

Chapter I
The Felon

"If what they say is true," the hangman murmured behind him, "then may God damn ye soon as he sees ye."

Breath steaming out in silvery plumes, Mogue Trench glanced up at the noose. Outlined by the glare, it looked withered and egg-shaped, a maw of agape nylon gently swaying from the traverse beam in the dawn breeze like a hypnotist's pendulum. He couldn't help but wonder how many necks it had snapped over the years.

Below the scaffold, a sea of faces was amassed. Some were emaciated, flat-eyed, staring up at Mogue, waiting to see him dance a Kilmainham minuet. It was an unseasonably drab day for mid-October. Flint-grey clouds skulked overhead, threatening to soak the city. To his eye, all things took on the general hue of pewter, as if the season had leached all colour away. Only the rich scarlet coats of the soldiers standing guard at the base, and the Kingdom of Ireland's gold-and-azure banner high above the yard, interrupted the dullness. As per the ritual of public execution, it had been hoisted to half-stand as he was dragged from his cell; it now hung toward the ground, as if in prayer, ruffled only by an occasional flurry of breeze.

A crow swooped down, perching on the granite; no doubt his corpse would make a fine banquet.

Mogue clenched his teeth and, though bleary from lack of sleep, scanned their faces as a sailor might scan the heavens for hints of an approaching squall. He had recognised the faces of both ally and adversary in the crowd all morning. Surely she'd be here, flapping a nicked brisé fan before her and trying her best to look incurious. And if she was, why wasn't she closer to the scaffold, where he might see her? Every face of every lady, he squinted to see; her presence would be comfort enough, proof that his departure from this world need not be fully devoid of hope.

But nowhere was she to be seen. Mogue stared ahead at the stone insignia carved above the prison entrance across the yard. *Let them gawk*, he thought. *You may as well be on parade for them. How many hope you'll break down and beg forgiveness through your sobs?*

He wondered if they felt disappointment upon seeing him in the flesh at last; no monster, no wild-eyed, bloodied assassin; just a young, feral-looking man with a limp, his cheek and jowl a patchwork of scars. His wrists were leathery beneath the heavy iron shackles clamped over them. He wore a torn, discoloured greatcoat; and to his gaolers' surprise, he'd asked for a shave before he was delivered from his cell, as a final request. Now, clean-shaven, he looked much older than his twenty-seven years; his face was drab enough to be forgotten as soon as it was seen. Sometimes even close friends had trouble recalling his features. Greying teeth. Hair soft and gossamer-thin, whiter than the soiled linen shirt he wore. Lean shoulders. But on the walk to the scaffold, he'd moved intently, despite his bruised legs, his hessian booted footfalls hard and cadenced as a drumbeat. And before that – as they had dragged him through the cobbled streets, through the mud and manure, through the loud jeering of the crowd, his clothes shredded, his legs cut; and pelted with anything they could hold – he had somehow kept silent.

From behind, he heard the hangman lumber forward, boots clumping on the rough oak boards. The noose was clenched roughly around his neck, pressed hard against his gullet; Mogue forced himself not to respond. Even here, in this place of extinguished hope, face encrusted in the filth of the streets and his own dried blood, some semblance of fortitude had to be maintained. They did not deserve the satisfaction of hearing him beg.

Far beyond the cracked parapets, over the rooftops, the Angelus bell from St. Michan's tolled grimly.

It was strange. He'd been surrounded by death and death's abettors since the cradle, yet his own mortality rarely intruded on his thoughts. But upon his arrest, a vivid expectancy had loomed in his mind. It grew steadily as a well-tended plant, watered by his interrogation, the hue and cry of his trial, the gavel's reverberation as the magistrate passed the verdict. It wasn't fear; at least, not wholly. More a sense of relentless, eclipsing finality.

He thought of shadows veiling the sun, church bells tolling their last, corpses of the long dead crawling up from their graves in revenance. Every precious second lost only enlarged the noose that now hung above him. Countless had stood before him, and millions more would after, for crimes both more heinous and more petty than his. Plenty more would stand there who bore no guilt at all, but the sentence had to land on somebody. All Mogue could think about now was that this would be his final glimpse of daylight.

Across the square, the chaplain intoned his homily: "Mogue Trench. You stand here charged, tried, and convicted of many heinous crimes within these realms. Verily, said crimes shall be stated herewith: murder, thievery, membership of a treasonable organisation, incitement to riot, the murders of Captain Joseph Shaw and Constable Ivan MacBride in cold blood, resistance to the police at Clonmel, together with a long catalogue of minor charges. For these crimes, you are to be sentenced on this day, hung by the neck, until dead. And may God have mercy upon your soul."

Months earlier, before the rebellion was even in full flare, he'd heard of the public execution by firing squad of a group of convicts suspected of seditious activity on the green of Dunlavin, in the County of Wexford. There had been no trial, no inquiry as to whether those men even warranted a death sentence. Suspicion was verdict enough. Yet he partly envied them the manner of their fate. With a firing squad, he'd at least have been able to look his killer in the eye.

Oratory completed, the magistrate called out, "Have you any final words to say?"

Had you been in the crowd that morning and were standing close enough to hear his response, something most peculiar would have been clear. Whether it was a trick of the light, some couldn't rightly say, but it seemed the man awaiting the noose smiled ruefully to himself – a crooked, upward tilt of the lips. Many felons before him had stood on that same platform, their hands bound, their bearings shrivelled. Perhaps you know how to read a face. Perhaps you've seen hulking murderers break out in tears, brigands cackle wildly at their subjugators, ill-famed madmen staring skyward with an uncommon solemnity as the final decree is passed, no doubt priming themselves for the union with death. To see an inmate smile, even dejectedly, is not unusual. It may be the only time in his life that a criminal would smile. But now the convict turned his forlorn smirk to the officials, before looking out again over the crowd. He held his fettered hands up, rattled them a little and demanded, "Does any man here know me?"

No takers. Strange question to ask at one's hanging. The convict's voice was cracked and hoarse on the air as his eyes darted expectantly around the clustered faces.

"Does any here know my face?"

Only silence answered him. He cleared his throat. Though known to pepper his speech with only the coarsest of invective, his voice now rang out with limpid appeal.

"Will everyone here remember my face?"

Again, he was answered by silence, with some people looking away. Most had no doubt heard his name long before today, shouted from pulpits and whispered in grog shops; now they had a face to go with it. He had no friends in the crowd; no one to cut his body down and drag him to the nearest grog shop, where they'd open his jugular and pour some mulled whiskey into it in pursuit of his own blessed revenance.

And afterward? Would they come to think him a martyr? Would ballads be composed in his name? Would he be listed in the almanacks among those who championed the cause of freedom? Would his name be spoken in hushed reverence, as if he were an unrecognised saint? Or most likely, would he be forgotten as the men in Dunlavin, his corpse dumped into some anonymous pit for the miscreant and the destitute?

The future be damned, his legacy also. In the precious seconds before the sentence was carried out, he decided to ruminate on the events that had led him to this place.

Chapter II
The Wait
Wexford, 1786

A mile out of the Tintern estate, the mail carriage slowed down. The horses snorted as the coachman drew on the reins. The two redcoats flanking the vehicle primed their bayonets. A half-moon hung awry amidst the stars; the sky looked polished as glass. Their timepieces stated it was an hour before midnight.

It was a clear night, and bitterly cold. The darkness of the road hunkered all about them like an audience, while the frost-choked ditches appeared like glacial pools of silver. Yet they had no need for lanterns; the moon was their guide. Its milky lustre flooded the road ahead, allowing them to see as far as the Abbey, standing silent on its grassy mound, fanged battlements surmounting the trees that surrounded it.

December was cloudless; the bare minimum of frost, drizzle and mist glossing the limestone, the trees defrocked of leaves.

Not a word was uttered by the coachman, the postboy, or the redcoats since Dublin. Departure time was 5 pm, and the sky had grown dark before they had even saddled up. As the city lanterns faded from sight, the postboy had tried softly crooning a ballad to himself but was glared out of it by the coachman. He'd held his peace since. The job ahead was too preoccupying, the silence too palatial to break.

This was the only road in Wexford safe enough for a carriage to drive upon. Ireland's hinterlands swarmed with highwaymen after dark, bands of armed brigands and rebels who hid in the roadway gullies, hands clamped over their pike handles. But they were not overly worried; the murk of secluded roads was familiar to them, and their destination was near. The driver flicked the reins, and they trundled on.

*

A mile away, the highwayman Joseph MacTíre crouched in the gravelly shallows of Bannow Bay, sea-green eyes scanning the darkness that surrounded him. He'd been there for over an hour, shielded by the lichen-speckled stone of the abbey bridge above him. The bridge lay just on the rim of the Tintern estate, its cutstone ribs straddling the Bannow's rapids in a crenellated series of arches and parapets, like the battlements of a fortress. At high tide, the river would hurdle under it relentlessly, spilling out toward the bay in a churning flow. For now, though, the shallows prevailed. The cold ensured some thin slabs of ice had frozen over it in parts, further curtailing the roaring rush.

MacTíre's breath was drawn in, and his ears were pricked for hoof beat thuds, the hollow commotion of a carriage. He lay on his stomach, the stony margent damp against his skin, even with the gloves he wore. Even under the moon's full scrutiny, he stayed hidden, his cheek and jaw swiped by the damp air. The tide's salty aroma stung his nostrils. He didn't mind the cold; in fact, he barely noticed it anymore. There had been a time when the damp chill would slowly infest his bones, leaching his body of all warmth, but years of sleeping under the stars had now numbed him to such sensations. His fingertips were grazed from crawling over the flint. The pink cuts and welts speckling his hands were a familiar irritation under his gloves, reminding him to keep vigilant. A few yards away, his horse stood tethered to a tree stump.

Ten minutes until the mail carriage reached him.

Every so often, his horse grew impatient, whinnying and pounding its hoofs, snorting hot grey tusks of breath into the air. Whenever this happened, MacTíre would creep over to the animal, stroke the grey velvet of its neck and make soft shushing noises, before sliding agilely back into position, tense from the interruption, breathing heavily. But he did not worry about getting caught; he knew the stream waters too well to give himself away.

Attentive to his attire, he was garbed in black, which allowed him to vanish among the shadows with great ease. This despite the weight of the guns with which he'd armed himself: a bayoneted carbine slung at his crossbelt, the blunderbuss he gripped upward away from the water, and a brace of smoothbore cavalry flintlocks, both pilfered from a redcoat officer. Although he wore a mask, mud also coated his face, along with the hilts of his guns and the buckles of his belt and baldric. Whenever he rode out in the glens, there was always the danger of the moon's glint catching one of the brass surfaces, so the highwayman never forgot to carefully darken his artillery.

Even so, whenever the moon crawled out from behind a cloud, pouring its light over him, he cursed it. It mocked his efforts to keep out of sight. *I see you*, it seemed to say. *Tonight will be the last crime you commit. I shall divulge your whereabouts without prejudice.* The highwayman saw nothing splendid or lyrical about the moon. It seemed to loiter in the firmament, keeping eternal watch on the proceedings of earth. A chalky orb, conspicuous among the stars. Even during an eclipse, it wasn't truly gone, merely hidden from sight. It swam behind clouds and sharpened to a creamy barb in warm weather. He never understood why poets and painters devoted themselves to scribbling about its loveliness, or daubing its acrylic likeness onto scraps of cloth. To him, indeed to all men who lived the life he did, it was one more thing to cut short his time as a lawbreaker, an informer Nature had set upon him as punishment.

Though still a young man, the highwayman had led his transgressive life for over a decade. Now at the age of thirty, he had on occasion marvelled that he had managed to survive for so long. Though he'd also remind himself why. He slept during the day, attending to his excursions after dark. He rarely risked showing his face in the daytime. The world smelled different at night, the stale dampness of the fields, the tang of flowers enhanced if the wind was calm, the salty whiff of seawater. Such smells he'd come to associate with his own genius for survival, and so he revelled in them.

A consummate practitioner of remaining hidden, Joseph now had only a vague notion of what the diurnal hours looked like. In early dawn, cold spindles of light rinsed the shadows from his hideaway, sole reminders of a world being blanketed in a timespan unthatched by darkness. Yet this was no cause for concern. Few men were better acquainted with the landscape and the secret places of Wexford than Joseph MacTíre.

Eight minutes until the mail carriage reached him.

For a while, the highwayman lay on his stony eiderdown and forgot about the approaching prize. His adrenaline dulled for a moment, before a sudden sting of energy caused him to tighten his grip on his guns. Now wasn't the time for rest. "Rest is for the grave," he hissed to himself.

Further down the saltmarsh lurked the dense and sequestered foliage of Tintern Forest, a knotted thicket of towering oaks and ashes that overstepped the riverbank. Their leafy ceiling was so impenetrable that no light, whether from sun or sky, seemed able to pierce them. Even the look of it, spiked and opaque, trees murmuring in a hushed frenzy as headwinds blasted through, was enough to daunt even the monks who lived nearby to walk in its undergrowth.

Again, his horse snorted, this time annoyed by a sudden gust of wind. For a minute, the silence seemed to evaporate. But it wasn't a big cause for concern. Both man and beast were accustomed to the wind, the jangling rainfall, knew to use them as camouflage and to read the deception in the noises it carried. MacTíre knew the horse was well concealed, for he'd trained it to keep from sudden whinnying or beating its hooves. There was no other strategy for attack. He'd wait for the carriage to enter his eye-line, then he'd leap up, pistols blazing, and shoot down as many as he could. He was an excellent shot, and believed that speed and not strength, the ability to move quicker and sharper than one's opponent, always won a fight. Yet the timing was also crucial. Attack too early, and a state of panic would ensue, and he might have to give chase. Attack too late, and the same state of panic would compel his prey to return fire, albeit haphazardly and without strategy.

With any luck, only two men would be manning the carriage, with two soldiers accompanying them. That was how it usually went. Four against one was a safe enough wager. And it was too much of a risk to follow them. Anything could give him away – a branch snapping underfoot, slosh of his boots through river rapids, his personal scent, or even a whiff of gunpowder drifting on the breeze as he drew back on the firing mechanism, upsetting the horses and lending awareness of his presence. He had to lay in wait, allowing some time alone with his thoughts. It was wiser to attack with the element of surprise, a lesson best learned under pain of wound.

Once, he'd waited for a carriage at the Campile crossroads, veiled in the rustling shade of a yew tree. He'd been barely able to hold his carbine up, he remembered, the weight of it lumbering his hands. There had been heavy snowfall that year, and so moving about was difficult. Not that it mattered: the footman saw him first. The orange afterglow of his campsite betrayed his position before he'd a chance to put it fully out, never mind the odour of smoke carrying on the breeze. A warning shot rang out in the dark, and the pellet grazed his jaw and cranium, leaving an ugly welt on his cheekbone. Though he'd returned fire, the carriage had managed to wheel around him and leave him where he was.

Lying in the grass, trying to dress the bloody issue on his cheek, he'd felt strangely thankful. They'd allowed him to live, rather than clap him in irons and drag him off to the nearest magistrate. He was young at the time. Hadn't even reached twenty. And he still had the scar, now a cord of white flesh running along the length of his jaw. People only had to see it to feel daunted by him.

Mercifully, no snow had fallen this winter. There had been a week of fog, but none tonight, for which the highwayman was sorry. Fog was a better accomplice than snow.

Six minutes until the mail carriage passed him.

Chapter III
The Courtesan
Dublin, 1791

"Will you be back the night, sir?" Still naked, the girl bunched her hair up in her hands before dipping it into the bowl of steaming water on the dresser in front of her. When she threw her head back, spattering a trail of moisture off the wall opposite, it hung, lank and darkly sopping, down her emaciated back. To his amazement, she didn't wince from the cold; just stared at him, questioningly, in the mirror.

Mogue Trench lay back on the divan, exhaled pipe smoke at the ceiling. It mingled with the steam rising from her bowl, smudging the mirror and windowpane like fog, curling upwards and needling his eyes. His shoulder was still numb from where her head had rested for most of the night; the ghost of her perfume still tickled his nose. He didn't answer right away.

"Did ye not hear me?"

"I did. I don't know yet."

He hadn't said a word since waking. The daybreak hours were his favourite time; that interval of grey tranquillity before the noise of the city fully reasserted itself, when he preferred not to profane the air with talk. In the laneway below, nothing could be heard, not even the odd dray wheel or a horse's brisk clop off cobblestone. The Charleys' night shift was over, he guessed; soon the first of the street-traders would be loudly declaiming their wares.

Without taking his gaze off the girl, Mogue softly patted himself down; his timepiece was right where he'd left it, as were both his folding knives. His belt lay sprawled where he'd left it across the chair, wherein most of his blades remained in their sheaths, oiled and polished of all gore and gristle. By the end of today, they'd be freshly reddened once more. His knives – the tools of his trade.

"Will the thief-catcher be there?"

"He better be."

"You plan to kill him?"

"I'll do to him exactly what he done to you. And worse."

"Worse?"

"Yes – my promise to you."

The girl nodded, and wordlessly laced up her bodice. She couldn't have been much older than fifteen, but she still knew better than to steal from him; everyone in this place did. They didn't like him, he knew, the girls and the madams and the bouncers alike; but he never gave any of them reason to turn him away. There'd be trouble if he did, and another visit that would involve cracked skulls and the parlour going up in smoke. But she'd no intention of robbing him; just wanted what he owed her, which was always a handsome sum. For that reason, she was the only one to whom Mogue enjoyed handing over his shillings, with the odd tip if she really outdid herself. He wasn't nearly as rough as most of the clients who darkened the place's door. And he preferred waking up in this room above all the others. She kept it clean, and her personal touch was evident throughout. The soft bedspread and the white cloth on the dressing table where she now sat. All things she chose to mark this room as hers.

She was pale, almost lily-white, as were all the girls in that place. The madam insisted on keeping them indoors; it gave them the look of courtesans. Of course, they painted themselves in rouge. Gentlemen and bowsies alike preferred pale and were happy to pay top coin for it. The gentlemen – the ones brave and depraved enough to venture this far east of College Green – because it gave them the conscience-killing illusion they were still fucking according to their class, and the bowsies because they got a taste of having risen in the world, if only for one night.

Mogue quite liked pale himself, though right now his own legs trailed out from under the blanket and an odd self-consciousness took him. They were tan and leathery like the rest of him, from years of sleeping in ditches and gulleys with nothing but rainwater to hold off the thirst.

Gaunt as she was, and despite the collage of scars marring her back, there was no sign of the pox on her, yet. The crisp dawn chill hardened her nipples, making them poke forward like soft jewels. The urge to reach out and take her back into his arms, shower her with kisses again, was overwhelming. He knew her bare flesh would be warm and delicate under his fingertips. Women like her weren't conjured in the poems he read in the book he'd lifted from a bookseller off Dame Street; yet he forgot how regularly he debauched her, how suited panniers would be hanging from her hips, her neck massaged with perfume. If she held her head high, she'd be nothing short of queenly. The tincture of a bruise marked her collarbone; he remembered running his knife-tip along it as she undressed for him last night, his breath quickening hotly as her shift fell to the floor. She'd winced as he traced over the bruise, her dark eyes springing open, but no more than a grimace, barely noticeable beneath the rouge dusting her bony face. Mogue was skilled enough that no blood was drawn, even accidentally. He knew all this about her, yet he'd never learned her name. Privately, he'd decided to call her 'Grace'.

"I don't know if anyone will be back tonight."

She turned to face him, her head slightly tilting. "What's that mean?"

"Just that and nothing more. What happens today, in the next few hours, could very well mean a different world for us all."

"So, this is goodbye, then?"

"Maybe. Maybe not. You'll know when you see my face in that doorway again."

"Assuming no one sets it on fire."

"It won't come to that. You have my word."

"How do you know?"

Mogue looked down; young as she was, she already had an instinct for when lies were being uttered. He knew because he had it himself. Life on the streets tended to sharpen such instincts. If he'd said yes, she'd be waiting for him.

"Why d'yis even have to do this?"

"I've commitments. I like to see them honoured. And what'll you care, anyway?"

She turned away, eyes unreadable in the glass. Mogue always noticed a girl's eyes first; hers had drawn him the first night he'd shared a bed with her. Now, they gazed right through him, piercing his mind.

Without a word, she stood up, wrapped a slip around her shoulders and left. Mogue made no attempt to stop her. Little point in compounding a lie with hollow reassurances. He didn't blame her; he was a reliable source of income that she'd now lost forever. After a moment he dressed and left the brothel, making for Meath Street.

An early sun crimsoned the sky, and Dublin was still dragging itself out of sleep. The caws of seagulls, shrill and high, resounded on the breeze. Everywhere else had a lone nightingale or rooster to herald the dawn, it seemed to Mogue; Dublin had a full choir of seagulls.

Mogue kept his head down, the tobacco in his lungs scalding anew. The pavements' cracks and dirt were all the more conspicuous in the dawn glare, but Mogue barely noticed it. It had rained heavily in the night, and puddles still blotched the cobblestones, thick as turf or porter. By midday they'd be burnt away.

At this hour, in the growing heat, the city was a riot of scents both pleasing and putrid, from sea-winds wafting coolly inland and barley roasting pungently from St. James' Gate; to the stench of vomit pooling in doorways and streets steaming with horse dung. All were eclipsed, however, by the Liffey's sulphurous reek, an odour every Dubliner knew intimately, mingled from brine and raw sewage that the wind whipped into a frenzy, causing people to hold their noses and quicken their pace. As he moved briskly across Essex Street Bridge, Mogue found his eyes stinging.

Glancing downstream, toward the harbour and where the river spilled into the bay, he saw a squad of navvies swarm over the humped, skeletal arch of the new Carlisle Bridge. Their pickaxes' heavy clink off granite and the orders they snarled and bellowed to one another as huge slabs of Portland stone were hauled into place glided on the wind like clarion calls. Mogue didn't let go of his breath until he reached the southside quays.

McClear, a lamplighter on Parliament Street, nodded wordlessly as he hoisted his pole into the mantle to douse the tiny flame within. Mogue knew his face, having bribed him for tasty information several times already, and had never found him to be a liar. He nodded back without breaking his stride, his blood starting to pump with each footstep; right now, he knew all he needed to know. The knives slung in his belt, hidden beneath his greatcoat, knocked gently off his thighs and ribs, goading him further, faster. If all went well today, McClear would get double what Mogue gave him originally.

Today was definitely a day for smiling, and to kick up a good dust.

Chapter IV
The Crucible
Wexford, 1786

Joseph hated nights like this. Clear, moonlit, bitingly cool. But he hated being so close to the Bannow River even more, for it dredged up memories of his older brother, memories he had forced himself to bury in his mind's inmost vault that now clawed their way back to plague him.

Despite this, there were nights when he found himself trundling out to its banks, hoping to drink in its ever-flowing calm. It was a ritual of sorts for him, a means of expunging any remorse he occasionally felt for his crimes. He would dismount and lead the horse over the bridge by its tether, moving slowly, instinctively, boot-heels scraping the gravelled floor, reverent as a pilgrim in the temple.

Whenever he did this, he'd often remember helping his brother and their parents drag a haywain laden with the day's produce to the community fair across that very bridge. The MacTíre family were cottiers, eking an existence living in a ramshackle, one-roomed cabin tucked away in the Kilmore foothills, proximate to the roadside on the estate of Fethard. They rented from one of the tenant farmers there, with less than an acre to their name. Redmond, Joseph, and their sister Fiadh were only three of six siblings to survive beyond childhood. As a result, they had grown up in a world of hunting for game in the dense forests in the neighbouring Tintern estate, poaching for salmon in the nearby stream, gathering bundles of tree branches for kindling.

The MacTíre siblings learned to read and write at a hedge-school near the limestone quarry at Herrylock – an illegal academy for children of the subtenants in the region. The school, a converted limekiln with red sandstone walls, was kept by a man called Hugh Ó Doirnín, a spindly, red-faced *spailpín* and amateur pedagogue from the County Louth, who harboured an undisguised fondness for poitín and who advertised his schoolmasterly services on the myriad, garishly painted signs adorning the hovel's door:

To Parents and Guardians. Wex. Such Parents and Guardians as may wish to Entrust their Children for Education in its Fullest Extent to Maestro Hugh Ó Doirnín, shall have said advantage at Herrylock of Church Street Chape. Also Licens'd to Buy and sell Liquor, Dry Goods, Etc.

The MacTíre children had been among dozens of local boys and girls to attend this covert academy, for as much as having a place to keep warm as for curiosity for the texts. Despite being in the direct path of icy sea winds that howled and lashed in from the peninsula, Ó Doirnín kept it heated by means of a small nook he'd converted into a hearth, periodically tossing slabs of peat – a perk from the seasonal labour he performed footing turf on the bog – from a steel pail onto its smouldering embers as he extolled the doctrines of Diogenes.

The promise of warmth and the thrill of reading kept Joseph and Fiadh returning, even as Redmond finally lost interest. From the bench seat where Joseph knelt, hunched over a tattered, coverless copybook he'd shared with his sister, he scratched out the rules of grammar with a grey goose quill, imitating the dusty white hieroglyphs Ó Doirnín – whose powers of erudition hastened to make him the literary guiding light of the parish – chalked on the black slate board pinned to the far wall, his haughty oration running through the full gamut of Ireland's melancholy history with endlessly aggrieved eloquence.

By the calming growl of waves and sea-wind buffeting the walls in hurtling, banshee-like screeches, the shaped splotches of ink on the flyblown page offered themselves to him, becoming more and more recognisable, fascinating him, luring him back. The solid weight of a book in his hand, the promise of what was stored within. Ó Doirnín showed them everything: the shapes and sizes of the alphabet, the gradual alchemy of sentences and paragraphs, the myriad dexterities they could be used for, and the sheer joy of a blackened page. Joseph murmured them to himself, forcing his tongue to take on their shape, his

xvi

accent to reproduce them, surround by the low hum of Fiadh and his fellow scholars taking in the day's lesson or Ó Doirnín's lordly voice urging them to heed their Greek. The master did not hesitate to wield his rod on the more unruly pupils, but there was little sadism in him. Joseph scraped his own name onto a bit of slate with chalk, admiring the skeletal cut of the lettering as a smith might admire a newly forged skein, realising he could use it against others.

"You, lad. On what isle did Aeneas make landfall after departing Buthrotum?"

"Eh, the Isle of the Cyclopes."

"Isle of the Cyclopes what, boy?"

"Isle of the Cyclopes, sir!"

"And whom do they encounter whilst there?"

"Sir, they meet the man Acha...Achamenides."

"And he is...?"

"Eh...the sole survivor of Ulixes' crew. Sir."

"Aye. Indeed he was, lad. Indeed he was."

A wealth of knowledge was before him. Fiadh's preferences ran to those of geography and natural history, but his own passions ran to English and Greek as fields of study. There were the laws of grammar, the declension that formed the ending of a Latin noun, the sussuration of Greek idioms. A verb held the glimmering of some grand adventure. As the rich aroma of peat smoke permeated the air like fog, Joseph's breath quickened as he traced over sentence after sentence, paragraph after paragraph, feeling himself steadily gaining mastery over it. It was like discovering terrain and knowing its dangers well enough to anticipate them.

And, of course, there were the stories relayed to him. The simple precision of a poem in octosyllables.

He could do it all day long if he were allowed. But he knew he wasn't. There was always work to be done, always another task to be aware of and executed. And besides, books were better for little more than firewood, his father and Redmond agreed.

Joseph recalled an afternoon their father had brought he and Fiadh to a market, the cart shuffling behind them. Their father had set up in the village square and asked them to stay put while he saw to some matters in the nearby tavern. Joseph sat back happily on the cart, unconcerned by his father's growing absence or Fiadh's boredom, ignoring the shadows' slow shift as afternoon morphed into evening, the tattered Euclid's *Elements* he stole from the school room holding all his attention.

It was then that he saw wolves for the first time: a local huntsman had dragged a wain into the square, and Joseph saw creatures trussed up in the back of it, bristly, blood-flecked legs hanging out over the edge, as if they were resting. The man had roughly drawn the burlap back to reveal three stiff, grey-furred wolfhounds trussed together by strands of linen, their maws still agape and faces burst apart from where the bullets had bit through them. Joseph still recalled his heart heaving to a standstill upon seeing them, while Fiadh's eyes were wide under the coppery thatch of her hair.

The walks to and from the places where such resources were in plentiful supply became expeditions unto themselves. The land surrounding their home was hilly and treeless, at the ongoing mercy of wind and rain. Morning dew varnished the grass on clear days. Lousewort infested the sagging thatched roof. Rainwater wept through the gauzy rafters. Decay smeared the walls. Driving winds cuffed the lone windowpane. Only the candles Joseph and his brother had filched from the cloister in Ramsgrange church kept the place well lit, and the turf fire in the hearth staved off the relentless cold.

Their schooling was cut abruptly short when it came to light that Ó Doirnín had been instructing them in Latin – a most grave offence that brought the local magistrate to his door. Arrested on suspicion of teaching seditious material, the school was shut down and its pupils dispersed - though not before Joseph managed to lift the few remaining books that hadn't been confiscated from Ó Doirnín's quarters to be used as evidence against him at trial.

Redmond MacTíre, his brother, had been a jack-of-all-trades, a hunter of work. As Papists, the MacTíre men hadn't a hope of toiling in any profession higher than that of water-drawing or woodcutting. Soldiering was off limits, as was service aboard one of His Majesty's warships. Nonetheless, the highwayman tagged along with his brother and their father on whatever donkey work they happened to be tasked with, helping however he could, his instinct and respect for labour growing, while Fiadh and their mother had worked as scullery maids in the Ely mansion. They spoke to each other in Gaelic, though both understood English well enough.

'Tis strange, he thought. *Since their deaths, the nights have become clearer.*

After the sudden deaths of their parents in the winter of '67, shortly after the school's closure, and with no other surviving relatives to turn to, Redmond assumed responsibility over the household. Fortunately, the years of working in odd jobs had served them well, and Fiadh for a time managed to keep her scullery position. Along with the farming, there was never a shortage of physical work for them to do.

The MacTíre brothers. That had been how people referred to he and Redmond. It was the name he responded to still, with habitual instinct born of familiarity. A name more befitting of a colliery, or a pair of local craftsmen. Yet it signalled them as Papist, suggesting immediately what church they attended and what prayers passed their lips. Not quite landowners or tithe protectors, yet still quietly respected by the Fethard tenantry. Their name was better than any title or style, for they'd no need to wield it over their peers with high-handed conceit. People trusted them, knew they were dependable. Yet whatever job paid, Redmond did it, much as his ability would allow him and with no complaint. He repaired carriage wheels, hewed timber in the bunched groves of Tintern Forest for the fair or the market, wove wool on a mill floor in Enniscorthy, burnt charcoal in the local kiln, helped the wagon-men haul slabs of crushed ore from the lead mines to Arklow port. Together, the brothers footed turf on the bogs in Ferrycarrig, plied the waterways along the peninsula for coalfish and whiting in a currach Redmond had built from the felled wood of a fir tree. Redmond led their horse, a seal-brown gelding christened St. Eligius in honour of the day on which he had been bought, on all these jobs, tethering him to the trees that bristled the shore. He undertook every job with the same druidic calm, the same quiet fervour of a man who prided himself on the severity of labour.

The highwayman remembered his brother's boundless strength. Redmond's arms had been solid as the kindling he chopped, his shoulders rounded and sinewy from years of labour in the quarries, his face leathery from raw lashings of wind that swept through that region. At times, he seemed to be born old, elderly before he'd even reached twenty; an air of yielding stoicism hung off him. Still, he'd been kind, had a pleasant voice and laugh, and was a frequent smiler. He was often seen at local dances and in the *sibíns* dotted around the country, played the fiddle at wakes and dances, and never seemed to want for company. He wasn't a heavy drinker, but he knew how to keep the laughter alive. In different clothes, he could have easily been mistaken for a lord's son, or a junior army officer, dancing with rouged ladies in the manor of a local viscount or leading a regiment of Redcoats into battle.

When he eventually found them permanent work in a local tanner's forge, heaving coal and chopped wood into the furnace to keep the flames going, he often returned home reeking of dead cinders. But that was the job that made both brothers strong. Their muscles swelled; their gaits became slower, more upright, but more assured, more ready for the world. People knew them, held them in quiet regard.

Redmond and Fiadh helped washerwomen carry their bundles from the river free of charge, Redmond's eyes appearing to dance. Joseph, by contrast, suspected they thought him surly, snivelling, too dependent on his brother to make a solid decision, yet dependable with any task set to him. Meanwhile Fiadh, with her sea-green eyes and uncombed auburn locks, was the subject of much malignant gossip from the women, and wolfish looks and remarks from the men.

Fear of what her eldest brother might do in retaliation should they ever lay a hand on her was all that kept them at bay. Not that she was ill-equipped to fend for herself. Once, she had been passing through the square in Fethard when a group of village lads outside the alehouse, already plunged in drink, had hollered all manner of lewd remarks at her. "I'd make a woman of you, Fee", and so forth. It would have been left at that, too, were it not for one of them attempting to make a drunken grab for her, and miss, much to his companions' lusty mirth. Joseph made to charge them but Fiadh's hand on his shoulder had stopped him in his tracks.

Without a word, she approached the leader, a butcher's apprentice named Tully, with a sweet smile ghosting her lips. Without warning, she grabbed him by the coat lapels and slammed her forehead against his nose, breaking it instantly. As Tully fell back in a haze of blood and screams and his comrades' drunken scrambling to aid him, Fiadh and Joseph had fled for their cabin, their laughter harmonious upon the air.

Because of things like this, he knew, they tended to invoke suspicion and wariness in the locality.

Popular and admired as Redmond was, people blessed themselves whenever he passed. Nor was he immune to the occasional rumour circling about him: he was a member of the Ribbonmen; he brewed poitín in a secluded distillery in the foothills; he and his brother were the illegitimate sons of a highly respected local magistrate. Redmond had always laughed such intimations off. But the highwayman had to admit, there were times when even he had felt slightly afraid of him, as much as he'd been enthralled. At dances and *céilís*, when called on to tell one of his stories, a savage brightness glazed his brother's eye whenever he told one of his deathly yarns. Under a murky pall of pipe smoke, his normally gracious deportment seemed to wash away, replaced by the raw wildness of the story being told. His voice sank an octave lower, shifted a pitch wilder, his accent sharpened. His stories were blustery accounts of crime and cruelty, of cave-dwelling hags who drank the blood of new-borns, cloven-hoofed men who seduced gullible young women over a game of cards before vanishing through the roof in a fiery blast, or convicts sentenced to hang who burst into flames the moment the hatchet door slid open beneath their feet; and, of course, of the

Sluagh na marbh – that horde of ghostly souls who ranged the air on the lookout for prey.

The stories he relayed seemed conjured from some diabolical source – yarns of robberies, or duels held in open fields; hangings and savage inclination, and roving bands of *ropairí*, those gentlemen of the road born into wealth now driven to lives of thievery; godless rogues and cutpurses who lurked on horseback on the high-roads and bye-passages in the dead of night, springing from knots of furze where they kept hidden, to attack travellers; all men with little or no hope of salvation or even the king's pardon, and all destined in the end to be fodder for the gallows. Given the current colour of his lens, Joseph often wondered how much of what he remembered of his brother were true, and how much was his own invention.

Whether Redmond had heard such yarns as a boy himself, or if he was simply making them up, the highwayman had never guessed. He and Fiadh revelled in hearing such grisly legends spill from their brother's lips, like starved travellers tucking into their first hot meal in weeks, feeling their brother's personal warmth flood the cabin like peat smoke as wind rattled the cabin's frail fixtures and roared down the chimney.

During the day, the country looked endlessly green, grassland mauled by the surging wind, fallen leaves everywhere. But at night, danger ruled the bogs and glens. Gangs of white-shirted men rode to or from a raid, setting fire to fields, barns and manor houses, maiming the livestock. Their hoof-thuds rumbling in the dark, grunted calls and clanking harnesses, echoed like wayward thunder. They'd storm in and attempt to strong-arm the men of the house into joining their ranks, or demand money, or else burn them in their homes.

On more than one occasion, they decided to honour the MacTíres with a visit, always unannounced and late in the evening. Redmond did not suffer them gladly. They would ride up, cowls drawn tight over their faces, a phalanx of white-shirted spectres with danger in their pace.

Redmond had been chopping extra wood for the fire when they approached that first time. As soon as he saw them, he told Joseph, who at the time had been only a lad of twelve, to go inside and bolt the door. Fiadh was darning something as he ran in, and the colour drained from her face as he urged her to hide. From a chink in the cabin's thatching, the boy and his sister watched the men line up at the wall in crude formation. One or two held burning branches. Horses snorted. Flames flickered in the dark.

He remembered wondering why they felt the need to hide their faces. Did they fear recognition? Were some of them neighbours, known to them? Evidently, they all knew him and his siblings, had no qualms about menacing them.

Their captain dismounted and sauntered up to Redmond, whose grip on the axe shaft had tightened. "Nice night for it, MacTíre."

"Aye, it's that," Redmond had replied, his voice calm.

The captain lifted his cowl with one hand so his mouth was exposed, and he spat on the ground. "I was wonderin', would ye mind if we gave your home a wee inventory?"

Redmond stood quite still. "What cause would ye have to be doin' that?"

"Only to see if things are in right order. Can't be having any…undesirable sorteen in these parts."

"There's nothin' here. You'll find nothin' and no one. Just me and my brother. Nothin' else. I'll ask you only once. Leave us be, please. We're not causin' you any harm. I'd sooner you did the same."

Joseph drew in a breath as the captain advanced a step. Fiadh's hand, ice-cold, clenched his.

"Mind your tongue, MacTíre. It may land ye in trouble one day."

"As will yours. Now leave us be, please. I will not ask you again."

The captain paused. Because of his cowl, his response was hard to gauge. For half a minute he stood there, facing Redmond, letting the silence build around them like a challenge, before grunting to himself and returning to his horse. They rode away, torch-flames rippling into the gloom.

Redmond watched them leave, finally lowering his axe and letting go of his breath. He knew they'd return. They always returned.

The worst of their visits had been on a chill March night two years later, wind and rain rampaging across the fields. Even over that din and huddled by the blazing hearth, the MacTíres heard the approaching hooves, heavy and deafening as the highwayman supposed the Four Horsemen on the Last Day would be. St. Eligius snorted frantically as they neared. They heard the heavy clatter of men dismounting and skulking toward them. A fist battered on the door and a rasping voice bellowed their surname, demanding that they show themselves. The door was kicked in before a reply could be made, and a gang of about fifteen men, all wielding either a blade, billhook, or club, piled into the cabin. Several more lingered outside. Fiadh had grabbed Joseph and drew them both back into the shadows of the thatch.

Joseph remembered watching them, their threat and their heaviness, with a boy's unafraid curiosity. Again, their faces were concealed by dirtied cowls, threaded crudely from burlap. The volume of the storm seemed to rise a hundredfold behind them. St. Eligius' howl rose as well, too strident to be ignored. Beside him, Fiadh's breath quavered, heavy and sharp, on the ear.

"Young MacTíre," said the leader, the same man as before, his voice once again muffled beneath his cowl. "It's a soft one we're havin' the night." He was a head taller than Redmond. In his hand he clutched a shillelagh, long and heavy as a bishop's crozier.

"What are you doing to my horse?" Redmond had demanded, attempting to make for the door, before being held back by his collar.

"Nothin', MacTíre. Nothin' you'd want to worry about, anyway."

"Leave us be," Redmond had murmured.

"Say again, lad?"

"I asked you to leave us be."

"Well, lads," their leader smirked, sitting on the stool by the hearth. "Did ye ever hear the like? Young MacTíre seems to have forgotten how to welcome guests into his home. Still and all, no harm done. Never too late to learn a new lesson."

It turned out the animal was being hamstrung, a forge dagger severing its leg tendons while this exchange took place. Over its wild grunts and tortured braying, the intruders demanded to know if Redmond was a tithe protector, a devotee of the Church of Ireland or, worst of all, of the Crown.

Although the MacTíre siblings had lived in the same hut all their lives, the intruders demanded to know what had become of its former dwellers, implying that a landlord had evicted them and put his more loyal tenants in place. They overturned the bed and hacked apart the kitchen chairs ("for firewood, ye understand"), tossed Redmond's Missal into the grate, made off with the last of the buttermilk, and left the door hanging on its hinges. All this was for their own protection, they'd been assured. It's better to know who you can trust.

Joseph, being only fourteen, hadn't enough sense to be afraid. As they shuffled out of the cabin, he spat at one of them. The man seized him by the throat, and with a strength that seemed to surprise even his comrades, lifted Joseph to eye level and slammed him roughly against the cold stone of the wall, hissing at him to stay quiet. That was all they'd been waiting for, it seemed.

As soon as Redmond tried intervening, two of them had pounced, elbowing him in the stomach. He grunted as he fell to his knees, where they treated him to a whirligig of fists. Alerted by Fiadh's screams, two more dragged her to the earthen floor, roughly pinning her by the wrists. One took her throat in his scarred hand whilst sliding his fist beneath her skirts. "Ah, you're a pretty one," he croaked under his cowl, anchoring her back. "Do ye sing as sweet as ye look?"

For years after, Joseph remembered the flinty bulk of his attacker's fingers jabbing into his flesh, cutting off his air supply, as well as the meaty thump of fist on bone and Fiadh's muffled screams as she flopped and squirmed fruitlessly beneath her attacker, who suddenly drew his cowl back slightly, exposing his lower jaw to clamp his mouth roughly over hers. He yanked her bodice and dress fully off, to his companions' bellowed encouragement. The sight of her bare breasts and shoulders, suddenly and cruelly exposed, drew a howl of choked fury from Joseph.

When her attacker was finally done, they all took turns on her, just as they had taken turns on Redmond, some flipping her over, until any fight

xxv

Fiadh had was gone, and she lay back in a pose of broken flaccidity. One of them was spent on her, and almost as an afterthought, drew his blade and gored the soft pulse of her throat. The blood bubbled and seeped, and neither MacTíre had the strength to cry out, nor could even expect the stealth of their movements.

Redmond, winded from the blows he'd received, was dragged to the centre of the cabin and held down before the fireplace. On his knees, like a man about to receive communion. The leader stood over him, holding the flat of the shillelagh to Redmond's cranium.

"I've always had doubts about ye, MacTíre," he said, the flames crackling behind him in the grate. "I don't know whether to kill you and that whingein' pup of a brother of yours the night, 'long with yer sister there, or else let yis live with the shame."

Joseph barely heard any of this. He was staring fixedly at his sister's bruised and bloody corpse, horrified. Nor did he quite see his brother's face, but, even over the din, he thought he saw him lower his head to the floor. "Not goin' to reply, no? Well, that says it all to me. The fact that you can't reply, that says it all to me, lad. Hold him out there, lads."

The two men had splayed Redmond out on the floor. Their leader turned to the boy, his voice cruel. "Mark this, lad. You'd do well to see it." He raised his club high before bringing it down with an efficient crunch on Redmond's left kneecap. Redmond's voice, howling from the agony, didn't sound like him; it didn't sound human.

Joseph had tried struggling, but the grip of the man's fingers on his throat was rigid as iron. For a full minute, the leader slammed his club several times more on the young man's leg and stomach. Every meaty crack, every harsh rumble of laughter, every strangled wail from Redmond, seemed to singe the very air. Eventually, the leader wore himself out. He stopped and leaned on the shillelagh's brunt. Even beneath his cowl, his panting was easily heard. "Even *amadáns* deserve mercy, MacTíre. Am I right, lads?"

The others cheered in affirmation. Their leader lifted his shillelagh and slung it back into his belt. "We won't kill ye, MacTíre. You or yer insolent brother there. But we'll need some extra payment off yis, just for that little…antic. A tithe, if ye will. But we prefer to think of it as penance for sins against yer people."

Despite the winding he took, Redmond had struggled mightily, but there were too many of them swarming to hold him down. The glint of a blade winked against the flames; the cabin rang with the men's hellish laughter as they slashed at Redmond's clothes, his shirt and boots, tearing it off him as a collector might tear a parcel-covering off an ornament. They dragged him to his feet only to kick his bloodied legs out from under him again, battering him stupid once more with their fists as he once more hit the earthen floor, the air driven from his lungs with each landing punch, tearing into him like dogs over a carcass. He coughed up hoarse gorgefuls of blood which sprayed off the hay-covered floor; his chest seemed to puncture under each boot-stomp. Redmond had tried getting to his feet but a swift, booted kick to his lower jaw sent him sprawling again, groping at the hay, spluttering tears and his own harsh grunts. The leader had stepped forward, a lordly hand raised to urge the others to cease, which they reluctantly did.

"Up, ye Judas melt," he hissed from behind his cowl. "On yer feet, MacTíre, c'mon!" He turned to one of the men who'd lingered by the door and beckoned him over, who in turn approached Redmond's stricken form. Kneeling, he lashed the elder MacTíre brother's hands together with a bit of hawser, the taunts and mockery and spitting of his fellows bubbling about them. A length of cord was tied around his neck and tightened; the tip of his tongue was forced out, and the leader sliced part of it with a *gralloch*.

Now naked, his mouth bloody and mangled, barefoot and with a few teeth missing and both eyes swollen shut, Redmond, his face a crimson, bruised pulp, was brought roughly to his feet and dragged outside to the horses. The men heaved him atop the unsaddled back of their boniest nag, slapped the animal's rear and laughed as it shambled off into the frigid dark, the pale form of Redmond's bloodied back still slumped astride it, shouting yet more insults after it until the clip of its trots vanished on the wind.

It was then the captain had turned to his men. "'Mon, lads. Let's make tracks."

Iron-Fingers dropped Joseph as the others shuffled out of the cabin. He lay there on the gathered hay, winded and overcome, struggling to breathe as wind roiled in through the damaged doorway and the fire still blazed over him like a witness. Outside, he dimly heard St. Eligius whinny again, his shrieks as shrill and as frenzied as Redmond's had been.

The intruders were gone as abruptly as they'd come, the pulse of their hoof-beats vanishing into the night. It was hours before Redmond, by now chilled to the bone and stupefied from the pain, had managed to urge the horse on which he sat back around. During that time, St. Eligius had continued to whinny across the *bóithrín* as if in desperate mourning, and Joseph had struggled to crawl across to Fiadh's corpse, which lay where they had left her.

By the time Redmond arrived back at the cabin, his wounds had congealed to blackish, crusty strips and his face had swollen hideously from all the bruises they'd inflicted. His mouth resembled a wound, crusted in dry, bloody flecks. Ghost-white, slumped over the nag's coarse mane as if desperate not to fall from it, he was shivering violently, the chill convulsions that jolted his body like a ragdoll in a wind never-ending. Joseph had found their skinning *gralloch* and slashed open his bonds. He could only watch as Redmond, overcome with fatigue, fell from the animal's back, collapsing supine on the dew-slick grass. His mangled tongue was hanging loose from his bottom lip, and his lips were curled underneath the blood that now encrusted them. Joseph had waited a long time before crawling over to his brother, who was still gasping for air. Slinging his one good arm over the young man's shoulder, and ignoring his grunts of pain, he helped him to his feet, tried guiding him back to the cabin, where he helped him to lay him on a bed of straw, keeping the fire going at low intensity. All the while, St Eligius' agonised howling filled the valley.

The next morning, after a whole night of the horse's painful bleating ringing through the glen, and Redmond lying across their sister's cold chest, his wounds still unhealed and he still feverish but endowed with some wild semblance of lucidity, Joseph's older brother had hobbled outside, and caved St. Eligius' head in with a boulder.

It was a memory the highwayman never quite pushed from his mind, the image of his brother in early dawn, among the netting of grass and weeds that tangled around the door of the salted cabin they'd shared, dragging the wagon up to the door to heave the animal away. Redmond's face, still addled with bruises, was the colour of claret, his workshirt and britches drenched in perspiration, his mouth slack as he hoisted the rock over his head and brought it crashing down on the horse's bloodied skull. The animal croaked, crumpled on its side, and lay still. Its blood pooled into the grass, dark as wine, mixing with the dew.

For half a minute, neither of them said a word. Then, without warning or reason, Redmond started to sing a lament, his voice a fluid, reedy tenor in the daybreak chill. He'd always been in the habit of singing while he worked, chanteys and street ballads mainly, to keep focused on the labour at hand. But what he sung now was slow, solemn, dejected, the words jumbled and slurred by his weariness, his voice gentle as the dawn breeze were it not for the odd moaning sound it now took on, owing to the mutilation of his tongue:

Is fada mise amuigh
Faoi sneachta is faoi shioc
Is gan dánacht agam ar éinne
Mo bhranar gan cur
Mo sheisreach gar sgur
Is gan iad agam ar aon chor
Níl cairde agam (Is danaid liom san)
Do ghlacfadh mé moch na déanach
Is go gcaithear mé dul
Thar farraige soir
O's ann na fúil mo ghaolta.

The clouds were heavy, shot through with red flecks of sunlight. The glare made them both squint. Redmond blessed himself, before limping back to the cabin to see how best to carry Fiadh's corpse away before repairing the door. He couldn't be certain, but Joseph thought he saw tears welling in his brother's eyes as he knelt to gather up their sister's cold body and carry it outside.

It was in that moment he realised how truly powerless he and Redmond were in the world.

Chapter V
Quayſ and Libertieſ
Dublin, 1791

What the moment required, Mogue Trench couldn't precisely say. He'd asked many people how exactly the conflict had started, but no one could give a definitive answer. Some posited it began the moment Cromwell's riding boots touched the slimy embankment at Ringsend. Others said it was later than that, with the Duke of Ormond encouraging those French settlers, or Huguenots, as they were called, fleeing hostilities in their homeland to set up shop among the back-lanes of the Liberties. Would the Ormond lads have had any reason to look for a fight at all, had he not done that? A wag in a groggery on Mabbot Street once insisted, between compulsive gulps of porter and subsequent belches, it was all due to what he deemed was the wretched machinations of the Pinkin' Dindies ("cursed Godless gowls!"), though Mogue very much doubted this.

In fact, the feud's origins mattered little to him, save as a point of curiosity. It was a safe enough guess that most lads on either side couldn't rightly say, were you to get close enough to any of them to ask without getting a carving knife in your gullet. To many, it was as simple a matter as asking which hurling team they supported; whomever they happened to be playing against on a given day was the established foe. But the more Mogue asked, the more fruitless his enquiries proved. Any excuse to crack a few skulls was grand enough. Once he got what he was owed.

Mogue never much cared for crowds, hence his keeping of odd hours. Yet he couldn't deny their usefulness in camouflaging himself. He could blend into a tight crush of people much in the way a phasmid shrouds itself among leaf-branches, undiscerned and indiscernible – a nifty enough skill, especially if the law were close. Nothing indicated he was a man of any consequence as he put more and more streets behind him. His tattered greatcoat and rawhide boots did nothing to draw attention, and this was deliberate.

But at this hour, before the daybreak swarm and hustle took off aproper, the likelihood of arousing suspicion was heightened. The streetlamps were long since doused. The City Watchmen were taking up their morning posts on the corners, leaning on bill-shafts and watching his every step. Mogue turned his face downward, as if contemplating the kerb, greatcoat collar hiked up to his jowl; half of them were thief-catchers, and, old as many of them were, they rarely forgot a face, regardless of the day or hour. For what other business has a man to be awake so early in the streets, allowing he is neither still drunk from yester-night's revelries nor opening for trade exceptionally early?

Mogue had the silence to himself but the clack of his bootheels off the cobbles threatened to expose him. This was Ivory's beat, he knew; the Petty Constable could usually be seen gasconading up Skinners' Row from the barracks, twirling his nightstick like a flail, eager to fight ugly at a moment's notice. His office's badge glinted from his lapel, as if he were a newly promoted colonel flaunting his chevron. People gave him a wide berth, stepping aside as he passed or looking submissively down if he deigned to address them. Others briefly stopped at the door of his constable's hut and handed over packages of swag; lickspittles of the streets paying tribute to their idol.

Mogue hadn't been in Dublin beyond two days when he was warned about the constable and his illicit dealings. A portion of Rob's takings were handed over to him each week on the condition he let the gang go about their doings unmolested. And he wasn't alone. The Ormond lads as much as the Liberty boyos delivered unto him their choicest palm-greasers. Lot of good it did them. Ivory was known for being a hard Charley, as likely to hit you a whack across the jaw and fling you into the cells as take a portion from you. All of Dublin knew his name. Mogue alone was one of the few who hadn't paid up; he was left alone so long as Rob's offerings kept coming.

Ahead of him, just as he'd expected, Mogue spotted Ivory, the blackness of his coat like a raven's enfolded wing, in hushed conversation with a man he didn't know. The constable was talking excitedly, but at a low volume. Mogue ducked into a doorway, peeped around the corner.

The old hatred for the constable fizzed under his flesh. His grip on the knife hilts clenched; there was no lie in what McClear had told him. Ivory abruptly stopped talking and eyed the man with an expression of cold expectancy.

Mogue watched the other man hand Ivory a small, bulging buckskin; the constable nodded as he shoved it into his pocket, and shook the man's hand before sidling off down the street toward the river, throwing sharp glances in both directions. There was nothing to stop Mogue from unsheathing his *gralloch* and plunging it between Ivory's ribs once he passed him. Instead, Mogue waited for the echo of the constable's footsteps to fade before making a run to the square. He'd see Ivory later, he was sure of it; but now wasn't the time to fall within his sights.

Though pressed, Mogue slowed his pace, as though he were merely taking a leisurely stroll among the rutted flagstones and granite. Bunching his hands into his pockets, he rested his palms on the reassuring pommels of his blades and whistled tunelessly into the air as he passed the constable's box.

He glanced up at College Green. Nothing but horse-shite-strewn cobblestones. The morning fog had thinned a little, though not enough to see clearly. The cornice and statues of the Parliament were veiled in creamy greyness; its colonnade's bone-white trusses were glistening as damp smeared them like oil. Their shadows slid across the Green like fingers. King Billy's statue loomed on its plinth, a cantering herald of doom now set in bronze.

Mogue moseyed on, down Castle Street and Back Lane, past the coal yards and Tailors' Hall 'til he cut down a dark laneway leading to the Liberties, that tangled and terraced warren of gnarled rooftops and alleys and side streets redolent with damp cobbles and cinders, far shabbier than anything the Green could offer. Where the lane sloped down toward the quays, a ghastly oaken carving of the devil stood like a sentry under the arched niche, its notched horns curving like scimitars, its claw gesturing to come closer, a deranged, saw-like grin etched into its features. No person of condition could be found here. Not even the Charleys bothered venturing out this far west of the city if they could help it.

The dawn air had taken on a scalpel edge, colder and closer on the bare gullet, but also reassuringly familiar. A few stray dogs wandered about, rooting for food. The drunks lying supine in the doorways were woken by Mogue's swift approach but turned back to sleep once they saw he was merely moving past. Liberties people were reputed to pride themselves on always leaving their doors open, but every tenement Mogue passed seemed bolted against the world; the traders had yet to open for the day. The Cornmarket House had a grim look to it, even in the glare.

Despite his poor sense of direction, Mogue barely had to think about his route; his feet guided him most of the way. Even with the fresh chill, his blood worked itself into a keen rhythm, a crimson tattoo thudding under his bones. He knew the old fury that now bubbled under his bones, the same lancet of savage intent that would grip him whenever he and MacTíre lay in wait under the Wexford trees for a fresh kill, when the element of surprise was thick in the air and the blaze of MacTíre's flintlocks as he fired on unsuspecting victims…

By the time he passed St. Catherine's church and down the narrow dogleg linking Meath Street to the rest of the city, it swirled through him like an opium rush. Finally, he reached a shabby corner house at a dead end. Desertion was the order of the day for the street it was on – an above-ground sewer, good only for escaping down, and never felt the press of a dray wheel. The building was a familiar one, a tenement block for the city's forgotten – prostitutes, street traders and the people who swept up after them, sailors left behind by their shipmates and weavers like Mogue Trench. As with all the others, its doors were locked, but Mogue paused for a moment, catching his breath. In a shadowy room somewhere high above, his presence was sorely expected.

Using his own makeshift key, he forced the door open and made for the stairs. Despite the foyer's gloom, and the mouldering chill that hit at the moment of entry, he didn't have to feel for the banister; he merely reached out and felt his fingers close over loose, unvarnished oak in the dark. His eyes adjusted to the staircase's narrow murk; it had probably been sweeping once, ornate, the property of some long-departed lord. Half a century's worth of accumulated dust and grime crunched beneath his bootheel. The steps' dull creak under his boots seemed like a violation of the place's deep shade, dense and tomblike as of a coalmine. He'd since stopped worrying about stumbling over a stray body stretched on the floor before him.

In any other time, had Mogue's ears been pricked, he'd hear wheezing and the hacking of throats from behind every locked door, in damp, stucco rooms where entire families of the great unskilled once shivered together, coughing up blood on dust-caked floorboards under a slumped ceiling. But the only sounds left to hear were the scratching and skittering in the walls; the evictions had been swift.

The urge to beat his fists off the wall, feel blood, warm and gluey on his knuckles, was overwhelming. He was ready for the day's hostilities.

As he climbed further and further up, past the first and second floors, Mogue's nostrils flared at the salty aroma of dried blood permeating the long stretch of the high landing, and he followed it to the far end to the only door that did not appear to be locked, also the only one behind which he could hear voices: one talking at length, as if holding court, and three more following in rapid succession. Mogue raised his fist, rapped on it three times before it opened with a clang.

The garret was grubbily hot. The smell of ordure, sweat and candle wax fumed up from the floorboards. The only light was a guttering flame from a stump of tallow placed atop what was once a mantelpiece. Shadows danced unsteadily by its glimmer, accentuating the bareness of the walls. The Liberty Boys' cramped meeting place, a cloister of cracked brick where the only decoration to speak of was the crudely sketched face of King Billy, staring down from a yellowed portrait propped next to the tallow. It was there at the insistence of Cobbe, a staunch Orangeman. Along the wall, glittering like a butcher's cutlery, hung an array of blades – machetes, cleavers, carving knives whetted to a silver edge.

Despite the gloom, Mogue recognised Ulick and Alf Guerin, both leaning off to the side and both with fresh welts on their hands and wrists from working the looms all night. Mogue nodded wordlessly at Alf, who'd let him in. Paul Cobbe was hunched by the room's lone windowpane, keeping an eye on the street outside. He glanced up as Mogue entered, a subtle sideward flick of the eye, before resuming his vigil. Perched on a weathered keg toward the rear, dealing a deck of cards with the easy absorption of a monk perusing a breviary, was the man who had done most of the talking before Mogue entered, Dagger Rob.

No taller than a shillelagh, Rob eyed Mogue with a smirk, his stunted legs thrown over the keg's rim and still far from reaching the floor. "Long time, Trench," he smiled. "To what do we owe the pleasure?"

Mogue's patience was worn thin. "You know well why I'm here."

Rob simpered. "You've that look in your eye, Trench, like you've seen how today'll go. Am I mistaken?"

"Not too mistaken," replied Mogue. "Ye have what I asked?"

"Never one for pleasantries, sure y'weren't?" Rob tossed the final card lazily and drew on his pipe. Mogue knew better than to be at ease; Rob's hands were huge, like those of a pugilist or a mason, rocklike when clenched and capable of dealing devastating blows; they appeared comically large for the stubby arms to which they were attached. "No matter, Trench. You're needed today. At Ormonde Bridge. As agreed."

"If that's where it's happening."

"It is." A sharp plume of smoke jetted into the air from Rob's ulcerous lips.

"Grand, so. And ye have what we agreed?"

"'Course – skills such as yours hardly come cheap."

Mogue let that hang in the air. Producing his own pipe from his pocket, he proceeded to fill it with tobacco. He struck a match, held it to the mouth of the pipe.

"Here's how it'll happen – you take out at least twenty of them, it's a half crown for ye. Take out more, and we'll talk of more. The oul' warchest don't runneth over, ye understand."

Mogue nodded and exhaled. For all Rob's friendliness, a glint of watchfulness flecked his eye. He thought he saw Rob glance quickly over at the Guerin brothers, for he heard a quick shuffling from behind, as if the two were standing to attention. At the window, he saw Cobbe's hand vanish up to the wrist in the inner folds of his waistcoat, where his own *gralloch* was sheathed, like a dignitary posing for a portrait. Not once did Cobbe avert his gaze from the window. Mogue ignored the others' eyes on him, how close their hands rested on their weapons. All of them stood at a safe distance, a man to a corner. He waited for his smoke to vanish against the ceiling. "And the other matter?"

"Which is?" Rob's head, shorn down to the scalp by crude means of a razor, gleamed thickly in the gloom. Despite the corners of his mouth coiling into a grin, his luminous eyes were now narrowed and fixed on Mogue. The latter forced himself to meet the stare; he knew when he was being scrutinised.

"The one we agreed to soon's we knew this fight was up. That your lads leave Ivory to me."

Rob sighed, leapt off the keg to stand to his full height – not much farther than Mogue's elbow. Mogue saw him a bit clearer now. A severe case of the pox had warped his face into a visor of dirty-red blotches, sprouting from his jaw, his nose, all along his bare scalp and across his bulbous forehead; whenever he smiled, the few teeth he had left flashed like the cutlery suspended behind him. Despite his affliction, he moved with kittenish agility, and Mogue's free hand moved to his blade-hilt.

"Well, Trench, we all see yer grievance. Ye want at Ivory, isn't that right? Sure, not a man here doesn't want to see the bastard under yer blade. And you've much better reason than most. But really, I can't very well ask any of 'em to leave off, sure I can't? Blood-blindness'll be the order of the day –"

"You assured me he was my kill."

"And he could easily be, if ye find him. Chances of him bein' there are excellent, too. He's never done tryin' to fuck us over, God knows. But really, what interest's he to ye? What's it matter who puts him in the ground s'long as it's done?"

"Matters to me. That should be enough."

"I know that, but you're not alone in this, Trench. There's lads we'll be fightin' later on who've an axe to grind with him also."

"That's all well and good, but when've I ever demanded satisfaction other than through pay? If you can order your lads to at least keep from goin' near him, you'll have my services for life. Your word's law this side of the river, remember."

"Perhaps, but once yez're unleashed out there, who's to stop anyone else from takin' him?"

"Not if I'm there."

"Ye don't really have a clue what's happenin', Trench, do you?"

"Have you ever had cause to doubt me?"

"No, but I'd lament losing your services. Murder is your business, after all."

"Too true. These are butchers we're up against. Killin's normal for 'em. I don't kill because I share your beliefs. I kill because you just so happen to pay me the highest."

"You kill for pay. Why should this matter?"

"Ivory's come between me and my sleep long enough. If my services are of no further use to you…"

"'xactly. Not a man here wishes to see him alive by tonight. No different for the Ormond boyos, either. It's one of the few things us and them'll happily agree on. But deny a man what he believes is his rightful kill, what do you think'll happen to him that's denied it?"

Mogue didn't reply.

Rob nodded a few times. "Precisely. Then I'll humbly ask ye not to attack any of my lads. Otherwise our fraternity ends today, and you'll be a hunted man."

Nothing idle about a threat from Dagger Rob, Mogue knew; but this was perhaps the best he could hope for.

"And he'll be there, for sure?" Rob asked.

"Aye. McClear told me as much."

"The fella lights the lamps?"

"Aye, the very same. And I saw Ivory on the way here, so chances are he'll show his face. The bastard can't resist a good dust being kicked up."

"That he can't. So, at some stage past noon, I want ye down at the Ormond with the rest of the lads. When the sun's high."

"And I'll see his face right enough?"

"You'll see all their faces, and the whites in their eyes before their gristle soaks your blade."

"There's no accounting for what happens today, Rob."

A flicker of fury lit Rob's eyes, and the poxy lips clamped together. The fact that Mogue's loyalty was measured strictly in shillings and half-crowns was something rarely touched upon between them; but today held a horizon of different promises to any other victories they'd scored on the streets.

"Just take who's ever yez can before the Charleys show up and don't be annoyin' me," Rob finally snarled. "Who knows, yez might even get double afterward. By the end of tonight, porter'll be warmin' yer cockles and there'll be a girl on yer lap. Now 'less ye plan on meetin' yer maker a bit earlier than necessary, I'd say start makin' tracks."

Mogue smirked. "Ah now, Rob. And here's me hopin' to get a game of whist in, at least."

"Is tha' righ'? Well, today's not really a day for games, Trench." Rob gestured, and Mogue heard Alf and Guerin move aside, and the door creak open. "Off ye go."

Mogue eyed each man in the room, steady but respectful, hands still on his blade pommels, and turned to leave. He kept them there until he was back out in the street.

Chapter VI
The Mark
Wexford, 1786

For years afterward, he'd often wake at night, tears salting his eyes, the sound of his brother's mournful song ringing in his ears.

Now, lying on the damp stones, he heard his brother's voice still. He wondered what Redmond would have thought of him, crouching on roadsides, waiting to plunder carriages. Redmond had been tall, serene, unshakeable. Born for hard work in rough weather. Even when wielding an axe, he looked contented, like he knew his strength was not easily knocked. Whenever the highwayman heard the word 'strength' uttered, he thought not of the Olympian saints and archangels adorning the stained-glass windows of Ramsgrange church, nor of soldiers marching at parade. It was the sight of his brother, singing quietly to himself over the dead body of a horse, that monopolised his thoughts. In a way, he knew exactly what Redmond would make of him now. He preferred not to dwell on it. Every man has at least one loved one to whom he fears making his crimes known. Then Joseph would recall Fiadh's corpse, bruised and violated and splayed on the earthen floor of their former home; and his resolve replenished.

Redmond was long dead now, a demise unrecorded by any magistrate and unmarked by any headstone in the many churchyards dotted throughout the region, just as Fiadh's was. Redmond had drowned while fishing for trout in the Bannow River, where even now crouched the highwayman. His currach was dragged into the clashing swells of a maelstrom, and Redmond had been unable to come about. His currach capsized, and the current took him. An angler who couldn't swim, his body washed away on the flint-coloured swells. Not unusual in these parts. A full year after the attack on their home. He was one of the many unmissed serfs buried in the soil they'd spent their lives tilling.

And because Joseph, then only in his teens, lacked his brother's business sense and could not work to keep the cabin as his own, Lord Baron Loftus of Ely, licensee of the Fethard estate, had him evicted. The uniformed cronies made him watch while they burnt his home to the ground, flames growling in the breeze. After that, he was cursed to mosey the dirt roads of Wexford, fleecing and begging for food. A Cain booted out of Eden, mantled in leaves, the cold snaking damply into his bones like an elixir, to never again know hearth nor home. The roads of Ireland became his new abode; in moments of crazed delirium brought on by starvation, he told himself they were his kingdom, not the holdings of merchantmen and absentee landlords.

Nobody took him in. He begged, but the sight of a grimy, flint-accented boy was not enough to stir people to charity. Somehow, they forgot he was Redmond's brother, and the last MacTíre. Poverty was what all people in that wind-torn region knew; charity a luxury few could ever afford. With no family or friends to speak of, the roadside became his bed, the hooting of owls and the wind's dry roars his lullaby.

He quickly learned that the nights were never fully deserted. Oftentimes he might pass one of them by, trudging out of the lowland shadows like scarecrows given life, the hollow tap of their canes off the road snapping through the fog, their filthy rags a caveat of what he might soon become. He had swollen their ranks a little more, these roadside beggars who tramped the boggy lanes and byways of Ireland, always en route elsewhere. Far from any kinship he might have felt for them, or they for him, he instead opted to avoid them, repulsed perhaps by the very rawness of want they presented in his eyes. A rawness that now also hung off him like an unclean odour, and which seemed to kill any instinct of kindness or charity.

They became easy enough to identify, not just from the tattered quality of their garb, but from the flat gloom that ghosted their eyes. Whatever menace or ferocity they might once have had was replaced only by paltriness. Joseph often saw them, packs of emaciated men with twig-like arms, bundled into rags that hung off their limbs like funeral shrouds, governed solely by starvation.

Some were barefoot, barely registering the bite of pebbles as they moved. They'd shuffle into town squares on market and fair days in the vague hope of work, importuning the locals for alms or warming themselves by the heat spilling from the open door of a blacksmith's forge; or else huddled from the cold at the roots of a beech tree. Others made their shelters in barns or under hedgerows, or in the roofless ruins of a monastery with the foxes and bird excrement. He saw many of them blind from the pox, limping from injuries that had never fully healed. Even death itself seemed quite unwilling to take them, content instead to circle about them like an invisible vulture, drawing out their suffering a while longer without quite administering its grim mercy. The wilier ones scratched a living where they could, doing seasonal labour on the harvests or singing ballads and scraping out tunes on a fiddle at *céilís* or on fair days, often to pockets as empty as their own. Joseph could barely fathom how they could bear to live that way.

On those frozen nights, he thought of a story Redmond often told him and Fiadh while they worked: farther north, in the counties of Leix and Offaly, there had been a lord, a crown-enforcer known as Cosby. "Not a man," Redmond would intone, "but a devil cloaked in a man's raiment." A former soldier, the Queen had granted him holdings in the midlands, along with a regular force of mercenaries to keep Gaels under England's yoke. The local people were doomed to feel the sweep of his malice, and without even suspecting it, for Cosby had pretended to be on cordial terms with them. But after he fell out with his main ally, a chieftain called Ó Mordha, he lured his foe, along with a hundred of his followers and kinsmen, to the shores of Mullaghmast under what he claimed was an invitation of truce. What none of the 'guests' knew was that Cosby had arranged to meet them in the encircled confines of a rath. For when they entered its doors, they were met only by darkness. Darkness, and the hidden blades of Cosby's men, who set upon them with a ferocity only well-trained murderers have the will to unleash. There was to be no escape for any of them, nor even a hope of it; no report of what those in power do to those they have enslaved. Nobody was to know about how they cut off the heads of their victims and collected them as they would trophies, the walls washed in the blood of all who met death that day.

"But d'ye know what?" Redmond would ask, eyes glowing with their customary fervor as he spun the tale's magic. "Only Ó Mordha survived. "He escaped and hunted down his vengeance on Cosby. He lived for the redress of his people. He alone made sure their deaths did not go unanswered."

The story lingered in Joseph's mind until he vowed to himself, although he could not quite remember the day or the hour, that he would never be made to feel powerless again. Especially not by cowards who worked in numbers. The life he'd build for himself would be friendless and unaided. The freedom he would know was not the idyllic tenet lionised by philosophers and poets in the few books he decided to steal, but a cruel state of self-reliance and brutality, where pistols and sabres were mere tools of the trade, and any man or woman sufficiently ill-starred to fall in his sights was an opportunity. No longer did he feel the want of a roof. He would know what freedom was, and what it was not, and could never be. His name would be a byword for it.

He no longer hankered for riches nor even for a life more comfortable. Never would he sleep on a stuffed feather bed, waking each morning to the scent of lilac and rosewater, waited on hand-and-foot by a retinue of servants, nor try his hand at the gambling tables in the gentry's gilded, candlelit parlours, nor lead a sarabande in their ballrooms during Parliament season, nor hear the stately thunder of their operas. Never would he inherit a title and sizable estate on the death of his parents. For all the sweat he and his brother and sister had broken for it, that was a world they would never and could never glimpse.

And yet, he did not care. For he alone would seek out his prey, and he alone would stake his claim on it. He became a day-sleeper, venturing out only after dark when the world is different and safety for the honest traveller is no longer assured. The backdrop to his excursions was the unlit solitude of Wexford roads, the rough boggy lanes which he knew better than any Englishman.

The shriek of powdered and wigged fops as he jabbed his gun in their faces. Never again would he be their slave or plaything. Never would he make Redmond's mistake. One must honour the memory of departed loved ones, true, but Joseph had no loved ones left. Let the sheep and maggots wander in droves, he decided. Let the lion find his prey unaided.

He made his hideout in a little cave situated in the cliff face that overlooked Baginbun Bay; it was high enough that the tide, even at its fullest, could not reach it, and small enough that it could not be spotted. He managed to reach it by lashing a coil of manila-rope to a nearby tree and abseiling down to the cave-mouth. There, in the clammy darkness, he drew up his plans by the campfire's dim flicker, ignoring the waves' hungry roar on the rocks below. He drank in the silence that lay beneath that, shrouding the countryside.

Silence became a language he spoke with great fluency. At night, he stole out and ranged the boreen, like a newly resurrected corpse climbing from his grave. He got to know every corner and turn, every preferred route, every stop-off point the peninsula had to offer him. He marked the times of deliveries, the shortcuts taken, the hidden paths that snaked through the underwood, taken by gypsies, journeymen and soldiers, the low troughs marked into the soil by wagon wheels. He soon came to feel that he owned it all, more so than the lords to whom it was officially granted.

A successful stand-and-deliver rested on agility, not strength. To catch a victim off guard was a skill in and of itself. Timing, swiftness, preparation, estimation, and sobriety were all key. Marked prizes moved with the expectation of being robbed and so were often the most difficult, but also the most rewarding. He wasn't always too concerned with claiming riches, though. Sometimes he just took what he needed, be it food, ammunition, or clothing.

Try as he might, he never managed to hunt down the men who terrorized him and his brother, who introduced him to his powerlessness. That was a thought he tried pushing from his mind. They used masks, as he did. Their anonymity protected them, as it did him. But tonight wasn't a night for melancholia; the mail carriage would be along soon, and the highwayman would have to be ready. The excitement, the perilous thrill of gaining some trinkets, never died for him. On the doors of alehouses, churches, and gaols, on the wharves of New Ross, in the timber yards of Enniscorthy, at horse fairs and travelling carnivals all over Ireland, a wanted sign showing his charcoal face hung for all to see.

He ingested newspapers and pamphlets like alms, keeping track of those who claimed to keep track of him, laughing at their wilder descriptions of his deeds and appearance. He laughed in equally scornful measure at the patriotic zeal adorning the pages of the *Hibernian Review* and the *Dublin Evening Post*, and the parliamentary reports, so rich with the pear-shaped cadences of oratory and fulmination. The lessons he'd learned under Ó Doirnín's garbled thumb were easily recalled. He read the speeches of a man named Grattan, cribbing for things like liberty and nationhood and rights for the land. Politics seemed like a rich man's plaything, MacTíre decided, all vying for their chance to run their gobs under the domed roof of some fancy stone-built edifice up in Dublin. A bit of ongoing theatre to ensure people were kept good and starved and docile while a few got their bellies full. 'Freedom' seemed to be your man Grattan's favourite word. MacTíre knew freedom long before any of those powdered, limp-fingered prigs made the word into their football. Out here, he was free as the stars.

The price for his capture was raised to 60 guineas in the last month, or so he saw. He grew accustomed to seeing his own face glare back at him from a stone-built wall. He'd grin at the image's crude lunacy whenever he saw it, the jawline's charcoal edge, the crooked nose, the hint of swinish fangs, the forehead's misshapen bulge. He was drawn with a sombre expression; anyone who knew him declared he never stopped smiling. And when he first read the call for his arrest, he laughed until his ribs ached. It was nothing short of a comic masterwork:

WANTED!

----------------------------**FOR**----------------------------

BRIGANDAGE & MURTHER

JOSEPH MacTíre

'**The Notoriouſ Highwayman**'

A Bounty of ſixty Guineaſ ſhall be pay'd to any Perſon

for the Arreſt and Conviction of ſame
DEAD or ALIVE
By Edict of
Hiſ Majeſty'ſ Kingdom of Ireland.

Beneath this flattering decree ran a description, identifying him as *"aged two and twenty years, a man of Loathsome mien and slouching Gait, middle height, pallid Appearance, scars on cheekbone, Often unshaved, black Tricorne hat, likewise clad entirely in black garb, teeth Filed down to Fangs... his Figure is spare, though his Shoulders are Broad, and His hair is a red, Lank mass... his Grin is crooked and his Eyes are green and Gimlet. He rides a seal-brown horse... his Hideaway is Called, in the Gaelic Parlance, Poll MacTire..."*

He'd laughed harder. He had a title now, if an uninspired one: The Notorious Highwayman. It must have taken a rare imagination to come up with that one. Still, how many gentlemen of the road could boast such a moniker? If the price for his arrest had been raised to sixty guineas, he thought, then the authorities no longer considered him a nuisance, a thorn in their regal side. A decade ago, they may have deemed him as such. But having his name share the same poster as the King's (an unsavoury honor, if there ever was one) meant one thing: he was making a fine impression. Now, he was an enemy of the peasantry and the peerage. Nor did he have a single hideaway, but many; various caves and crannies dotted all over the county that were known to him and him alone; some for shelter, some for storage, some for both. Caves on the sea cliffs, ditches dug in the undergrowth by the high road, caches where bullion and supplies and hunting fodder, firewood and amassed weapons and shot were stored, should he need them. It always paid to be prepared.

Yet there was one hideaway, one above all, in which he cached his most treasured takings. The hideaway he considered his main storehouse and stronghold, his territory, his own manor was sequestered far off in the dense undergrowth of Tintern, on the brow of a cliff facing the southerly coast. Though only a few miles from the high road, no path unwound to it; and it was far beyond the notice of travellers or redcoat scouts, veiled by leaves and overgrown nettles, and leaning hollows and alders speckled in white, scar-like lenticles. Its dark mouth he kept covered with a knotted sheaf crudely woven from underbrush and mangled ferns; he alone knew this tapestry of greenery indicated the cave's location amidst the dell.

'Twas was not the lure of silver and gold and heavy, richly coloured stones – these he could fence or easily sell to anyone suitably enamoured of their brilliance. Into this cave he placed not treasures but tools. Leather cartouche boxes, fully loaden with shot. A box of carpenter's chisels and gouges. A water canteen. Tobacco. A bronze, pot-bellied cooking pot and iron cauldron seized from one of the encampments, and tapers for lighting fires. His musket. Sailcloth. His books. A coil of rope, a ship's rusted quadrant. Hewing axes and shovels and adzes. Pails and nets. A soldier's haversack filled with soap and powder and timber and pitch. A bottle of perfumes, stolen for Gráinne.

Along with all this, he stockpiled his true trophies, the prizes he always hoped would fall into his hands – the spoils of sin – in this very grotto. The brick-thick books of hours. A weighty almanack. The tome by Defoe that detailed the life of a man, a merchant sailor, shipwrecked alone on a desert island far beyond the seas. The handwritten notes scribbled on their folio pages, the black solidity of their texts. These he kept piled together in bundles like a pyre, all around the grotto, reading them by the blaze's dusky flicker as night closed in.

There was no need to return to Gráinne. She was neither wife nor paramour, and he foresaw having no sons or daughters by her. Yet leaving her to fend for herself seemed too cruel an act for even MacTíre to contemplate. Many times, he had shared her bed in the alehouse's farthest alcove and whispered of who was next whilst lying in her arms. MacTíre had known so little of love he feared he would not recognise it were it finally offered to him.

Not once did they whisper words of tenderness to each other; neither would have believed the other if they had. There was little about devotion she cared to hear, and he had naught but silence on that subject.

Loneliness she understood, the struggle for survival in a land bereft of second chances she knew with a fluency that matched his. He had made plenty of enemies; there was no need for them to be hers as well.

And so, here, deeply sequestered and spreadeagled on his bed of black earth and ash, cocooned by the grotto's thick flint walls, images spun through his brain and left a spasmodic chill juddering his spine. The mellowness of blood. A snow-headed barn owl gliding through a forest, its bleached wings thrashing in the dark. A forest in flames, the hollows and pines and oaks scalped to kindling in a congress of flame. The hellish light hovering, combing the shadows for fresh prey, its glaring luminescence quaking as yet more leaves and saplings were roasted. MacTíre often saw the woman's death – a bullet puncturing the soft flesh of her throat, a blade slicing through her belly – and wept at the notion.

On other nights as he lay there, sealed off in his loneliness, he envisioned massacres – for no massacre, he knew, ever occurred without good reason. Bloodshed was in the future, of that he was certain – how it would manifest remained a question he harboured no desire to see answered.

Three minutes until the mail carriage reached him.

A cloud covered the moon, and the highwayman let out a thankful sigh. His breath slowed; if the weather was rainy or gusty, he needn't have worried, with the chattering raindrops or howling breezes to stifle the noise. Great care was needed on calm nights. The silence could be either a friend or a foe to him. Even a sigh of relief would carry and betray him. His natural aroma carried a piquant whiff of gunsmoke, laced with rainwater. He hoped his scent would not be detected by either the men or their chargers.

The redcoats would be vigilant for attack. His plan was to gun one of them down while crouched and take on the other before he could rally himself. A carbine ball through the throat or skull would do. But his finest weapon, he knew, was the element of surprise. His guns were useless if he were spotted. He'd wait until the coach was less than a foot away before even drawing his flintlock.

Rarely did he target anyone in the same place twice. His vantage points always changed. His victims were as diverse as the curving roadway. A sailor on the dirt road from Slade village, made to stand and deliver the locket he wore. A ploughman and his lad driving a cart from the New Ross market, their horse shot in the eye from behind a sheaf of heather. A Redcoat scout left naked and trussed up under the trees, his uniform torched and a mesh of scars carved into his back, the high road before him.

Yet it was rare for the highwayman to fire his gun anymore, he met so little resistance. Murder featured rarely in his repertoire now, though it had once been an inevitability. Now, the threat of it was enough.

Such a strange manhood he led. His life would end proudly, he'd make sure of it. He was no gallows bird; he wouldn't die as food for crows. When he died, it would be in the heat of a skirmish, or cradled in his deathbed. This he promised himself. Though he knew the former was more likely.

Only through apocalypse would he and this place know absolution. He dreamt of blood with a vindicator's fury, weight of a hundred more crimes holding little in his mind, until full command of the fens and townlands rested with him. He deemed himself a man old before his time, wizened by exile. His head bore such spectres well, away from the timeworn lore of campfires, his skull fizzing like a cauldron, the rioting coal – the power he'd relinquished. The Kilmore Quay he never returned to, the sister he could not save. The lashings of yellow fever that might finally take him. The faces of women he never learned to love or keep. The blood, the shite, the horse tails sheathed in bronze. The recurring dreams of leering skeletons, of thunder whispering to the horizon, of the rabid kraken enclosing its tentacles like anacondas in the branch of a fruit tree around the cannon, shark fins slitting with slow ease, saltwater filaments shimmering to a dead lee, the anchor's arms thrown wide.

Such wolfish scenes, fit for a proscenium, to be carved from seashells and handsome scrimshaw, perhaps, focalised in a watercolour mural to be set above some steward's fireplace in the Colonies, or else a marble, candlelit altar in a minor Balearic Basilica, ash-soiled, dead-eyed saints withering in gilded craquelure, tide-blue rosettes and a scarlet, oaken keel, all forfeited, even unto the sandy ocean floor, where his brother rested. He was known to the sword edge where harquebuses are set and tactics are key. It was strategy favouring him, not gods; the workings of weather and muggy nightfall reminding him what to expect.

Were he so able, he'd have ordered the waves to hit England, to swallow without trace her ruby salamander pendants and leonine crests, to drown out the haughty drone of her court composer's harpsichord as the plump strings of a mandolin are strummed and cut like the anchor cables at Gravelines. He had all the quiet in the world to dream of this, to tiptoe around the reef's spiked eggshell, eye the quartet of weathers slowly bleeding into one another over a year's calendared extent:

Lead and spark, muzzle flash, small fires scalding the channel at Ross. Towering prison hulks anchored off Wexford's arid shore and coccyx. Hired cut-throats lying in wait amid Wexford swells at sundown, their bevelled and saw-like sabres bared for a reckoning. The screech of bar shot clear-cuts the bay, rapid as lightning. Footprints char the sand like the kiss of a branding iron. And all for the recoiled surety of liberation, felled masts and sails blackened by the gun-ports' agape stern rake.

Toledo alloy, a vanished star, genteel stones plucked from the earth and strung together on a thread: the perfumed hands resting on rosewood globes, the stainless sceptre, baroque cathedrals toppled by swells of wrath, smearing rust over their agate-strung pillars, a belaying pin's shaft, the snapped rope, a plumed bowsprit, sunk to a sunless brine. Like the flood deployed by God's fist, men, planking, and sovereignty broke to detritus, lofty squadron rear-guard and gargoyle snarls breaking as if in ritual, cannon and crown-piece submerging.

He wasn't a man who took dreams seriously, unless they could be realised. He trusted in plans, maps, bait, and blood, keeping his notes carefully on file, his unpatriotic labour in calm order of signet, cartouche: a rebel, a dog, a man too caring by half. The sea was never far off, the horizon untouchable. The ships were awash in the hollow throb of a drum-major, rallied to his commission, to his imported duty, who dreams of the ancestry he'd no choosing in and sweated with pride over. The anchor's wide arms. Lashings of yellow fever. The reef's spiked eggshell. The faces of women. And the women noticed him. Almost as much as he noticed them.

Lying in the shallows of the river where his brother had died, his head bubbled with such thoughts. He had killed, yes, deprived wives of husbands, children of fathers, with a single blast of his pistol. Murder trickled over his record like a spillage of ink. He'd face God for this, eventually...

The carriage may still double back, there was still time for it. Perhaps they'd decide to put up for the night, with a fire burning, and stay on their guard throughout. Then he would have to come to them, and who'd be the loser in that tussle? Or they might take a shortcut to the abbey, beg for shelter from the lord there.

The highwayman snarled an oath to himself, tried shaking off such cumbersome notions. His quarry was too close to be passed up now.

Chapter VII
The Thief-Catcher
Dublin, 1791

"Thief-Catcher! Pleasin' Paul! Filthy thief-catchin' bastard!!"

Mogue threw his arm back and flung the torch across Ormonde Bridge. It somersaulted, trailing a smoky fantail behind before cracking off cobble, right at the feet of a charging Ormond lad. Clear as the heavens were, the sun blazed pitilessly down; he'd have to squint to see his way through the madness. All around him battle cries and fiendish shrieks thickened the air, a strangulated chorus of fury as the two gangs swarmed across the bridge at each other. How many were mustered that day, Mogue did not care to guess. A small army. There'd be no camouflaging himself this time – his tools, greatcoat and knife-belt set him apart easily. Mogue kept his pace, walking as Cobbe, the Guerin boys and the rest hurled past him, like a man merely strolling through a meadow. His knuckles whitened on his *gralloch's* hilt; it caught the light as he drew it out and surged past two Ormonds, wading headlong against them.

Below his feet, the Liffey churned lazily at high tide; its waters would soon be an eddy of scarlet, a deep gush of blood from fresh corpses. Behind Mogue, Rob's hoarse bellows died echoless over the clamour.

"Gallows! Show your face now and we'll send ye to hell!"

This was no army he faced, but a thronging horde seemingly unleashed from the hell's lowest ash-pit. Faces gnarled with drink and rage, bellowed for any kind of blood. Mogue had fought enough grisly battles to know what to expect. It wasn't hell this horde had come from, but the city's slums, which, he supposed, resembled hell strongly enough. Animal fury gripped most of them, and were Mogue less skilled in knifework, the chill snaking through his blood would have pierced all the stronger. The desire for blood, the crimson mist through which so many of them blindly surged, could almost be smelled. He could no longer tell man from woman, child from adult, as all mouths were drawn back in tigerish snarls, all faces wizened and burnt clean of compassion, rabid with bloodlust and pouring towards him, demon carapaces and witch-like features, wrinkled and deformed, unholy faces marred by disease and the despair of poverty – the least of the city, its refuse and its forgotten, now bellowing with battle-fever.

Though fashioned from stone, the bridge shuddered under the crush of bodies. Lads from both the Liberties and Ormond Street, loose-limbed and dressed for the most part in their work gear, wielded the implements of their trade, blades, cudgels, slash hooks, tailors' scissors and cleavers whetted to a biting edge, as weapons now. Across the river, the new Four Courts, bristling with scaffolding, loomed. On both banks, the quaysides were deserted. The city was standing down.

A blizzard of steel jangled around him; it was music to Mogue's ears, a symphony of strife. Wild cries ripped through the air like locusts. Clubbed skulls and men hitting the ground like sacks of shit, coughing blood. A blunt cleaver was planted in a Liberty lad's skull with a loathly crunch. An Ormond fella screaming as he dropped over the side over the bridge, splashing into the river like a boulder. The stain of grey sinew and gore puddling glutinously at his feet. The symphony would reach its caesura with a flourish, a viciously shrill bell and whistle ringing out and breaking into echoes downriver, before erupting again with rekindled fervour.

Mogue knew those bells and whistles well – the City Watch were on their way, charging down the quays, their cudgels drawn and shouting for order. Ivory would be in spitting distance soon enough, his truncheon cracking skulls open. Mogue needed only to see his face to get at him; his eyes peeled for any man garbed as a Charley.

But keeping a weather eye proved difficult when he was in sight of men who desired to see him dead. His *gralloch* hissed in the air and punctured flesh, its steel lustre soon smeared crimson. Despite the sun hovering high and bright, a vicious chill jolted his bones, and he charged again, teeth clenched. Mogue pounced, stabbed, grappled, lashed at eyes, kept his teeth bared for a stray throat to bite down hard upon. His arms swirled, hands like lightning, slicing men in butcher's aprons, their blood mingling with the fresh pig guts still dripping from their smocks. Most of his opponents were trained butchers, and it showed; their movements and stances were heavy, trundling, easily seen coming. The heavy splash of corpses dropping into the river never even reached his ears. Despite his frenzy, Mogue moved quick and light on his feet, thanks to the tailor's delicacy, easily dodging and weaving with the grace of a dancer.

No longer could he discern between ally or adversary. Who he cut and sliced at, whose blow he dodged or parried, who scarred him or whom he scarred back – it mattered little now. His world was nothing save the *gralloch* in his hand and his foes' deliciously soft gullets and ribs as he drove it in. Neither gang wore any sort of uniform, no tunics nor colours to mark each other out. No Charleys among them, either. For the moment, at least. Butchers' aprons and loomers' smocks were indistinguishable; greatcoat and hat offered no indication. The blades and bludgeons bore no visible signs of variation. If Mogue hacked off a comrade's arm, it wouldn't have mattered in the chaos.

Blood now speckled his face, warm and sticky, vivid as pimples or mud. Just as he tried to wipe some of it out, a uniformed figure barrelled at him, black greatcoat flapping. Mogue swerved to the side and managed to slash at the man's sleeve. The man was a Charley; at some point they'd shown up and simply joined in the melee, rather than at least attempt to break it up. More and more of them broke through the line, their cudgels in groups. Even as bodies crowded about him from all sides, Mogue saw the figure of Ivory among them, throwing punches in the air. The one face he'd hoped to see the day. His cudgel swung like a crozier and Mogue saw the whites in his eyes.

"Thief-catcher Ivory!! M'ere to me, ye fucker –"

The cudgel orbited at his cranium in a black, dizzying arc, cutting him off; he ducked and managed to hook Ivory's side; the constable fell back over a dropped body. Mogue drew out a second blade from his belt, the sticky gore on his palms causing it to tighten in his grasp as he thrust it forward, raking Ivory across the jaw. The constable staggered, blood trailing down his jaw. Fair play to Ivory; already, he was already back on his feet, eyes flaring and a beastly snarl coiling under his moustache as his billet flashed.

Like wildfire, Mogue whirled his *gralloch* at Ivory, but the constable was already at him; he parried the blow away, the cudgel knocking hard off Mogue's carpals. Before he could register this, a huge weight slammed him square in the belly, robbing him of breath. Mogue staggered and slipped, his back smacking off the gory cobbles. Ivory vaulted for him.

A heavy boot slammed into his ribs, while the cudgel thudded heavily into his chest. Ivory loomed over him, tall and livid, his billet-point thrust at Mogue's gullet. Blood still leaked from where Mogue had managed to cut him. He spat in Mogue's face, a globule of phlegm and gore, as coughs racked Mogue's body. Ivory didn't let up; his cudgel kept hammering down, and his heel suddenly clamped over Mogue's throat.

Yet some of Mogue's wits had resurfaced. Though blind for blood and shite, and with the cudgel whacking down harder, and Ivory's blood-soused face roaring above him, his free hand reached for his belt, where he kept the folding knife sheathed.

Mogue flicked the blade free and whipped sidewards; it cut across the man's shin, hamstringing him. He dropped with a pained snarl, his billet clattering, groping for his wound. Mogue forced himself to his knees, breath still hacking out of him. Ivory would bleed hard and fast into his boots, he knew. He'd made that move before, whenever at a disadvantage.

Ivory was supine, grunting and grimacing from the pain. His watchman's coat was now in shreds, soaked by all the blood. He turned on his side, scrambling to pull himself to his feet or at least to safety, but the wound Mogue had inflicted hindered him. Mogue already saw his blade plunging into the constable's ribs, or slashing fast through his throat, throwing him even further off balance, blood spurting heavily from his main artery out onto the cobbles. The man was hated throughout the city; he'd have few enough mourners. How colossally stupid was he to enter a fight such as this?

Mogue kicked the billet away and lurched toward him, panting heavily, knife-hilt clasped in his palm.

All around them, the battle was a rabid blur as men stabbed and hacked at each other under the sun. By now, plenty had fallen off the bridge into the river below, and the heavy splashes accompanied their screams in fraught harmony. An Ormond lad fell on his back as a club slammed into his chest. A Liberty boyo was roaring out of him as he sloshed through the water, trying to hold an enemy down in the water.

Though still blind, and now tasting blood, Mogue saw a pack of them, Liberties or Ormonds he couldn't say, rushed over as one, clasping Ivory by the collar and hauling him to the ground, blades flashing anew as they closed in on him in a whirligig of fists and gnashing of teeth. Ivory growled, as he struggled to be free; a hard blow to his brow seemed to knock any vestige of sense out of him. His face had lost all fury, was a riot of bruises, both eyes by now swollen shut.

The constable lay slumped at the feet of every man on the bridge, it seemed. Ormond and Liberty lads alike crowded over him, raining down blows with the ferocity of demons; Rob was somewhere among them, as was Alf. Even some of his fellow Charleys appeared to be joining in. Finally, someone leaned down, grabbed Ivory's torn collar and hauled him up one-handed. Senseless as he was, the constable seemed to cough, a wretch of bloodied bile. The hand holding him was Rob; the little man somehow seemed to throw him above, until the Constable was lifted onto someone else's shoulders.

"Afternoon to ye, Constable," Rob bellowed. "Would ye ever look at the fuckin' state of ye now? Callin' yerself a Charley, yet happy to crack skulls whenever it suits ye. Did ye not think this'd come back to bite ye eventually, no? Did ye not think makin' a foe of every man on this bridge might one day be yer downfall? Did ye think it would last, did ye?"

Howls of "Let him swing!" and "No mercy, no quarter!" filled the air. The blood on the cobbles now ran so thick Mogue's boots were drenched through – sacrificial wine, shed from the flesh of sinners, whose sins remained stubbornly uncleansed. He stared as the mob hauled the constable off, raised high above their shoulders like a mascot. Despite the operatic volume of their cries, his thoughts were as clear as a bell:

This kill was mine. Rob assured me as such. He takes this from me, he takes everything. This isn't how it should end.

Ivory was hunched in horrible relief against the summer sky, his face a soiled pulp, as he was carried off toward a lamppost by the bridge's abutment. He'd slashed somewhere on his person, for he bled freshly, the scarlet trail behind him. Odd thing to think of, Mogue thought as he looked past him and at the lamppost to which he was being carried. McClear had doused that lantern only this morning. Someone flung a rope around its upper crosspiece; it tightened into a loop and fell fast, swinging faintly.

"You've plagued this city long enough, Ivory," bellowed Rob. His voice was raised for his audience, both eyes kindled hideously. "You'll be tastin' fire soon enough, for all your sins against us.

"You'll burn long before you die, Constable, knowing that the city you claimed to serve ordained your death." Rob strode forward as the noose was hooked around Ivory's gullet, lifting him off the tiny man's shoulders. The man seemed lost for sense; no longer a threat to anyone for the foreseeable. Mogue watched as someone handed Rob a burning torch, its flame guttering heavily on the noon breeze. The little man walked forward, touching the torch against the tattered remnants of the constable's cloak.

The flames burst up, engulfing the constable's corpse as it swung to the wild cheers of the onlookers. The heat and reek of crackling flesh needled Mogue's nose, but he tried not to look away as his prize smouldered and the flames burned higher. The man's hair glowed, the crackles and sparks hissing viciously over the bridge, and streaks of ash trailing to the ground strengthened as his greatcoat and flesh mingled as one in the vengeful heat. Smoke swirled on the breeze, which had only just picked up as if to fan this tiniest of conflagrations, smudging away the sunlight, and the frantic cheers around him doubled in frenzy. The constable's body, thudding slightly off the lamppost, was charred beyond recognition.

The satanic, rejoicing chants of "No mercy, no quarter" were bellowed ever louder the more the flames swallowed, then finally began to subside, flickering as the crackles stopped with them, the incentive to resume fighting also seemed to die. Mogue noticed lads from both gangs starting to turn away, limping across the bridge and back to the city or else wearily seeing to the corpses of their fallen comrades that littered the cobbles. Plenty more floated in the river, like swollen wrecks.

Mogue sheathed both his blades, resigned that he would now never know the satisfaction of hearing Ivory's dying scream. His brain had dimmed. Not even the thought of stabbing Rob and suffering a similar fate as the constable crossed it. As he withdrew from the mob and bridge back toward the Liberties, he was glad for the blood drying on his face – it obscured the tears in his eyes, and the pale, ghost-like sheen that now tinged his cheeks.

Chapter VIII
The Mark (Refumed)
Wexford, 1786

When he heard the timber clip of the approaching horses, Joseph smiled. The carriage was right on schedule, the noise swelling with each step. His fingers tightened on the flintlock. Only forty seconds left.

He wouldn't give them due warning; all three would be armed. The postboy wasn't a worry. If he shot one of the horses first, he could gun two of them down in the thick of the chaos. The horses would dash about, frenzied and whinnying; with any luck, the riders would be thrown off, the carriage would overturn, hopefully before any returning shots were fired.

Thirty seconds until the mail carriage reached him. He wondered if his Irish blood impelled him to be so mutinous. The Irish loved a rebel, after all, and a good story to tell and hear about him. He felt no loyalty to them. He did not speak their creeds or their prayers. His cause was one of survival, not sovereignty.

Still, the Irish spoke of felons such as himself in fond tones, drank to either the health or the memory of a known rapparee during the *Samhain* festivities. They turned out in droves to witness the hanging of a local brigand. The stories they told their children reworked miscreants into heroes. Common criminals were praised as martyrs, murderers as champions of some doomed, private crusade. The Irish held thieves close, in the ballads they sung and in the silence they kept. They were a strange, treasonable folk, after all. The villains of the law were the darlings of the people, it seemed. And their rebellions were always quiet, devious affairs. Sparse gunfire, hushed clarion calls. Low-voiced meetings held in torch-lit caves. Pamphlets written in secret and intended strictly for private perusal.

Yet how they also scurried toward their churches at the clanging of a bell, to grovel on the freezing marble and fling their praises at the alabaster figure of Christ upon the cross. Or kneel before the pulpit as some priest, in his starched collar and dress, paced about the tabernacle, droning on in Latin about sin and salvation, damnation and deliverance, as the censer's stern, pious perfume fumigated the altar and aisle. Or else huddle in dungeon-like confessionals, whispering their sins and quaking in the meridian light that spilled through the stained glass, babbling their prayers into the ether, thinking themselves blessed once they had ceased speaking and returned to the world.

That would never be MacTíre's fate. Never would he allow himself to be swayed by priestly pleas for his soul, nor fall at the feet of some perfumed pontiff to beg clemency, yanking at God's apron-string. He would sleep through a drab sermon, diving like a dove to catch in the bishop's craw, designed to persuade him to defect from his warring self. Yet from what or whom did he need saving? The road where a death blow missed him by inches? The yesterdays, the tomorrows?

Perhaps in league with their religious fervour, the Irish also spoke hotly of the independence won from Britain nearly ten years before in the Americas, as if a similar blow for national deliverance might take place any day now in Ireland. The Empire would die, as empires often do, from within. The flame of liberty would wax hot as perdition. The cracks in its foundations were stretching wider; soon they'd run right to London, its gilded heart, and freedom would be theirs. This would happen for the glory of the nation, they often said.

How lost they seemed without their creeds, how empty their lives without their legends. The burning of a rich landowner's barn; the hold-up of a lord and lady returning from the annual revelry in Loftus Hall; the chase and escape at the hands of a party of Redcoats – these were the fabric from which such legends of Joseph MacTíre were woven. The handiwork of men tired of their own powerlessness. The highwayman couldn't blame them for this; a subject people will always concoct their own means of resistance, however sly or covert. He suspected many locals, farmhands, blacksmiths, and washerwomen knew and recognised his face all over Wexford. By never informing on him or attempting to hunt him down, they told him what any criminal longs to be told: they supported his deeds.

Twenty seconds until the mail carriage reached him.

It was the women who noticed him most of all, his aloofness and how he stood apart. Noticed him the way they'd once noticed his brother. With his mask off, walking freely and leisurely through the fairs and *sibíns*, he was just one more anonymous traveller, passing through until he set his sights on wherever he was headed. Most took him for a courier of some description, who came in, drank his fill, kept to himself, didn't cause any grief. Occasionally he'd join in with a song or a game of cards.

Yet the women seemed to know better than to seek love from him, and he knew better than to offer it; if hatred weren't his vocation, then loneliness certainly was. He knew very little about the modes and means of courting, but he sensed loneliness was never a pleasing quality in anyone, man or woman. Nor had he any desire to be a husband; to bind oneself to another – even one who vowed to give love and affection and support – seemed like the gravest folly to the highwayman, proof that freedom was too much for anyone to bear and the lure of marriage a more convenient option. Just lying with a woman and loving her with all the casual feverishness of a one-off paramour, to savour the dawn afterglow before saddling up and going on his way – that was enough. Better to leave them pining than to reveal who and what he was. The man MacTíre did not exist. He died with his brother in the stream; only the man in the mask remained in his place. Women don't need men in masks. Such men make terrible husbands, and even worse fathers.

The colleens plying their wares in and around the alleyways and riverfront taverns of Arklow and the town of Ross knew him best. They remembered him chiefly because he always asked their names, the wolfish countryman with the pink nicks on his hands and the gimlet eyes. No one else ever did such a thing. How eagerly they threw their arms around him; how firm and feverish the kisses he shared with them and embraced him under the smoky, lurid lamp-glow. He knew he was no longer capable of love or caring or faith, the ordinary things a man should come to feel with age and experience. Any moral code or even any sense he could make from the way he lived his life had lost all hope of ever emerging. It was as if he now walked in some frozen, lonely waste-ground, at a remove from logic or decency or honour.

He did not operate like any normal man; more like a beast in survival mode, crouching in a hiding place before springing to attack or flee. He knew he could not stop, start over and make his amends (not that there were any amends he particularly wanted to make). He was of no use to anyone, least of all to himself.

The highwayman prided himself on never falling under illusions; the women merely earned their keep, their sweet, breathy words in his ear, their scented breasts and limbs, the milky powders and rouges that kept bruises and pox scars out of sight, their groans of put-on rapture as he entered them, forceful and grunting – all of it was an act, a standard trick of their trade, as the cowl was to his. He was one more handful of coins for their night's work, as they were temporary redeemers of his loneliness; nothing more. He knew it could only be loneliness that made him sentimental over a whore's touch.

He could go to them whenever he pleased, knowing he'd be received with a studied warmth that he supposed resembled affection. Never once, however, did he force himself on any woman. To resort to rape, to rob a woman of her final vestiges of dignity, seemed to the road thief the lowest measure of cruelty, made worse by the fact that it required virtually no effort on his part and would be attended to by no meaningful consequence. Murder he could stand; brute force against an enemy as well-versed as he in savagery he understood with limpid intuition. But the women he knew had been brutalized enough. To add to their suffering was to admit that no true law existed.

And then, of course, there was Gráinne. Hazel-eyed, dusky-haired Gráinne. In her arms, he knew some semblance of peace.

She worked out of a pub not far from here, on the Tintern estate, which became their general place of rendezvous. Not much older than Joseph, her knowledge of the comings and goings of the various travellers who put up in her premises was revelatory. She'd quite the knack for prising valuable information from her gentlemen callers, about carriages due and cargoes delayed. Always Joseph gave her a cut for tipping him off, some token from his nightly excursions – a handful of pearls here, some scented water or a lady's finely silken shift there, or a ring set with sepia and enamel, or even a porcelain brooch, along with her usual fee. These he would hand to her with a thorny smile and a murmured thanks for her help, for not once had she been mistaken or mendacious. Once he showed her how to fire a pistol, and in return she taught him how to cauterise a wound with the heat of a poker, a loathsome task she often had to perform on her girls if they happened to spend the night with a less than pleasant patron. She'd also shown him a second, if even rougher means of cure: if no poker or even steel was to hand, a twig doused in black powder and set alight was equally effective.

He remembered sitting back in her bedchamber one morning, the sun a molten halo striking the tenebrous fields with delicate, spectral rays. He'd watched as Gráinne took aim out of the open window at the trees opposite – where he'd hung a small wooden board midway up in the boughs – with the flintlock he had primed and loaded for her. Her back was to him, so he could not see her eye, but he sensed her squinting firmly in her sights, intent and unblinking as any rebel or redcoat he'd yet encountered. Her hand was steady, enviably so given the barrel's steely weight, her finger hooked snugly behind the trigger guard. She took enough time to rivet her attention on her mark, her breathing heavy and slow, before jerking the hammer back with her thumb. When she finally fired, the report echoed with devastating bite through the chill dawn air, the recoil juddering sharply through her body and throwing her slightly off balance. When he'd walked up to look at the board, it hung askew from its place in the trees, half burst apart from where the bullet had hurtled through. She had stood back and faced him, the smell of smoke mingling richly with her natural musk, and she could barely hide the satisfaction in her smile.

It was a pleasant memory, one that stirred a strange, claggy ache in him for things he knew better than to ache for, that he never would or could possess. Like a steady, decent woman to come home to and share a bed with. A woman to embrace, who found neither him nor his means of earning his keep contemptible. A woman with whom he could build a life, unless he was shot during a nightly raid, or the redcoats finally caught up with him and his body was left to swing from a roadside gibbet without so much as a trial; or he was dragged before a magistrate in irons. They both knew that life in these parts could be short, brutally so. It did not pay to get too attached to any one person. Yet, after a while, she stopped asking for payment in cash and requested he simply pay her with his embrace and manhood instead. In the mornings, they practised shooting together, side by side at the window and taking turns, and no one dared object.

Joseph paid her well for her company, and for what she knew, with her preferred currency. Lying in his arms in her squalid bedchamber, her breasts gently pressed against his torso, her dark hair spread sleepily over his chest, the sweet, amber aroma of her perfume filling the air (yet another gift he'd stolen for her, taken from the carriage of a merchant's wife) as she told him about the mail carriage, about when it was due. Said she'd heard about it from one of the redcoats who'd taken her the night before. It was headed for Tintern Estate, with letters intended for Sir Vesey Colclough himself.

She'd planted a fond kiss on his lips then, a kiss both tender and greedy enough to reignite his hunger for her. He returned her kiss, felt her breasts heave welcomingly against him…

Rarely did he have such luck elsewhere. Once, in a saloon on the Arklow quayside, he made the mistake of letting one girl – a Nordic little nymph called Amelia, who always left satisfied, both physically and financially – play with his gun when they'd finished. He'd been getting dressed and she accidentally fired the pistol into the wall opposite, shattering the Roman vanity mirror and missing the highwayman's skull by a whisker. There was commotion; her pimp had burst into the room to see him struggling to wrest the weapon from the girl's hands. For his trouble, the highwayman was beaten black and blue and kicked sprawling into the mud, his plunder for the night lifted from his pocket as damage payment.

For the most part, the rebel gangs, such as the one that terrorised his brother, left him alone. Never had he been approached by them, to be persuaded or strong-armed into joining their ranks. Nor would he have joined them if they had. He decided early on that it was always cowards who worked in numbers, whether they be masked louts who saw themselves flying the flag of national liberation (even as they burned their countrymen's farmsteads to the ground), or well-heeled agents of government decree, enforcing laws that seemed to keep humanity at bitter, perennial odds with itself. Mongrel curs each of them, all believing themselves to be wolves. The only thing he had in common with them was the mask he wore.

Never would he plan to rob carriages or attack convoys of regiments-on-foot with such men. No doubt they knew his name from the posters, while he knew none of theirs. Perhaps he did know a few of them, had done business with some and shared a drink with others. They deemed him a useful, if tacit, ally, he supposed. Dead Redcoats were all the rebel gangs wanted or cared for, anyway. He only ever preyed on the well-off. The ferment of a chase, the red-handed exhilaration of spoils filched from a powdered fop's pocket, the sturdiness of the gun as it erupted in his hand: these were the highwayman's true impetus for crime.

Ten seconds.

His breath deepened, heart walloping under his flesh. His flintlock shook as he raised it, the coach trundling into his sight. The scarlet of the soldiers' livery was dull by the moonlight. They rode in procession, one rider to either side of the coach, like mourners flanking a coffin. Their bayonets glinted, as though noticing the highwayman.

He saw the fixedness in the soldiers' eyes, making them almost lidless. The coachman sat huddled in a sodden greatcoat; the postboy shivered next to him. He was a scrawny lad, sporting the first tinges of stubble, eyes agape. Away from home for the first time, the highwayman presumed. The coach itself was appetizing: a four-wheel prize painted black and maroon, inscribed with the royal coat of arms and scarlet-daubed wheels that spun like gaunt rose petals, drawn by four horses, four coffee-furred geldings. Fine beasts, those geldings. Best be careful where he aimed. He wanted a claim on at least two of those horses.

Five seconds. Four…Three…Two.

An exhaled breath, and the highwayman leapt up, discharging his flintlocks in furious succession. A pair of white flashes burst through the gloom. The horses drawing the coach reared up, hoofs flailing in the dark, keeling the carriage over with a rolling crash.

One bullet passed through the stomach of the nearest horse, another burst the coachman's head apart like a melon. Blood splashed over the road and the horses and the postboy, who was too startled to cry out. Crawling from the fallen vehicle, his leg sprained from the fall, he stooped under the wall of the bridge, hands tight over his ears.

The mounted soldier wheeled around, wasting bullets on the darkness. The man on the ground tried scrambling to his feet and was shot in the belly. The flashing volleys lit up the highwayman. He didn't stand still but bounded up and crouched again before firing a round. His flintlocks rung out a cruel rhythm, a tattoo of cordite and powder. Tossing his guns aside, he wrenched the carbine from his belt.

The remaining soldier's horse gave in to its fear and made to gallop off along the bridge, throwing its rider off. A final blast from the highwayman put an end to him. The sudden quiet was overwhelming, the tang of smoke heavy in the air.

The boy, enveloped in the shade, watched the villain pace among the debris, examining the bodies, untying the horses. He kicked open the fallen carriage door and began rummaging through the sacks of packages stored there. In the dark, he was only a black outline against a cloudless sky, a wraith in a tricorne hat, moving with questioning stealth. He didn't look over his shoulder or even around him.

To his right, the postboy saw the coachman's gun lying, having dropped from the old man's hand. A speckle of moon flashed for a moment in the flinty barrel. The pain in his leg from where he'd fallen jolted through him; he longed to scream.

Holding his breath, one eye fixed on the black figure, the boy reached as far as he could and managed to pick up the gun by its barrel.

He tried not to scrape it off the ground. It was heavier than it looked, and for one terrible moment the boy nearly dropped it. Cocking the muzzle, he held it over his wrist.

The highwayman stood up and took off his hat, cursing to himself. He ran a hand through his rumpled hair. There was nothing of value to be gained. Just stacks of mail, parcels. No trinkets, no gold, no guineas. Waste of an excursion, he decided. Then again, he shouldn't be too surprised. It was only a mail coach. All mail coaches carried an armed escort. With any luck, he could pawn off whatever takings he found. He'd have to make tracks sharpish; someone was bound to have heard the gunfire.

Moving among the bodies, he snatched up any stray trinkets or powder he could find. He stopped, inhaling the smell of smoke. It was a comforting smell, aromatic with victory. And a hollow victory this night had proved. On top of it all, the postboy had gotten away! But no matter. He'd given the lad a night to remember. If their paths crossed again, the highwayman would say he was welcome.

The soft click of a gun being cocked made him start. His eyes darted about, as if to puncture the darkness. The sound was so unexpected; a cold flare of shock stung his flesh. He saw the dull glint in the shadows, heard the rough gasp of heavy breathing. Under the wall, the boy's finger nestled the trigger as he took aim. The highwayman saw him at last and appeared to smile. The boy shut his eyes and fired, shattering the silence.

Part II

Chapter IX
The Resurrection Man
Wexford, 1786

"Ye have a name, lad?"

The words, and the low, rough-accented voice that uttered them, arrived from nowhere. As if they were conjured. At first the postboy thought them imagined, for they echoed unnaturally, as if in a vault or a high-roofed church. He blinked and tried to see forward, hoping to glimpse the voice's owner, but only an immense gloom met his eyes. The darkness was near and thick as the air in an especially dense and tangled forest. Glancing upward, he thought he saw, far above, a jagged sliver of reddish light bleed faintly down, like the fantail of a comet; shrill gasps of wind rung through this cranny like banshee howls. The soft, far-off hiss of a waterfall and damp grit of stones beneath told him he was somewhere near water, possibly on a strand. The cold seeped through the linen of his shirt and his teeth chattered. Something tight was wrapped around his forearm, like a piece of sailcloth. As he sat up, a sharp jolt of pain spasmed through his arm as he feebly tried to move it, and he couldn't help but howl out.

"Well?"

The voice was closer now, as if the speaker had moved forward. But the postboy heard no footfalls. Yet he was now certain he no longer imagined it. Someone was definitely there, in the deep shadow that reeked of cold soil and damp.

"Even *Sassenachs* have names. What's yours, pray?"

"What place is this? Where in hell am I?" The throbbing in his arm seemed to pulse now, slithering through the rest of his body like a witch's pestilent brew. Whatever was tied to his forearm was too tight, and he tried to reach up and undo it. But every time he moved, the pain seemed to reignite.

"Lay still. The more you move, the worse it'll be." Despite its softness, the voice in the shadows cut through his howls like a sabre. "It won't stop 'til ye lay still."

lxx

The last words were spoken with icy emphasis. The postboy lay back, choked gurgles heaving from his throat; curiosity about whom he was speaking to could wait. He took a deep breath and tried remaining as still as he was able.

"*Cia as duit*? You're of English blood, aren't ye? Ye speak bettern' I thought ye might. Ye must be of English blood. I'll bet ye feel a bit like Odysseus. Down in the underworld, eh? 'Cept I'm no phantom, as ye can see. I'm as real as the cold on yer flesh and the pain in yer arm. So, I'll ask ye 'gain, only the once. Your name?"

"Mogue...Trench," the postboy managed to splutter. Squinting through the pain, which was now simmering to a steady, brookable throb, he discerned the tall, spare outline of a man leaning at an odd angle several feet away. Though Mogue couldn't make out his face, he saw the man's eyes peering at him through the gloom, narrowed and glassy and strangely calm.

"*Céad míle fáilte duit*. 'Twas quite a fall you took on that bridge yonder, Mogue," the man said.

"Is my arm broken?"

"It is. Sorry to have done it to you, but ye left me no choice."

The man's voice had a muffled, rasping quality to it. As if he hadn't spoken aloud in a long time. That, and Mogue noticed, he was very still, almost like a statue. Hardly any movement at all came from his person, and he was powerfully built.

"Where are the others? The mail driver?"

"Dead, it saddens me to say, lad. Don't know if ye remember all that happened."

"Why'd you attack us?"

"Yis had some things I wanted. It was either me or your mates."

"Those men weren't my mates."

"Mmm, I'm sure. I'd say count your blessings you were spared, so. 'Tis not me habit to spare people I attack."

"Aren't you generous?"

"When I want to be, I am. And by rights, you ought to be dead by now, boy. If I'm bein' honest, I'm the only person who knows you're still alive."

"Yeh, well, I'm breathin' yet. So why don't you open me throat and done with it?" Despite the venom in his voice, Mogue was secretly glad for the conversation. It took his mind off the insistent throbbing through his limbs.

MacTíre laughed at the boy's defiance, giving a livid half-smile. "Oh, you've vim and verve, that much is clear. Even with yer arm in the state that it is. But have ye the energy for me?"

In the dark, Mogue saw the man reach down, take something from his pocket. The sudden, sharp hiss of a match being struck echoed throughout whatever vault they were in. The flame puttered, and Mogue saw the man's face at last, eyes glowering greenly by the tiny, dancing light. The patchwork of scars covering his cheek and jowl was monstrous. Despite a rash of stubble speckling his jaw, he was disarmingly pallid. Mogue knew that face; many a crude rendition of it had stared him down from the wanted posters hung across the city.

"You're him, aren't you? The one they call Mac…MacTíre? The road thief?"

"Aye, lad, I am he, truly, I am he." His lips hooked into that sour half-smirk. Mogue tried not to flinch; smiling did not become the man. Running the length of his cheekbone was a livid, barely healed scar, from where a sabre once slashed his flesh, while a mass of shaggy red hair fell to his shoulders. "Captain Joseph MacTíre, at yer service. I'd bow, were I the bowin' sort. And you're probably wonderin' where y'are, I daresay."

Mogue's mouth had dried; he found he could not summon an answer. MacTíre dropped the match and they were in darkness again.

"I'm after bringin' ye to one of me hideouts, as ye might've guessed. I've many lurkin' place, but no one'll find us here, so let yer worries die on that. I wasn't wild on leavin' ye for dead. Try not to move now, lad. Ye lost a quare amount of blood as it is."

Straining, Mogue glanced down at the sailcloth binding his arm before looking back up at the road thief. "You're a man of many talents, clearly. A surgeon as much as a road thief, is that the way of it? And they say there are no more miracles."

MacTíre's smile softened somewhat as he responded: "No miracle at all, lad. Thank the woman who showed me how to do it. Ye just might meet her someday."

With these words, the highwayman stood and approached Mogue. He was taller than he initially seemed; his eyes flared with a stony glint. He wore some sort of heavy cloak that brushed off the stones; a brace of vicious-looking flintlocks was hooked to his baldric, their pommels glistening like pearls. *The weapons that nearly ended me*, Mogue thought dimly. MacTíre's movements were agile to the point of being soundless, as if he were hewn from silk; despite the heavy boots he wore, Mogue barely heard his footsteps. The urge to flee was suddenly unbearable, but Mogue couldn't move – his legs were bound tightly together.

Hunkering beside him, MacTíre gently pushed the linen sleeve of Mogue's shirt up and lit a fresh match. The light illuminated a soiled rag wrapped tightly around the boy's forearm, wetly darkened from what looked like pus or blood. Several dark, ugly blotches, like waxen seals applied to stamp shut an envelope, dotted his arm.

"Y'were shot," MacTíre mumbled, eyeing the marks. The hot stink of his breath made Mogue's insides seize up. "Glad I got ye in the arm, not the head."

"Is that where you were aiming?"

MacTíre made no reply. His gaze was fixed on the small chain of wounds along the boy's arm. Drawing out a bit of hemp rope and a leather powder horn, slung next to his flintlock, he tipped the black, peppery-looking contents onto his open palm. The dry, sulphurous reek of gunpowder filled the air as MacTíre smeared it into the boy's wounds; Mogue winced at his touch.

"Take my hand, lad. Ye won't like this."

"What are you doing? Wha–?"

"Save yer breath. If I don't do this now, infection'll spread. Take this."

He placed the rope between the boy's teeth. Mogue bit down as MacTíre, with deft slowness, held the match's scorching tip against each powder-filled wound. Mogue's screams echoed off the flinty walls as sparks and smoke hissed upward, and he barely noticing his flesh's crackling odour as a blindingly luminous flash needled his eyes and pain flooded his marrowbones. He'd never before smelled it. The powder coating each wound ignited that which lay next to it; his entire arm seemed to sizzle, and the smash of blood hammered in his temples as he thrashed and convulsed. MacTíre's gloved hand kept him pinned against the stones, his other clamped over his mouth.

"It'll be over soon." MacTíre's voice was a dull flurry of syllables, somewhere close to him. His fingers, like the clamp of an iron vice, clenched Mogue's one good hand, his rigid grip preventing the boy from falling into convulsions; if he gripped any tighter Mogue's arm would surely shatter. The urge to writhe was unspeakable. Not once did the highwayman's stare falter, even as Mogue went limp and was engulfed, unable to muster any further screams, into dormancy.

*

The smoke did not leave him. Everything else was swallowed in darkness, but not the scent of smoke. It seemed to come from every direction, sustained without being relentless, and never quite faltering. It crept into his skull like fresh mist off the sea, swirling through his pores and steering him through whatever fresh, painless oblivion he now found himself ensconced.

From whence it came was of little interest to Mogue. It had doused the pain as rainfall douses a scrub brush torched by the summer furnace. There was no light punctuating the darkness, not a glimmer of a candle or even the brief glint of a spark. Whatever mercy he was shown, he would take.

Opening his sluggish eyelids was an effort. The darkness eased, but only by degrees. The notion that he had died drifted in…and was gone. An orange blur thrashed at his vision's outermost rim. The stony damp still chilled his flesh, but now a welcome cocoon of heat swept through him. Light flickered dimly off the cave's craggy walls, and the jagged sliver in its roof far above him was once more in gloom. As if it were sealed shut.

The smoke drifted; sparks churned and billowed in crackling spurts. Mogue's lips were dry, and his nose twitched slightly at the smell. The flames spat and glared, and on the opposite side of the fire MacTíre huddled, his expression both alert and far away.

"Ye alright?"

Mogue tried sitting up. A fresh cast swathed his arm. "Y…yeh."

The highwayman tossed a bit of snapped branch into the flames. "Good. I was worried y'wouldn't last the night there."

The boy ran his fingers over the cloth, just where his wounds resided.

"But sure, you're on the mend now, thank Christ. Be a shame for ye to lose that arm." MacTíre tilted his slightly; in the light, Mogue saw his hair was streaked with premature strands of white. The highwayman smiled his clouded smile. "And there's me thinkin' the resurrection wasn't possible."

Mogue's brain was still too fogged to reply. He merely nodded and croaked, "It seems so."

"A woman taught me how to do that, as I said. Mayhap ye'll get to thank her." After staring wordlessly into the flames, the highwayman murmured, "Ye ever killed before, boy?"

"Not to my knowledge, no."

"Ye'd some fine blades with ye. Don' worry, I kept them. 'long with everythin' else."

"Everythin' else?"

"Takin's from the carriage y'were driving. Books, mostly. Which suits me grand."

"You're lettered?"

"Aye. Can write, too."

Mogue blinked. "Who taught ye?"

"Me brother, God rest him. Tell me, lad; did ye dream at all?"

The oddness of the question barely registered. "If I did, it's lost now."

MacTíre fixed his eerily serene eye on the boy once more. By the flames' red glow, his face appeared spectral yet flushed; the only sound was the sharp crack of sparks puttering before him. His grogginess fading, Mogue had the strange sensation of being appraised, a side of mutton under surveyance for market.

In a voice hushed by the fire's crackles, MacTíre spoke, his words mingling softly with the sparks and smoke as they hurtled heavenwards. At first Mogue thought he was praying. In fact, the highwayman was chanting, his luminous stare never once leaving Mogue:

> *"Hunting (and men not beasts shall be his game)*
> *With war and hostile snare such as refuse*
> *Subjection to his empire tyranneous:*
> *A mighty hunter thence he shall be styl'd*
> *Before the Lord; as in despite of Heaven,*
> *Or from Heaven, claiming second sovranty;*
> *And from rebellion shall derive his name*
> *Though of rebellion others he accuse..."*

As MacTíre continued, Mogue thought of those barnacle geese that soared and wheeled in black clusters with the winter wind, like ink-stains on the sky. Word by word, the highwayman's voice took on a strange mellifluousness, as though he were reciting an incantation to some baneful god. It resounded off the flinty walls, swelling in volume throughout the glacial depths of the cave. Time was suddenly non-existent, each passing minute obliterated by the dark modulation of the speaker. Even the roaring flames seemed to quiet to a smoky putter, as if they, too, were transfixed by the highwayman's intonations, though their heat blazed all the stronger.

MacTíre spoke like a minister sermonising from the pulpit, as if his audience were a congregation of thousands, and not the mere cowed boy before him. By the thrashing light, Mogue's mind raced with many unbidden, unforeseen visions. MacTíre's voice locked him in its godless sorcery, until he finished with the words, "gracious things…Thou hast revealed", and sat back, his eyes closed.

"Fine words. Would you rather I applauded?" Despite his gall and the heat, a sudden, strange chill snaked its way down Mogue's spine.

"That's from Milton, lad. Paradise Lost." MacTíre's eyes didn't lose their savage lustre.

"What's that?"

The highwayman tossed a fresh branch on the flames. "Are ye lettered too, lad?"

"What? You mean, like...books?"

"Aye."

"I'm not, no."

"Ye should be."

"What's the use in it?"

MacTíre grinned. "Plenty. Yer mammo never taught ye?"

"Never knew my mother. She died years back."

"And yer da?"

"The same."

The highwayman nodded to himself, as if having reached some unuttered verdict. He stared at the sparks flitting into the air. His silence unnerved Mogue. "This where you live?" the latter ventured.

"'Tis, aye," replied MacTíre. "Meantime, I've somethin' you'll need."

His gaze lingered on Mogue as he took a small vial from his pocket. The substance within looked clear. "I've removed the bullets and staunched yer wounds. You kept sinkin' in and out of consciousness. If ye wish to die, lad, ye need only say the word. But if ye want my help, I'd advise ye to drink this. The pain'll be back soon. This stuff's all that stands between you and the agonies right now."

"And why should I trust you?" Despite the snarl Mogue put into his voice, he was cowed.

"'Cos, weren't for me, ye'd be long dead by now." MacTíre looked abruptly away and placed the vial at Mogue's hand. "And I've seen enough death for one night."

He finally stood up. "It's nearly dawn, lad. Ye best get some rest. You'll need it. As for me, I've to be about some business."

With that, MacTíre turned and started walking in the direction of the waterfall. Mogue, too cowed to call after him, watched the highwayman stalk off into the gloom, his boots clipping heavily off the stones and sloshing through the water, barely the ghost of an echo trailing behind him. Already, the fresh pangs of the boy's injuries were beginning to bud and sear through his marrowbones, rending his frame into a husk of agony.

With his one good arm, he reached over, and lifted the vial to his lips. He gulped back the heavy, bitter-tasting drug, grimacing as the taste ravaged his tongue and throat and the rest of it spilled down his front. Lying back, the damp beneath Mogue's flesh dissipated as the soporific mist slowly engulfed him.

Chapter X
Into That Dark Fold

His sleep was dreamless. Or perhaps he forgot them the moment he woke. Either way, the red sliver above was brightening as dawn got underway, like fresh blood brimming to a wound. Wherever this place was, it was too remote to hear birdsong or cockcrow. Mogue thought of the many times he'd wakened to the sky's dark blushes, the sun flecked with scarlet as it burned through the morning mist, like a skull adrip with blood. Had he been cursed to always rise early with such ominous morrows?

Beside him, the fire had smouldered down to a smoky clump of cinders. Wind gusted icily through the overhead crack, and as he sat up, he realized MacTíre had put his greatcoat over him as a blanket. It smelled harshly of tobacco, rain, and damp soil; as he shook it off, a dull ache, though not as severe as before, blossomed in his arm. Clenching his teeth, Mogue rose slowly to his feet.

The cave was lit, albeit dimly, by the slender column of amber sunlight beaming downward from the fissure. The soft roar of the waterfall and bubbling glint of black water like a slick of spilled tar some way off sounded as clear as it had after dark. Glutinous shadows still prevailed, as no doubt they had done for centuries. Mogue's nervous breathing sounded faraway even to his own ears. As his eyes began to adjust, he still had to strain and stare into the vast gloom before scanning the heights around him. The craggy walls were dark and damp from rainfall; in the half-light, they shone like the eyes of some watching, waiting creature. A carpet of pebbly mud seemed to crouch under his boots. Yet, the rancid-looking sailcloth tied to his arm didn't seem as sullied as before. Gingerly turning his arm as best as the pain would allow, he ran his fingers over it; MacTíre had tightened it well.

He was not yet ready to venture into the shadows and seek a way out of the cave; or, indeed, to even find his captor. The highwayman was no doubt more accustomed to darkness in a way that few men ever are. Not only had his eyes grown acclimated to the shadows; his body now moved instinctively through dark places with nary an echo to betray it. He could move and hide as he pleased, knowing every nook and cranny as if they were his own home; for all Mogue knew, he could be lingering there in the shadows, undiscerned and indiscernible, keeping grim watch while he fumbled about this accursed tunnel with only a single good arm.

An odd, ghostly hum slowly knifed through the silence, echoing off the cave walls.

As it turned out, MacTíre was doing precisely that. From the shadows, he watched the boy attempt to get his bearings on the clammy shingles, wincing every so often from the pain in his arm. It would be a good while before his wounds fully healed, but when they did, MacTíre had plans for that arm. The lad was clearly frightened and somewhat disoriented, but he was attempting to regain some semblance of control. His slow movements told Mogue he had caution, the bulge of his eye told him he was aware of being not quite alone in this dank vault. Adjustment to the shadows always took time.

MacTíre drew one of his flintlocks and began to hum to himself. He knew the cave well enough to position himself exactly to ensure that his voice echoed with just the frightening volume he intended. The sound of his voice, humming a quiet air, bounced and trembled off the black stone and dank gloom. He saw the boy start and glance agitatedly around, his eyes wild. With practised quiet, MacTíre forced the shot down the carbine's barrel, humming all the while. He cocked and aimed it, kept it trained on a delicate point just past the boy's ear. The shot ignited, the crack reverberating loudly off the cave walls. Mogue started and nearly fell to his knees as the highwayman stepped forward, his boots crunching off the stones, and lingered on the rim of the light. The barrel of his flintlock glinted pallidly. MacTíre, smelling of smoke, advanced.

"And Endymion wakens! The drug should've kept ye in a stupor far longer than it did. Any pleasant dreams at all, lad?"

"Why'd ye do that?" Mogue spluttered.

"To see I've yer full attention. Now, I know yer arm's still hurtin', but I'd still suggest ye raise yer hands high above yer head there. I've no desire to waste another shot on ye. On yer feet, lad."

Mogue, his heart now at full gallop, raised them as best he could, baring his teeth.

MacTíre stepped forward without lowering his gun. By the beam's glimmer, his scarred face was even more terrible to behold. The hand gripping the flintlock was white as a fish's backbone, yet a disquieting calm pervaded his hard eyes. What those eyes were witness to, what nightmares lurked behind them, what fresh horrors they intended on seeing, Mogue had not the heart to consider.

"I know nothin' of who ye used to be. Mayhap ye'll tell me, mayhap ye won't. But I just may know exactly what ye'll become. It's time." He moved toward the boy.

"Time for wha–" Barely had the words escaped Mogue's lips when MacTíre tossed something into the air. Instinctively, Mogue's good hand reached up and caught it. It was a skinning dagger, its hilt carved from undamasked whalebone, its rusty, rain-grey blade nonetheless keen and long. *Feels lighter than it should*, a voice whispered from within.

"A few hours from now, we'll be leavin' this place and I'll lead ye into somethin' few lads yer age ever get the chance to witness," MacTíre said, clipping his flintlock. "If our luck holds, as I'm fairly sure it will, ye'll be on the road to yer fortune quick enough. But I've to verify a few things 'bout ye first. That blade in yer hand may well decide whether ye live or die the day."

Mogue squinted in confusion. 'You…you want me to fight you?"

"If ye wish to leave here alive, and to earn some hot grub… yes." MacTíre grinned at the boy's sudden twitch. "Ye must be hungry, lad. Go one round with me, and it's yours."

"Why not just let me go?"

"You've skill with knifework, lad, 'tis clear. But I want to see if ye can fight without earnin' any extra scars for yourself." MacTíre nodded at the *gralloch* Mogue held in his hand. "I fleeced that from the belt of a fat merchantmen en route from Dublin. Make of that what ye will."

MacTíre tapped something tucked under his coat and ripped a gleaming bayonet from its sheath with a hiss. "Shall we?"

Mogue had crossed blades with men before, but never one with so hideous a reputation as MacTíre. He cast an eye toward the highwayman's stance as he extended his weapon and assumed a fighting position. If the man's scars and bruises were indicators of anything, it was his brutality. No gentlemen's rules would apply in what was to follow. Nails, fists, or teeth were all potential weapons. No point in even trying to emerge unscathed; getting cut or sliced was inevitable. The wounds would not be inflicted cleanly and whoever drew the most blood would be the victor.

MacTíre seemed to fill the entire cavern, his movements tight and regimented like a soldier at parade. A flicker of misgiving darted through Mogue. He almost seemed to be planning each move as he swished the bayonet this way and that, carving the air.

"Have a care for the rocks, lad. They could upset yer balance."

Suddenly, MacTíre lunged, lightning quick as a dancer, his bayonet clattering hard and heavily off the boy's dagger in a hail of echoing clashes. His body became a fever of movement, limbs snaking and dashing at the boy, the force of his attack enough to bring anyone to heel.

Were Mogue a novice, it would have happened too fast for him to even react. But he was versed as a scholar in the alchemy of knifework. Of the two, he was easily the nimbler, and his boots as much as his blade were lighter. Big though he was, Mogue noticed MacTíre moved slowly, not from deliberation but from necessity. His forearms also lay exposed, their tendons waiting to be severed.

Parrying each blow with the flat of his dagger, Mogue managed to sidestep the highwayman, briefly blindsiding him with a rapid thrust to the rib. MacTíre's curved, deadly stroke narrowly missed him, and he was left chopping at the air, butchering dust. As he gathered his bearings, his breathing was shredded, laboured. Somehow though, Mogue knew the highwayman's gnarled smirk was curling back in the dark.

"Not bad, boy. You've good form."

MacTíre charged again, but Mogue was the nimbler of the two, his legs whipping between stones, just as he lashed between blows. Surprisingly, his lame arm was not a hindrance – it allowed him to dance more freely, dodge more nimbly. He was manoeuvring around the agony that threatened to stir from any sharp movement as much as he was the gravel beneath his feet.

Sparks spat into the air as their blades jolted together and swung apart again. The boy's blood pounded, a hot tattoo in his ears. The dagger in his hand seemed to ring with a life of its own. It gave him courage, fearlessness almost, an ability to know precisely which stroke to land and where to land it. If the brute touch of steel were to assure his survival, and perhaps even the besting of this reprobate road thief, this MacTíre, then he liked these odds. Regaining his balance, he loosened his grip slightly, and with a flick of his dagger sliced a sharp pink graze across the highwayman's sternum.

It wasn't a deep cut, certainly not enough to warrant victory for Mogue, but enough for MacTíre to grunt and stagger backward, dazed. He glanced down, and his free hand located the laceration as blood bedabbled the linen of his shirt and seeped out onto the stones. The splashes, too, echoed loudly and they both stood back, appraising each other and the damage. Mogue saw his smile was askew and his breathing heavier than before. *Holy through his own blood*, he thought.

"Very good, lad," MacTíre panted through clamped teeth, something like approval flaring his eyes. They stood now on the very lip of the water, their feet crunching damply through the stones with each parry and riposte. MacTíre's back was to the water, and the more ground Mogue gained would ensure he'd fall in.

Dagger and bayonet flashed and blurred, rang and clanked; steely clatters echoed through the cave like the shrieks of ill-fated souls. To anyone else, that sound was murder to the ears. To Mogue and MacTíre, it was sweet as an aria.

Desperate now, MacTíre raised the bayonet to resume the advance, gashing and whirling through empty spaces where Mogue had managed to swiftly sidestep away from his assault, his dagger blocking a hard downcut and biting fast through MacTíre's black sleeve. The highwayman kept his teeth bared before spitting, his movements now rattling with fury. Yet his strokes were also sloppier, his breathing ever-more laboured.

He was starting to break one of the cardinal rules, the one Mogue had known by instinct when he first picked up a blade: never get angry in a duel. It blurs concentration, makes one clumsy and more likely to be beaten.

MacTíre was no less dangerous for it, though. Droplets from the cut on his chest sprayed over the rocks; his boots kicked up stones in his wake as he swung and kept missing. He was flailing now, aware that a shift in the air had occurred and he was no longer at an advantage.

Weakened, he managed to ward off another of Mogue's slashes, blocking the boy's riposte somewhat, but it was far from enough. He forced the boy back somewhat, but Mogue charged, and the highwayman listed against a rock, grabbing on to it to catch his fall.

With raspy breath and mouth agape, MacTíre stepped forward, blade lowered. There was blood in his eyes now; even in the dark, that was clear. His empty hand found the nick and the blood pooling around it, warmly soaking his fingers. The cut ran deeper than either of them thought. His face now seemed to register something alien, for in truth, he had no facility to fathom defeat.

He tried hacking again, in a downward arc, but Mogue's counter was too quick as his dagger raked over his gloved wrist. MacTíre yelped sharply; his blade seemed to spring from his hand as if by magic. It clattered off a nearby rock, a hair's breadth from the waterline. All that MacTíre felt next was the cold sting of the dagger he'd handed the boy pressed to his gullet. His head canted slightly, avoiding the steel as best he could. A single wrong move spelled death for him.

For a moment, neither man nor boy moved. In the half-light, even the echoes no longer sounded. Only the ragged gasps of their breathing were clear.

"Yield," Mogue hissed, his jaw clenched. "Yield, damn you, road thief!"

MacTíre wondered if the boy truly had the sand to kill him then and there. Silently, he deemed the risk not worth it. "Good form, lad," he mumbled. Despite the pain snaking through him, and unbeknownst to Mogue, he was grinning. He seemed to give no care at all to the wound on his sternum and the blade at his throat. "Truly, you're as good as I imagined. And faster than any man I've yet come across."

"Hunger'll make anyone good at knifework," Mogue replied.

"Aye, that it will, lad."

"Stop calling me that. My name is Mogue Trench." Saying his own name aloud, in the cavern's flinty depths, to this stranger but also ostensibly to himself, seemed curious. Until now, he'd never uttered it aloud as a declaration. It was what he'd always been called, but of its origin he couldn't rightly say.

"Well then, young Mogue." MacTíre's voice was strained from the pain that was no doubt coursing through him, but it had lost none of its mesmeric edge. "Me hat goes off to ye. Had I known any better, I'd've thought twice about engagin' ye in a fight such as this."

Mogue scoffed. "You mean, if you weren't the notorious Captain Joseph MacTíre, scourge of the Kingdom of Ireland, you'd have been just as easily disarmed by a mere boy?"

MacTíre didn't reply at first, one hand by his side and the other still pressed to his wound, staunching it. Mogue kept his eyes warily locked on him, tightened his grip on the hilt. He liked how snugly the knife fit his hand, how sharply its blade glimmered despite its dullness, how light it was to the touch and yet how efficiently it had served him. As though it was a part of his own body. He kept his grip strong, fingernails digging into the sweating flesh of his palms.

"Even boys can be skilled in knifework. As you've just made admirably clear, an' you with only one good arm. But there's somethin' yer after forgettin'."

MacTíre's hard eyes slid down to meet the boy's, and that notched grin of his spread slowly. Mogue barely had time to register any startlement at the blunt force of a punch that seemed to knock the breath from his chest. A mere split second before, he'd been clutching the dagger with the whalebone hilt to MacTíre's throat; now that same blade was pressed to the curve of his own gullet, poised to bite, and his back now pinned to a rock, forced to look up at MacTíre. The force of the stone revived the pain in his lame arm. The highwayman loomed over him, a deadly calm knotting his features. Mogue froze where he was, his throat suddenly arid and his tongue heavy and sour as a stone in his mouth.

"Inflict the killin' blow while yer able," MacTíre growled. "Otherwise, you'll see yer throat opened."

Benumbed with fear, Mogue attempted to swallow, his throat bobbing dangerously close to the dagger's edge. He tried reminding himself that he was still on his feet, at least. MacTíre kept staring him down, until finally, to the boy's surprise, his expression softened, and he lifted the knife carefully away.

"But as I said, I've no desire to kill ye. You've also earned yerself a hot meal, after all. If I mistake not, me terms were, ye fight and emerge without scars. And ye have no scars that I can see."

Mogue's eyebrows lifted as the highwayman loosened his grip, releasing him the hardness of the rock scraping his back. Relief billowed up from his chest and out of his mouth in a single unmediated sigh. The mention of a hot meal suddenly reminded him how hungry he was, and how long it had been since he'd last eaten.

With the same steely grip as before, MacTíre helped him to his feet, and allowing the boy to lean on him, led him down a passageway to another part of the cavern, farther back into the stony recesses. Not a word was uttered between them; only the highwayman's heavy footprints and steady breaths echoing in the profound dark were all to be heard. Mogue glanced warily around, wishing he had a torch or even a candle to guide his way, until, from the corner of his eye, he saw a dim flicker of light in the distance.

As they neared, a feint whiff of smoke tickled his nostrils, and he saw the light to be a hot little fire blazing amidst a deep-set nook that resembled a crypt. Ash and embers and tiny furious coals crackled beneath, and the air was thick and closer with the smell of it; the chill in Mogue's bones wilted. Suspended from a rack above the flames was a black iron pot; tendrils of steam wafted forth over its lip, mingling with the smoke as it billowed through a crack in the ceiling. The smell of whatever was cooking made his famishment form a gurgling knot in his belly.

Against the far wall Mogue saw, by the flame's thrashing light, Mogue saw a great heap of treasure: spoils, no doubt, from MacTíre's past excursions. There were brass coins, silver brooches, signet rings, and baubles; many blades, guns and bags of shot, and a settle-bed. But mostly there were books, a great stack of books, rolled-up sheafs of paper, their green and wine-coloured leather spines facing outward, the gold and silver lettering of their titles shimmering like coral in the firelight. All of Ireland could have been plundered to make this underground library. There was also wood stacked beside them.

MacTíre eased the boy down and handed him an oil-cloth blanket before feeding a few more branches to the flames. The blaze ignited, and the highwayman began stirring whatever was in the pot. Mogue drew the oilskin around him, rubbing his shoulders down. After the freezing conditions of the cavern, the warmth was an intoxicatingly welcome reprieve. He desired not to think too much; merely savour the glow while it lasted.

The highwayman poured a scoop of steaming stew into a small, rough-hewn bowl and handed it to Mogue.

"Eat, lad. Ye fought well today. You've earned this."

Mogue grabbed the bowl, attacking the stew without grace, shovelling the hot, salty substance between his lips with his good hand. He cared not for his scorched fingers or tongue or the stew dribbling down his chin, or even the gritty sensation that entered his eyes from the smoke. His belly was soon filled as though he'd tucked into a banquet. MacTíre sat a-ways off, humming quietly to himself while he staunched his wound. When he concluded, he began polishing the mechanism of his flintlock with a bit of cloth, occasionally looking up to pensively watch the boy.

"Ye made a good mess of me back there, Mogue," MacTíre smirked, a note of wonderment creeping into his voice. "Glad I was able to stem the blood where I could. I wouldn't have expected a man to have fought with your fervour, much less even take me on."

Mogue eyed him warily. "You left me little choice."

"That I did." MacTíre went back to polishing his flintlock. The fire spat and cracked.

"I don't fear you, road thief. Am I clear?"

"As clear as day, lad."

Mogue did not reply.

"When I first saw you, after you took aim at me on that bridge, I knew instantly there was promise in you. Ye saw more death in that moment than most men see their entire lives. Yet there was no fear in you. Only an ardour for survival, to see another morning. Perhaps it's hard to believe, I was there myself once."

"Is that right?"

"I don't keep much company, lad. I much prefer workin' alone. Means I've less to worry about. Means I alone enjoy the takings I bring in. Neither the Redcoats nor the constabulary will make any kind of move to stop me. Nor will the secret societies that infest this place. Make no mistake, Mogue. Long as I breathe, this place may never call itself civilised."

The flames crackled. Mogue looked at the sabre-cut face, incredulous. Fearsome a form as MacTíre cut, to hear that voice, rich and dulcet, fall from his mouth was like a charm. The boy thought of when he'd heard it for the first time, merely the night before, when MacTíre had chanted the lines from Milton. The same honeyed cadence, the same wistful tone, yet the voice retained its guttural coarseness. To hear such a crude mouth speak so sagely and hold him mesmerised was an unnerving thing. It stirred up darkness while convincing the listener of light.

There was sorcery in how the highwayman's speech floated from the roof of his mouth and hooked the boy's ears into listening. As if his tongue were silken and his throat sprayed with silver. As if he were delivering oratory in parliament or reassuring a prisoner that he was absolved of his many crimes; or tempting a man to commit some unpardonable sin against God and his own fragile nature. This was a voice that could either break or raise the spirits of whosoever's ears it reached. It would make murder sound reasonable, thievery a judicious course of action, rape a tenable instinct. A balm to the ears, or a killer of time, Mogue forgot how long the highwayman had been speaking, so rapt was he in hearing the voice weave its magic. Regaining his bearings somewhat, he cleared his throat.

"Well, you've done very well, but –"

"I'm not askin' ye to understand. I'm askin' ye to join me."

"What?"

The highwayman stared into the flames' thrashing glow. "I'm a rumour to many, Mogue. A mere phantom who emerges from the shadows, kills quickly, and vanishes, leaves only blood in his wake. A secret that cannot be retracted once revealed. But ye've just seen what most never would. You've not only willingly fought me, but almost had me bet. You're probably the first to know that I am merely a man like any other. So, I'm offerin' ye a chance to live a life where eventually you'll be free from wages, from hunger, from the petty laws men devise to keep each other shackled. I'm offerin' ye a chance for freedom, real freedom now, not the abstract fancies they fill their books with."

Mogue glanced over at the books. "What do you want from me?"

"Ye might be the very stuff of a *meirleach* yet. We shall see."

"How?"

"If ye can fight me one-armed, just imagine what ye migh' do once that arm heals."

"What're ye talkin' about, road thief?"

"Make no mistake, lad. You're still at my mercy. So, I'd advise ye to lend me yer ear, unless I decide to cut it off. Have I yer attention?"

Mogue looked down. The highwayman reached into his pocket, drew out an unsealed sheaf of parchment, held it up for Mogue to see. It was crumpled, its blood-hued waxen seal rent in two. To Mogue's horror, its edges were flecked with dark-red stains, and slightly burnt.

"Good. Now, do ye know what this is?"

Mogue shook his head. The dim glow of the embers danced.

"Mmm. Well, there's some things that need explainin'. See, I've gone over all me takin's from that little carriage ye were on. Books mostly, letters, pamphlets, bills of ladin'. Wouldn't be much of inth'rest or use to an unlettered man, 'cept as firewood, maybe. But I'm quite an avid *leitheoir*, it so happens. Had meself a good few hours perusal while ye were healin'. But one in particular's after grabbin' me inth'rest 'bove all the rest. Found it concealed in a bag of shot, on the chance it might be discovered and its contents exposed. It's this letter here, marked with the seal of a particular *Sassenach* lord I'm quite familiar with. Not face to face, ye understand, but his name's well-known in these parts. Addressed to Sir Vesey Colclough, bart., of Tintern abbey. But don't be fooled by the title, lad, he is no officer of justice. He owns half the land we're standin' on right now, though he's also a man of much-depleted fortune."

"We were to deliver mail to him, what of it?"

"The contents of said mail could be very, very ruinous to many people, Mogue. So, I've been thinkin'. P'rhaps the time has come for me to...rejudge me situation, and me methods. P'rhaps we can both help each other. You're no good to me dead, sure. What say ye 'bout joinin' me?"

Mogue blinked foolishly and made to speak several times. When he spoke, it was as if reciting from memory, as if the question were new. "You...you want me to be a road thief? Why?"

"I've no fam'ly either, lad. They were taken from me. I'm alone, as I suspect are you. To be alone is to be damned, perhaps, but it's also to be free. Why not join me, fight by me side? There's perhaps a better life for you in it." He spat on the ground. "And need I remind ye...ye won't go hungry again."

xc

"And why not just let me go?"

"'Cause I can see, despite your tender years, there's great fight in ye. Perhaps it can be put to good use. And perhaps I'm the one to help you see what use that might be. This life isn't one that affords men the opportunity to grow old and enjoy the spoils. I'm only offerin' ye a choice. Otherwise, you're free to leave. Nearest road to Dublin is a day's walk from here. Ye can find your way there 'less the aul' *Buachaillí Bána* find ye first. Not a fate I'd wish on anyone. Now, I imagine…since ye've little 'nough to look forward to, you'll be wantin' a place to sleep. You're welcome to stay here 'til that arm heals. After that, it's up to yerself whether ye wish to stay or no. Though, if ye wish to hear more of Milton and suchlike, I can show ye. Might show ye how to read him yerself, if ye'd be so inclined. If that's the case, here's where I'll be."

The boy dropped his eyes.

"Well, lad," MacTíre murmured. "What say you?"

*

To the forest they returned. Despite the heavy cloak MacTíre had given him, the chilly night air still managed to slither down into Mogue's lungs. A hard dusting of frost carpeted the rutted *bóithrín* like sugar. The sky had been slate-grey for much of the day; a heavy fog had rolled in with the twilight, bestrewing the fields and roadside in a flint-grey gloom. The forest's hulking, tangled shadows seemed to ooze profoundly, impervious to any light and brimming with hellish intent. A sabre-sharp wind sighed through the leafless boughs and their rattling was to Mogue as a skeleton stirring awake in a crypt. His lips were cracked, the coldness biting into his jaw, his breath huffing in spurts, grey-white in the dark.

Country darkness was as divergent as daylight to the darkness in the city, which was at least punctuated by chains of lamplight along the streets and the glimmer of candles in tenement windows, and even the alleyways, where a man could expect to find a blade slid between his ribs for his timepiece, had the benefit of braziers. Out here, the darkness seemed fathoms deep, tended on by the frost and cold that managed to pierce glove and greatcoat, with the smell of sea salt prickling the air, and not a sound to be heard save the clop of their mounts' hooves and his heart's fitful thud. Were it not for the fog, the moon would be hovering, curved and luminous, in the heavens.

The tall, upright figure of MacTíre rode ahead of him, his black horse blending with the shadows. He seemed to know his way through the looming blackness, and the outline of his greatcoat, gleaming filthy from rainfall, told Mogue he had not vanished. Since leaving the cave, he had barely spoken, except to grunt a few husky commands to his horse. The dearth in conversation suited the boy; his own horse, a bony skewbald, was led by MacTíre, for the highwayman understood Mogue was not a seasoned rider. It struck Mogue again how, despite his hunter's garb and rough bearing, MacTíre could be easily mistaken for a lord. "Stick to the road, lad," he had snarled as they set out, throwing a contemptuous glance at the moon. "Not even the shadows sympathise."

"How far away is Tintern?" Mogue had ventured.

"Beyond them trees," the highwayman returned. "As long as we keep to the river."

Those were the last words to pass between them. After an hour's riding, they reached the river-mouth and began edging inland. Mogue thought of his companions killed in the mail carriage raid and the shots he'd fired at MacTíre. That same gun was now slung into the highwayman's belt, already loaded. On that frost-choked road, in this country that seemed utterly purged of daylight, the memory was already a distant one.

Suddenly, MacTíre hastened his horse to a canter, and Mogue's horse broke into a dutiful trot behind, knocking the boy clear of his thoughts. He gripped the reins, praying he would not be thrown off. He had to keep ducking his head to not be struck in the eyes by a low-hanging trunk. Before long, the sluggish growl of the Bannow reached his ears and soon they were racing along its bank, kicking up pebbles and squelching through muddy flats and snapped reeds. The river's dark shallows swirled and gushed without even a shred of moonlight to illuminate them. MacTíre took a sharp swerve and even in the sudden, swift blur, Mogue recognised the cut-stone and crenellated battlements of the bridge hurtling by on either side of him, mottled with lichen splotches and centuries of storm. Through the fog, he glimpsed the bridge taper off into a road that cut through a wide demesne, wooded thinly with ash and oak.

MacTíre urged the horses to a stop, and, as if by some sorcery, the fog seemed to lift somewhat, allowing slivers of lunar radiance to glisten down. At that moment, Mogue's chest seemed to hollow itself out. For there, under the sabre moon, a pistol's shot away on the rising mound, Tintern loomed into view, its frowning casement windows void of all light. Wind howled icily through its arches and parapets, which to Mogue's eye resembled the dread fangs of some fantastical beast.

"Is this it?"

"'Tis," MacTíre replied. "Abode to all manner of *siógs* and *púcaí*, where the cacklin' of banshees does be heard echoin' down its passages every Samhain night. So the local whisperin's go."

Mogue continued to stare charily up at it, as MacTíre dismounted and led their horses toward the edge of the trees, where he tethered them. He moved as nimbly in the dark as Mogue did in the daytime.

"Don't get too excited, lad. I need ye alive for what comes next," murmured the highwayman, his jaw clenched as he drew out the pistol and handed it to Mogue.

"Beg pardon?" Mogue's eyes narrowed.

"Make no mistake, the man who dwells up in that ruin yonder's mor'n a bit dangerous. I need ye to be as swift as ye were back in the cave." MacTíre's expression was one of furrowed solemnity. Mogue forced himself to return the stare without blinking.

"I…"

"I've seen ye shoot tha' thing before, lad. Just stay close, keep it cocked and perhaps we'll both see another sunrise." With absurd poise, MacTíre abruptly turned and set off toward the castle, scuffed leather boots crunching through the frost-starched grass, as if he were merely taking a stroll amid the grounds. Mogue glanced down at the gun he held. The urge to shoot MacTíre in the back kindled in his mind. He knew he was unlikely to encounter a better opportunity:

He saw the muzzle flash blazing as the bullets tore through the road thief's rib, making him stagger and crumple heavily to his knees, his fingers brushing the sudden crimson burst that now leaked darkly from his wound and stained the grass.

Yet Mogue also knew he was alone, in a strange terrain that he had no knowledge of, peopled by thieves even worse than the one who was quickly vanishing into the shadows ahead of him. MacTíre was a reprobate, but right now he was the only person within a hundred miles who could perhaps ensure his survival. And that was why Mogue Trench broke into a fevered run after the highwayman.

Like a scimitar of alabaster, the half-moon briefly swam into view from behind a wisp of ragged cloud, casting sickly light on the Abbey. As Mogue caught up with MacTíre and fell into line beside him, he got a better look at it. No doubt it had been a sumptuous manor once; but now, its stony central tower, though still standing regal and stark over the trees surrounding it, was draped in great knotted tapestries of ivy and vine. The nave and mouldings were a row of rain-worn lancet windows, empty and arched and overgrown as rotted teeth. He heard the squawk of crows somewhere high near the broken roof, echoing on the night wind. Shadows seemed to crowd upon it as if offering tribute; as with the forest, they also seemed to emanate from its nave and chancel. It looked as though it had been abandoned, most likely during an outbreak of plague. Whatever money had been poured into its maintenance had been shamelessly squandered. Closer now, Mogue saw a glow of lamplight visibly dancing from a lone mullioned window high up in the tower, several storeys above the gables. Were it not for that light, an observer would have concluded the Abbey to be deserted by gods and men.

The edge of the forest tapered off into the gloom. Under the half-light, a dozen tree stumps were knotted together, crudely notched from many axe-blows, powdery scatterings of dust and bark mulch sprinkled into the grass surrounding them; and the sharp, sticky odour of sapwood still permeating the air. Piles of freshly felled timber strips, most of them three or four times the length of a man's arm, channels sawed into their tips, or else sharpened into spiked points like giant skewers, were stacked nearby, as if waiting to be hauled away. MacTíre's pace did not waver, but his eyes narrowed at the sight of them.

"Sir Colclough..." the highwayman fumed. "See that light there? That's his chambers. All tha' money wasted on buildin' fortifications, and yet he can't afford men to guard 'em. Never thought I'd see the day that the deluded *Sassenachs* would be of use to me." He seemed to speak more to himself than his companion.

"What's he to you? An old friend?" Mogue holstered his gun but kept his palm resting on the hilt.

"Friend is puttin' it gen'rously, lad. But whatever history I have with him can be forgotten after tonight. A fresh start, as 'twere." MacTíre did not look at Mogue, instead appearing to peer up at the manor's tower.

"What do you want with him?"

"Oh, much." The road thief's voice had gone flat, void of its usual melody. "And I think ye will as well."

Mogue blinked. "Me? What possible use could a destitute baronet be to either of us?"

Even in the dark, MacTíre's frown was clear. "I'd suggest ye keep your eyes peeled. Tonight's an opportunity for a lad like you."

"A lad like me?" Despite Mogue's leeriness, the road thief's words intrigued him.

"As we've seen, Mogue, you've some skill with knifework. And you haven't shied from a fight. There's grown men in these parts who can't say nearly as much. But I've a feelin' yer skills might be put to better use elsewhere. Somehow, I think there's more you'd care to do than simply stayin' alive."

Mogue drew in a breath. "And you know this how?"

"A will to survive is always more than just that. A man clings to life 'cos he knows he has yet to savour all of its possibilities. I know what freedom is. What it truly is. Perhaps ye might know it also, as long as ye keep to my side." MacTíre spoke all of this without affectation or without even breaking his heavy stride through the frost and grass, as if he were merely describing facts. Mogue's mind was beginning to convulse with conjecture. Nonetheless, he kept his tone defiant.

"I still fail to see what any of this has to do with this Colclough man," he said, staring ahead.

"You'll know soon enough," the road thief returned. "But mark you, lad…I take no man for granted, nor do I ever underestimate the skill he displays. The fact that ye chose not to shoot me the moment I'd my back to you tells me you're able to think things through. Instead you chose to follow me, and you just might follow me into a life of…untold bounties."

They walked on in uneasy silence, the older man's footfalls getting lighter by the pace. Finally, Mogue spoke. "You certainly know how to keep a person interested. A rare enough skill."

MacTíre spat on the ground. "There's no survivin' without skill, lad. I've seen yours and hope they might be put to better use. The man up in this elegant ruin just might know what to do with ye."

"I find it interesting that you seem to discern such qualities in me," Mogue said. "Though our acquaintance is no more than two days old. I could just be lucky, for all you know."

"Ah, but ye aren't. I see what many either cannot or will not. I suggest ye trust me on this, lad." MacTíre smirked before coming to a sudden halt. "First, though. Findin' a way of gettin' inside is our first challenge."

They advanced and climbed over the cut-stone wall that led to the immediate Abbey grounds. MacTíre sniffed the air and drew his pistol, glancing furtively at the boy. Instinct told Mogue to hold his tongue, yet the question buffeted against his mind like a wave.

"Will we have to fight anyone?"

The highwayman was not listening. He stared up at the Abbey as though it were a beacon that might point him to a better place. After a time, he exhaled. Mogue did not see him move, exactly. All he knew next was that MacTíre's hand was suddenly clamped around his gullet, the barrel of a pistol pressed to his temple. When the highwayman spoke next, his voice had dropped to a sharp whisper, his face knotted into a thunderous scowl.

"I need ye to listen carefully, now. Follow my lead and do whatever I tells ye. Don't speak 'less I speak to ye. Else you'll be under me loadin'. Am I clear, lad?"

MacTíre let the boy go without waiting for a response, and stalked towards the Abbey, to the main door, glancing up constantly at the light shining from the tower. An instinctive caution seemed to enter his steps, for here not even the crows overhead nor the wind could reach them, and a deadly silence engulfed all things; even the crunch of their boots off the gravel seemed unduly loud. Across the courtyard, as well as Mogue could see by the moonbeams, was the main door, carved from rusty oak, and barred heavily from within. Above it, yellowed by weather, hung the Colclough family crest: a black eagle with wings outspread, standing astride a shield of ashen brass.

"Watch yer step now, lad," he muttered. "It's likely we can get in through that door there, but withou' given' ourselves away. Colclough has few servants, and no guardsmen, but I could be wrong about that. So, stay silent as the grave for me 'til we get to his chambers."

Mogue breathed in – the night air had grown cooler around him. He couldn't tell if it was excitement or fear that now crackled his nerves.

A sudden wild barking filled the night, accompanied by the harsh rattle of chains, puncturing the heavy winter silence. They were as unexpected as a lightning bolt, jolting Mogue and MacTíre where they stood. Before either could register the clamour, the mastiffs to whom the barks belonged came racing around the corner and bounded straight for them, slavering hellishly as their spiked collars jangled.

Guard dogs, thought Mogue, gritting his teeth.

The inevitable shouts of men alerted to a disturbance followed close behind. Each of the men who rounded the corner seemed to wield – alongside billhooks and hoes – some sort of bizarre scythe, their tips keenly tapered and their edges jagged, like the leaves of some venomous tree, glinting fixedly in the darkness.

Chapter XI
The Learned Loft

"Curious," Sir Vesey Colclough purred in a tone of vinegary archness. "I don't believe I've heard the name Captain Joseph MacTíre yet uttered without the speaker blanching in fear. Yet, seeing you here, in the very flesh and blood at last..." He trailed off, letting the sentence hang momentarily in the air, like the answer to a particularly troublesome riddle, before finishing, "I cannot say I am impressed."

Those were the first words he had spoken since Mogue and MacTíre were brought before him and cuffed to the chairs in which they now sat. Prior to speaking, he had simply stared across the table at them for what seemed like an age, bloodshot eyes unblinking as though viewing artifacts in a cabinet of rarities. The arms of the mahogany carved chair he sat slumped in were blackened with grime; books and folios cluttered the surface of the table separating them. By the candles' dancing glow, his pallid face, smeared with trickles of sweat, reminded Mogue of molten wax. Cherry-dark splotches of presumably claret stained the baronet's lips and teeth; a matted, unpowdered tangle of silver clung to his scalp. His scarlet coat, once so grand, was soiled and torn from cuff to collar.

Mogue had never seen the inside of a gentleman's house before, much less knew how to comport himself in the presence of one. Yet, under the circumstances, such thoughts were trifling. Besides, the sight of the Colclough, even in the gloom, put him in mind of a walking corpse. *Must corpses also be afforded courtesies?* Mogue was nonetheless taken aback when the man suddenly whipped his head to the side, hocking a clot of phlegm over his shoulder.

Beside him, MacTíre's jaw was clamped as he returned Colclough's stare, a bright purplish bruise the size of a musket ball swelling beneath his eye from where a volunteer had struck him with his flintlock pommel.

"I hope you realise it is in my power as baronet and MP of this county to have you both shot on sight," he continued, his voice thickened from too much drinking, "without interrogation or trial."

Even from across the table, the slur of the man's speech and the stale fumes seething off his breath like some invisible, unclean fog made Mogue grimace. Neither he nor MacTíre made a reply, though the latter's eyes narrowed to a glare. Mogue shifted a little in his seat, eyes to the floor, ignoring the harsh rattle of leg-iron manacles that entrammelled his wrists, ankles, and neck. The chain's weight forced him to lean forward, almost bow; its black, rust-flecked texture was long and thin, sickeningly similar to charred bone. Charred bone that could not be broken. As he sat cuffed to the chair, the iron biting into his wrists and gullet, he tried his best not to meet the eyes of anyone else in the room. Blood roiling, he forced himself to sit perfectly still, a study of incurious poise.

Nonetheless, the urge to flick his eyes about and take in the library in which they were now chained was overwhelming. Situated in the tower's east wing, it reeked of something stale and arid and forbidding, and he tried not to inhale. There were no sconces giving off light – or, if there were, Sir Vesey did not bother to have them lit. Even with the two oil lamps, and the few tallows and wicks placed on the desk in front of him, deep pools of shadow continued to hover about him, on the very cusp of his vision.

The logs and coal piled in the grate had seethed down to a knot of russet, glowering ash; wind panted in muffled bursts down the chimneybreast. Rain chattered off the mullioned window, beyond which he saw naught but even more unfathomed darkness. He had to remind himself he sat within a library on the topmost floor of a converted abbey tower, and not a crypt. *Though a crypt may well be my next destination*, he told himself.

The gloom notwithstanding, and the sense that mildew was slowly devouring its woodwork and wallpaper, Mogue could see that the room was yet palatial. Tall, mahogany bookcases seemed to reach for the crumbling plaster ceiling on all sides, creaking dryly under the weight of all the volumes stowed carefully on their shelves, manifests and codices and leather-bound folios among them, manuscripts no doubt lavishly decorated with monograms and marginalia, tinted in pigmented woad and crimson lead. From where he sat, Mogue barely discerned the calligraphic lettering of their titles by the quavering light, editions antiquated and freshly bound, bindings both exquisite and economical, gilt and vellum spines pressed closely together like bricks in a kiln. The books were neatly shelved – those which seemed to serve the purposes of metaphysics, of theorems, of equations, of polemic and rhetoric, were ornamented at the most elevated shelves; whilst those which interrogated history, scientific inquiry, matters of morality and ethical nuance, easier to reach. On the small table before them lay a compendium of Dr Johnson's wittiest epigrams, and Rousseau's *Confessions*. Above, the faces of marble busts placed atop shelves swam in and out of the glow and shade like bone-smooth spectres, carven eyes staring flatly ahead like those of a blind man.

There stood surrounding them a posse of men, about five strong, half-shrouded in the sickly glow, watching him and MacTíre, sitting or leaning against shelves, labour-calloused palms resting on the walnut hilts of their pistols. A mere ten minutes earlier, those same hands had rained basalt-hard blows down upon Mogue's face and limbs. His jaw and facial muscles still throbbed from those blows. Dried ribbons of blood crusted his face. The surprise at not being killed right away had not yet worn off.

Of one thing he was certain, however: these were no Redcoats, nor any kind of soldierly troop he could name.

His nose bristled at the earthy reek of soil and horse dung which many of them exuded. Habited as farmhands or labourers, in drab, unwashed waistcoats and work tunics, the various flintlocks they cradled said they were more than mere serfs. One or two even had scabbardless swords slung at their belts, alongside bulging pouches of shot, their mud-crusted boots thudding heavily off the floorboards' unwaxed timber. For the most part, though, they carried billhooks and loys, some still smeared with leavings of earth or moss – tools of labour now wielded as instruments of war.

All of them to a man, however, gripped the heavy truncheons of pikes, fashioned from ash, the tips of which seemed to scrape the ceiling overhead. By and by Mogue found himself staring at these crudely wrought javelins with something that amounted to considerably more than mere curiosity. Now that they were in full view, he noticed the ash of their staffs were unvarnished, and most measured three or four times the length of a man's arm. He recalled MacTíre's glare at the many piled stacks of timber and tree stumps at the cusp of the forest not half an hour earlier, and suddenly comprehended. The iron of the pikes' hefts was whetted, as if from repeated rubbings of flint. Some were conical spearheads; others were hinged and bent narrowly over into curved clasps, like hooks. As with his own blades, which had been confiscated, these pikes could skewer the pliant flesh of a belly with devastating ease. Such a weapon must surely have been used to puncture Christ's rib on Golgotha. They were blades that needed neither embellishment nor exaltation. Workable, yet ruinous, the roughly tempered truncheons seemed capable of slicing through the sturdiest steel.

As to their bearers, Mogue saw that the closest they had to a uniform were the hooded, muck-stained, crudely stitched cowls of sackcloth that completely hid their faces. By the candles' soiled shimmer, they took on an uncanny, spectral quality, 'til they seemed to Mogue less like men and more like fetches conjured by some obscure sorcery. Colclough's face was the only one he had seen since crossing the abbey grounds.

For his part, Colclough sat back in his chair, a syrupy smile warping his lips. "But, as you both can no doubt see, I am also a man who enjoys a rollicking good story. Pray tell, then…who are you to intrude upon my home like this?"

A hush crept through the library. The dignity of the man's words and the degraded state of his person was staggering. Smoke puttered upward from the tallow; waxy tears welled and oozed beneath the flame. Mogue lifted his eyes. Beside him, MacTíre cleared his throat. "You're a man for the stories, m'lord?"

"Amongst other things, yes."

MacTíre seemed to nod at this. He looked down as if in deep consideration of his reply. Lying on the table before him was a book, its smooth Morocco cover wine-dark, even by the frail glow, its brass edges slightly worn. Mogue heard him mouth several words under his breath, in a language he did not know. *"Hai Ebn Yokdhan."*

Evidently, Sir Vesey had heard him too, for he said, a note of surprise tingeing his voice, "You know that work?"

The highwayman nodded impassively. "To an extent, sir."

"Mmm. In truth, 'tis not one of my favourites. The title alone is enough to put me on my guard. Though, perhaps, that particular translation is also rather lacking. In any case, those Mohammedan savages have little eye for reason, and even less so for a story well-told. Far too eager to cut up the corpse of a doe and slaver over the entrails and so forth. Not to mention his assertion that the Kingdom of Heaven lies too far beyond the hearts of men to even conceive of. Tell me, Mister MacTíre, are you a praying man? Suspicion tells me you are of the Popish persuasion. Most of the men in this room are."

"I am not."

The baronet's brows poked upward. "You aren't? A Church of Ireland man, then? Like myself?"

"Wrong again, yer lordship. Nor am I even of the devil's party. I pray to nothin' and no one."

Sir Vesey's head tilted slightly, his eyes narrowed to watery slits.

"Does that surprise yer lordship?"

"Not as much as the fact that a man of your…inclinations, shall we say, is also lettered. Though, I suppose, anything is possible in these…strange times. Even savages and heathens can find their way around basic sentence structure if they possess the will. And be most assured, these are strange times indeed. Like the Romans, we find ourselves dancing upon a precipice. Polemic and profane thought are the literature of the day –"

The baronet suddenly turned his head to cough violently into his soiled kerchief, an ugly, hacking sputter. When he had finished, his smile was haggard, and crimson droplets stained the fabric. "Forgive me, gentlemen. Mild complaint of the lungs. Quite common this time of year. But to return to our original mode of discussion." Resuming his position, the baronet exhaled. "The rather small matter of your intrusion upon my cherished abode. By all means, MacTíre...edify us."

Without a word, MacTíre climbed slowly to his feet, standing as close to his full height as his shackles allowed. The expression did not change on Sir Vesey's face, but a sharp glance into the shadows made his guards prime their weapons. The baronet raised an eyebrow in a silent question at the highwayman, who intoned in a voice that flowed like wine:

"Whether for life or death, in the presence of God Almighty I voluntarily swear that the Tree of Liberty shall be planted and reaped by the holiness of blessed water and by the strength of our arms. I solemnly and sincerely swear to always heal and conceal and never to reveal any point, part or act or letter of what I have got from this secret lodge to any person with whom it is not concerned, 'til the ashes of my body are cast on the seashore. I sincerely swear to see tithes and royalty abolished, these two kingdoms separated, and that all our enemies are put to death. I will firmly stand and uphold the present cause and purpose, according to the express intention of our emancipation. So help me God."

He ceased, and let silence engulf the library once more. Throughout this oration, Mogue sensed a flicker of confused shock roll amongst the masked men in the shadows. They shifted about uneasily, heads turning beneath their cowls as if to glance at one another, grips tightening on their flintlocks, whispered questions passing between them; MacTíre's words clearly carried some baleful familiarity to them, unsure as they were what to make of them. He heard a pistol being cocked from somewhere behind him, and the heavy footfalls of a man stepping forward.

Sir Vesey's eyes, meanwhile, were like rheumy flintstone, the beginnings of a frown lining his brow. His mouth was now open as if he meant to make some reply. But, to Mogue's surprise, words seemed to fail him. After a moment, he cleared his throat: "How is it you know those words? Answer truly, if you can."

MacTíre remained standing for a moment longer before seating himself again, his fetters clanking harshly as he did so.

"Not a man beyond the walls of this abbey ought to know those words. How do you, pray?"

The bruise beneath MacTíre's eye seemed to pulse. "When your men apprehended us in the yard, they indeed searched us, but not, I fear, thoroughly enough. I suggest you have them search me again."

Sparks sizzled and spat in the hearth; a fresh flame suddenly ignited, dancing jerkily on its ember-red stage of coals.

"Banville," Colclough hissed, without looking away. "Would you kindly do as our guest asks?"

The man standing nearest to the baronet stepped forward, the crude linen of his cowl keeping his face obscured. Levelling the barrel of his carbine to the highwayman's cranium, he patted him roughly down. MacTíre's face remained unreadable, marine-green eyes neutral as the man reached into his breast pocket and drew out a crumpled sheaf of parchment. He held it up between his middle and index fingers: the broken wax seal, maroon as an old bloodstain, was clear for all to see. He handed it to Colclough, who snatched it from him unceremoniously, discoloured teeth bared like the unlacquered keys of a harpsichord.

"Banville," he seethed, after a time.

The man who had searched MacTíre replied, "Sir?"

"Would you be so good as to leave us for a moment?"

Banville shifted a little on his feet. "Beggin' yer pardon, sir?"

"I'd like a private audience with our guests. Wait in the hall, please."

Banville and the others did as directed, filing slowly out of the room and shutting the double doors with a heavy click.

"I thought it a clever falsehood at first, I must admit," said MacTíre, his voice oddly cordial. "But as ye can see, sir, it bears your seal and your signature. 'Less, of course, it was forged, which I very much doubt. This lad here was postboy on the carriage that was set to deliver it to you. I apprehended it last night. Hauled a pretty swag for it, too."

The baronet stared down at the parchment, scanning the inky squiggles and splotches that were no doubt inscribed there, before staggering back into his chair. A hand reached damply, quivering, for his forehead.

"If me understandin' is correct," MacTíre continued, "ye plan to garrison this…illustrious ruin. In preparation for a fight that's yet to signal itself. Nor are ye alone. In my travels, I have seen similar such convenings. Packs of men, all over Ireland, meetin' in secret or under cover of darkness, all in the name of some mutinous purpose, swearing oaths to causes, to nation, to family. Farmers, charcoal-burners, horse knackers. And what ye just heard me say? Are those not the very words ye would have men say to you?"

"Why is this of any concern to you, MacTíre? Or to this boy you've press-ganged into your loathsome life? What could you possibly want of me, then?"

MacTíre's responding chuckle was hard and dry and arid as slag from a gravel-pit. "Come, come, Sir Vesey. 'Tis readily apparent you're plannin' somethin'. Says as much in that missive, addressed to yer good self. All me and me young friend here'd like to remind ye, such operations are punishable by law. Sure, isn't the country a measure for lawless these days?"

Judging by his brows' coldly amused curl, the baronet seemed to know what MacTíre would say next. The highwayman neither seemed to notice, nor care.

"Now ordinar'ly, I'd take a dim view of men with a cause – idealists and would-be emancipators adrift in a haze of utopic delusion, fuelled by too much perusal of rabble-rousing pamphlets and chain-breaking polemic. Many of them, I suspect, secretly yearn for the hangman's noose, if there's even the slenderest chance of history veneratin' them as martyrs for the cause. If the cause happens to be a lost one, then all the better."

Mogue nearly coughed on the sawdust that had now settled in his throat. Whatever MacTíre's plans were, divulging them now might spell death for them both. Had the road thief brought him all this way just to see a bullet puncture the flesh between his eyes?

"But, that being said," MacTíre continued, "men who are willing to fight that their lot might be improved…well, even I can see there's much to admire there. I don't know how willin' any of them masked yahoos are to shed blood in yer name. Ireland does be simmerin' with bloodshed, sure. But worse'n blood spilt is blood waitin' to be spilt, I shouldn't doubt."

MacTíre paused as if awaiting a response, before turning his attention back to Colclough: "Perhaps we can help each other, sir. The contents of that missive could very well spell ye a visit to the hangman. 'Tis yer signature, after all. I merely came out here to see it is was true."

"And for what purpose? Turn informer?"

"Ah, it needn't come to that. Per'aps I can make yer life somewhat more bearable. I know the land, its vagaries; sure, the dark's no obstacle to my eyes. I move through shadow as easily as I do daylight. I know where the redcoats drill and where they parade. So, may I suggest we need not call each other foes? May I suggest, sir, that you accept us both into the fold and see this fight carried to greater purpose? Let us go here and now, and ye'll be free to carry on as ye were unmolested. Perhaps even intelligence can be sent to ye. For a price, of course."

The highwayman spared not a glance at Mogue, but had he, he'd have seen disbelief plastered all over the boy's face. Opposite, however, Sir Vesey's lips were hooked into a smirk.

"Impeccably said, road thief. You're a poet, truly. And as for your offer, well, I don't deny its enticement. But answer me this: do you deem any of my men to be soldiers of fortune?"

"Ah, their loyalty's to you, that much's clear. Whether you've bought or earned it, that is a different question."

"I'm afraid their loyalty cannot be measured in gold, MacTíre. Something I doubt a man like you can appreciate."

"Don't you talk down to me –"

Sir Vesey's voice was steady. "You give no orders here, road thief. How little you know of what I intend to do, and how little I imagine you could even begin to comprehend. You know the life of secrecy, yes, you know the ways of living in the dark and by the roughness of the road. But you know little, I suspect, of overseeing men's lives. You know even less of their concerns, the daily pangs that see their livelihoods and their families tormented by hunger, by threat of eviction, that may see them fall as low as yourself. "And yet, I find myself wondering. Well, men like you are wasted on sneak-thievery –"

"You've seen yerself what a fight we put up before ye had us in fetters. I can bring a great deal of harm with what you say next, Sir Vesey. Speak carefully."

Once more, a laden silence reigned in the library. MacTíre's voice dominated the room long after the cessation of his speaking. Stirring was its timbre, forceful like a reveille, and as it settled on ears and minds, the highwayman sat back, savouring the effect of his words.

Sir Vesey laughed. "You have as much to lose as they do."

"And what would that be? A life of knavery? I'm afraid I'm not really one to be wedded to a cause."

"No. You stand to lose life itself. Fervour for insurrection scorches the very air we breathe. Who among my men would be the first to join the fray or fall beneath it, soon as it happens? Well? Even a man such as yourself, who makes daily survival his vocation, can see this. Everything that can conceivably lose, they'll lose many times over before the end. Their homes, their families, their means of labour...which has of late yielded little. Yet I imagine their grievances must seem strange to you. You who live by the roughness of the road, in service solely of your own interests. Unlike most, I choose instead to help them rather than see them evicted. For that, they'll stand together and burn together, if need be. Can either of you say the same? I doubt it. But having you may yet be viable."

"How so?"

"We speak of different things. I mean to challenge an empire, with the full weight of an army at its disposal –"

MacTíre smiled. "Ye risk little. We risk all."

Sir Vesey spat again. "I risk much, and far more, road thief. Should this operation be discovered, it isn't just my body that will swing over the walls of Wexford. Every man here, thyself included, will be made an example of. No magistrate I know of will show leniency to members of an organisation branded as seditious or that is convening with seditious intent. Many of them pass their sentences with the help of a well-placed bribe. I must know every man here has loyalty to his fellows first and foremost, not just his purse. That when they swear that oath, I can believe them. As for you, worry about the fight that's coming. The battles to come will no longer be fought in Parliament. And I think we can both agree, it's only a matter of time before we all must face it or perish. I could show them how to properly fire their weapons. How to strike fast and vanish before their enemy even knows what's upon them. We could build walls, train men to guard them. Reap their labour in defence of this place instead of filling the pockets of their overseers."

"And don't ye believe me when I say I must respectfully decline your flatterin' offer?"

"Even less than I believe Mr Grattan whenever he spews forth one of his dreary monologues before Parliament. Every man here has loyalty to his neighbour."

"And if ye knew anythin' about me, Sir Vesey, ye'd know my feelings towards me neighbours are decidedly less than Christian."

The baronet ignored him. "These men have their grievances, but they are not ready to take on the full weight of redcoat regulars. And you care not a jot for that pledge you've memorised. Soldiers of fortune desert, betray the causes they swore upon their lives in sight of God and men to defend. Oaths mean nothing to them. And they mean even less to you, I should wager, MacTíre. You have no future to look forward to. These men do. The risk they are taking with theirs far outweighs yours. They look to me for hope. With you in our ranks –"

"Fuck you!" MacTíre snarled.

Sir Vesey raised a wizened hand for silence, which to Mogue's surprise seemed to work. The baronet sighed before addressing the highwayman, his face betraying not an ounce of worry. "Tell me,

MacTíre, what do you know of what's said about you? The rumours to which your name is attached?"

"Beg pardon? Rumours?"

"It never ceases to amaze, how much more adept at surviving are rumours than truth. To many, men like you are mere phantoms, conjured from the shadows to frighten children, an entertaining fantasy. In truth, you're lower than the beasts of the field, setting on innocent people for your own selfish gain. Yet the fear you inspire in others is a result of these rumours. Without the rumours, there is very little left of you."

"I'm sorry, but I don't understand –"

"Have you not heard the rumours? I can't imagine how you haven't. You live only for yourself, they say. Kill purely for your own pleasure and spoils, so it goes. So, tell me, in this fight ahead, what sense is there in not having such a man in my ranks?"

"As opposed to seeing us both swing?"

"Heavens, no. But have you ever thought about how you'd like to die, then?"

"Not really."

Sir Vesey cast a sour glance at the window. He did not seem to be staring out of it, at the gnarled, shadowy trees and the dark river that frothed coldly and relentlessly out to sea beyond, but rather observing the solid, oily blackness that soaked through the mullioned panes of the glass. Something about the man commanded silence, an anticipation of his next words, even with his decrepitude. Even the crackle of rain and wind outside seemed mute, as if also eager to hear Sir Vesey's reply. When he spoke at last, there was frost in his voice. "I've never had much luck as a gamester. Why, then, would I gamble with men's lives?"

MacTíre frowned. "You tell us."

"The fact is…these men are quite happy to make that gamble themselves. You're wrong, MacTíre. They also risk all. And given what lies ahead, the term 'bravery' does not even begin to describe them."

"Bravery and recklessness are oft confused," MacTíre replied, his brows converging.

"Not on this occasion," said Sir Vesey. "War is on our doorstep. The time for parliamentary prattle has come and gone – and with so little achieved! Those powdered fops who crowd to interrupt one another in Dublin and Westminster have little idea of what is suffered out here. Men like you, MacTíre, are only the least of their problems. I am left with little choice but to raise a covert militia, exercise them in arms, have 'em swear upon their lives to protect my good name and lands. As long as this place and the identity of every man herein remains secret."

The scorn in MacTíre's sigh wasn't quite concealed. "And ye plan to do that with pikes against English cannon and blade? I must say, I'm surprised a man of yer standing would even permit a serf's weapon in his private quarters –"

But the baronet was talking himself into a frenzy, his voice growing with conviction. "But eventually, word will spread. Rumours will gather, be repeated, and repeated enough times over until they are taken for gospel. And for a while, we'll be able to hide up here in our glorified sanctum, provisioning ourselves with whatever food and arms we can procure, whilst the burnings increase and the Redcoats become ever more numerous. Before long, all our main outposts will be overrun 'til there's only here left to besiege. No escape route will be devised because we never felt the need for one, and yet here my men are, cut off and ready to be shot like dogs. The forest can only conceal us for so long until we are hunted down."

Sir Vesey kept his eye on the dark window, as Mogue and Joseph exchange furtive glances. "But we shall not be hunted down," the baronet continued. "While I breathe, I can see a way of none of that ever occurring. I can pledge to you to lead these men as your captain and see them through whatever bloodshed we know to be inevitable. It's a danger we all face, and whatever differences we may have had before, now they are irrelevant in the grand scheme of things. Martial law sees itself imposed and we are left to scatter into the trees. Beyond that window lies a country deathly quiet at night, but not from peace. Far from it. That quiet, to my ears, is similar to that preceding only the worst storms. And that because there are no more wolves to be found in these parts. Wolves have fascinated me always, MacTíre. They hunt, and yet were hunted themselves. Their howling at the moon has long since faded. Now the nights are silent as a tomb, and only the moon lingers. At night, as a boy, I'd often hear them, and O, how they froze my bones! At first, I thought it just another breeze, but how it rises, like a crescendo. Then one joins, and another, until finally it's an entire chorus, howling to the heavens. The hunted, talking to one another. Reminding each other they are there. Even the hunters find themselves as prey eventually, I suppose. Myself, I would not object to my slaughtered carcass being tossed to a pack of wolves. After those self-same wolves had concluded killing me, of course. I would see God Himself dethroned before that, and these men are no different. This is a land without wolves, MacTíre. God knows I have sat through enough caterwauling of sheep. I intend to hear them howl once more."

Mogue's head danced. The urge to protest that he did not and would not have any part in this was drowned out by the need to see what might transpire.

"We are all endangered eventually, road thief," Vesey went on. "You pay no regard to an oath of allegiance. And yet, like the wolf, your appetite is at its most keen when it hankers for blood."

"The fuck're ye talkin' about, Colclough?"

"Lend me your ear now, MacTíre. This little rebellion of mine? It won't succeed, I'm well aware. Whatever His Britannic Majesty intends for this place, not a man among us will not feel it. Either we stand together and ensure for ourselves a greater chance of survival or it will swallow us whole. You see these polemics, declaiming freedom and sovereignty? I suggest you join us in putting those fine notions into action. Engaging the enemy in open conflict is futile, at least until our ranks are sufficiently swelled. Our advantage lies in knowing the land around us, this terrain of furze and gorse. And you, road thief? We could use a man like you. Not a fair-weather rebel. Not a petty defector who'd tuck-tail and flee under fire. Captaincy is yours if you pledge that oath again and once more declare yourself and this boy our loyal comrade. Join us now, sir. I, myself am most desirous of your service."

Not once throughout this did the baronet lower his gaze from the darkness of the window. MacTíre kept his eyes level as he spoke. "Never, as long as I draw breath, will I subordinate meself to you or any other man. My shoulders will bear no yoke; I will submit to no oath or pledge of allegiance. Of that I am resolved. My place is out there, on the road. I do not belong in the service of anything. However, myself and this boy are now in the know of your little operation. I'm sure there'd be others most interested in hearing of it, too. But I am no friend of humanity."

Sir Vesey's smile was mirthless. "And the minnow deems himself a leviathan. I see."

"And I see that you're willin' to die for a fancy. And take your tenants with ye. Men with families, means, as ye say. You'd take the shovels from their hands and replace them with pikes?"

"Aren't you doing no different with this fine lad here? You're raising him to the rank of man long before he has the will to behave as such."

"Whilst ye think an army can be raised from a gaggle of lime-burners and cottiers? I'll be frank, then, Sir Vesey. I have an offer for you. One of supreme value."

"For me?"

"Damn yer blood, sir, damn yer blood. Damn yer militia, yer oaths, and everythin' ye bring with ye. Ye know nothin' of this land. I sensed that about ye the second I saw the whites of yer eyes."

"I...?"

"How many men ye buried on yer estate? How many prayers did ye fling at the earth in their name? Not many, I'll wager. Make me yer puppet, will ye? Tell me, why do I feel you would happily direct one o' yer men to shoot me and this lad once we're at safe distance?"

"And why do I feel that were you to be left alone in this library, you would not endeavour to escape but instead fill your mind up with every volume I possess?"

"Perhaps I am a tad more predictable than I care to admit, sir."

"Then perhaps you're familiar with the dour scribblings of that most choleric of chroniclers, the Right Honourable Mr Thomas Hobbes.

Leviathan, after that sea monster from the Testaments. Not a book for the faint-hearted, I'm sure you'll agree, MacTíre. He presents the most chilling vision of what might be should we as men forsake our better natures and return to that savagery wherein every man shall make a home from a cave and find himself at perpetual war with every other man. No alliances, no compromises, no agreements. Just enmity with everyone and anyone. Can you even imagine it? Freedom at its most true. We become the barbarians we have always been but have told ourselves we are not. For could barbarians build stone walls, write books of eminent doctrine and bend both the land and the seas to their prowess for sustenance? Yet look at how skilled we are in the arts of atrocity and carnage. Look at how efficient our arms become by the year, and how ironclad our laws become! How different are we really to rats that scuttle forth from the blackness of caves to leave yet more pestilence on the earth? But seeing you here before me now, I am reminded of something else." He paused. "There is a bounty on both your heads, is there not? Seventy guineas at the most recent estimate, if I recall correctly."

MacTíre glared, eyes like polished marble. The words spilled from Sir Vesey's lips like a poisoned river, fluid and sure, as a ghoulish gleam kindled his eye. Yet throughout the baronet's monologue, the highwayman's own gaze lingered not on the speaker, but upon the two oil lamps shimmering away on the table before him. They were starting to wane and dim, Mogue saw; jaundiced orbs of light wavering within their cages of glass. MacTíre moved his cuffed hands, folded them on the table in a gesture of loose concentration. As if Sir Vesey's words held some minor interest for him.

He was moving before Mogue or the baronet even realised, seizing the brass loop in both hands and swinging it in a wide arc toward the nearest bookshelf. The brittle noise of glass shattering off the oaken casing echoed through the room. Oil splashed thickly over the shelves and books; the smell of it was as acrid as Mogue imagined sulphur to be. Flames suddenly roared up over the many books and frames, a flowering of fire bursting upon the gilt spines, on the unvarnished oak of the shelves. Sir Vesey staggered to his feet, wide-eyed and clumsy, his chair crashing to the floor. "No," was all he could manage, stepping backward with both hands raised.

But there was no time to be transfixed. Smoke and scorching light swirled through the room, devouring the shadows as MacTíre hurled himself to the floor and rolled. Survival instincts stirring, Mogue leapt under the table, coughing, where for a moment he lay still. Already, the smoke's pungency was heavily choking the air. Against the weight of his fetters, the boy forced himself into a sitting posture, coughs and gasps still retching up from his throat, his face pale. Through salt-stung eyes, he dimly saw that the guards, meanwhile, burst back through the double doors, immediately scattering to escape the blaze. Pikestaffs clattered as grips were lost, and confused, garbled shouts were drowned out by the fiery roars all around them. The library was turning swiftly from a scholarly refuge to a powder keg.

Even with both hands fettered, MacTíre had managed to get one of Colclough's guards in a headlock, wresting his carbine from him. Slamming the butt of the carbine into the man's cowled face, he managed to send him reeling back into the flames, which broke furiously over him like a molten wave. The man's screams as he thrashed were lost on MacTíre, who was now taking aim with his carbine. His index finger wrenched the trigger back and, miraculously, there was no misfire.

The resultant shot thundered forth, gunsmoke mingling with that of the flames. Two more guards were sent sprawling to their knees; both were frantically attempting to load their own pieces. Their blood sprayed the floor, and as they fell, some of it even found Mogue's face and shirt, spattering his jaw and brow. Shutting his eyes, his stomach curdled at the warm sensation of crimson goo oozing down his cheek. When he opened them, through the salty tears that welled under his lids, he thought he discerned the fourth guard shove a spluttering Sir Vesey towards the double door, hurrying him out.

A wall of flame had now ignited the library, a blaze of heat and incandescence eating through the rafters; salt welled in Mogue's eyes as the world morphed into a hellish flurry of choked cries and wild, staring eyes and books flaring into tiny infernos. Any kind of weapon or means of escape would have been welcome now. Another guard with powder burns singeing his cowl came at him, his pikestaff levelled. Mogue swung his chains at the man's ankles, doubling him up. He leapt out from beneath the table, kicking the man in the face for good measure, sidestepping around the eagerly-dancing flames, smoke billowing all the heavier.

Someone's hand roughly gripped his shoulder, and an upsurge of sparks struck Mogue's face, scorching his jaw. He let out a growl of pain, wincing at the hot fangs of fire biting through his flesh.

The burning was too much for him to notice MacTíre's fist draw back, nor hear the mullioned window smash open. It was too much for him to protest nor reply to the highwayman's snarled command for him to hold on, nor that he inexplicably held the other oil lamp slung to his belt, which banged heavily and hotly off his thigh. It was too much for him to notice the sudden blast of chill winter air and rain scraping his flesh nor the sensation of gliding, trailing, plummeting downward, swift as a boulder plummeting from a precipitous height, the black ground below yawning up at him. It was too much for him to notice his feet hitting the ground and MacTíre bellowing at him to keep up, as they raced headlong through wet grass and dank, icy soil, towards the bloated gloom of the waiting forest and the river's wild swirling.

It was only when Mogue finally risked a glance over his shoulder and saw a heavy pillar of fire and smoke belching forth to the heavens from the broken window of what was once Sir Vesey Colclough's grand library – the dark, rain-lacquered stone of the abbey's central wing lit up around it in an ugly amber radiance – that he comprehended his situation. From somewhere far off he heard dogs barking, and the enraged voices of men.

Stoked by the heavy winds, the glow spread over the abbey's parapets and the treetops, licking through the shrouds of moss that clung to the tower, and gleaming off the metal of MacTíre's carbine. The abbey's entrance door burst open, and a crew of men and dogs raced out in pursuit, harsh, tumultuous voices and barks echoing horribly like the voice of a legion over the abbey grounds. Outlined by the inferno's hellish glow, they gave chase down the slope.

Only the forest could shelter them now. MacTíre and Mogue made a run for its shadows.

Chapter XII
Prey For The Hunted

MacTíre tore along the dark forest path, head bowed so as not to suddenly blind himself with any low-hanging branches, sweeping leaf and ivy and underbrush aside with his free hand. His legs already ached but still he managed to press on, the soil bare and rutted and cold underfoot. The lantern he gripped wasn't much against the dark, throwing a sickly orb of light around him, the path barely offering itself to its lambency, as trees slowly revealed themselves before retreating murkily back into the gloom like spectres. They provided a gloomy shelter, though their leafless, frost-varnished branches made it more difficult to hide.

But this concerned him not. He had hunted in this forest many times in his youth, and little of it had changed. Even fettered, he moved nimbly, his familiarity with the night hours permitting him to run with ease, bobbing and weaving past fallen, moss-coated logs with nary a sound, despite his boots' suppleness. The path was narrow, yet it also sloped and dived, veering into pockets of shadow, and forcing him to stay alert. Thick knots of leaves lay bunched and encrusted with frost, crunching harshly underfoot; briars and nettles thrust sharply from the ridges like pikeheads, stinging his flesh and tugging the loose linen of his shirt as he passed. The soft, calming growl of the river swirling into a cataract along the gravel bank was a relief; it meant their scent was concealed from the snouts of Sir Vesey's mastiffs.

Not far behind, the dull, frenzied rattle told him Mogue Trench was close by, gasping thick, heavy plumes of condensed breath into the night air. He did not know the forest; yet his pace did not seem to falter. *Fair play, lad*, MacTíre thought. *You've kept up this much.*

His own breath now ragged, the highwayman slowed to a halt, pressing his back against the soaked, wrinkly bark of an ash tree. Beside him, Mogue, still half-dazed, came to a stop at the clearing, wheezing heavily. He seemed on the verge of collapse as he stooped over, hands on his thighs. The burnt scar on his face now resembled a blackened vein in the dim lamplight.

It was several seconds before either of them spoke, or even had the strength to. MacTíre, his head thrown back, took a quick inventory of their surroundings. By the lamp's glare, he saw they had reached a dense copse on the far riverbank, far from the main trails used by Sir Vesey's huntsmen. Here the trees loomed tall as church columns, their lowest branches a good foot above the soil, and – though he could not see it – heavy, gnarled branches overhanging were ensnared like skeletal fingers, forming an obsidian roof, so thick that no light or sound could puncture through. Not a star nor even a patch of sky was to be seen.

Darkness hovered around them like a shroud, redolent with rainwater and pine; MacTíre knew the forest on the cusp of the Tintern estate well enough to know it was never fully still, even on the coldest nights. It had its own music, covert and yet riddled with the frenzied calibre of night-time: caws, frantic scurrying, chirrups, abrupt, blood-freezing hoots. Yet here, in this icy clearing, the silence seemed almost like a deathly, physical weight, as heavy as the manacles they still wore. Here, the woods offered no noise: not the whispering of leaves in a flurry of wind, not the gushing roar of the river, nor even a bird calling off in the distance somewhere. That's what made it perfect, by the road thief's reckoning.

The lamp in his hand still glimmered away, a cocoon of radiance against the sheer density of the dark. Almost like a pocket of air in a sunken vessel. It would give them away eventually, he knew; and he had to act fast.

Before the boy could protest or even understand what he was doing, MacTíre grabbed him by his manacled wrist, simultaneously smashing the oil lamp off the tree, engulfing them in pure darkness. The air was so close here, there was little concern to be had about the sudden, echoing crash of glass alerting their pursuers as to their whereabouts. Nonetheless, he clamped a hand over Mogue's lips as the lamp shattered and the hot, waxen oil from within spilled slickly out, trickling over the boy's cuffed wrist with a squelch. No doubt the pain was excruciating, but Mogue's inevitable screams remained muffled under the highwayman's gripped palm. He gritted his teeth, silently urging the lubricated hand to be free, tugging mightily on the wrist bone. The oil seared through his own flesh, a hot bite worming swiftly down into his bones. The exertion caused him to exhale heavily, his fatigued grunts sounding hideous even to his own ears, his entire body now tensed from anticipation of the release.

Finally, he felt it, the boy's hand starting to pull loose through the iron clasps. With a final mighty tug, he felt Mogue's wrists finally slip free of their cuffs. The boy stared in disbelief at his now bloodied and sticky flesh as MacTíre doused his own wrists in what was left of the slimy liquid, wriggling his arm out. Grimacing, he let what little breeze there was brush icily off the wounds and peered into the thickened shadows across the clearing. His flesh still smarting, MacTíre moved carefully across to the thicket, careful not to kick up any leaf-moulds. He stood there and held his breath, kept as still as he'd trained himself to be over all these years. The solid blackness would not be so for long; even the tomb-like silence had to reach its end. The cool closeness of the air ruffled his jaw. Such a silence told MacTíre that even the dead might be listening.

"Hold yer noise now, lad," he murmured. "They aren't far off. I know it."

Far away, the noises he anticipated reached his ears at last: wild baying of dogs and voices of men calling harshly to one another, distorted by distance and echoing and the thick linen of their cowls, voices crashing over one another like some savage choir, puncturing the stiflingly still forest air, and yet no words distinct words could be discerned. How many there were, there was also no telling. Dense as the forest was, it was not huge. The men had split up and were racing in separate directions; any one of them was bound soon enough to chance upon the clearing.

"Mogue," MacTire muttered, nodding. "Get over there opposite."

The boy obeyed, moving lightly over to where the highwayman pointed.

"Now, keep yer eyes open. On my signal, you'll know."

Guttering of torch flame slithered through the trees like fireflies, beads of thrashing, smoky amber against the enormous gloom. Soon enough, he'd smell smoke, both from the flames and from the flint sparking the men's rifles. The dogs' frenzied yowls told him they had his scent, and Mogue's too, no doubt. Glancing over his shoulder, the boy's shivering, wide-eyed stare told him he, too, could hear them.

Yet the reflex to run, to flee into the dark safety of the leaves, did not touch either of them. Not into the shadows, nor back towards the river. Even as the torches and barks neared. The mastiffs scuffled full-bore through cracks in the underbrush and over immovable crags, easily outrunning their masters, incited by the sweetness of their quarries' blood. MacTíre's grip on his now-loose fetters tightened. A nod in the dark at Mogue, and the boy drew his own back. They kept well out of sight, listening.

From the thicket, a glimmer of torchlight illuminated the trails leading into the thicket, followed by heavy footfalls, not far off, crunching over the leaves. Mogue whipped fully around in their direction whilst MacTíre's eyes merely snapped to them.

Into the clearing stumbled one of Sir Vesey's masked men, his breath muffled behind his cowl's heavy lining. A brace of hunting pistols was slung at his waistband. The torch he gripped guttered wildly, the pike he wielded unfit for dragging through the leaf-mould, and though his face was hidden, it was clear he'd lost his way amidst the trees.

Just as the torchlight fell on them, MacTíre sprang as if on fire, whipping the manacle chain above his head in a black arc. It locked around the man's throat like a cobra, clamping his gullet before he could scream or cry out. Dropping both his pike and torch, which snuffed out with a hiss as it hit the soil's considerable damp, he crumpled to his knees, still grunting and clawing weakly at his unseen attacker.

Mogue saw his cowl, saw MacTíre's face contorted into a determined snarl at his shoulder, and dove for the pike, seizing it by the shaft. Smarting from its weight, he raised it and ran its owner through, feeling the sensation of the spear bury itself deeply and up to the langet in the soft recess of the man's belly. Through the shadows, he heard the man croak and his body sag over the leaves and fallen twigs.

MacTíre swiftly knelt and unbuckled the pistols from the man's waistband, acquainting his grip with their roughly chiselled hilts. With a meticulousness that did not quite suit him, he recharged them and handed one to Mogue.

"I trust ye know how to use this?" he smirked.

Before Mogue could reply, the hungry raving loudened. The hounds were closer now, dangerously so, their barks echoing among the trees like alarms. The highwayman threw wild glances around the clearing, as if to which direction they were coming from, and the sound of his pistol being cocked was drowned out by the noise. The barrels bristled through the dark, awaiting their targets. The entire forest seemed to thrum with the barking and guttural shouts and calls, but Mogue couldn't tell if it was due to the road thief's silent expertise or the ringing in his ears drowned out all other noise.

"Now what?" Mogue muttered. The first shot almost punctured his ears, a noise like a branch snapping sharply, thundering through the small space as if in answer to his question. Readying his flintlock, Mogue took aim at the spaces between leaves as MacTíre kept his aim up, trying to ignore the trembling in his hand.

"Hold yer fire," the road thief snarled back. "Await me signal."

It was impossible to tell how long they stood there as masked men and dogs charged for the clearing, alerted by the shot. It could have been seconds, minutes, even an hour. From behind the hammer and frizzen, Mogue saw the torches and several mastiffs scuffle through the trees head-on, trailing his scent. They moved swiftly, hungrily, as if in flight. The men who lunged after them seemed to swarm in from all directions, spilling out of the shadows like trundling wraiths. Even as three beasts broke through the foliage and streaked right for them over the leaves, he barely had time to fire his newfound weapon. They were mastiffs, possibly the same set upon him back at the abbey, their snouts tingling with the savoury richness of his blood. He was sure of it.

Meanwhile, MacTíre wasted neither time nor bullets. His aim was careful, taking down a pikeman through the throat before managing to stop a mastiff in its hungry tracks. Both man and beast reeled backwards, landing bloodily in the teeth of the underbrush. He fired and brought down a second hound that had its jaws ready to clamp down on his outstretched wrist. Then he ducked and rolled by the treeline, reloading and firing on two more.

From his spot in the foliage, all that Mogue could now register were the billows of fresh gunsmoke and black powder, vicious snarls, growls and shouts from their pursuers, and bodies frantically swarming from all directions. As he fired wildly into the shadows, doing his best to divert his aim away from MacTíre, he managed to fell two more dogs at close-range and slam the hilt of his gun into a fourth man's cowled face.

Unsure of reloading, he grabbed the still-hot barrel to use as a club, the chain he carried now swinging wildly, just as a darting mastiff's fangs grazed his linen-covered wrist. The chain crashed into the beast's snarling mouth, cracking through bristly bone and throwing it aside with a whimper. Mogue leapt over to the animal, bearing down upon it, and a final slam of the chain into the creature's swollen neck saw it crumple to the forest floor.

Mogue crouched down sharply and drew the pikehead from his belt. He skewered a man's shoulder from behind, slashing from the dark with his natural dexterity. More hounds and men lay toppled around him, blood seeping darkly from under their cowls and from erupted heads.

MacTíre managed to fire and reload, taking out a pair of volunteers at a time, bullets biting through skulls and guts and eyeballs. Nor did he linger in a single spot for too long, managing to evade the torchlight's betraying flicker. Rarely did his shots miss their mark, close range or long. The volunteers were certainly not trained in attacks such as this. Their knowledge of the forest and its many uses paled sharply beside his. Confused panic now seemed to roll amongst the few that remained, as more of them dropped like flies. Yet the road thief also knew his shot was steadily dwindling.

The boy had managed to sidestep past the chaos, where MacTíre had managed to snatch up a fallen flintlock, of longer range than his pistol. Cornered now, with five more volunteers bearing upon him as if they knew his shot was spent, he managed to fell two of them before wading into the brawl. A frenzy had gripped the road thief; his eyes flared with brutality as he stared his attackers down, slamming the stock of his gun into a man's face or slashing hard at another's throat with the bayonet. His own snarling breaths were sharp and streaming white on the air as he pivoted, flailed, slashed, and parried blows, meeting steel with the solidity of oak.

And for their part, his enemies were equally as determined, thrusting their pikes at the highwayman as if trying to skewer a beast for market. All their mastiffs, it seemed, were slain. Only the pungent reek of smoke and powder and now the odour of new carcasses filled the air. By now the only hope was to see him killed and hope he either tired or was just a fraction too slow with his parries. How long it could go on for, no one could say.

The final four volunteers, the last of the hunting party, were all he had left to contend with. They had forgotten entirely about Mogue. Under their mantles, their voices were demented, desperate. He managed to finish them off and only then did a final mastiff, the last of the raiding dogs, come surging from the trees at him again, hollering wildly. Its fangs bit down into the highwayman's ankle, throwing him to the ground with a demented shriek. Furiously, it readied with jaws poised to rip his face off. MacTíre managed to bat it off with his flintlock handle, forcing it to let go. Raising his weapon again, he fired, but the shot missed the beast by inches, flying astray to graze the bark of the young pine behind it. The mastiff was on him again, gore wetting its fangs, lips drawn back in a starved snarl.

Several bullets tore through the creature's neck and side. It jerked and spasmed before crumbling to the soil. MacTíre fell back and kept still. The mastiff's eyes closed slowly, the bloody holes in its neck leaking crimson waste. Looking up, he saw Mogue, one of the fallen rifles smoking in his hands.

Bodies and weapons littered the forest floor all around them, mantled men and butchered mastiffs and fallen pikes. The wind had died down, and a deathly silence now descended upon the forest. Not even the gentle rustling of trees could be heard.

MacTíre stood still in the clearing for a long time, his breath ragged as he surveyed the carnage. The volunteers and dogs lay at their feet, blood seeping into the soil beneath them. He at last allowed himself a sigh of relief. Turning to the boy, he saw crimson flecks of blood misting his face, like warpaint, in addition to his scars.

As he approached Mogue, sidestepping around the corpses, the road thief saw that the weight of the rifle was straining the boy. He was breathing heavily, adrenalin still gushing through his veins. He had seen more death, witnessed and partook in more carnage and gained more scars in the last few days than ever before in his young life. Yet no fear could be read in his features now. He dug the rifle stock into the yielding earth, leaned on it and tried catching his breath.

MacTíre lowered his own flintlock. A strange calm, such as one that always appeared following a long fight, was beginning to spread through him.

Then it happened, as he expected it would. Mogue leaned on the rifle stock shuddering, but not, MacTíre could see, from the cold. His breaths deepened and quickened, and the boy vomited into the scrub-bush, his retches loud, and bitter to hear. The smell of dead dog and blood and flesh seemed to sheath them. He couldn't quite get to his feet for a while. MacTíre gave him a moment and looked at the dead men and dogs. Walking among them, he gathered up bags of powder and shot from their waistbands, knives, blades, anything that was worth salvaging. He realized, throughout the entirety of the night's excursions, that he hadn't yet seen any of their faces.

He gave Mogue a few minutes more to gather his bearings; the boy's ragged splutters and retches had yet to relent.

There were many hours yet before daybreak.

Chapter XIII
Meeting of The Waterſ

At the alehouse's weathered door, MacTíre halted and glanced skyward. The clouds had darkened to the colour of ash. He threw a surreptitious eye over his shoulder, watching the roadside, and then he looked at Mogue.

The boy was whey-faced, and the hideous scar had suppurated to a crusty, ink-dark gash that was mercifully well-hidden beneath a stolen labourer's cap. Nonetheless, and despite his hair being wildly tangled, he was well-rested; for as soon as they had arrived breathless at MacTíre's hideaway, the lad had collapsed into a desperate sleep. They'd spent most of the day there in hiding. Only as the noon light began to wane did MacTíre deem it safe to venture out again – yet longer they had waited.

Now, as they sat here in the cold, Mogue's teeth were beginning to chatter as he kept his head down and his clothes drawn tight about him. Experience told the road thief that a bone-deep chill would soon be upon the lad, burrowing into his flesh and jolting his body with shivers, a torture his rain-drenched garments would quickly aid. Though he had ridden faithfully behind MacTíre all the way, it was clear the lad needed rest.

"Be dark soon, Mogue," MacTíre said, making the boy glance sharply up. "We're better off here, with a fire to heat our bones and a hot meal in our bellies. Besides, there's someone here I've to have a word with."

"Right," murmured Mogue, his voice arid as sawdust on a carpenter's floor. He ran his fingers through soaked hair as MacTíre drew the brim of his hat over his eyes, swung down and led the horses around the back to the stables. He decided a pint or several of something amber and nectary to soak the boy's craw would not be remiss. It had been an age since he'd had a drink himself.

The alehouse's faded signboard swung creaking in the breeze; smoke uncurled from its chimney to mingle with the sea fog rolling thickly in from the peninsula in silver wisps. Soon that fog would pervade everything, the bocage and shelterbelts, the rivers and earthen banks; even the places where their boot-prints and any other traces of their activity had been scrupulously covered.

Since the events of the previous night, there was no doubt in his mind that word of his escape had spread, a greater sum attached now to both their heads. Experience told him that travellers were numerous on this road, and came by this inn regularly enough, outnumbering the regulars by an unhealthy amount, a multiplicity of strangers all either heading to or from the townlands: couriers and mail carriages, *spailpín* tramping from one day's labour to the next, patrolling redcoats a day's march from their garrison, pedlars and merchants and *bochtáns* alike, occasionally walking together and grimacing under the weight of their haversacks. The risk in entering the place was entirely MacTíre's and Mogue's, yet the former retained some cautious confidence that the rough labourers' garb he had them don would enable their blending in.

They'd managed to escape with only the shirts on their backs and this same garb pilfered from the corpses of Sir Vesey's fallen men; these they supplemented with heavy smocks from the road thief's hideaway. A brace of flintlocks were slung, concealed, under each of their cloaks; and MacTíre strongly advised Mogue to keep them out of sight. Though certain there was no shortage of huntsmen and off-duty soldiers and outright *maistíns* to darken this place's doorway on such a bleak night, he didn't care to arouse suspicion. Their scars and mud-stained attire alone would either set people on edge or permit them to blend in and be left well alone.

MacTíre frequented the alehouse as irregularly as he was able; as he'd expected, its clouded windows haemorrhaged waxy light and the discordant babble of voices accompanied by a fiddle's tuneless whine sounded from within. But mercifully, the roadside was deserted this night, and few enough horses were tethered outside. No noises were heard ahead or behind them, no hoof clops nor splash of a puddle nor the rustle of damp leaves.

"Mind ye keep yer face well-hidden, lad," MacTíre urged.

Upon barging through to the dim, smoky taproom, no landlord approached, but several pairs of narrow eyes threw glances in their direction, taking in the scars and the filth on their clothes before turning sharply away. Yet MacTíre's apprehensions were ill-founded, for the majority of small farmers seated there – and the girls who, as he expected, lounged on their laps – were more absorbed in their meals and slurred chatter than in a pair of mud-spattered itinerants just newly wandered in. There must have been easily thirty to forty crowding the room, and none, he was thankful to notice, clad in a scarlet coat. Plenty were fellow travellers themselves, set up for the night.

The floor was bare, unvarnished, smeared with dark, muddy patches of boot-prints and spilled beer. By the wall, a horse-faced chancer cheerfully sawed through shanteys and ballads on a bedraggled fiddle. The bar ran all the way across one side of the room, and a group of haggard bogmen were gathered by the taps, their voices low, their accents whiskey-garbled. On low benches and stools, under palls of pipe-smoke and wavering lamp-glow, the drinking was quick. Blister-handed tanners clinked mugs with quarrymen still coated in soot, a stonecutter dealt a hand of cards to a waiting faggot-cutter and fellow cottier. Their faces could only be seen by the murky light thrown from the candles on each table.

Ladies of easy leisure moved about the room, exchanging enticing looks and accepting the offers of whomever had extra coin, leading them by the hand up the narrow, rickety staircase to various bedchambers on the upper floor. Every so often, two more emerged from a room, coins crossing each other's palms, and two more took their place.

One of the girls, a hazel-eyed nymph swathed in a blue manteau gown, started when she saw them, locking eyes with the road thief as he passed. Had Mogue been less wind-drunk, he would have seen the briefest and subtlest of nods exchanged between them and would have felt the girl's eyes follow them.

Most of the men, it soon became apparent, wore white linen shirts. MacTíre fought the urge to swear, gripped his flintlock's hilt, and kept his eyes low as he threaded his way through to a low wooden table by the brew kegs at the room's far end, Mogue cautiously following.

A peat fire seethed rosily in the stone hearth, a pair of horrendously sized antlers, prized takings from some long-ago hunt, perched on the wall above it. They sat opposite each other, MacTíre lighting a pipe. Mogue continued to shiver with chattering teeth, but his relief as the aromatic warmth took hold was palpable.

"Hungry, lad?" MacTíre quietly growled.

The boy glanced up at him blankly and nodded. "I am, yeah," he managed to reply.

MacTíre nodded and barked for a platter of salted ham and two mugs of ale from the place's wizened barman, pressing some shillings into his palm. The boy seemed reluctant to either eat or drink at first, but after a moment he descended on the food ravenously, the ham's hot, juice-marinated flavour throwing his famishment into stark relief. MacTíre remained silent, just to give the lad a moment to feel like himself again. With an ear cocked on the general thrum of conversation in the room, he studied various faces over the rim of his mug.

As they ate and drank and savoured the heat, it occurred to MacTíre once more that for one lucky rifle shot, he owed the boy his life. Mogue had seen more death and bloodshed than anyone of his years should see, had more scars and wounds to his name than most, and here he was, supping a small banquet with the killer of his old workmates. At any point, the lad could have tried to make his escape, or at least make an attempt on his captor's life. He certainly had the grit and spirit to try it. Yet why hadn't he?

"Mind ye drink slowly, lad," the road thief muttered, brushing suds from his beard. "Goes down better."

But the boy was ravenous; there was no helping it. MacTíre relit his pipe and blew smoke, letting his clothes and flesh slowly dry by the flames. He now reckoned about fifteen to a man in the room wore identical linen shirts. He caught more than one of them glancing furtively in his direction but made little of it.

The girl he acknowledged earlier sauntered towards them, skirts trailing off the floor. He pretended not to notice her approach, but neither surprise nor tantalisation crossed his face as she slid onto his lap, her petticoated arm coiling lazily around his neck, breasts partially bared to his sight.

"Fine evenin' for it, Joseph. *Cá raibh tú?*"

The road thief bristled at the sound of his own name, even as his free hand clasped her waist. "If ye say so," he conceded, ignoring her question. "'Ow's business, Gráinne? Countin' yer shillin's?"

Her lips parted demurely. "Look 'round ye. Sanctu'ry for all."

"So it'd seem."

The girl glanced over at Mogue, who was lifting his tankard to his lips with both hands. He slurped loudly through the suds, his gullet heaving with each gulp. He finally banged it down on the table with a hollow thud, breathing heavily, beer sluicing his front. "And who's this charmin' rogue?"

"Ah, just a stray pup I've made me travellin' companion."

"And does the pup have a name?"

"Mogue Trench. Late of Dublin, and of the mail carriage ye were kind enough to tell me about. Very handy with a blade, he is." The road thief's smirk faded, like the sun drifting behind a pall of cloud.

Gráinne's brow was raised. "I wasn't expectin' ye the night."

"Well, I wasn't expectin' to be here." Gráinne eyed him. "Ye were right, by the way. 'Bout the pikes, I mean." Reaching into his greatcoat's tattered folds, MacTíre drew out a pikehead, iron-forged, long as a cook's carving blade and sharper than a lion's fang. Traces of the ash shaft he'd sawed it from still dangled from its socket. He kept it low to prevent it being seen by prying eyes. The girl stared at it, tracing her finger along its cross-section; the dried bloodstains smeared along it had dulled to an unsightly bronze tinge. "It's forged well. Had to see 'em for meself."

"You went to the abbey, then."

"Aye – me and him both. We were even made guests of honour – they had us in chains."

"And yis broke free?"

"Aye. I did say he was quite handy with a blade." MacTíre glanced at the bar. The wizened barkeep had placed a tray laden with several freshly poured tankards in front of the bogmen. "Gráinne, me love…any whisperin's?"

Her smile was wry. "Ye know well that costs money, darlin'."

"Money I have. Enough for several nights runnin'. C'mon. Make this night an easier one for yerself." Holding out his hand, several brass coins winked up at her before he pocketed them again. "There's more o' that if what ye tell me's good."

"Isn't it always?"

"Don't be coy, now. Ye were right about the mail carriage, ye were right about the pikes. And I can't help but notice, I haven't seen hide nor hair of his nibs since we walked in that door. Where is he, pray?"

The horse-faced chancer was re-adjusting his fiddle. The hubbub of voices, though still audible, had grown noticeably quieter. The fire's smouldering crackles seemed to echo. Mogue leaned in closer, as if to hear the road thief's reply.

"If we're to talk," Gráinne said softly, her hand brushing slowly along MacTíre's thigh, "then we best head upstairs. No one here needs to hear us. Not even yer…friend. Wouldn't ye agree?"

Her tone was grave, but an arch hint flecked her eyes. It was a look MacTíre knew well, and missed. The softness of her breath tickling his ear drew an involuntary shiver from him. Downing the dregs of his ale, he called for another round and addressed Mogue, who was now studying the taproom in its entirety, much as a ship's lookout studies an unfamiliar horizon.

"I'll be upstairs for a bit, lad. You stay down here and try to keep ou' of trouble. Another round should keep ye busy, but mind ye drink slowly. Anythin' odd, let me know. And have a care. We're still on Sir Vesey's land, remember."

Without awaiting a reply, MacTíre turned and slunk up the rickety stairs, Gráinne just ahead of him, her hand pressed in his.

Mogue watched them go, and then ate the last of the ham. All around him the room moved as though he had never set foot in it. The chancer started up a hearty jig, to spirited yips and hollers from the bogmen, many of whom pounded the tabletops or stomped their feet in time to the rhythm. His skill with the fiddle was haphazard, his singing hideous and reedy. Yet he sang with a passion of sorts; enough to get the revellers around him sufficiently riled into hearty clamour.

The barman approached Mogue with a fresh platter and more ale, and skulked away without taking, or even waiting for payment. The chancer was pacing about the room, elbow sliding nimbly as he worked through the melody. One or two of the girls threw Mogue a tempting look, but apparently sensing his age, slinked on.

Sitting back, Mogue did his best to remain out of sight, swirled the beer around in its tankard. The ale had purged the cold from his bones, yet he couldn't shake the sense that he should really leave this place soon. He folded his arms, felt the barrel of the flintlock pressed against his rib.

"'Tis a curious thing," a voice murmured behind him. "I daresay tonight shall be unlike any other."

Mogue tensed and looked over his shoulder. The aged man who spoke winked and took a long swig from his tumbler. His elbow rested on the tabletop, and the cape-collar of his greatcoat was creased and travel-stained, though not to quite the same extent as Mogue's. A think, untrimmed moustache bristled above his liquor-stained lips, giving him the look of a scholar much out of favour with his peers. His eyes glittered shrewdly, like polished marbles.

"'Course," he continued, his voice sodden with alcohol, "I may be wrong. But ye do keep the company of a most dangerous man there. Hope ye realise what *milleadh* ye be courtin'."

The boy turned to face him fully, eyes narrowed. "'Fraid I don't quite get yer meanin', sir."

The man glanced at Mogue's half-full tankard. "I see you're grand for a gargle. And the girls here want men, not lads. One of me most lucr'ative girls upstairs right now with her friend. Always pays 'andsomer than he looks, mark ye. And bein' quite honest, that's why I'd much sooner see 'im alive'n dead. No matter. But surely ye've some concern for yer life. While ye still have it, o' course. To know that man, to call him a partner, to have his trust in matters adversarial – that is to know darkness. It's also how ye gain an idea of how ye just might meet yer end."

Avoiding his stare, Mogue replied, "My association with him is strictly one of necessity."

"A likely story. Shall I regale ye with an even likelier one? Not too far from here, only just last night, in fact, a house of local repute was torched – ah, ye know of it, I see – and some local men vanished, without trace. Few were neighbours of mine. Landlord of this fine establishment and his son were among 'em. His wife there's worried sick abou' where they might be. Fierce dang'rous for a woman to be alone in these times, I'm sure you'll agree."

Mogue studied the man's thin face. "I'm afraid I haven't heard anythin' of that, sir. We're just travellers, on our way to Dublin. I barely know this place."

"Yer accent'd suggest that be the case, and yet that pretty little cut adornin' yer cheek there tells me diff'rent."

"You have me confused with someone else, friend." Mogue cursed himself for not hiding his scar more thoroughly, even as his hand moved toward his cap.

"Confusion's easily cleared up. Assumption far less so. Some in this very room are Papist, others Protestant. Would ye be able tell me which, pray?"

"Couldn't tell ye. Is not flesh and bone all that unites us?"

"Perhaps, but I also know this much," the stranger spoke slowly, savouring each syllable. "Sir Vesey sent out a summons there. For the landlord and a few others to ride out to the abbey and to bring their keenest blades and pikes. Perhaps ye seen it, on your travels, like. They don't say why they're goin' or how long they'll be. But his missus is goin' spare, 'cause it's been a full day now since he left. And the fires at Tintern are burnin' away. Sir Vesey won't say what happened. Silent as the grave, so he's bein'. But there's been search parties convened. They're scourin' fields, ditches, fens, the river. But the one place they've delved deeper than any other, the one place bound to yield them any clear answer, is the forest. And they'll only just be back, I should say, in less than an hour. They'll have much to tell, I shouldn't doubt."

Mogue felt the cold stares of the others fixed upon him as a hush swept the taproom once again. Once more his hand reached for his weapon as he fought to appear nonchalant. His heart was hammering relentlessly under his cloak. Reluctantly, he sipped from his mug.

When he looked up again, the man's sly grimace had vanished. Despite his drunkenness, his eyes were clear as polished stone, unblinking and flared with cruel intent. Never taking his eyes from Mogue, he reached downward and jerked out a *gralloch* that was slung into his sash, its blade lividly notched along both edges, and placed it bare on the table before him. Mogue fought to keep his eyes and bearing level.

"Someone tries burnin' Tintern to the ground," he continued, tapping the knife dully off the oaken surface, vaguely in time to the chancer's tune. "They didn't get very far, only that big library of his was engulfed before any real damage could be caused. Sir Vesey lived, but I don't doubt he's been driven fully mad by it. Few of his men did, too, but whoever tried settin' it alight fled into the forest. Chase was made, but it seems that the man who fled had skill with a blade as well. Nor was he alone. He was aided by a mere boy. A boy with a sabre cut on his cheek. Much like yours."

He belched hoarsely. They sat in silence for a while, before the renewed whine of the fiddler striking up a barely recognizable version of the 'Ballinafad Polka' filled the room. The stranger chuckled and banged his hand off the tabletop in time to the music, having seemingly forgotten Mogue was there. Grey ribbons of tobacco smoke snaked into the air as raucous yips and cheers crashed around the fiddler as the polka took hold. The stranger then stood and ambled off toward the keg, his coat swinging. As he moved off, Mogue saw that people seemed to know him, the girls letting him pass with deferential airs, the men hollering his name in hearty greeting.

It was only then that Mogue noticed he'd left his knife on the table.

*

The chamber was silent, save for the heaviness of their breathing. As always, Gráinne was the first to break the silence. "I see ye lost none of yer skill to break hearts."

MacTíre's smile was wryly arched. "And I see you've lost none of yer skill for whisperin' sweet lies in my ear."

"I should really thank ye for the custom. Most 'em know by now I'm yer woman."

"That don't scare 'em off?"

"God, no. Why should it? They all desire what the road thief can have, free of charge. Whenever you're gone, me reputation keeps me in coin."

"Such is the market."

"Mmm."

Gráinne was the only girl on the premises in possession of a key to every room in the alehouse, from the scullery to the master bedchamber. Ensuring the room stayed locked for as long as necessary was something MacTíre could trust in, always. The walls and floorboards were thick enough to keep the noise and revelry in the taproom below pleasantly muted. A fire was lit in the far corner, but the bedside lamp was doused, and the blinds were drawn on the gathering dark without. The scent of turf smoke was heavy in the air. It was an arrangement that suited them both, secrecy being a language they spoke with great fluency.

The warmth of the room and of her body was just what Joseph needed. Gráinne didn't lack scars of her own from previous gentlemen callers, but MacTíre was one of the few men who never endeavoured to hurt her. Consequently, her bruises and scars had dwindled over the years as it became clear the road thief favoured her above the other girls. Few desired being on the receiving end of his flintlock.

As they lay there, sweaty and breathless in flushed afterglow, MacTíre lay back, allowing her head to rest on his shoulder as she huddled beneath his free arm. The steady, consoling heave of her chest was lulling. His fingers recalled the magic they'd worked between her legs, and the gouges on his back left by her nails were smarting. It was a familiar ritual, the smooth curve of her cheek pressed close to his, the tempo of his breath in lazy harmony with hers. Her hair was spread in a cloak of brunette, and every so often her lips, still tasting of wine, managed to gently find his, despite the gloom. Her fingers traced through the hairs on his chest, the softness of her touch enough to deceive any other man. But with MacTíre, she had little need for deception.

"Still have that pistol I gave ye?"

She reached under the pillow and held it up. He smirked. "Smart girl."

"Ye shouldn't be here," she finally murmured, her breath tickling his jaw.

He stared up at the filthy ceiling, envisioning the night sky beyond it. There'd be no poxy moon in the sky tonight, and that was a small comfort. "I know that. But I also know I won't see ye for a good while."

She gently traced her fingers over the various scars and remnant bullet-burns that blotched his torso. Each one felt the soft graze of her touch, with the freshest ones lingered upon the most. It was her habit, and he'd never once asked her to stop. "It's as bad as I said, and worse. There's been talk of insurrection for months now. Sir Vesey gallivants up to Dublin for those parliament talks, and little is ever changed. Meetin's were held in the taproom after hours, but I always kept my ear to the door. Whatever else happens, the roads are no longer safe just because of you."

MacTíre sighed, the weight of things now clear. "I saw the pikes, the cowls, heard the blatherin's about revolution. The man's deluded."

"Well, deluded or not, he does have his followers. Volunteers willin' to take up arms for any cause of his choosin'. 'Tis easy to scoff at now, but ye know better than most what zeal is in desperate men. Pity ye made enemies of 'em all. Would that ye might join them, don the uniform, maybe."

"It was men in uniform who destroyed my fam'ly. There's no joinin' 'em now, even had I the will. Price on me head's been raised tenfold. Any man would happily knife me if he could. And I know this place's landlord was among the ones we killed. Tell me, what's bein' said about him?"

"He's been gone more'n a day now. Him and his boy. The missus has been goin' spare, but when a few of the local lads returned, they swore the fire in the abbey was an accident. Others say it was redcoats, or yeos, or rival Defenders. Most say it was you. No one holds a secret like a bogman, believe you me. But the rumours are already in full flow. And with the price on your head raised, bounty hunters will be upon ye. If ye don't leave, I'll be in trouble, too. They know what we share. Just knowing you has me in grave danger. That boy, too."

MacTíre shut his eyes, conceding the truth of it. Anyone who touched her could fear his wrath, but sooner or later they would join forces and hunt him down. The dread of facing him in a fight was too much, but only for now. He thought of the zeal shown to him back at the abbey. There had been little enough fear of him then, and even less as they pursued him through the forest.

"The boy can look after himself," he said finally. "I seen as much."

"Ye left him downstairs in a room full of wolves. How long d'ye think he'll last?"

"I was younger than he when I first killed –"

"He isn't you, though, Joseph."

"No. He's not. But he might be."

She turned away from him then, facing the velvet blinds. "Ye never took on partners before. Always said ye'd work alone, and that no one should know the life you do."

"Maybe I'm gettin' soft in me old age. Feel like bein' a Good Samaritan."

Her smirk was arched. "Old age. You're a young man still."

"Young men don't last long in this game."

"So why force him into it, then?"

MacTíre bristled. "I'm after givin' him every chance to flee, yet he hasn't. He's been cut, burnt, starved, and ran off his feet, yet he has not fled. I left him down there to see will he run or keep watch. If he's not down there when I leave this place, so be it. But perhaps the time has come to reinvent me methods, as it were."

"You left alone him with a dang'rous man, Joseph." Even in the dark, her glare managed to puncture through his thoughts.

"Who?"

"A man walked in here only two hours ago, askin' about Tintern and where he could find it. I knew from his accent he wasn't local. He was coy enough, but I've me ways with coy men, as well ye know. Anyway, he said he was a hunter, who specialised in tracking wolves. I told him we had no wolves out in these parts, not in years like, and he did not seem at all surprised. Said never fear, there was one wolf in partic'lar he was after. He seemed to think I didn't get his meanin'."

"He could well be that. A hunter in the wrong place."

"No. He could very well be sniffin' out the bounty. But he's down there now, and he's done little but keep his eye on you and that boy since yis both walked in. I even offered to bring him up here mor'n once, but he refused every time."

"More's the pity."

"Don't be so cavalier. I know his intentions. He won't be the only one, either. They're amassing for your blood as much as that of the crown. Who's to say the man down there is your equal, if not your better, at concealment and moving with stealth? Who's to say he won't strike a bargain with anyone down there who's lost their closest at your hand?"

He sat up in the bed, reached for his baldric. "Ye were right about somethin' else. I didn't believe it 'til I saw it with me own eyes. They go out in packs to the forest, and fashion pikes from the trees they cut down. They're no army, but they're gettin' close to it. Whatever it is they're plannin', it's comin' soon."

"You don't seem perturbed."

"As long as it means more pickin's for me, I'm not complainin'."

Gráinne shook her head. "I knew ye'd say that. But know this: soon they'll stop fearin' ye and start huntin' ye, once the pay's right. Far as most of 'em are concerned, you'll be preparation for the bigger fight to come."

"The bigger fight? Do they seriously expect to stand against the might of cannon and musket with those pikes?"

"Yes. Entire empires've been toppled by men wieldin' pikes. You've often said so yourself."

It was true; often he spoke of the vastly outnumbered Spartans challenging the might of the god-king Xerxes, reducing his splendour to bronze ash even in the shade of countless arrows. A stolen, calfskin-bound copy of Herodotus' *Histories* had taught him that story. He thought he'd spied a copy of it up in Sir Vesey's library, too. He wondered, with no small measure of wistfulness, how many magnificent volumes had been claimed by the blaze. So many magnificent worlds rendered to ash, so many fantastic wonders wrought in ink and folio gone forever, and all so his wretched survival could be ensured! He cared little for Sir Vesey or for the cowled animals he'd set upon them, but even if he'd managed to salvage a few books, it would have been worth the grief of raiding the abbey. If the man was redeemable in any way, it was for his extensive collection of books. And besides, young Mogue had much to learn by way of being lettered. The few volumes he kept stowed in his hideout would only do much on that account. It occurred to him that, had he taken better care, he might have been able to sit with him and debate their contents. Nonetheless, he brushed that story aside, trying to keep his voice steady.

"Sir Vesey said the same last night. When he says it, he sounds like a madman."

"And when I say it?"

"Like a seer." He turned back and drew her to him. "And I fear yis're both right. But I doubt victory is at hand for anyone here. All hearty declamations aside."

"And why is that?"

"'Tis one thing to drunkenly trade fists on fair day with yer neighbour, knowin' yis'll share a pint after. Quite another takin' on trained soldiers. And takin' *me* on is far more trouble than it's worth for any of 'em. Rebel or redcoat. I hope they at least realise that."

"Ye seem very certain."

"Not too far from here, in a forest clearing, many of their comrades lie dead because of me. And waitin' below are enough *Buachaillí Bána* drinking to their hearts' content before they head out to menace some poor smallholder. I know those shirts, Gráinne. Men who wore them robbed me of me home once. And every year my hatred for them grows a little more. Twenty men against one's man's rage? I don't fancy them odds, meself."

"You're forgettin' somethin' else. Me. How safe am I if this all escalates?"

"What do you mean?"

"They won't fear ye forever. Unless they go for that boy, they'll come for me also. They also pay me well from their takin's."

"They pay you for orgasms, not whisperin's."

"That may well be, but I've lost a good few customers thanks to yer antics. Mayhap it's also worth yer while to join up. Lend yer fightin' skills to 'em, at least. Yer knowledge of the land, yer way with letters –"

"Stop. Never in my life would I serve another man's cause. Truth is I care not if I fall under a rebel or a redcoat's hand."

"Then why keep runnin' from 'em?"

"Ah, they do prate of revolution, but who among 'em actually possesses the will? Ye won't make a convert of me to any cause. Not now or ever. My life is my own. Join a cause, and ye lose yerself eventually. Become subject to their minor tyrannies, for the sake of some abstract common good. It isn't something I want any part of. Far as I'm concerned, they can wage their filthy insurrection without me."

"And that may well be your fate, from the way you're goin'."

"I may subject myself to certain death, but I'm no slave. Those men down there, and in that forest, go only where they're told, with no recourse to themselves. They are won only by the most persuasive argument in the moment. It'll be the crown one day, the pikehead the next. And let's not pretend they talk of honour or sovereignty with any understanding. Those men down there took my home. Destroyed me brother, violated and murdered our sister, facilitated me into this life. Do you think I can ever forget any of that? They are all slaves, and they wear their chains willingly. So long as I draw breath, I join no army, no movement."

He did not see her roll her eyes in the dark. "Yet ye plan to make that lad down yonder a martyr for your cause?"

"He's alone in this world, just as I once was. I'll see he has a home and a means of survival. Sooner a boy enters a man's world, he must know this."

He lay back, stared at the ceiling. "And he will."

He did not see her careworn face, nor hear the silent prayer she mouthed. What he did hear, however, or thought he heard at least, was the deliberate, gentle tread of footfalls in the corridor outside, nearing their door. Slowly, he reached for his flintlock.

*

Every time a tune trailed off, the taproom seemed to shift a little towards somewhere darker.

Amidst drunken hoots and frenzied hollers for another tune, the chancer was strolling spasmodically around the tables, worn cap proffered for the bogmen to toss a few coins. Mogue had little in his pockets save a few copper shrapnels; he rolled his shirtsleeves up, his hand resting upon his pistol.

The chancer was leering as he approached. Mogue's guard had been up from the moment he'd entered, and the chancer did little to ease his nerves. A smallish man, his face long and coppery, white-streaked curls fell to his collar like a hood. He held his fiddle and bow by his side while holding his cap out with a wizened hand; the light clink of coins landing within its cloth was numerous. A goblin-like leer was slashed across his face; the aromatic reek of dead clay and smoking turf hung off him like a curse.

Everyone in the taproom seemed to know him, raising glasses to him as he neared, calling out his name heartily. Mogue was in no humour to trade either jape or coin, though, even less to hear him strike up again.

But his vexation was ill-founded. The chancer's grin vanished the second he locked eyes with him, and, despite the cloddishness of his movements, he seemed to slink past Mogue's table with considered deliberation, making for the bar instead. Mogue swished the remnants of his ale around. The man to whom he'd spoken earlier was engaged in a hushed chinwag with two of the bogmen, throwing the odd furtive glance upstairs. Mogue sipped more ale, attempting to look more pissed than he really was. Narrowing his eyes in a hazy imitation of comfortable drunkenness, he subtly took in the room. At every table, someone seemed to be staring fixedly at him, looking away when he sensed, the girls as much as the men. Each glance seemed inveterate in its antipathy, each furtive stare luminous in its resentful suspicion.

The man's *gralloch* was still lodged on the table. Despite the notches and rust, it was a handsome weapon, its scrimshaw hilt marked with woodcuts and the slender blade forged from good steel.

Mogue's eye now caught a third man, this one huddled not far from the door. Initially he took him for just another corbeller or the like, or even a fellow traveller. Unlike the majority, he was not clad in the customary white shirt favoured by the others. Nor did he seem to know anyone there; none of the girls slid a flirtatious hand along his shoulder, none of the men seemed to engage him in conversation, though he did flip a coin at the chancer as he passed. He drank slowly, as if in meditation, one hand resting within the folds of his waistcoat. He was also the only one not to cast hostile glances in Mogue's direction. Putting his tankard down, he rose, seemingly to approach the bar.

What happened next was a blur of movement and noise for Mogue. The man made an abrupt cut for the staircase, ascending each step with a soft, measured pace, clearly trying not to waken anyone. Barely a creak could be heard. His hand remained in the folds of his waistcoat and his eyes were narrow with intent. Snatching the *gralloch* up off the table and hiding it, Mogue lingered a moment before following him. Mogue had never encountered a blade that did not seem to fit snugly into his hand. This *gralloch* was no different.

The corridor was narrow and led to a far end; the few lamps intended to illuminate were on the verge of sputtering out. Dim slivers of light seeped from under some of the doors, but not from the one the man was approaching. The din and revelry of the taproom faded quicker than Mogue expected. He had to keep his pace measured and his breath drawn in – no point giving himself away by a foolish clump of boots. He had a clean enough shot of the man, but he cared not for the attention a pistol would draw (and anyway, he was not yet the marksman MacTíre was).

Step by step, the man ahead, now a quiet, hulking shape blending with the shadows, moved with his back to the wall, head turned toward the door at the corridor's end. Slowly, he withdrew his hand from his waistcoat, and Mogue tensed at the sharp glint of a gun barrel in the dark.

The man moved over the bare floorboards with catlike care, his boots barely making a sound. The terrible thought of him suddenly glancing back down the corridor to see if he was being followed hit Mogue, who was relieved for the deep shade that filled it. No doubt the door was locked, but even in the gloom it was clearly worm-eaten; the man looked more than capable of knocking it off its hinges with a single well-placed kick. He stopped in his tracks, levelling the gun at the doorhandle. His hand reached up, fingers poised to pull the hammer back.

Does he mean to shoot his way in, perhaps, and storm the room in the chaos?

To Mogue Trench's predatory eyes, there was scant time to find out. His senses, as they so often had been over the last few days, were now afire with primitive alertness. His weariness from the road and the ale in his belly forgotten, the former postboy gnashed his teeth lividly, and sprang. His free hand clamped tightly over the man's mouth; his wrist pivoted as though he were turning a key through a lock as the *gralloch* plunged through the soft meat of the man's neck.

The man's head fell back, and he dropped his gun, his hand wildly clawing at his neck. A dry groan retched from his muffled mouth. Blood seeped down onto his smock as his knees buckled and he fell forward.

Mogue's breathing was heavy and fast. Warm viscera snaked down his forearms, like wine leaking from a burst sack. More of it stained his front and fell in warm, blotchy splashes to the floor. Yet in that moment, there was no horror at what he had just done. No sudden realisation, no deep shock of remorse or alarm that broke over him like a tide. Just an odd contentment, as if he had completed an especially laborious task, and had completed it well. In the dim of the passageway, a smile of satisfaction gnarled Mogue Trench's young face.

The man's deathly grunts could not possibly be heard from below, but clearly they were heard from behind the passage door, for Mogue thought he heard frantic footsteps and voices.

The door creaked heavily open. A half-dressed MacTíre stood in the door, his own flintlock primed. The girl Gráinne he'd been with appeared at his shoulder, her young eyes wide and a pistol in her hand, primed and angled toward his face. The sight of Mogue, breathing as if he'd just run a marathon and holding the man's prone corpse, his blood pooling heavily onto the floorboards, caused her to momentarily freeze, before reaching up to grip MacTíre's hand; a gesture the road thief returned in kind. Mogue returned their stare, but without any fear on his features. If anything, MacTíre noted, a satisfied flush now tinged his cheeks, and his teeth flashed in a grin of pride. The road thief steadily lowered his gun, his breathing heavy.

"Time to go," he said drily.

Chapter XIV
Upon Their Wordſ
Wexford, 1787

For days after Tintern Abbey's central tower caught fire, the flames could be seen for miles around, a great spiralling pillar of smoke mushrooming angrily at the winter sky. It glowed through the night like some hellish beacon, warning whomever saw it to keep away rather than come closer. Naturally, many people's curiosity proved greater than their caution.

Crisp sea winds rolled in and fanned it well, kept it roaring heavenward like the endless gushing of a volcano roused from slumber. Sir Vesey's library and chambers fuelled it; the mantle of smoke reeked of burnt parchment and cremated leather, a smell few were able to identify. It lingered in the air for weeks after, a sulphurous reminder that seeped into clothes, stung eyes to tears, left throats horribly raw, and anchored hearts yet further into dread and despondency.

Many locals volunteered in the efforts to put it out, tossing bucket after bucket of water scooped from the nearby Bannow, but most were too entranced by the sight of great smoky veils blocking out the sun. Even those who had lost loved ones in the fire found themselves mesmerised, even as the hope of recovering their fathers' or husbands' or sons' masked corpses faded with the inferno. In one of his sermons, delivered with portentous ardour from the tabernacle of the Enniscorthy cathedral, Bishop Caulfield of Ferns was heard likening it to the flaming pillar, now rekindled from the pages of *Exodus* (quite literally, perhaps, given where the fire was started and Sir Vesey being a known possessor of many now-incinerated editions of the Holy Scriptures, in choice volumes and all of tremendous worth); it was, therefore, a sign of many more holy and unholy things to come.

Little of this reached the ears of either Mogue or MacTíre. The smoky stench that took hold of the land caught their nostrils, but they were in hiding now. In the days following their escape, when sheens of hoarfrost still crusted hedge and road and tree branch, they had kept to the ditches just beyond the forest border, ever wary of encountering one of Sir Vesey's men hoping to visit revenge on them for the deaths of their comrades.

Mogue could not help but notice the abnormal calm that seemed to descend over MacTíre during this sojourn, his unconcern at giving himself away in the night's starry, smoke-parched quiet odd to behold. The sky above was curdled with cloud, and the first stirrings of a hard wind swiped his cheek, needling his nostrils with the charred vapour. It was only when the road thief wordlessly got a fire going that he finally unburdened himself of whatever grim thoughts rioted behind those livid green eyes.

"We'll lay low here a time further. Tomorrow I'll let ye know what our next move'll be."

"And why not tell me now?"

The road thief's eyes darted sharply toward the cave mouth, now cunningly hidden by a thick sheaf woven from brush and sapling, and he sniffed the close, humid air. "'Fraid I don't know what that is just yet, meself."

Before Mogue could offer a reply, MacTíre murmured gruffly for him to get some rest. His face had kept its mild blankness, and the sabre-cut on his cheek even seemed bland to look at. He had not the strength left to argue. Muddy and still trying to ignore the dull flecks of red that stained his shirt, he collapsed upon the piled straw, his bones anchored with fatigue. He then watched the road thief stand and select a book from the makeshift shelf on the far wall, before sitting lazily back against the opposite wall to begin reading it by the blaze's crackling shimmer, his face unreadable.

MacTíre turned the pages slowly and meticulously, eyes tracking the words with absorption, lips moving slightly. The heat in the grotto grew, causing the tight set in MacTíre's shoulders to loosen, and inducing Mogue to sleep after a few jaw-straining yawns. His lullaby was the hollow, heavy crackle of the flames as MacTíre tossed a fresh log onto it without even looking up from his volume, and the road thief's low murmur as he mouthed whatever was inked there.

The following days and more passed in similar fashion. Neither had much to say to one another, but sometime later, after hours spent in quietude, Mogue had wrestled himself away from the morbid weight of his thoughts and tried engaging his companion in some conversation. "S'pose you might enlighten me as to what our plan is in due course?"

MacTíre had not looked up from the heavy folio he now perused. The silence was perturbing Mogue more than he cared to admit. "When I know, ye'll know," the road thief said, his voice distant.

He leafed again through the pages, his dirt-speckled finger running beneath the sentences printed there. "By helpin' me, they'll be after yer blood as well, but they know nothin' of ye nor what I've got planned. I shouldn't doubt they'll let rumours of our deaths – and those'll be doin' the rounds too, mark me words – discourage 'em from raisin' the price."

Mogue knelt by the fire, warming his hands. Another of MacTíre's books lay where he'd left it, weather-worn and open. He picked it up and examined its pages, his brow knotting as his eyes ran over the inked shapes of letters and the elaborate, full-paged engravings. Rough markings marred the edges of the pages.

"Ye can't read, sure ye can't'?"

"And so what if I don't?" A defensive edge marked the boy's voice.

MacTíre nodded slightly. "Care to learn at all, lad?"

His voice stabbed through Mogue's absorption like an insect's stinger, and the boy looked at the array of books on the shelf. "You've read all those?"

"Every one of 'em, yeh. And I do intend on readin' more, once I'm able. They're a happy reprieve from killin'." MacTíre smirked. "Have ye a problem with lettered men?"

Mogue grimaced, but kept his gaze on the page, angling his head over the various blocks of text before finally facing the road thief. "No. Why should I, but? Learn to read, I mean?"

"Cause ye never know when ye might need it. Ye might see yer own name on a wanted poster and never know ye were hunted." A flicker of amusement crossed MacTíre's face as he remembered seeing his own name scrawled above the price on his head in some village square.

Mogue had much to learn by comparison, even learning the mechanics of the most basic combination of syllables. His skills with a knife would only serve him so well. With scant knowledge of tactics or navigation, how could he hope to accomplish a successful raid or kill? "Ye fight well enough, lad. So why not the word-savvy to match it?"

"I've never had any cause to, you understand. But..." his thumb traced the ending sentence of a chapter, "...curiosity does be prevailin'."

Had the boy been given a choice to run, forsake whatever lay ahead of them, it might have been the end of it. Yet at no point had he made a move to run. The events of the past few days seemed to weigh on him, making him reluctant to abscond. Or was it curiosity for what might unfold for them both that kept him in place?

Disquiet lodged in Joseph's chest like a stone hitting the seabed. He had noticed the boy was not much of a conversationalist, and that suited MacTíre – aimless chatter made his skull ache. Yet the boy needed to occupy himself until they ventured out again. He needed a skill besides knifework. Even now, watching his mud-flecked fingers comb carefully through the folio, eyes squinting in concentration at whatever was written there, it seemed the boy had more curiosity than he cared to let on.

The boy had much to learn, and there was no better time than now, while they were in hiding. He'd pushed Mogue too far in the last few days. Whilst they gathered their bearings, out of range and out of sight, what other opportunity was likely to present itself?

Mogue still clutched the book in both hands, a cheap, goatskin-bound edition of Clement's *Protrepticus*.

"Teachin' ye to read could be worth both our whiles. I'm no scholar now, but I can grasp enough. Neither of us are stupid, I wager. Ye may learn as much from them words as much as from hearin' men talk."

It did not escape MacTíre's notice that the lad was now turning the pages slowly and much more thoughtfully. "Ye've never had the value of it. That sense that ye can achieve what most cannot. To master those inky scratchin's, decipher their meanin' as if they were stars and trackless seas. To keep it concealed and then surprise yer enemies with yer el'quence. Ye do be like a sailor who's after washin' up on some unknown strand, with only the knowledge that it's yours and yours alone to explore. 'The things ye shall know hereafter', as 'twere. And in battle, ye might be a literate predator, holdin' both reason and ferocity under the glare of the moon. The world's never quite the same once a good read has been done."

Again, there seemed to be the sense from the boy that he held something profoundly precious in his hands, something touched by God, perhaps, or consecrated by the ministrations of a saint.

"The more ye read, the more yer appetite swells for greater scribblin's to devour. Yer urge to fight and kill is no different, surely?"

Mogue wondered if there was even a name for the language this volume was printed in. Like all the books, it was no doubt ill-gotten, although, Mogue also suspected, it now rested in far better hands than whatever library or drawing room they had been originally charted for. At the very least MacTíre seemed to turn to these books for a few hours' pleasant distraction from the nightly excursions of blood and fire he embarked upon.

"I feel most alive when I'm takin' the lives of others. Is that so terrible in a world such as this?"

"Tis best to kill swiftly, lad. Less time to have it weigh upon your mind. And more to expand it."

Mogue ran his finger over the spine of another volume, this one bound in wine-dark calfskin, and spread it out before him. The embossment gracing its cover might have been grand to look upon once, but too many years in this subterranean hole had taken their toll. Finally, he found the words to reply. "I imagine it's better than waiting. There's only so many times I can keep whetting my blade."

"In a manner of speaking," MacTíre replied, reading Mogue's expression and grinning knowingly. "It prob'ly won't be of much use to ye in battle, but I can guarantee it'll keep yer mind in fine condition. In a fight, with the element of surprise at your command, it might lead to the best outcome."

"Whilst you fire the opening salvo."

MacTíre nodded. He walked over to the shelf and withdrew one of the larger volumes, bound in bottle-green leather – a compendium of Milton's prose works – and handed it to Mogue. "Tell us, what do ye know of letters?"

"Not much. They go in no real order, yes?" Mogue's eyes were fixed on the page, as if trying to decipher a riddle. This one felt even more precious in his hands.

"We'll start with the basics, so." MacTíre opened the title page and traced his finger beneath the words; they dominated the page, similar to a wanted sign. "This one's by Milton. *Areopagitica; A speech of Mr. John Milton for the Liberty of Unlicenc'd Printing, to the Parlament of England.* I managed to fleece that off a man in a high carriage. He'd a chest overflowin' with documents and ledgers. Milton's book was among 'em."

"He still alive? This Milton?"

"Long dead, lad. But that's no matter. He speaks to us still, through them pages ye hold. Keep that book close, and ye keep his ideas alive:

> *'Many a man lives a burden to the earth; but a good book is the precious life-blood of a master spirit, embalmed and treasured up on purpose to a life beyond life. 'Tis true, no age can restore a life, whereof perhaps there is no great loss; and revolutions of ages do not oft recover the loss of a rejected truth, for the want of which whole nations fare the worse.'*

"He's easily one of me favourites, lad, and if this goes well, he might be yours, too. To read him is to know the language of freedom. I do much prefer when he does be sayin' this, though:

> *"... what in me is dark, Illumine,*
> *what is low, raise and support;*
> *That to the height of this great argument*
> *I may assert eternal providence..."*

He trailed off. "Though I do quite like what he's to say here. He was a man who knew what freedom truly is."

"That it always comes with a price?" Mogue leafed through the pages.

"Aye." There was a grim twist to MacTíre's smile. "Once ye know that, Milton might just be a breeze to ye."

"I shouldn't doubt it," Mogue replied, no levity in his voice.

MacTíre once more looked down at the book. "I hope that, when ye're finally lettered, ye'll proceed with this one. Of all the books and doc'ments I've stolen in me time, that's the one I keep returnin' to. When it was written, it was to expose falsity wherever it lay, and to allow ideas to be freely discussed. To silence a man, to rob him of his voice and his convictions of free expression and enterprise – well, frankly, I'd prefer the noose or stake, meself."

Mogue picked up the book, savouring its finely wrought weight in his hands with even more reverence than he had the others. It was cool to the touch, its cover and spine a burgundy map of tiny indentations within the leather. His eye settled on the lettering on the page, taking in the thick, finely printed ink, and great blocks of script marked with thorn-like curlicues and curved, rune-like shapes. "You're suggesting I start with him?"

MacTíre nodded. "Yeh. Milton's for the cutthroats, lad. There's many across this world who'd gladly see every last copy of this volume burned. To read polemics is to invite danger into yer life. But you've had enough danger for now. Learnin' to read will be your punishment – readin' with ease, that'll be yer paradise."

"And what's paradise to you?"

"Anything within. But first we must needs see ye lettered." The road thief wondered why such an instinct had taken hold of him, for he was no pedagogue. It was unusual for him to care, and in the last few days he felt in himself a curious protectiveness toward the boy, a desire to see his own skills for survival and thievery imparted and carried forward. The boy showed no sign of wanting to be rid of his presence. Whatever life he had lived prior to boarding that carriage was in a way superior to hiding out in a cavern, at the mercy of the law. There would be few riches or reward, and certainty of death. Yet the boy did not fear any of these possibilities. If anything, he was compelled by them.

Just as he intended, MacTíre pulled a few scraps of parchment and an unused bottle of ink down from the shelf. Handing them to Mogue, who took them wordlessly, he dipped the quill into the ink and scrawled the letters of the alphabet. He glanced up at the boy for a moment, curious as to what his face would reveal, but the boy's attention rested strictly on the shaped lettering before him. They whiled away the hours like that, MacTíre scratching letters onto sheafs of parchment, Mogue copying them out with sharp, silent, fervour.

And so Mogue Trench began the slow journey of becoming lettered. Some instinct of pragmatism told him that it was not worth his time – learning how to aim and fire a pistol might be far better use – but he found he enjoyed it far too much to pay his instinct much heed. His mornings were devoted to the study of linguistics, and his evenings to the perils of knifework and marksmanship. MacTíre said January was usually a slow month with little opportunity to hunt, so his lessons made for a welcome divergence. They'd managed to stockpile enough venison and salmon to keep them sated in the meantime.

Mogue often murmured the sounds of the letters to himself, his voice mingling with the smoke as it billowed up from the flames. Letters formed easily on his tongue, and his skill with writing improved. Words, letters, syllables rioted through his dreams, and monopolised his thoughts during the day. When he turned in for the night, his dreams were replete with the ebb and flow of language. He whispered and stammered in the dark the words MacTíre had assigned him that day, his voice slipping and sliding over each syllable, his tongue adept and overcoming their shapes, their coarse diction, their strange music.

It helped that the boy had enough English already – MacTíre knew plenty who had none. Lying in the dark, he kept watch and ward, finally succumbing to sleep as the boy's confused murmurs echoed through the grotto like smoke.

Time passed like this, MacTíre rising just before dawn to hunt for any deer or fish that he could snag, cooking on the fire as the boy woke and dressed, aiding him in keeping the flames stoked and silently chewing on whatever poached, fried, or salted game resulted from what the road thief managed to ensnare and bring back. After cooking, he sat down to review the boy's progress. By the flame-light, their reading lessons continued, MacTíre deciding which book to go from.

"What word's that?"

"Ah, bastardy. Daresay ye know the meanin' already."

"Bastardy? Right." He read on: "W-why brand they...us w-with *base*–? With *base*...ness? bastardy? base, base? Who, in...the lusty...stealth of nature, take more com...more..."

"Composition, lad."

"...c-composition and f-fierce quality than doth..."

It was strangely endearing to see it, the artless manner in which Mogue's eyes would dart to him whenever he stumbled over a word or could be certain he had it right. The silent, sullen youth who wielded a hunting knife to lethal effect was replaced now by a makeshift scholar who studied the page with an engrossed, child-like frown.

Throughout those frostbitten days, Mogue gorged himself on the books in MacTíre's rough-hewn library with swollen, almost obsessive avidity. His face was lit by the flicker of the fires MacTíre kept burning by a steady mix of saplings and peat. By degrees he deciphered the shapes of words, straining his tongue to their pronunciation, and soon began to apprehend their meaning with a diligence that seemed almost unbecoming of someone of his unripe years.

This surprised MacTíre not one jot, as the boy had clearly kept himself alive throughout his short life by keen deployment of his wits. Ever since they had stood together in the forest surrounded by the bodies of their foes, and again when the boy had narrowly prevented his assassination, he felt a kinship with the lad he did not believe he had shared with any living soul since the deaths of Fiadh and Redmond. That same primal intellect now lent itself well to his newfound, rough-hewn scholarliness. He devoured with a readiness of mind MacTíre found enviable. The boy's nose would be buried in *Meditations* or some firebrand pamphlet, already two decades out of date, calling for the emancipation of slaves from His Majesty's plantations in the Americas, or even an end to Crown rule in Ireland; he seemed to forget his surroundings. Engaging himself at study proved far better than any other pursuit to which he had yet inclined his attention and industry.

And he was proving to be a promising student. Images and emotions hitherto foreign to him flooded his brain and bosom. It was as if some inner torchlight had been shone upon subjects about which he knew nothing. The more he read, the more his circumstances seemed to unveil themselves to him. He wept with Dido for her fallen city; he revelled in the triumph of Odysseus reclaiming Ithaca after so many years of intractable voyaging.

His knowledge hoard swelled. As he gained sufficiency in the written word, so too did his taste and discernment augment. Breaches of erudition were made upon his mind. The authors of antiquity intrigued and tantalised him as much as the daily findings of the newspapers MacTíre stole for them. Yet more recent authors held their delights, too. His capacities of truth became clearer to him and increased his focus. The names of Milton, Cicero, Spenser, Hobbes, and Johnson became as known to him as the passage of Marlowe's *The Tragicall History of the Life and Death of Doctor Faustus*, in which the jaded healer declares, '*The god thou servest is thine own appetite…*'

He was in turn taken by the line spoken by Satan in the fourth volume of *Paradise Lost*:

> "*…Can it be a sin to know,*
> *Can it be death? And do they only stand*
> *By Ignorance, is that their happy state,*
> *The proof of their obedience and their fate?*"

Often, he returned to part of the verse, re-reading it with a bittersweet understanding quavering in his breast. Of the vehemence of Macbeth in the Scottish tragedy's morose fourth act, he resolved to crown his own thoughts with acts, the edge of his blades serving as coolly as his newfound purpose. MacTíre, seeing his dexterity with language had now borne palpable fruit, had smiled to himself with no small hint of pride.

And MacTíre's library, gathered over years and robbed from all manner of targets, was easily the broadest and richest an ill-gotten trove of bibelots could hope to be, and certainly within a hundred leagues. He thought of the books in Sir Vesey's library catching fire, with a wistfulness that he'd never have the chance to read any of them. In some ways, Sir Vesey's collection was as much an ill-gotten stash as his own. Some were wrought from the finest oxblood leather and semi-limp, others barely kept together by the frailty of their spines, and from years of the road thief browsing them. The immensity of the mysteries they contained; the length and variety of journeys they tempted him to embark upon. He found himself carrying them with the same reverence of a pilgrim carrying a chunk of the One True Cross.

Dusty polemics and pamphlets; despatches and red-sealed letters of introduction; years-old newspapers and periodicals, irreversibly yellowed by time. Epistles to strangers, compendiums of wittily trenchant epigrams, prayer books, dictionaries that carried the aggregate weight of many octavos; instructional tracts on chivalry, navigation, hunting, fencing, table etiquette, histories of witchcraft and craven superstition, robbers and pirates, travels and voyages. Edicts on army disbandment; oratory, scripture, dialogues between senators on matters of state and honour. A tattered King James Bible, with a faded codicil scribbled into its opening blank page in garbled, blue-black lettering. Catalogues of loan exhibitions, indexes of yet more bibliography. Greek tragedians, Roman scribes, Italian courtiers.

It was, Mogue came to believe, true of MacTíre's mode of living and of his own curiosity that seemed more rapacious with each word devoured, and testament to the strange power each book seemed to contain. He came to view them as Pandora's boxes, brimming not with all manner of evil and shadow, but prized vessels by which sacred precepts of honour and survival were inculcated into him with great precision from the inchoate rubble of antiquity.

Mogue came to admire the deeds of heroes and machinations of the gods, all those shadowy figures that swaggered through the pages of so many accounts, seeing parallels in their pride, and glorious downfalls reflected in his own life. His joy in Livy's account of Hannibal and his army marching on Rome through the Alps' snow-coated plateau kept him feverishly awake at night, the thunderous beat of elephants' hooves echoing around the chilly crags like a lachrymose drumroll. Republics founded and empires toppled, gods who wielded the fate of men as their holy plaything, angels cast out of heaven and resolved to rule the very darkness to which they'd been consigned, the disconsolate sorrows of poets and the lofty tenets of philosophers.

Nor was he content as the years went on to confine himself to these subjects alone; history and engineering, the science of time and of material mass, held his interest as much as that of the classics. The hours passed in dog-eared reverie, and he found an affiliation with emperors and generals as much with the common thieves so often left to swing from the walls of Dublin.

One evening MacTíre, who had managed to procure a jug of whiskey from Gráinne, rose unsteadily to his feet and cleared his throat. Over the crackle of the flames and the lad's smirking bemusement, he recited fragments from a poem, something he must have picked up from one of the schoolbooks crammed in the back:

> Lone on the midnight steep, and all aghast,
> The dark wayfaring stranger breathless toils,
> And, often falling, climbs against the blast…

> Where now, ye lying vanities of life!
> Ye ever-tempting, ever-cheating train!
> Where are you now? and what is your amount?
> Vexation, disappointment, and remorse.
> Sad, sick'ning thought! and yet deluded man,
> A scene of crude disjointed visions past,
> And broken slumbers, rises still resolv'd,

With new-flush'd hopes, to run the giddy round.

His voice was flat and slurred from the drink, and his accent seemed to rip over half the words, like breakers erupting over a shoal. It echoed off the cave walls with the hollow thud of a pebble clattering into an oaken keg. It was a moment before his head rolled back and thick, garbled snores rose from his heaving form.

Before sleep took him – and because he and MacTíre conversed in English as a matter of necessity, and in Gaelic as a matter of expression – Mogue found himself wondering if language perhaps carried as much worth as silver and gold. In Dublin, he'd never cared to learn. If it didn't allow him to survive another dawn, whatever was the use? He knew the booksellers, loudly plying their wares on the warren of thoroughfares netted around the quays. Yet never had he cared to pick his pockets with the brightly coloured folios they were peddling, unless he was pushed to desperation. Now he cared for little else; their contents held his young mind in the way little else ever could.

*

At daybreak on a given day, as a faint sun rode the sky and MacTíre shook off the dregs of another hangover, they walked toward the low treeline that crouched opposite the cave mouth, and they drew their blades. They circled one another briefly but steel met steel, and the daybreak birdsong fell silent as if the crakes and thrushes were viewing the performance with great fascination.

Mogue was as fleet of foot as he was now of mind. Even with a throbbing skull, MacTíre was viciously thorough with a blade, but Mogue managed to meet his strokes every time. The blades clattered and clanged in the dawn air, their echoes stemmed only by the river's low burble. A slash bit into Mogue's white sleeve; his riposte swiftly grazed the road thief's torso.

Soon enough, both bore cuts and scars on forearm, shoulder, cheek. The half-frozen ground beneath their feet grew increasingly trampled into damp, rot-rich soil. After an hour, their blades were notched, their flesh pocked with cuts; but their heads were clear. MacTíre grunted some affirmation to the younger man's skill and shuffled back inside, and that was it. MacTíre did not let the lad see it, but he was privately grinning through the grimace he wore from where Mogue had cut his tendon.

It was understood that their sparring sessions would always be of the morning. They sparred in the cave and on open ground, around the trees and on the riverbank, when the tide was low enough. Wind, rain, or whatever meagre shine the sun could offer mattered little. Their only concern was of being seen and their hideout discovered, but they were secluded deep enough in the forest to avoid even the few travellers who dared pass under the looming trees to venture farther than the trail. MacTíre knew he was far from the only threat that haunted the woods. Besides, the screech of blades ringing out in the dense midst of a forest, as jagged and piercing as that of a barn owl, tended to repel rather than elicit curiosity. They also took the time to venture out among the trees for Mogue to learn to shoot, and the air was so thick from the trees that their gunshots carried little echo.

Mogue's judgement sharpened along with his fighting skill. His appetite for blood, first whetted at the alehouse, now agitated him with restless fervour. His hands trembled even as he clenched them and silently willed them to be still; his blood waxed hot as gun-oil as he imagined his blades drawn and biting into the flesh of some luckless traveller; the raw, gimlet fear in their eyes as the realisation that death was truly upon them at last a thrill. How he thirsted for that moment, for the taking of a prize!

For Mogue, the world seemed to be made of slate, and the river ran as coldly and clearly as a strip of fortified pewter. Gradually, more and more travellers made the rounds on the forest, and MacTíre would sometimes steal out alone to the alehouse, gathering more intelligence from Gráinne. Much of what she had did not bode well.

"Will yer beard ever know the scrape of a razor?" she had asked one day after bidding him enter, grabbing him in a tight embrace and holding him with no small relief. The road thief held her back for a while; she smelled of aloe and ambergris. Few other women could calm him so. "There's little left of ye that's handsome."

"Little of me ever was handsome."

"Matter of opinion, Joseph." She kissed him gently, and led him inside, careful to keep him out of the other patrons' sight. "Though, were ye to shear it off, I may not recognise ye."

And that's what I fear, he thought, but kept his lips sealed. The temptation to follow her upstairs to her bedchamber, to rip her bodice off and lie amongst the sheets, drinking in her scent and naked flesh and forgetting of all other things, was needling him. Such were the things he wished to remember of her, and the things he hoped to know again before a bullet took him. But more pressing matters were at hand.

"Spare me yer *plámás*, Gráinne," he murmured. "There's things we've to discuss."

Her eyes narrowed. She poured some grog into an empty tankard and placed it before him. "What more do ye need? Don't forget, the risk is as much mine as yours."

"I understand that. Ye have my protection whilst I still draw breath, though."

"And that could be over any day now."

"Perhaps, but it's been a time now, and they haven't found us, nor have they dared bring ye any harm. Nor will they, not while they know I still walk free."

Gráinne sat opposite him. The taproom was silent, and the evening crowd were still a few hours away. "What more need ye know?"

"Men come in here, their pockets bulgin' with coin and their heads with whisperin's. What more have ye heard?"

"Enough that'll keep any man with sense away."

"When've ye ever known sense to be my strong point?"

"Since I saw ye last. Ye'd be wise to stay in the shadows and cease these visits. If ye weren't a hunted man before, ye certainly are now. Half still think you're just a *taibhse*, the others know there's money to be had from yer death. The garrison at Duncannon's been added to.

More redcoats are on the road than ever before. I don't know what it is yer plannin', but you and that boy best keep yer wits about yis."

"The boy can fight," MacTíre sipped the grog.

"Not against trained soldiers. Ye know this. And the volunteers are rallyin' too. There've been midnight meetings, regardin' both you and the redcoats."

"And that's why I'm here. Also, to see if you were unharmed. And it's only a miracle that ye are."

"And how long before I'm not? There's only so long before they decide to send ye a message. Don't make me that message."

"What be yer worry? Ye said yersef, most of them are too fearful to move on ye."

"For now, yeh. But what'll become of –"

"The lad's safe at my side. He's a skill for knifework. Once he's ready, there'll be plenty at his mercy, rebel or redcoat alike. While he stands with me, he needn't worry. And nor should you."

"I'm not the one who has a hideout to flee to."

"Nor were ye ever one to let fears of an imagined shadow daunt ye, Gráinne."

She reached over, her palm folding over his. Her eyes were steady. "I hope you're right. But anyone who knows ye well must also know the price."

"Trust me with this, then." MacTíre kissed her, and, to his relief, she reciprocated. For a brief moment, he cared not for the other patrons in the taproom. The urge to keep her close, visit his heat upon her, was too much to bear.

"I don't know when you'll see me again," he said, already dizzy from her aftertaste.

"Ye can't stay a while longer? There are many empty beds upstairs."

"Ye've risked enough, Gráinne." He paused. "How's yer shootin'? Still practisin' at cock crow?"

"What do you think?"

MacTíre smiled before handing her a full cartouche box. "Good to hear. Ye'll be needin' this, so." He kissed her again, before prowling out the back door.

*

MacTíre had returned from one of these irregular visits, hunched in his greatcoat and with mud crusting his boots, and Mogue barely glanced up from Hesiod's *Theogany*, even as the road thief hunched opposite him and tossed extra birches into the flames.

"Ye best keep a weather eye on the cave mouth as much as them books, lad," he finally uttered. "Mayhap we'll make tracks soon."

"Are we to leave?' Mogue responded.

"I'm after findin' us a lead. Due tomorrow evenin'. You'll have to forego scholarly pursuits for one night, I'm afraid. Put yer skill with a blade to work."

"And what are we after?"

"Not a question of what, lad, but who. I'll need ye to be rested."

"Redcoats?"

"Aye."

Not for the first time, Mogue noticed how seamlessly the road thief wove the two tongues together in one breath, how he'd sprinkle Gaelic words in and among English phrases, like sand amongst stones. From far without, a roll of thunder sounded, heavy and low as a timpani tattoo. MacTíre glanced up, a faraway smile twisting his mouth. "D'ye know, lad, that could be an omen. It's said that when lightnin' strikes, the crack of thunder that follows is actually yer ancestors callin' out for ye to join 'em. What make ye of that?"

"I reckon it's about to piss rain any second."

The road thief smirked at that, took up his gun once more and left the cave in search of firewood.

On such nights, Mogue would remain in the cave, practising knifework and gorging himself on Swift's *Letters* or some other stolen volume by firelight; or else keeping watch by the entrance, his flintlock at the ready. His eyes had adjusted to the flames' golden seethe. At times he did not practise parries or thrusts but instead moved the blade about as if to cleave the air, its weight in hand both reassuring and pleasurable.

The hours of lingering solitude he came to cherish like the choicest dish at a banquet. Settled against the hard flint wall, a concentrated squint gnarling his brow, he turned to the next volume. The grotto was lit as much by the revelatory sortilege of lyric and ode presented in the pages of the road thief's many purloined books as it was by the fire. These were no fruits he was forbidden to taste, but feasts he was only too welcome to devour without restraint.

MacTíre would return with his night's takings, perhaps deer or salmon; and after eating, Mogue would finally approach the road thief with some question as to the contents of his latest literary conquest, which then led to them exchanging their sometimes coarse thoughts. They spoke of things MacTíre suspected few others could ever hope to understand. Their night-time discussions often passed like that, until both were too fatigued to speak any further and drifted off to sleep by the fire's puttering cinders and the lingering smell of smoked fare.

"Damn them all," MacTíre would snarl, his scar all the more livid for his grimace. "They claim to hold all men equal and yet are content to damn any man who shares not their delusions of altruism. 'Tis naught but the stoking of vanity. Pretty words are but pretty words, lad. A song sung by a siren. Have faith in nothing, language least of all. When the very words we speak are made into weapons, be on your guard. If you'll use your reason for anything, make it that. Let them fool ye not. Men need their myths, after all."

They sifted headlong through the opuses of poets, essayists, pamphleteers, like sailors scrutinising the angles of a chart in hope of sighting a much-anticipated shoreline. Occasionally the road thief spoke with an eloquence that did not become him, in a voice dangerously tremulous with feeling, of the woe which cuts men off from all hope of salvation; of the tragedy that leads unto death; or of the charms of women and the rule of the senses.

Fire and blood seemed to soak MacTíre's memory. In the grotto's flinty confines, his mind seemed to become a torture chamber, wherein a thousand grisly scenarios played themselves out with vivid, grinding inevitability, to which he could not help but give utterance.

Always his fondness for the bludgeoning cadences and mercurial genius of the great John Milton crept into every conversation, and he was given to bursts of quotation. He raged at the tyranny of emperors and kings, mocked the insurrectionary efforts of peasants to better their lot.

Several times Mogue wept as MacTíre raised a point of ethics, calling himself damned and the boy along with him, before scoffing about the outburst later. He had the gruffness of a man far beyond his years, who knew disappointment as an old companion; his wonder at a story recounted from the Holy Scriptures or a Shakespearean sonnet was that of a child.

More and more, Mogue wondered how such zeal for learnedness and brutality could be so equally present and fully formed in one man. He was intrigued that MacTíre's rough manner and bristly accent did nothing to lessen the considerable command he wielded over the English tongue; or that through that same tongue wielded vocabulary, ideas, hypotheses, and theorems with the same vigour he applied to wielding a gun or a blade. He knew the meanings of certain words with a seeming scholarly assuredness; stumbled over others with the clumsiness of a child.

MacTíre sensed Mogue's delight in finally being able to converse with another human being at length, to deliberate over matters of liberty, metaphysics, and nature; as long as their colloquy remained confined to such lofty notions (their loftiness being as much a source of contempt as it was of clawing fascination), his verve did not falter. Nor did his own curiosity as to the lad's burgeoning literacy abate; occasionally he found himself gently correcting Mogue on matters of pronunciation, even though he knew his own to be far from the best. Occasionally the lad could not only engage but even best him in debate, deploying a point the road thief had left unconsidered.

That they both lacked any full comprehension was beside the point; both sensed that minds far greater than their own revealed themselves in the way stalactites seem to in caves, glorious and forcible and revelatory. Years in solitude would trigger dreams, Mogue understood, perhaps the same dreams that once held the Revelator captive on Patmos' dim coast. With neither method nor modality nor bearing, his own ardour for scholarship waxed hotter and hotter, the vines of ignorance that twisted and tangled in his brain unravelling as if by some inner sorcery, and he found himself scaling previously unconceived heights of imagination.

It was as if a great flare had been ignited in Mogue's head, and the trail of gunpowder it now sizzled along would soon ignite some shadowy nether region in his psyche where understanding had yet to be roused. Like the butterfly bursting forth from the gluey incarceration of its cocoon and spreading its newfound wings, no longer did he fear any of the world's myriad shadows. The dead hand of barbarism no longer gripped him. He deemed himself to be his own beacon, his sole torch against the world's many and matted shadows. Only by his own lights would he decide and act, not according to the perfunctory prescriptions of morality or health or line of thought dictated to him by any outside force. Much of society seemed content with submitting to such precepts; he'd have little part of it. Ideas that once thrummed vaguely at the back of his skull now increased in volume and gleamed in clarity. His own ignorance of such matters melted pleasurably away, just as frost dissolves from the branches of trees with the radiance of the sun's daybreak beams. The sheer depth of his old benightedness sowed pestilent seeds of shame in his breast. To keep its weeds from sprouting, his appetite for study swelled as he and the fermentation of thought now roiled in his mind.

Not a second could now be wasted. He now wished to know it all, to trawl through his newfound and roughly devised curricula with the fervour of a catechumen: the truth of an institution's purpose, the faculties of men all proving equal, regardless of birth or circumstance or level of prowess, the strange harmony of the sciences. His mind was a tool as useful and as germane as a blade or sickle. He came to see himself as a citizen of nowhere – not of Ireland, nor England, nor the Empire, nor of any place neatly marked and tabulated on a chart and curbed by countless borders and imagined boundaries – nor as a subject to any king or potentate, or any man who might declare himself vested with powers of rule. On no man and nothing would he now depend, save his own whetted wits and reason and conscience. No doctrine would he mindlessly accept, no man's word would he fully believe until his own investigations had proven a fellow's claim. Oaths of office were merely dainty declarations; promises were false until kept. Like the master mariner setting sail into perilous seas, he alone would determine his voyage. He had no preference for light or heavy reading. To unwind he perused some of Pope's hardy cantos, his willowy eye following a mock-heroic verse by the light's dim gutter, reading certain phrases repeatedly, sometimes hammering the pitch to cacophony or else pressing it back to dulcet accord. He read until the fire burned down to ashes, savouring the hushed moment. *'Twas neither the age of darkness or enlightenment when the pages burn, or the verses cease*, he decided. MacTíre, meanwhile, grafted through the whirling cold, nimble machinist of the raw season. *A being darkly wise, indeed.*

The sheer multiplicity of manoeuvres to which language could lend itself dawned on him steadily but surely. His aptitude increased; guided by MacTíre, his handwriting gained legibility, his wrist and hand unsteadily piloting letters and sentences into slow, heedful existence. He found himself especially drawn to the writings of Hobbes, themselves bound and spined in a plain burgundy cover that put him in mind of the dark, thick substance priests pour into goblets in a vampiric simulacrum of holy blood. But there was nothing holy about this book. To read Hobbes was to cast off any vexatious yoke of morality, faith, law. There was little in the world, it seemed, capable of resisting any claim he was of a mind to stake.

Throughout this baptism by words, he hoped to one day be able to recite great swathes of this noble work by heart. To read Hobbes was to recognise the nationally agreed-upon sham of each and every dogma one could name, the fetters and shackles men so willingly wore. In devouring the library, he now deemed himself to have cast off some monumental shackle that he had hitherto been unaware of wearing. Some things he came to believe in wholeheartedly and others he found repugnant; yet none escaped his contemplation. Freedom was not possible for all men, he knew that; to live free would be to retreat to a cavern such as this. The masses would rather turn to their self-appointed guardians in all matters of magnitude. Kant and Machiavelli's understandings of princes left him thinking; Hamman's rejection of the cold sleep of dogma enthralled him.

In another life, he had lived only by the hounded beast's instinct to survive, working whatever circumstance he found himself to ensure another morning would be seen. But now, curiosity of the world's strange workings offered itself to him, with each completed text. He knew all too well, from his time among the kip houses and soot-ridden lanes of Dublin, that scarcity was real as the cold whirling in off the sea, dirt and hunger as unshakable as the stone against which he propped his back; Hume's *Treatise of Human Nature* needn't remind him of that.

How the questions so often outnumbered the answers! The unmoored rage he had once felt at such things now had a rudder, so like MacTíre's, now had its point and purpose. For now he believed the rough existence led by the road thief was the only acceptable mode of living in a world where men happily tore one another apart. Notions of liberty were delusion; notions of equality were laughably meagre; eradicating the natural inequalities that had always divided the masses seemed a struggle worthy only of Sisyphus. Men becoming like God through the rigorous study of industry and science, and ethics and natural history – it all seemed so laughably roseate.

And well it was for such men – these fops, these self-appointed statesmen, these powdered, slippery, limp-fingered prigs, these bewigged sons of the gentry with ample time and sustenance, who had known the benefit of wealth, letteredness, a respectable surname, and many friends of similar standing and situation since birth! Honour was saleable to them as silverware, the lives of men profitable as the porcelain from which they sipped their tea. What did any of them know of poverty beyond an abstraction to prate over in their saloons, parliaments, and coffeehouses? Who among them cared to know, who spoke with all the cloying decorum of the Crown? Who among them had fired a gun, wielded a knife in self-defence, lived by the blisters of frost, swirling blasts of wind and rain, all of nature's bitter buffetings, or had been forced to ensure they would live? They clamoured for revolution, for a great overhaul of the very society from which they benefited; and yet some wry instinct told Mogue that just as these men would be the first to express dismay at even the vaguest inkling of any such uprising, they would also be among the first to slake the mob's thirst.

His own thirst for hunting waxed. Every day brought a new lesson in combat-readiness as much as philosophy. His mind still swarmed with the day's reading as they crossed blades and the harsh ring of steel on steel sent birds scattering from the trees or bounced off the stony ceiling. Every time MacTíre knocked him to the ground or bested him with a blade pressed to his gullet or inflicted a fresh bruise on his eye was an opportunity.

A few days before the carriage's arrival, they found themselves chewing on burnt salmon in the cave. After opening his *Leviathan*, Mogue kept his knee rested. The warmth of the fire on his flesh was welcome.

As he continued to read, he noticed MacTíre open a jug of whiskey in his half-lit nook. He wordlessly offered it to Mogue, who grimaced at the taste. The scorch in his throat was enough to keep alert.

"Gettin' used to it, I see," the road thief frowned, scratching his stubble.

"And to Hobbes as well," Mogue returned, without looking up.

"What make ye of him?"

"He's difficult going, right enough, but I think I shall wrap my head around him eventually."

The road thief sipped again. "He's one of the few I can make full sense of. That dread state of nature…"

Something in his voice made Mogue look up. Introspection was not MacTíre's wont, the lad had come to learn. Rarely did he share his thoughts beyond whatever the topic was.

"Ah, that state of nature," the road thief went on. "Every man at war with every man, unto death. That is the true, final destination, lad, when men must become reacquainted with their own savagery. 'Tis liberty at its truest, it saddens me not to say, and the only true law that cannot be broken. Tomorrow night, when we wash our blades in fresh blood, they shall be reminded of that. There's a reckonin' in the air, lad. Of that I'm very certain."

Mogue noticed the highwayman was staring off into the distance. He kept very still. He could tell MacTíre neither sought nor expected any answers for whatever it was he was about to say.

"When I was a young lad, with even less years than you, they had a name for me. They called me 'Tíre-gasur'. Means 'Wolf Child.' I know what their names for me are, lad. They'll dream up ones for ye as well. Me entire life, I've never been thought much of. I see little cause for remorse if I kill."

"Did you ever?"

A calm entered the road thief's voice. "I no longer recall. So many deaths, so many moments of seeing the end open up to you. So many secret societies here, Irishmen harassing Irishmen in secret, while redcoats do the same in the open."

"And you never thought to ally yourself with any of them." Mogue merely stated a fact, but it sounded like enough of a question for the road thief to respond.

"I need no army, lad; just one true companion."

"And the redcoats?"

That required no answer. Mogue knew full well by now the road thief's contempt for both rebels and redcoats. How he'd managed to survive with so few allies was beyond him.

"Devil take 'em all," MacTíre snarled. After a brief pause and a few more sips that steadily became gulps, he added, "'Tis strange, but I might've happily joined one or the other once upon a time. The whiteboys are doing what they do for a reason. I've seen it."

"And more redcoats are on the way?" It was a suspicion Mogue had long held.

"Seems so. But it's the same story since men crawled out of the sea, just retold in crueller colours. They squabble over land, resources, men. Whatever they can claim to possess. But there's a reckoning coming."

This time Mogue refused the proffered jug. "*Milleadh*?"

"Aye."

The boy tried ignoring the hollow knot of disquiet harvesting in his gut. Again, he heard that eerily convincing edge to MacTíre's voice.

"This entire nation will be given over to bloodshed. I know it. For every redcoat, there'll be a thousand would-be firebrands to stoke local resentment over their presence in this land. I'll never don the uniform, white, red, or otherwise. Men in uniform took me home. That's not easily forgotten. Once ye enlist or swear fealty, there's no escape. One faction speaks of control, the other of emancipation and reform one day, and both of fire and the sword the next. Believe ye me, there is only fire and the sword. 'Tisn't freedom they seek, lad. Merely to trade one tyrant for another. Delusive notions of liberty, runnin' rampant. Before long, the carnage'll be unprecedented. And I'll keep to the only law I know, which is one they forget. I'll keep huntin' at me pleasure. What of it?"

"Why not ally ourselves with them?"

The silence that followed could have weighed many tonnes burden. The boy scanned the road thief's scarred features for any reaction. MacTíre's eyes tapered into a sea-green glower.

"'Cause I don't believe in rebellion, lad. Or in revolution, for that matter. And neither should you, if that's the notion you're takin'. In rebellion, sense is often lost. The initial thrill for justice only gets warped into a need to bend all persons to one will. All things have their cost, Mogue. Revolution's no different. Have ye the patience to see change occur incrementally?"

"And do you desire to see the world burn, or see it progress?"

MacTíre leaned back, his eyes closed for a time. "Only that I can survive in it."

"I lost my people," Mogue said quietly. "In Dublin. Lost them to the streets, to the hunger." The road thief could not understand why the lad was telling him this, though he was listening. "And I knew so little else." The boy looked down, all feral defiance waning slowly.

MacTíre grunted and took another swig. Mogue looked up at him, confused.

"When did I ever say I wanted to know any of this, lad?" But there was no mockery in MacTíre's voice, no dismissal.

Mogue's glower put him back into pensiveness. "We both lost our people."

"I didn't *lose* mine. They were taken from me. My sister was defiled and murdered before my eyes and my brother was scarred 'til the waves took him. I was only a young lad, younger'n yerself." MacTíre leaned back, fatigue blanketing him. "No easy thing to forget."

Mogue looked down.

"And in many ways," the road thief continued, "I do be wonderin' what else we've to expect. Every place I look, *tá dreach cíocras fola ar gach rud ann*. The reach of sin was curbed by nothing, nor was that of chaos. What Hobbes dreaded and what Calvin inveighed against – yet there's no God to be found here, not even one who visits fire and fury and cities in ashes on his stricken creation. And so, I take a notion that maybe God long since gave this place up for dead. Then I take an even worse notion." He took a final swig, with a parched man's grateful desperation. "Maybe... just maybe, He was never even here to begin with."

MacTíre was shocked to find he was on the verge of tears. The needling moistness entering his eyes nearly brimmed over before he brushed them away. The lad had no need to see him like this. His throat was still scalding from the last of the whiskey and he poured the final dregs onto the flames. When he spoke again, the lethal resolve in his voice told Mogue he was warding off a hideous impulse that nonetheless gripped him in a state of fervent exhilaration. "Even the ones who claim to want your best interests will find a way of muzzling you. You don't seriously think they'll let you go once they know your knee is bent, do you?"

"And execute us like they do in the stories?"

"I wouldn't be so cavalier. Men were once burnt at the stake just for the books they saw to print."

"They had fellas burnt alive just for writin' somethin' down?"

"Not for writin' *somethin'* down, lad. It was *what* they wrote landed 'em in the cells and then at the stake. The pen's as much a weapon as a gun, lad. Don't forget that." The road thief paused again. "Ye know, there's nothin' to stop ye from leavin'. You're free to wander outta this cave at any time. And yet ye linger by my side. Why, pray?"

"You mean, apart from the guaranteed warmth, the food, the thrill of adventure, and an endless array of volumes to peruse?"

"Ye could always return to an honest livin'. Yer old habits of industry, and all tha'. Now that ye can work yer way 'round basic sentence structure, I'd say yer options have opened somewhat."

"I believe I've a better opportunity standing by your side than anything else. I don't look forward to the cold, the running, the unrelenting sun and bludgeoning rain, the hours of lingering in one spot in the hope of a prize entering the crosshairs. As for any bounty on us, sure they could hunt us for the rest of their days if they so desired. They'd never find a trace."

The road thief didn't reply, and the lasting silences induced by these ponderings became a regular occurrence within the cave. MacTíre would rise before dawn and see to it they ate, and at night they would ride out.

Chapter XV
The Red Carriage

Lying flat on his belly in the undergrowth, trying not to squirm against the chill snaking through him from the peaty soil, MacTíre glared into the shade. The winter twilight left a cloudless sky; yet the glen was shrouded in shadow. His pocket watch was in hand, moonlight glinting off its smooth, cream-coloured face as the hands ticked the precious seconds away. It was dark as oblivion, but he was accustomed to that. The silence begged to be broken. Not even the chortle of a blackbird, or an owl's heart-stopping shriek, dared disturb it. Perhaps they sensed the road thief's presence.

The trail ran like a muddy trough between the leafless trees, with lingering patches of hoarfrost, and the moon flickered ghostly overhead. It was used often enough by travellers, but rarely after dark. With tales of MacTíre and his dangerous young companion growing, only hunting parties and troops of redcoats willingly passed through there now.

A faint glimmer of torchlight fluttered through the trees. The dim pounding of hooves grew louder; low voices and barked commands would soon follow. By their movements, it was clear they knew not the land they patrolled. It was too far distant for the scarlet of their coats to be seen. MacTíre exhaled and angled his flintlock toward the trail, shifting his gaze to where the lad stood, a-ways off on the trail.

"Calm now, lad," he quietly urged. "Calm 'til the fire."

Mogue Trench, of course, made no reply. The approaching torchlight would reveal him in time – a feral-eyed youth standing stock-still, boots planted far apart in the trampled soil of the path, staring fixedly ahead as they neared. The various blades he had concealed about his person, in the folds of his smock and shirttails, would not be so easily discerned. He was so still as to be mistaken for a statue; only the occasional sharp turn of his head to sense better angles of fire would tell you he was living. Truly, the lad possessed a sagacity far beyond his years. Unless he was standing still from all the sawdust in his mouth.

It was strange, thought the road thief, knowing he was no longer acting alone; yet Mogue seemed fully aware of the situation. Experience told MacTíre there was no better hour to commence hunting than the one that brought twilight. He could lie in wait for hours until a mark entered his sights. Rebel or redcoat, only a fool would venture these parts unarmed.

The element of surprise now had the addition of the sight of the figure on the trail. The road thief sensed and saw them before Mogue did; his only concern was for the lad's vigilance faltering at the crucial moment. A single false move would be the end of them both.

Torches flickered through the trees like fireflies; anticipation stirred in MacTíre's chest. He wondered if the same feeling had Mogue in its grip; it was too dark to see, after all.

"How many?" he remembered asking Gráinne.

"Only a few regulars, from the regiment, no more'n fifteen," she'd replied. "Not very many, but enough."

"Where're they headed, d'ye know?"

"The fort at Duncannon."

MacTíre nodded at that. Any section patrolling the forest had to be one of foot.

She hadn't tried to dissuade him of this. No words of reconsideration, nor even to prevent Mogue being a part of this. This was to be the lad's life now. She understood that, as Gráinne understood many hard things. All she wanted was her share of any valuables claimed, and MacTíre's body to warm hers in the night.

Unlike Mogue, the road thief knew what to expect. He'd carried out many raids like this before, and even the extra concern Mogue's presence gave him did not deter his focus. Even trained soldiers could succumb to panicked disarray if nudged the right way. They expected to be attacked but could seldom gauge how such an attack might manifest.

Try not get us both killed, lad, he prayed, though there was enough poise in Mogue's stance to still his anxieties.

He heard the footfalls first, boots squelching into damp soil and brush. His breathing slowed as his keen eyes finally sighted them and the meagre flicker of their torches, so dim against the gathering heap of shadow that spilled into the glen with the hour's decline. The redcoats marched in twos, an orderly phalanx even under cover of the thicket, passing knotted branches on either side, rolling into view like phantoms in broadcloth. All carried muskets and blades. But, as MacTíre suspected, they moved with caution – this trail was unknown to most of them. The sudden hammering in his ears was molten. He raised his flintlock and cocked it, wincing a little as the walnut stock jammed into his shoulder.

On the trail, Mogue Trench stayed still until the edge of the torchlight fell upon him. Pale, unblinking, he looked as if he were moulded from marble and affixed to the soil, were it not for the heavy smears of ash rubbed into his face and hair in crude emulation of a skull. The whites of his eyes glowered at the soldiers as they halted in their tracks. For a few precious seconds, not a word was exchanged, nor a sign made.

From the undergrowth, MacTíre watched one of them – a sergeant, no doubt, judging from his black-laced epaulettes – move forward. His measured pace – careful and cautious, his boots sinking heavily into the soil with each step – signalled uncertainty, despite his calm appearance. Meanwhile, many of the redcoats had their muskets at the ready, trained on the dense blackness of the trees.

The officer was so distracted by the strange, unblinking youth standing before him, like an apparition made from ash, he seemed cognizant of little else. MacTíre sensed he was trying to say something to the lad, but was clearly stumbling over his words. In any case, Mogue did not respond, as the road thief had instructed him; merely stood where he was and stared the man down as he approached.

MacTíre's finger extended to the trigger. He had a clear shot from where he lay; demanding a stand-and-deliver was of no more use.

Rough estimation told the road thief that the officer was easily twenty yards from Mogue, and a good fifty paces from where MacTíre crouched. The glow of his torchlight guttered on the wind.

Is mise Ifreann, he thought. *Anois, beidh aithne agat ormsa.*

The shot that rang out burst apart the wooded silence. MacTíre ducked instinctively as the bullet whistled through the air, felling the officer where he stood. Alone, this was the moment MacTíre relished the most when on a raid; the sudden panic of his mark, the alarmed, frantic shouts and calls to either run or fight back, the heavy rustling as men loaded guns and dove and hunkered for cover, the smell of gunsmoke cauterising the air.

Now with Mogue at his side, he couldn't savour it very long. He managed to reload and get two more targets before they realised the attack was coming from the trees. Several more were already clumsily returning fire, shooting blindly into the trees from where they crouched. Yet the boy had managed to slip into the trees, moving with the reflexive stealth of an acrobat.

MacTíre's gut tensed as he moved on his belly, firing from behind trees, and never from the same place twice. The smell of cordite and smoke thickening never failed to keep him alert. Every shot fired sounded like the dry-throated hiss of some unearthly serpent. Surrender would not sate him; mercy was no longer salvageable to Joseph MacTíre.

Savage excitement was all he knew now. Some spirit of rapacity had him in a stranglehold. A desire for murder as much as plunder gripped him; blood was his bondage. Shots whizzed past him, but never quite close enough. He moved too quickly to remain in one place.

The redcoats in their confusion had forgotten about the ash-covered youth on the road. Mogue was rushing through the soil, both blades drawn, light as the breeze. His blades sang through the air, pinning men in the back and shoulder. Choked snarls and cries were cut off by yet more firing. Bullets passed through shoulder and gullet; blood spewed over leaf and bark. Fingers were pressed to wounds before men fell into the sodden leaves beneath.

MacTíre's breathing was heavy as he stood and looked at the scene. The odour of death and smoke filled the air that would now know more tattoos. He walked into the clearing to see Mogue ambling about the bodies, pulling blades from the flesh with a juicy wrench. Only one or two of the redcoats' torches were still blazing; the rest had been snuffed out where they lay, dropped amongst sodden leaves. The lad looked out of breath, and the ashy smears on his face were now streaked with sweat and dripping like tears. He squinted against the haze.

"Good work, lad." The road thief, his voice more raw than usual from the smoke.

Mogue's ash-covered face made his expression difficult to read. His teeth were bared and his hands appeared to be shaking, yet he did not drop his blades. His eyes kept running over the various bodies that lay felled around them. Barbarism seemed to whirl off him like a cloud of smoke.

"Should we get them off the road?" was his eventual response.

"Nah, leave 'em where they fell. Sends a better message."

Neither had taken injuries, aside from a few minor scrapes of bullets hurtling past. The throb of battle fever, thunderous in his ears mere moments before, had worn itself out; nor was there even the thrill of victory to soften the road thief's mood. Only the odd serenity that only ever seemed to attend on him after a fight, leaving him calm and refreshed and temporarily at peace, began to fall through him like a cool mist of rain.

Above the trees, the sky had turned fully dark and still no moon was afoot. Whatever threats were left among the trees, MacTíre neither sensed nor cared to sense. The forest held no fear for him. They gathered up what spoils they could from the fallen bodies, pouches of shot and any muskets found. There was little on the redcoats' persons that could be bartered later, but that never stopped the road thief from being thorough. The sight and smell never repulsed him; if anything, he'd grown fond of them both. As he rifled through pockets and withdrew bullets, cartouche boxes and other valuables, he noticed Mogue was doing the same.

It was a while before the smell of gunsmoke would leave the forest.

Chapter XVI
Aſheſ of Legend

As they knew it would, the story of how the notorious highwayman Joseph MacTíre, the Wolf of Wexford, the storied road thief – already with a hefty price on his head for innumerable crimes – had evaded capture from right under the nose of Sir Vesey Colclough of the Tintern Estate and had brutally slaughtered a great deal of his men in the depths of the nearby forest, was on the lips of every cottier, bogman, and redcoat for miles around.

His infamy became such that even the least superstitious were heard to assert that he could be neither caught nor killed, that he preyed on man and beast, tearing them to pieces with equal frenzied savagery; that he roamed among the leafless oaks and river valleys girdled in wolfskins instead of a greatcoat; that he grew clawed and fanged and furred by moonlight, and that he growled and howled to the heavens after making an especially savoury kill. Given the dearth of wolves in the county for several decades, it was rumoured he was among their last, preying on any wayfarers unfortunate enough to wander into his territory. That he must be aided by some malevolent force far beyond this world, that kept him informed of when and where to strike, was never in doubt. Whether mantled as man or beast, however, his ferocity was unchanged, his rabid, myriad hungers perpetually unslaked.

It became a favourite tavern yarn by those who claimed to have been there that night and witnessed the road thief's savagery against their fellows; a subject for fulminant damnation by the priests in their pulpits; and a ghost story with which parents frightened unruly children into obedience – *"Beware, beware, the Wolf of Wexford is near"*. There were the inevitable embellishments that circulated around his legend as well, speculations of his sinfulness, hearsay of his hatreds, torridness of his temper, disingenuities uttered with such supreme confidence that seemed to spread with so little allay.

It was widely rumoured, in allegedly less benighted circles, that he was not a man at all but a phantom conjured by some dark necromancy;

that he was a sworn member of the Whiteboys or the Defenders or any one of the seething morass of militias and secret societies blighting the Irish countryside; he was an English mercenary, charged by the Crown to provoke fearful uncertainty amongst the ingrate bastard Irish; a disgraced colonel of the 105th Regiment who saw action in the Americas, and who now sought revenge on his former military superiors following his company's disbandment. That MacTíre seemed to prey with little reluctance on prince, peasant, rebel, and redcoat in equal measure did little to slow these whisperings.

MacTíre frenzy swept through the nation. The newspapers, both gutter press and respectable dailies alike, were only too happy to stoke as much frenzied interest in the lupine rapparee as they could. By their alleged reportage, MacTíre soon stood accused of everything from brigandage, gunrunning, cattle houghing, street brawling, debauchery, conspiracy to treason, and generally wilful and enthusiastic denigration of the public good. His genius for knavery saw fresh crops of posters appearing in the towns and harbours, offering as much as 200 pounds reward for his capture.

Before, he visited no further mischief on his intended prey once he had stripped them of whatever wealth or finery they carried; now, the urge to kill and see blood rush was impossible to ignore. He cared not for life anymore; staying his hand was out of the question. He would have their blood as much as their riches, and no doubt the devil incarnate would drink from the same cup.

He fled from no war-heat; better always to die in the face of a pike's lunging hiss, or retreat through underbrush where armoured horse couldn't follow, than kneel before a blood-blind banner.

The price on his head was raised; the townlands scoured by all manner of would-be fortune hunters seeking to put him down with the same measure of savagery he saw keenly foisted upon his victims. Yet for all the prices, there were just as many who refused to venture out upon the Wexford trails after dark, knowing that an invisible, silent hunter who knew the land far greater than anyone, lay in wait amongst the shadows.

As for the cavalry, they would call his name as if he were commonage to rack or rent, or one of their hunting bitches called to heel, even as he cut and run across his own country.

But, to Mogue's delight, the story of Joseph MacTíre was expanded upon; he apparently travelled with a companion now, a youth who moved too quickly to be seen, who wielded skinning blades and whose face was smeared with ash and soil in crude imitation of a human skull. MacTíre's Cub, he soon became known, striking fast from the shadows even as MacTíre distracted their mark with his usual stand and deliver spiel.

*

"This matter, I may probably set right another time, and only observe for the present, that the pirates at sea have the same sagacity with robbers at land. As the latter understand what roads are most frequented, and where it is most likely to meet with booty, so the former know what latitude to lie in, in order to intercept ships –"

MacTíre's heavy, tobacco-rich laugh hacked through Mogue's full flow of reading. "If I knew little better, I'd say this Johnson fella nearly admires the likes of us."

Mogue frowned at the interruption. "You think little of him?"

"He writes well, and the rovings of those sea-dogs never fail to tantalise a mind such as mine. He claims to write of these men in order to educate those who would endeavour to apprehend them. But he is also answering a more primal need."

"And that is?"

"The morbid curiosity of the masses. Observe a man relaying a ghost story to a crowd; how greedily they hold onto his every word. They are ever seduced by tales of death and depravity. 'Tis neither justice nor vengeance that draws them to watch a knave's body swing from the gallows. He invokes laws of reason, but it is the abandonment of reason, the slow plunge into the abyss, that truly holds his attention. He cleaves to his own delusory sense of morality, which really has been thrust upon him since birth, and he lacks the imagination to devise any other ethical code according to his own lights. His faith in the laws of men will let him down eventually. He cannot understand why men so willingly embrace their darkest impulses, why they unmoor themselves from reason. A part of him envies them, for having the shameless will to cast off any yoke of duty and live with true freedom, unchained by some self-imposed code of ethical consideration."

"You seem very certain of this."

"What those men understood, that ye too will soon have to realize, is that they knew how to make their fortune outside of the law."

He polished his flintlock, held it up to test its grip. He looked up at the crevice, and then glanced at the flames smouldering before him. "They turn to their institutions. Their kings, whatever version of God they've been instructed to worship, the structures they believe will stand forever. There is no reason in any of this, however much they insist on reason and its infallibility."

"Is that what you believe?" Mogue ventured.

"'Tis what I know," the road thief answered. "Their anthems whirl in my ear, their prayers conjure up naught but ash and shadow. For ash and shadow is all this life is. Vanity and vexation is what the Bible names it. And that is why I live without apology. The world doesn't care for men such as us, 'cept for when it calls for our deaths. Believe me when I say…keep outrunnin' them and strike when you have to. They have little to offer you, save the noose."

He put his flintlock away and began honing his knife with a lump of flint that lay close by.

"Aye, that is the crux 'n certainty of this life." A harshness now entered his voice, and he spoke low, as if willing himself not to bellow. "I've nothin' to fear from God. If He truly was as merciful, as wise, as the scriptures say, then why, pray, are neither of our prayers answered? Ye ask what kind of life this is, but I then must ask of you: what's a life of labour without end, of yer wages bein' snatched from ye to keep a lord's life upheld, a church standin' tall? Look at the both of us. Able for war, we might don the scarlet coat and shoulder a musket, venture from these shores, kill some other sad bastards a world away, all in the name of what? A king who cares nothin' for us? A church that deems us beyond salvation by dint of our very existence? A lord can easily fall under my gunshot as much as a peasant, and what difference has been made? Men live and die because I have made it so. 'Tis their time, and I am the emissary that the reaper has sent. When my time comes, as it most assuredly must, I'll welcome it."

"You don't fear death?"

He paused. "I've...made my peace with it. Most likely I won't live to see many more years. When death finally comes for me, he shall be greeted as a friend."

"Is that not also to despair?" Mogue countered.

"Perhaps it is," MacTíre replied. "But I cannot tire of this life. 'Tis all I know."

"Sleeping in the cold and evading capture from *Sassenachs*. Some fuckin' decision."

MacTíre laughed harshly. "Ah, there is plenty of that, I grant you. But there are also fortunes to be made. If you've the *misneach*." He gave a low, wry chuckle, nodding at the book. "Take the lads he writes about, the sea thieves. If there was anythin' they understood, it was ambuscade, how to lie in wait for prey, hold a position as long as necessary 'til a prize wandered into their sights. No, easy thing, as well ye know."

Mogue put the book down – the text was distracting him now – and rubbed his eyes. "And when they choose to fight, as they've been known to, they eventually pinpoint where we're firing from."

"Not 'less we cut n' run," MacTíre said, his smile one of concession. "The trees'll keep us concealed, once we know the season. And at the mention of me name, any will to fight is soon lost."

"And if there's a will to fight, knowing who we are? What then?"

That reply was not expected. MacTíre's eyes narrowed as Mogue picked the book up and pretended to resume reading. "Then we sally forth and meet them," he whispered. "As we've always done."

The boy did not look up, but MacTíre saw exactly where and when his words had punctured him. Mogue's brow was furrowed, mouth curled in a glower.

"I've no death wish, road thief. Don't pretend you don't know this. And I'm not sure I want any part of yours." The boy closed the book abruptly, tossing it back toward the shelf, where it knocked off the wood and landed face-down on the ground, spread like the wings of a felled bird. MacTíre watched it land. The sea change in Mogue's voice, thick with disquiet, was troubling to hear.

"'Tis what must be done, lad," he said.

"What must be done." The boy stared, nostrils bristling with raised choler. MacTíre didn't quite know how to pilot the conversation. His death – likely to come courtesy of a bullet or blade and long before his hair turned silver – was an inevitable fact that had never let him be since he began following the gun, a truth as undisputed as the cold and the dark from which he engineered his raids. It had been years since the first grim comprehension of it broke over his mind like a rogue tide – the same comprehension this boy was only no doubt beginning to feel.

"While yer by my side, no real harm'll come to ye," he said, trying to keep his voice conciliatory. *The boy should count his blessings – at least he's someone to explain all this to him.*

Mogue's throat was dry and he had trouble sipping his water. "Tell me, do you like this life? The way you earn your keep?"

Now MacTíre seemed lost for words. "I…that is…well, 'tis naught but what it is. Solitude pleases me; wind and rain suit my spirit, I shield myself well enough from the moon –"

Mogue put his mug down and tossed a fresh log onto the flames. "And you care not for a wife? Family? You've no thought of earning a proper home for yourself, even?"

"I hanker not for domesticity. Sure, why would I, after all this?" MacTíre replied, his voice edged with annoyance.

"And how long must we stay here, then? 'Til the food runs out or we're found? By now, the price on both our heads must be soaring –"

"We won't be found 'cause no one's hunting us. Sir Vesey is long done looking, and they can send an entire army to scour these woods if they wish; none know it as well as I –"

"Which is why I sincerely hope you have a plan." Mogue spoke distantly, his gaze fixed on the flame's sparked burst, but his eyes pulsed with something equally fiery.

"If men such as we must live under the vile appellations they give us, branded outlaws, hunted men, it is only because by their appellations can they hope to understand us – that we take what's ours and live without fear."

MacTíre hooked his thumb into his belt buckle, fatigue suddenly freighting his bones. How much of it did he believe, really? "This war was once mine and mine alone. It's yours as well now. Death is a daily companion for us both. I'll need ye ready for –"

"For the moment when I must put a bullet through a man's head before he puts one through mine."

"That's the way of it, yeh. Not that ye haven't done it yet, lad."

Mogue picked the book up again and thumbed through it, his lips moving along with the words as the flames crackled and the sparks bounced upward like fireflies. MacTíre sat back against the cave wall, the base of his skull resting on hard stone as he watched the fire. The growing heat slowly washed over him, making him yawn until sleep finally took him. The lad was still working his way through Johnson and his chapter on the infamous Blackbeard as his eyes closed.

He found himself dreaming, unbidden, of Gráinne. Her absence weighed heavily on him, and no flame could thaw the chill of loneliness that raked his innards with strained regularity. Lying awake beside her in those small hours of the night, in her chamber at the alehouse, her soft whispers brushing his throat, as she told him of new prizes and of her own loneliness, weighing as heavily on her whenever he was away (and that she staved off with her acerbic tongue and scalding wit); her worry that this would be the last time they had together before he was felled by blade or bullet.

Even the thought of relinquishing this life and attempting a life with her, with an honest living to his name, seemed unattainable. He had made too many enemies from both rebel and redcoat now to ever fit into a life of normalcy. If Gráinne's shade was to join Redmond's and Fiadh's on his account, what abyss then lay in wait for him?

He had always found some semblance of peace in her arms, some inkling of intimacy and perhaps even love. He suspected, or deigned to suspect, it was the same for her. She consented to his kisses and embraces with greater ardour than he suspected she did other men who chartered her services, and often waiving her usual fee for him. She needed no alms; none had yet dared harm her, knowing her intimacy with him. True they despised him for his crimes against their families, but fear of his wrath far outweighed any urge for vengeance. She had no sensibility for marriage, or even for attaining higher respectability for herself, whether through marriage or embarking into some mercantile venture. The alehouse was sustained solely by her shrewdness and her ability to keep her girls looked after and herself in coin from their wares. Visiting her over the years told him she was satisfied with her station, inasmuch as she could claim to govern it, and his last visit to her was no different.

Like him, she was marked by a certain loneliness that all people of self-forged strength must endure; it was what drew them together so naturally and irresistibly, why they so often sought anchorage in each other's arms, why she was such a willing abettor in his crimes, and why he was so happy to bestow upon her a cut of the spoils. She'd said many times she had little need of a man, except in bed; MacTíre found himself oddly at peace with this. Yet his affection toward her ran too strong and too deep to fully detach himself; his own loneliness, kept easily at bay in the rush of a night-time chase or the heart-pumping wait to strike at a valuable prize, felt so horribly underscored by it. MacTíre loved in his own manner, in the silent manner of those who have long resolved to lock their finer feelings away in one of the heart's murkier recesses, never quite uttering a word of it. His need for solitude was too great as well; he counted his blessings that she understood such a thing. And yet, despite his understanding and all of the pragmatism they shared over the situation, he could not escape how dark and forbidding the nights were without the warmth of Gráinne's hand in his, and the wry mirth of her voice.

Upon waking, the road thief saw Mogue was still poring over the book, his eyes gimlet. He had lit a small tallow candle to provide what meagre light he needed to discern the text. MacTíre sat up and yawned, and only then did the boy acknowledge him.

MacTíre glanced over at the fire. Only a few wisps of smoke now drifted up from its ashy remnants. MacTíre left the cave to perform some ablutions, throwing himself into the river to wash away the smoke in his head.

On returning, he told the boy to put the books down. Mogue glowered as the road thief dipped his hand into the still-smoking clump of ashes at his feet and then smudged the grey particles of dust over his face and hair, running it down his jaw by his fingers, pressing more of it into his brows and mouth until his entire face resembled a human skull.

MacTíre nodded down at the flames, and Mogue reluctantly accepted that he was expected to do the same. He reached in, sneezing a little as some of the dust got into his nose. He rubbed it down, eyelids closed, until a crude rendition of a skull also graced his features. Once again, he was ready.

Chapter XVII
To That Foul Revolt

In the halcyon years since the fateful flight from Tintern, as the seasons blasted and buffeted high road and field and forest floor, and the tenants of that sea-girdled region lost more of their families and fellows to the road thieves' nightly raids, MacTíre grew less and less careful in who he targeted. If rich or poor had made little difference to him before, it made virtually none now. He understood the danger making enemies on all sides, yet he cared little for how it affected him.

The forest became their natural fortress, thick and tangled enough to deter any pursuer. No fear of redcoats nor bounty hunters nor even a troop of mounted yeomen venturing too deeply in to prey on them. There wasn't a hiding place under that ferny canopy the road thief and his protégé didn't know; there wasn't a tree they could not blend themselves into. MacTíre knew the terrain well enough now to sense that even the birds and beasts were in sympathy with his and Mogue's savage enterprise. So accustomed had they become to the road thieves' presence that they still sung whereupon they passed; only when they fell silent did they know a foreign presence had slipped past the forest's nets.

The outstretched limbs of oak and chestnut were as salient a refuge as any garrison. With blades neatly slung to his ribs, and now fully accustomed to the damp of the soil ever seeping into his shirt with each newly laid plan to attack, Mogue's eyes had adjusted to the wildness, the merciless way the sun gilded the forest path and made his prey squint, and he now moved quick and readily as any beast.

The dell still rang with steel and MacTíre's grunted instructions as they sparred daily, and the silence that filled it afterward, so heavy and close, was enough to set any traveller on edge. They spent hours trudging through dells and glades, marking out the best positions to attack and working out escape routes, hours lying on their stomachs in wait for the approach of a uniform. The winter gales blew crisp and savage off the river where the sea blustered them in, rustling the leaves like an emerald whisper and ensuring they did not nod off. No chance of being hunted in their own forest, either. They owned it as the lord-lieutenant owned the kingdom of Ireland. Of course, they did more than merely hide and run.

"The element of surprise is with us. Once it becomes clear what's happening, any will to resist will have deserted them," MacTíre advised his now not-so-young protégé. "Take the river. Ye could lie in wait there on the banks. But then ye've nowhere to run, save the water. 'Course, the water'll hid yer scent from both man and beast."

And always he kept up Mogue's crude education, the knowledge he gained from the books they stole expanding and his understanding of the world's troubles growing. More books lined the hideaway's crude shelf, and goings-on across the globe held his fascination. The lad could not kill as readily as MacTíre, could not descend on a victim with as much desire for slaughter.

Mogue's fighting fitness steadily increased, and with this his hunger for taking a prize. He would look into the shadows for imaginary targets, listen for the crunch of boots in soil or the smart splash of soldierly red. His wrists throbbed softly but steadily, the hammering of his pulse sending him into a trance that was broken only at the moment of striking. He slid through the underbrush with instinctive finesse, ducked and dived past trees like a surveyor. The air of the forest, so close and secret and nearly solid, kept him well fed. The soft growl of the river after dark, barely muted by the moss on the bank, reminded him he was close to home.

Working with the boy did take some getting used to. MacTíre found his attention was now divided between their approaching prey and gauging Mogue's alertness. It concerned him that his advantage in both the ambush and the fight that followed might be compromised. Yet Mogue was not governed by youthful recklessness on these nightly excursions. He listened to MacTíre's orders and followed them to the letter, striking from the shadows with a nimble flick of his wrist. His *gralloch* flashed in the dark and was gone; he moved like lightning made flesh. Neither rapier nor rifle seemed to deter him.

The real trick, MacTíre had told Mogue, was about knowing when the time was right to take advantage, when to catch a prize off-guard and outgun it fast.

The search for meat and fresh prizes was never-ending. They might go days without nabbing anything at all, and then have several nights' worth of bullion. Many a hapless traveller came to know their works, trundling by horseback on the Dublin high road, always laden with some manner of bauble, tantalisingly small and valuable. Mogue learned when to spare and when to unleash bullets. They retreated rapidly and without warning back into the shadows. MacTíre knew what twists and turns in the road went unnoticed by the traveller's unfamiliar eye, what bye-ways could provide adequate shelter and which would aid a swift escape.

Only Gráinne could be trusted with leads, they knew, and yet they avoided visiting her too often so as not to raise any further suspicion against her. They visited the old tavern where she plied her wares, handed in some small tribute to her and were on their way. Mogue found welcome reprieve in filling his barren belly with as much food as Gráinne could give them before they rode off. They spent most of Christmas lying low and letting their wounds heal. When the food stores ran out, they made for the river and speared some fish for the evening. Always their ears stayed pricked for the baying of dogs, the echoed shouts and calls of men amongst the trees.

The road thief had long since resolved to see Gráinne and her girls kept safe from all this. She continued to fill them in on what were soon to be passing through, what cargos they were likely to be carrying, how many men were protecting it and how much of a fight they were likely to put up. From here, MacTíre visited her only at night, and made sure to leave as surreptitiously as he'd entered, the hot scent and flavour of her pubis still coaxing his tongue. He left with both some lingering trace of her and the secrets she passed on. On the occasions Mogue accompanied him, one of her girls would take him up to the back chambers, and rarely did he emerge until dawn. "Prizes come in many guises, lad," MacTíre once told him with a smirk.

The first time he fucked one of them, it hurt, the tumid throb from his pelvis obscured by lace and perfume and soft, scented flesh. He'd gotten excited by the words of flattery she whispered, the soft, inviting snap of the kisses she planted on his cheek and throat, and had let out an involuntary moan as her palm curled around his swollen member and she gestured intimately to the bed. Her fingers had raked through his hair, hair that had never once known the scrape of a razor or comb, as she undid his shirt and her free hand stroked the bare, scar-streaked flesh of his torso. His cheeks felt suddenly aflame. Her kisses had left him groggy and flushed, the aftertaste of rouge and salt gnawing his lips; her humid breath and sweat were crisp to taste, her breasts fell free as he tore off her shift; her nipples swelled under his fingertips' knead and then between his teeth.

She'd coiled her tongue past his lip, allowing it to moistly meet the tip of his, pinching out the oil lamp as she let him slip deep inside her. He'd gripped both of her wrists and spread her back hard against the bedstead. He'd wanted to see her face in the dark, see her cheeks tinged with crimson as she grimaced avidly beneath him and their torsos moved together in increasingly feverish rhythm; instead he settled for savouring the warm glisten between her legs, her thighs' welcome tremble, and even the rough tingle snaking down his spine and reddening his cock as she quivered and heaved. Afterward, he'd fallen asleep in her arms in a calm euphoria, waking to find his share from last night's raid taken in full. Try as he might, he couldn't summon the requisite anger over it. There'd be other prizes.

But the road thief appeared to have lost interest in merely taking prizes now. He was a hunter without any specific prey. Anyone stupid enough to pass through his forest was fair game. It wasn't as if they'd no warning; Wexford was a county of wolves once more. They doled out death like monks dispensing alms. Soon more and more uniformed corpses were seen lying prone in a frosted ditch, cold, open-eyed, the frost nibbling at the edges of their bones.

The cool, quiet country nights, with their temple-like silence and ever-present moonlight bore a cruel luminance over the fields and townlands of Wexford. Wind, hail and rain volleyed and screamed through cedar and ditch and briar; Mogue's flesh grew immune to their icy prickle. The reek of dead leaves and drenched soil soared, borne upon heavy breezes whirling in full, chilly force from the coast, occasionally tinged with the aromas of salt, gorse-vanilla or chimney smoke, depending on what season they found themselves in. He came to view the silence as resembling bated breath, reigned in just before a moment of devastating truth or choice.

Save the cavern which MacTíre used as a hideout, never did they linger in the same place twice. The road thief insisted on that.

Whatever deformed home life Mogue had come from up in Dublin, he readily forgot. If ever he felt fear, his skill at hiding it matched that with which he wielded a blade. He had the makings of a killer as much as the road thief, striking quick and sharp, his veins seemingly flooded with ice-water. After a raid he gathered up trinkets from the corpses, as indifferent to each face as he was to the cold air. In the dark, moonless Wexford nights, he felt his hand becoming more claw than limb, clamped in the same hooked position from clasping his *gralloch*-hilt. Were he a soldier, he may have held it to salute at the funerals of comrades, at parade, instead of drawing it furtively out in the dark.

They managed to take many prizes in that fashion, with MacTíre firing the opening salvo and Mogue striking from the shadows. When the entire company was slain, they retreated silently with their plunder to the cave, just as the first crows began to circle. MacTíre wasn't one to pick and choose. A consignment of lumber and a finely decked coach were equally fair game to him. MacTíre had little concern for gold. Some things they divided between them, others they kept if they were of no foreseeable use. Once, an overturned cart turned out to be laden with muskets and over a dozen pikeheads and handles of no paltry workmanship; the mangled body of a youth no older than Mogue in calvary armour was found half-buried in a ditch, carpeted with soil. Cartouche boxes loaden with powder and shot were always kept, and whatever monies they could find. Lengths of rope, saddle bags bugling with bullion or keepsakes – shawls, silks and kerchiefs and other items of clothing for lads and ladies alike, in many variations of finery. Books, too. MacTíre always made sure there were letters and documents to take back and store. None of these ever saw themselves traded in at the hawkers' stalls.

MacTíre did not care for hoarding silver and gold, deeming them instead as useful for procuring food or warmth, or pleasurable company for the night. A priceless gold crucifix, studded with rubies cut into the carapace of tears, bound for the Ramsgrange church, was hawked at Fair Day; a velvet-lined snuff box was traded in for a bed in one of the brothels in the town of Ross, the dubious upward slant of the innkeeper's brow patently ignored. They divided their plunder into crude heaps, letting the other take whatever he hammered the most for, or else haggling when it was called for. What they didn't need, they sold or traded at Fair days. This was how they gathered intelligence on the world around him, apart from what Gráinne had to tell them. It was how they learned the price on MacTíre's head had been raised again and had come to include that of the young ward who now abetted him in his crimes.

The hour of danger was never quite finished. They returned to the cave shortly after, keeping to the shadows as the first crows began to swirl overhead. After they had settled in and a roaring fire was lit, it hit him. As was quickly becoming his wont, Mogue was frowning his way through Dryden's Essays when, with a hiss of frustration, he finally placed it aside and addressed MacTíre. "How much longer are we to keep hidin' out here?" His jaw had an inquisitive set to it as the road thief faced him, looking up from the flames.

"We're not hidin' here, lad, am I not after tellin' yeh? This is where we live. And we're not hidin', but lyin' in wait." MacTíre's voice was as steady as he could keep it. He didn't relish the thought of this conversation.

"In wait for what, exactly?" Mogue drew one of his blades and began rubbing a bit of flint against it, the saw-like rasp of stone on steel echoing in the gloom. MacTíre waited for him to stop. The boy's restlessness was nearly as dangerous as the sparks dancing before him.

"There must be a bigger reason for this than mere survival. We spar, but there's little enough you've shown me of strategy. If we're bound to take a major prize, I'll need to know your ways beyond just the blade and the gun. Will you show me that, at least?"

MacTíre glanced at the knife, hoping the stiff set to his shoulders and his own steely tone would calm the boy. *How much of the lad's curiosity could be sated?* He fought well enough and struck enough times, but there was no denying luck played as much a part in a successful raid as fighting prowess. It was a conundrum he himself had to address in his early days of thievery. MacTíre tightened his lips into a bloodless line and winced a little at an especially sharp crackle of the fire. The boy had some right to strategy as much as he did a share in the plunder, after all.

Mogue's eyebrows were raised inquisitively, and he had sheathed the *gralloch*. "Well?" he asked.

"It'll be more'n just wayfarers we have our sights on from here on," the road thief murmured. "Redcoats patrol these parts often enough, as well ye know, but now their numbers'll be doubled. And that's before ye consider the bounty hunters, too. Both are trained in this type of thing. If we're to cross paths with a fella or even a gang of fellas who're out with the express purpose of huntin' us down, what might be the best way of dealin' with them?"

The silence that followed was protracted. Mogue was clearly turning about as many possibilities as his mind would allow, his face set in that musing expression he so often had. "Shoot before they do, I'd imagine," he finally suggested. "Make sure they haven't got a chance."

MacTíre shook his head. "Ye'd think so, but no. If ye attack too recklessly, guns blazing and no strategy, then you're no use to me as a partner. Ye have to know what yer advantage is, not when's best to start wastin' precious shot and gettin' yerself killed."

"And our advantage is what, then?" The frustration in the lad's voice was poorly hidden.

"The land, the trees. Attack from a place that's both good for yer aim and also good for lettin' ye slip back into the shadows where even their huntin' dogs won't know where to follow."

"A group of four, even eight men we can take down, 'specially if we can shoot at least three of 'em. That time in the forest…"

"Which time was this?"

"After Tintern, ye daw! Only us two, 'gainst twenty men. Unarmed, need I remind you?"

"But who's to say the hunt won't be given again?" Mogue said. "They know you're flesh and blood now.'

MacTíre's lips clamped together without anything in his expression betraying any kind of fury. He instead scanned the flames, as if in the hope of seeing something empyrean and otherworldly emerge. "Careful, boy," he murmured at last. "The stories they tell 'bout me exist for a reason."

"I've yet to hear any."

"No, ye've heard plenty. 'Tis a small island. Whispers travel swiftly."

"Whispers are hardly facts."

"No…they are merely the shadows of fact." MacTíre's jaw tightened. "What I'm gettin' at is, those men weren't soldiers. Much n' all as they perhaps yearned to be. Nor, it was clear, did they know the forest as well as I. They weren't plannin' on bein' invaded that night, less so the two of us escapin'. They now lie dead in that very undergrowth as a result. Half of that was because the element of surprise was with us –"

"And the rest because Sir Vesey didn't drill them well enough."

"'Twould surprise me if he drilled 'em at all. They could neither plan ahead nor improvise. And they called themselves Defenders? I ask ye, what the fuck've they got to defend? Unfallow fields and homes right for the burnin? Their main weapon are them pikes they carry – not very effective 'gainst a well-aimed musket, I shouldn't doubt. 'Mon, lad. Let's go huntin'."

Mogue was growing used to MacTíre's gruff habit of ending their conversations on an abrupt note. It allowed him to return to his reading, after all; the road thief prided himself on speaking only when necessary, and not yielding any potential points of weakness.

Truly, justice was being delivered at its most rough. Their slogans and songs began as whispers, and soon were shouted defiantly at a troop of passing horsemen. A day would perhaps come when such bare-faced calls to arms would warp and shrivel into cliché, but never obscurity. *Let our word of mouth tempt you*, they seemed to say to their more timid neighbours, the ones in their thousands who yearned for little more than, *Be martyrs with us. Trade the red for the green. Force the hand of hatred to clench into a bristling fist. The world is old enough to outlast us all, but still young enough to outgun us in every ambush we inflict from the wayside. Let us abide, then, by our engulfing decision.*

Rumours of their doings must have reached Dublin Castle. Enough people had vanished or had been robbed of their effects for it to have become unmanageable. They ambushed drays of fowl and fish on their way to the docks at Ross, left the bodies to be claimed by the insects and the soil, or else dumped them into the Bannow's eddying rapids, where they were carried off out to sea. A trail of bloated redcoats, drifting out into the Atlantic like funeral barges beset by the mortis. How many of them were Irish-born Mogue pushed vigorously from his mind.

They chanced upon a group of Whiteboys drilling and marching in the dell at one point; Mogue's unearthly howling soon drove them off. *Tin soldiers, the lot of them*, MacTíre had scornfully decided. He'd spat on the ground and hadn't quite noticed Mogue's eye stayed trained on them a little longer.

Mogue, meanwhile, continued his studies by the dim firelight. The newspapers MacTíre stole for them held his interest for much of the evening, and they debated reports of distant mutinies and revolutions, the toppling of tyrants and ascension of even more in their place.

"Lettered men insist that our age is one of supreme indifference," MacTíre would declaim, "that reason's icy edict alone may hold sway. I'm afraid I'm not inclined to agree. I deem this to be an epoch of blood-blindness and bloodthirst. Some say it's that spirit of liberty, awoken at last. An endless search for freedom is now beginning. But to me, 'tis readily apparent that too much reason will drive men to barbarism; I see they are driven to it already. They clamour for freedom and yet call for a government's aid once confronted with misfortune. We are barbarians, Mogue; no livery may conceal that fact."

"Is it not that they have faith in a better world being brought about?"

MacTíre smirked. "Faith? Faith, lad, like all superstitions, lies croaking on its deathbed, I fear."

As he soon realised, both Dublin Castle and the lads in Parliament had far greater concerns than a few missing redcoats and waylaid stock. At times, after an especially bloody encounter which left the majority of their prey lying dead on the trail, he would ruminate on what voyage into darkness was he piloting the lad. But these moments were mercifully rare. Enkindled by a ruthlessness that the road thief had no doubt inspired, Mogue took to both his studies and the way of gunfire with a zeal only the newly converted tend to display. The more prizes they took, the more he desired to attain more. At night he devoted a solid hour to reading whatever tome he had managed to claim before joining MacTíre in a sparring session. He fought swiftly, his blades flashing like miniature thunderbolts, clashing like the shriek of a banshee. He countered MacTíre's swings and thrust with rapid litheness, his parries instinctive and more artful than the road thief's brutal hammerings. Blades bit into flesh and soon both of them had a varied collection of scars inflicted by the other. Nocturnal raids were carried out; fear stalked the moorlands.

They sensed this whenever they entered a Fair Day garbed as wandering merchants to ply whatever plunder they'd gained. The risk of recognition was becoming greater by the day. The air itself throbbed with such grave mistrust. Agitators were widespread. People in the markets moved with a more pronounced wariness of one another. Suspicion was in every eye MacTíre met. Evictions, much like those he had known, were becoming more common. Fires were lit from the crests of Mount Leinster in the night, their luminous flickering serving as apparent signals. Often they'd see them when they set out, blazing beacons after dark, and with little sign of abating. They blazed throughout the dead hour of the night, and the sun rose upon them still smoking vigorously.

One afternoon in the Fethard market, as they moved through the village garbed as roving traders, they saw a heavyset redcoat sergeant standing on the church steps, going hammer and tongs at a small cluster of keen-eyed local lads, who seemed to lap up his words as if they were nectar. A snot-nosed drummer boy stood nearby, thwacking out a cadenced tattoo in accompaniment to the speech. The sergeant's face was as red as his uniform as he declaimed:

"There is much to be said for soldiering, lads! No rhyme or reason in the wide world why a young man should not want to earn a few shillings more. And The Royal Irish red offers no better opportunity!"

MacTíre, wearing a broad-brimmed hat inclined low over his brow, had smirked and gestured to Mogue, whose hood kept his own features concealed. "Gettin' desperate, so they are. Wonderin' what he's after?"

"I already know," said Mogue. "Uses the power of his voice to inflame passion in men's breasts; make them believe someone else's war is theirs too, and therefore worth fighting. The price of labour becomes the price of battlefields. He who now tills the land will soon work the munitions. But they must be convinced first to do so. How will he go about it?"

"Look around ye, that's easily seen. Farmers and cottiers, most of 'em. They've mouths to feed, homes to uphold. Labour in fields for shite wages and hand over tithes for when the landlord's man comes callin'. Plough and shovel are their shackles. They live on little more than spuds and water. The next winter frost could easily be their last. Now here's this *Sassenach*, promisin' adventure and glory and reg'lar meals and pay. A bayonet for a bale-hook. One indentured for another. Mark ye this, though – takin' the king's shillin' isn't the worst decision when you're starvin'."

"That true of all of 'em?"

"Not all. Look closer at a few of 'em. Like them two there." MacTíre indicated the entryway to a nearby tavern. Two young men lounged beside an empty barrel, one smoking on a clay pipe. They, too, were listening to the sergeant's oration, but the wariness that graced their features told Mogue they were less than stirred by it.

"They've been marchin' in convoy through this place for centuries. Can ye see the red from the green? I know I can't."

"They want possession of what's theirs restored. Can you blame 'em for that?"

"The land belongs to no one, lad. A fact far too many are content to ignore. They want possession of what was never theirs in the first place."

England was no longer at war, not officially, if the newspapers were to be believed. But MacTíre knew that nations, like men, tended to seek out fresh conquests soon after the jubilation and enervation from the former had subsided. There was little to be gained or gambled in a state of victory, he'd long decided. The more remote regions of the Empire required protection. Fresh effusions of blood, as copious as if spilled from a winepress, were an acceptable loss in ensuring His Majesty's dominion remained unscathed. Restlessness was a dangerous thing, he knew. Work for idle hands and all that.

Morale was low during those years. Weapons and manpower were in short supply. The loss of America ensured the Empire no longer stood on firm ground. Reports of a potential uprising in Paris was greeted in Parliament with the customarily stormy fulminations. Trouble seemed afoot all over Europe, enhanced rather than mitigated by the declared peace. Mayhap the prefatory lines of the Empire's obituary were being written at last, and page upon page inked with self-governing poesy, or so MacTíre hoped.

Meanwhile, the reek of corpses sullied the air all across the continent, and the years did little to heal the scars left by the war. Irish carcasses lay dead and tainted on battlefields all over Europe, clad in scarlet tunics, reeking of cordite and Brown Bess oak. Fodder for someone else's strife. Many more were wounded, maimed, blinded, with little hope of ever being relieved of their condition in this life. They had given their youth and their vigour for the bulls' wool, only to be rewarded with bodies shattered from French and Prussian bullets, and minds brittle as dead wood. Boatloads of their survivors were returning home to the green sod, scattered back to their appointed garrisons.

MacTíre had seen plenty of them, disembarking at the quayside in Wexford and Ross, shambling into formation.

Many, he knew, had seen action at Gibraltar and in America; some had even battled their neighbours who had emigrated and joined the revolutionary forces. Few seemed proud of their service, beyond the extra few shillings they were accorded as pay. There was nothing triumphant in the scarlet coat now, nothing to give it a sliver of dignity, even in defeat. Countless lives were lost, if not to rifle and rapier than to the steady contagion of typhoid.

Their experience on the battlefields of Cuddalore, Saratoga, the Balearic Islands, Minorca – not to mention their glowering hatred for the jacket red, that enlisted their service and squandered their spirits and saw their fellows lying in bloodied droves all over Europe, and even further afield – left them perfect recruits for the secret societies; those masked men who ventured out, ghost-like, after dark and razed the cabins of their neighbours to the ground. Rumours in pubs spoke of yet more secret societies, men giving themselves to strange oaths and disreputable allegiances. Corps of yeomen patrolled the open countryside; people rallied to homesteads after the midnight hour. Reports of maimed cattle and fields set afire became daily occurrences; and MacTíre could not read them with any surprise.

In the backrooms of pubs, the cellars and attics of country lodges and townhouses, men congregated as if in clandestine worship. Men both landed and landless rubbed elbows. Illiterate farmers spoke freely and readily with those who held the benefit of a formal education, their zeal alike ignited by the polemics MacTíre hadn't yet managed to steal. Differences in religion seemed to matter little to them. For indeed, the god they allegedly came to worship was liberty, and their prayers were uttered loudly, in tones of wrath and ruin, while the devil they swore to reject was the dead weight of the Crown.

If these meetings were discovered, they were broken up at the point of bayonet and their chief agitators arrested. More soldiers were quartered in the usual outposts. Such a struggle, nay, such an uprising, would be gilded by the poets, with their linguistic smoke, their rhyming mirrors, their enemies' blood mottling Hibernian pillars. People were no longer afraid, but avid for something more.

Yet darker things, such as MacTíre had hinted at, were now afoot. Times were changing. General disaffection was giving way to a swelling thirst to rise in arms. Acts of outrage and perfidy were soon rampant. Gangs of men, hooded and cloaked, ranged the pasture and sloblands in the night, scratching crude insignias on gables, leaving the scrub and heather blazing and entire herds of cattle houghed. Whether by fire or by hacksaw, it did not matter. The wheatfields and stubble were soon littered with smoking husks of doomed cabins; neighbours lived in holy dread of one another.

Those who worked the fields threshing corn were sent by the scoreful into forests, chopping down trees to fashion into pike shafts. Their foul revolt seemed on the girding, and the Crown finally had them marked. The number of soldiers escorting mail coaches doubled. Phalanxes of faceless, white-shirted demons roamed the countryside, and whenever MacTíre spied them in the distance, the knuckles on his fists seemed to bleach to an equal severe shade of colourlessness. Men of even minor standing feared being butchered in the night; Papist and Protestant alike took to sleeping with a brace of pistols by their bedsides.

After dark, the roads were neither asleep nor awake. Still as statues, they drank down the cold by the moon's bleached radiance. A cap was angled like a helmet, an unlit pipe was clutched, quivering, between a man's lips, fingers tight as fury, oak-hilted pike shafts held at a savage tilt to the dust of the road. *Enjoy the green-gold of summertime, lads,* MacTíre thought. At the rate they were going, there would soon be no more cabins left standing for them to burn. Soon, by MacTíre's reckoning, only smoke rings would drift and stretch across dew-rinsed hectares.

What, then, would the eye surrender to? It was readily apparent that all the years of playing at soldiers were over. They were rebels now, uniformed and eager, pikemen and gunmen marching on foot through rocky *bóithrín* and crouching at the foot of every hill, perching on their stomachs as the road thief and his young protégé did, enmeshed by a field's emerald limbo. Yet you would be forgiven for thinking the country they claimed to fight for was attempting to dismantle them with lashings of rain, Atlantean fog rolling in, thick and heavy as a burial shroud. *Repent lest ye perish*, the clergymen seemed to declare as one. A line from Milton inevitably resurfaced in the road thief's mind:

> *... we may with more successful hope resolve*
> *To wage by force or guile, eternal war*
> *Irreconcilable ...*

But of course, they were far from the redcoats' only concern.

If MacTíre had ever killed sparingly and perhaps kept mercy as a keepsake, now he slaughtered with abandon any who crossed his path. It was becoming painfully clear the road thief nor his legend would not fade into obscurity just yet. Stagecoaches were attacked and set alight with their passengers still within. Bodies littered the roadsides where the crows happily dined. Rarely did he go long between prizes, for black and forlorn moods tended to take him; the thrill of the hunt and the satisfaction of making a kill seemed to stave off these miseries most keenly.

Through seasons of full leaf and hoarfrost, these moods seemed to hover over him like birds of prey, awaiting just the right moment to descend. The price on his head now ran into the hundreds. But rarely did any poacher or bounty hunter find him; inevitably he found them, his footfalls never discerned through the trees, his moment of attack always one of grim surprise. Whether the accusation possessed any merit was immaterial.

MacTíre had little to gain from incessant worry, however. Enough close shaves with death can sharpen a man's resolve.

Chapter XVIII
That Dark Empyrean
Wexford, 1790

Four years became the strange crucible in which Mogue Trench's young manhood was melted down and reforged. Four years of hiding and moving with calculated stealth. Four years of crouching in ditches and taking cover beneath the furze. Four years of striking camp whenever and wherever they were so able. Four years that tasted of burnt venison and unsalted salmon plucked from clouded rivers. Four years that smelled of sea salt, sea air and gunsmoke. Four years of learning the intricacy of the hunt; and, whenever and wherever possible, the primacy and majesty of the written word. Four years which saw Mogue Trench's youth ripen to a blood-flavoured and death-dealing manhood.

And so, for Mogue, it seemed like there could be no returning...

It began and ended with the sudden hush of birdsong.

It was late in the summer of 1790. The day had dragged on, humid and tinder-dry, turning the sky a sullied amber, even as a brazen sun squinted from the heavens like a glazed shield. Its rays did little to puncture the dense, emerald shade; the forest floor lost little of its gloom. All throughout the forest, from the bone-like branches that hung knotted together, the lashings of pitch that splashed and soaked the pines at their very roots, a hundred small fires were lit. A match was dropped here, a taper flung there, and by and by flames erupted as if in unison. They licked at bark and twig, shrivelled leaf and bramble with equal intensity, leaping swiftly from oak to beech to ash to pine, fanned by a crisp sea-breeze that sizzled in from the southeast and coaxed the smoke to whirl higher, parching the soil as the sun rose ever higher, swelling the heat and making martyrs of the trees, sending smutty cinders drifting downward like a macabre Christmas present, each drifting to the ground like confetti.

The flames did little to augment the light; the smoke heaved and spread like a plague through the trees, clouded and toxic, as though its chief intent was to see the road thief and his ward choked, if not burnt, to death. The flames leapt and caught leaf; the smell of smoke became unto normality. To see their beloved forest go up in smoke was a sacrifice seemingly tolerated by all, a sacrifice to some odious and unreachable god. The very glow of it seemed to outdo the sun.

Mogue Trench heard the birds go silent, his vigilance piqued.

Crouched on all fours, his hand went instinctively to his *gralloch* hilt, lips curled back with the ghost of a snarl. He readied his blades, the ugly tang of burning oak now unmistakeable. He saw neither smoke nor flame, but never had his senses deceived him. Standing, he sniffed the close, lush air and stepped out of the foliage. This was no accident of heat, no early gorse fire ignited at random by the sun. There was a definite whiff of pitch on the breeze; soon the flames would be upon him. He could already see the baleful glow bejewelling the gloom; he broke into a run, dodging through the trees.

*

Flames soon sprang and danced from all corners of the forest, rushing rampant from bramble to canopy. Trees ignited like towering candles. The sky seemed to bronze and then blacken as smoke weaved in and out, its avid curl blanketing all things. Sparks spat and sprinted fervidly like comets in miniature, eating through leaf and loam. It had been several days since rain had fallen, and so many of the trees were bone dry. Roots incinerated to ash, and their trees toppled with almighty cracks where they stood, providing yet more kindling for the hurtling blaze. The conflagration had a beauty of its own, as if one might be inclined to stop fleeing from it and eye its reddish approach.

His breath already ragged, and with ash already seasoning the air, the road thief smelled the smoke before he saw the fire. He felt no surprise, however. It would only take so long before this day would be upon him, he had known. There was never any doubt even in MacTíre's mind, and virtually no fear, that reprisals would eventually be visited upon him. It was never a question of when, but whom would do the visiting. There had been so few signs in recent months of Sir Vesey or any other local authority deciding to move against him. Whether the fires were lit by redcoats or volunteers (or, he thought with a sour grin, some brief and absurd coalition between the two), he could not say.

And of course, it was only a matter of moments, he sensed, before he would hear the frantic barks of hunting dogs. Racing through the many trails known only to himself, he made deeper into the forest, where his cave could be found. Outrunning the fire would be his sole priority for the time being. Given the season, chances of rainfall were slim, but even a heavy downpour would do little to quench the coming inferno. Mogue would find his own way, he knew; he had trained him well in the unique topography of the terrain, what directions were the safest to take and what unfamiliar noises to keep one's eyes and ears pricked for. As with knifework and letters, the boy had a keen grasp for it all.

Suddenly he became aware that there was someone else in the forest, someone other than whomever had lit the fires. Not an intruder or a hunter tracking his movements, but an unwilling wanderer, forced to find their way amid the forest's countless concealed trails.

The road thief darted past the rim of the flame, his throat drier than ever.

*

By rights, Mogue Trench was too young for cynicism, but he was certainly old enough to see the white furnace engulf the trench and sear Tintern's olive trees to leafless bone; old enough to see Death wriggle in rapid-fire spurts, lucent shrapnel punch through belly and skull and limb; old enough to see eruptions of blood, grey sinew, raw tissue cut loose from organ and bowel; to see the air muddied with fumes, the ground redden to a dusty concussion; to see the eye of every man who hunted them melt to a waterless pothole, lidless graves bored into skulls, unblinkingly sheer; old enough to see men robed in a collective cerecloth of smoke, and to see Death make off with war-time plunder.

The summer dusk might have been a brother to him, with its amber gold piercing through the dark green leaves, but there was nothing brotherly about this spitfire, bayonets of flame stinging the air around him, the heat scalding him to the marrow, massacring sleep from his head and clemency from his dreams for many nights to come. The forest was a riot of writhing red-gold and bilious orange; it resembled the very core of hell.

It was then that Mogue saw her, and his throat felt as though it were seasoned with sawdust.

Gráinne staggered blindly through the fumes, her feet bare and her face a mask of confused, unblinking dread. Her dress was in rags, her shoulder exposed, a vicious-looking gash streaking blood down her temple, and dark stains of what appeared to be yet more blood glistening and dried into her bodice. He saw her stagger through the trees, shorn of her magisterial composure, as the flames roared behind her like some monstrous fanfare.

"Gráinne! Why are you here? What's happened you?"

Abandoning all instinct of caution, he rushed toward her. As he neared, he saw she was shaking slightly, and her eyes were glassy as she stared right through him. He grabbed her by the shoulders, tried bringing her at eye level. "Gráinne, it's me, Mogue! What happened ye?"

The cut on her cranium was even worse close-up; fresh blood oozed steadily down her jaw, thick and crimson as wine from a ewer. She was babbling to herself, almost as if reciting an incantation. "They said they were coming...they are not yet here...more dry fuel needed...tinder and pitch..."

Mogue barely registered her words, for the sharp, ear-rending crack of a long-smouldering birch readying to fall cut across her. The tree was a mere ten feet from them, and it fell as if toppled from a plinth, hitting the dry earth and spraying great bursts of sparks into the air like loose birds; patches of wild flame burst over the brushwood and the ground itself seemed to shudder from the impact. Then a huge plume of smoke mushroomed upwards, daggering his eyes and nostrils. He had to force back a cough as he dragged Gráinne away with great urgency, the heat breaking over his face as he tried shielding her, even as she continued to babble. The very air around him suddenly seemed to be choking.

"They're ready...to hunt...they have his scent..."

Mogue kept her near as he took a sharp dodge back towards the river, and as he slipped past the still-green leaves, he saw fumes cresting the treetops, a blazing pavilion, a swirling nightmare of angry gold, its minarets of smoke slithering and fading through the air. Famished flames gulped down elm and oak, whitened birch and pine to leafless bones, engulfed green crowns in a burning stroke. The breeze's gurgling hymn churned the blaze, forcing shorter fuses to eat oaken fruit. Oddly hypnotic as it was, Mogue forced himself not to watch and kept running, his hand tight over Gráinne's, swigging down what was left of the clear air, this glowering sacrament of haze and soot; an inferno's smelted prayer detonated his heart, a choir of heat, an altar of ash, cut out daylight's homily, brimmed over dawn's chalice.

Eventually he found one of the many hollows known only to him and the road thief, and he slipped beneath it, dragging Gráinne before him into the cool, dry crawlspace. Relief that Gráinne only seemed to speak in low, inaudible tones kept him going, as he crouched next to her beneath a shroud of leaves, the cold emanating up from the earth into his chest. The baleful glimmer was all around them now, as were thick drifts of smoke. And of course, now he heard them, clear as a funeral knell: the hungry yowls of bloodhounds, hurtling through the undergrowth.

The beasts raced past them as if unleashed from the pit, dark shapes bounding and bolting past the trees, hungrily as the flames surrounding them. Tendrils of saliva spilled from their maws. In the dark, Mogue heard their arched growls, how they seemed to spike the air; but the small space where he and Gráinne lay crouched put them out of reach of sight and scent. Their owners would come rushing forth soon enough, allowing the flames hadn't reached their meridian. For her part, Gráinne seemed barely aware of her surroundings, muttering on and on to herself about wolves and hunts all the while, as blood glistened on her cheek.

"The wolf shall walk no more..." she rasped. "The forest shall know his flight..."

"Gráinne?"

She ignored him, continued her aimless, barely coherent cant. "The harp is newly plucked –"

"Gráinne!"

Mogue then grabbed her ripped sleeve, tried to bring her eye to his, and for a moment, that seemed to have her attention. If Gráinne always carried herself with guarded poise, her expression was now nigh unreadable – yet the whites in her eyes indicated only fear.

"What happened, Gráinne? Who did this to you?"

"Men...in masks...who are not yet dead."

"What men? *Buachaillí Bán*? Redcoats? Who?"

"My room was afire –"

"They burnt the tavern down?"

"As a warning...they said. Then sent me out here...to find him."

"Find who? Joseph?"

She nodded vacantly. "His scent's known to them. They're following."

*

He'd have fewer and fewer hiding places soon.

With barely any alert, hellish sheets of wildfire thrashed amidst every tree he saw, a fiery marauder, a swelling inroad, interring every hidden trail under its torrid appetite. Even with his face lowered to avoid the noxious fog, he still saw flames eating into the trees like swollen tapers, turning the slope into a furnace. A wall of red-gold heat was to his back, and the wind was beating it to his bare flesh; it seemed the very shadows, his constant allies throughout all this, were themselves ablaze. The sky itself was blurred out from the smoke, a plane of sullied orange, filthying the air and nibbling at the leaves. His eye was peeled for Mogue still, but the smoke and sparks and nearing howls of the bloodhounds kept him racing forward. Somehow, they'd acquired his scent, knew with canine certainty that he was afoot. Of that MacTíre was certain.

The thickening smoke, almost as heavy as the worst sea-fog, now made it more difficult to see even ten feet ahead. MacTíre knew that if he could just reach the banks of the river, his scent would be camouflaged and escape would be within his grasp.

Then a black blur leapt out of the low ridge from where the undergrowth reached down toward the riverbank. It moved so fast MacTíre barely had time to register it, and by the time its jaws were locked around his wrist and its fangs punctured deep into his flesh, he found himself on the cold stony ground, its snarls and foul breath in his face, and his own agonised bellow ripping through the trees.

Yet his free hand managed to draw his bayonet, and he managed to roughly thrust the blade through the beast's gullet as if through a wine-sack, letting it collapse with a startled whimper on his belly. The pain erupting through his forearm was monstrous, but the road thief managed to haul himself to his feet, his teeth clamped and his skull ringing. Even over the inferno's roar, the dogs' barking had increased in number and ferocity; they had him. A trail of red seeped warmly from his wrist's mangled flesh in heavy droplets, staining his jerkin sleeve. He began to stumble on toward the river, aware of his pursuers. Even through the smoke, the raw, ripe scent of his life source would have them in a frenzy.

He couldn't help but throw frantic glances over his shoulder as he ran, and so he overlooked a root protruding from the earth. The fall threw him into a ditch, and fresh agony flared through his arm. His face scraped along the hard span of flinty earth, the brunt of the fall pumping air from his chest where he fell, his heart racing.

Then and only then did he hear the growls.

There might have been seven or eight of them, an entire pack of slavering, black-furred mutts, their noses no doubt sparked by his blood, though his field of vision showed only three. They prowled slowly from the burning dead foliage, fangs bared and tongues lagging wet from their mouths. They sniffed his blood on the air, mingling with the smoke. Their eyes glistened with narrow intent, their jagged growls low and garbled, yet unmistakable. They padded to the edge of the ditch from all sides, smoke and flame dancing all around them.

In that moment, Joseph MacTíre saw the shade of death standing over him, and he felt no fear, only the thick flavour of blood rippling on his tongue and teeth as he readied his flintlock for a final time.

Had he any time for God, he might have knelt before this shrine of charred undergrowth, scattering whatever impious birds were left into the smoke-soused air, its sermonic flare leaping from muddied coal. Was it ever a crime, or even a cruelty, for a man to explore or ignore his own soul at his leisure, to let his words swim in waiting darkness, to look the swirling seasons in the eye? To make his heart wretched, cut his voice loose, dismiss Love as the chief of pleasant lies, to baptise himself by brushwood, by tinder, or cherish the naked inferno of his life?

The road thief knew he dreamt none of this, he had conjured none of this from his skull's oozing hideaway. His frozen solitude never smudged the night-air, pearls of rain did not kindle upon his jaw. *Do old dreams scuttle like crooked flowers, to bloom amongst the trees' molten shade?* He'd often imagined statues of the saints in the churches wearing wolfish smiles, as trees sweat beneath winter's load. Had he any vows, he would but spit them into the throbbing wind, his heels digging into the vinegar of snow. Briefly he wondered, *Am I the only man to witness this crackling spectacle, this woodland inferno?*

The first one to pounce got a bullet in the throat, and another staggered off at the bite of his sabre, but that was it. The rest fell upon him as scavengers upon a rare and much-hunted trinket; as the flames closed in, torching the last of the brambles and gorse, their razor fangs tore through the road thief's clothes and ripped flesh from bone, between ragged, feverish howls. They chewed and fought over scraps of his guts. His blood spewed into the soil of the burning forest, and his dying screams were rumoured to still be heard echoing amongst the pines of Tintern Forest for many years to come.

*

Mogue Trench had little need to smear his face in ash, as per his habit – the smoke had left his features thoroughly blackened. When the redcoats who started the fire finally found him and Gráinne huddled in each other's arms in the charred undergrowth, there were concerns they'd both been burnt beyond recognition. After hours of trawling the blackened remnants of the forest, they were the first human faces Mogue Trench had seen since he had given Gráinne shelter. As the last of the flames died out, only the hovering drifts of smoke and sooty stumps of what had once been the trees remained.

Mogue was arrested within minutes of discovery. His age and bearing and armament indicated he was indeed the highwayman's accomplice. Locals identified him as having had covert dealings in the taproom of the now-incinerated alehouse with some of Gráinne's girls, several of whom readily joined in his identification. Were he a more lowly class of miscreant, he might have perhaps been shot on sight, but orders were for him to be taken alive.

For his trial to begin, he was to be brought to Dublin to await hearings. In practise, this meant he was to be detained during the interim at Newgate Prison. After three days of being held in a caged cart like swine ready for market – without food, drink, warmth or anywhere to take a piss or a shite – Mogue Trench found himself back in his home city, that dismal metropolis that hunkered between mountains, low on the seashore. The crisp country air he had inhaled for the last four years, that had lent him a vigour and sturdiness of foot, steadily evaporated by the capital's stony haze. O Dublin, City of Fever! The close, pestilent air, a miasma of mingled diseases, ten people to every fetid room in every slum! Through the carriage grating, he thought he recognised the Palladian dome of Parliament buildings, the thicket of ships' masts berthed at the Liffey quays, before the procession trundled across the river.

Not that he had much time to take it all in – after entering the city from its southerly gates and clacking through the narrow, filth-strewn lanes, he saw he was being ushered along the north quay-walls, the Liffey placid and azure as a lagoon beneath the noontide sun, toward

Little Green. How the sun could roar down was beyond him. The stink of the streets seemed to greet him like an old friend; the frowning edifice fitted with the appellation 'Newgate' that hulked above them appeared to glower at everything in sight.

Despite its name, the New Gaol put Mogue in mind of an ancient, ruinous temple dedicated to some malignant god, its squat, black limestone pilasters and iron railings like caryatids, or cannon muzzles trained on a defenceless sky. Even from without he heard a vague cacophony of what he knew to be screaming from the grated windows that no doubt lined the cell blocks (he later found the prisoners had christened the place 'Cox's Hotel'). Its portcullis, held by together by fragile-looking mortar, hulked over him as he approached, outlined by the glare resembled to his eye a mausoleum of weathered Wicklow granite. The entire city seemed to be built from granite gouged from the earth of Wicklow; why should the prison have it any different?

The paved parade ground, where the cart came to a halt before a troop of waiting Charleys and gaolers, reminded him of a bed of snuff. Over two dozen uniformed police constables stood drawn to attention upon the shallow flight of steps leading up to the entrance as he was hauled from the carriage, their pistols primed and unholstered as if they awaited a riotous horde, and not a mere youth with his hands and feet entrammelled.

Just as he was led through to the hall of the prison's main entrance, the clank of his fetters loudly echoing off the flagstones, he'd glanced upward and saw, just above the doorway, the execution platform jutting out over him like a gangplank, the lines of the trapdoor through which hanged prisoners swung clearly outlined. Perched atop it was the iron gibbet flanked by its quartet of pulleys, its black carapace like charred bone, a vestibule for the dying. Men were known to hang from its scaffold for hours after death, in full sight of the punters. And so, Mogue Trench's last glimpse of the cloudless summer sky included the city crane's stygian silhouette.

Mogue had no notion of dying just yet, however. After they searched him and found nothing, he was frogmarched, chained, starving and sore, into the lower cellarage, toward what were known as the Felons' Side, where only the wildest and most refractory prisoners made their abode (as opposed to the State Side, where criminals from more estimable walks of life were held). The turnkeys led Mogue down a winding staircase and into a dank, narrow passage of granite topped by an arched ceiling; the dripping darkness seemed to swallow everything. The passage was so narrow Mogue's elbows banged off the stone on either side as he walked them.

The vague screams and groans he had heard from without the prison now assailed his ears with operatically agonised sounds, accompanied by a bedraggled orchestra of clanking chains, slamming bolts and the echoey grating of locks. After the sun's August glare, the murk of the dank, piss-redolent corridor came as a shock, even with the spare, lazy flickering thrown by the few torches on the wall. The iron cell doors, narrow and very foul to the eye, glimmered dully through the gloom like unmarked headstones.

Moaning from the cells soon grew louder and rose to meet him as if in grim welcome. The dripping from the ceiling and the squeak and scurry of rats occupied the cavernous dark. Slender bones of light bled through overhead fissures, giving the faintest of outlines. Mogue had never actually ventured underground, into the city's sewers or the labyrinth of tunnels reaching out toward the city's artery-like rivers and canals, but he imagined this was as close as he would get in his lifetime.

Pinioning his arms, the gaolers moved with ease, accustomed to the gloom, tossing him unceremoniously into one of the lower dungeons, their boots echoing heavily off the rusty stone as they walked away. The cell was a fetid, windowless box blacker than pitch, as numbingly dark as the seafloor on a winter's night. The ceiling was so low he merely had to reach slightly upward for his palm to press against its cold, craggy texture. He was buried in complete and utter darkness as the heavy door swung and thundered shut; had he not emerged from the afternoon sun, there would have been no telling whether it was day or night. The turnkeys threw him so roughly he ended up sprawled on the cracked granite floor, which appeared to be covered in rough sheaves of hay; the stale, mephitic reek of faeces and urine and unwashed flesh caused him to curl his nostrils. The smell of ruination and mouldy airlessness seemed to be the place's natural scent. What hit his ears, however, was somehow much worse.

A cacophony of voices, warped by hunger and confinement, raved at him in demonic greeting. The raspy whispers and rattle of chains like coins nestled in a pocket told him he was not alone in his fetterment. Thirteen other bedraggled, grime-coated wretches like himself – he did not need to see them to be aware of their presence. Squalid figures clad in the filthiest tatters skulked and languished in the dark, curled up into balls or else rattling their shackles. To Mogue's eye, they resembled fish gliding blindly through the depths of an undersea world. The noise of thirteen voices, raving, whimpering, cursing, snarling hungrily, recoiled off the walls like failed gunshots as the dim light from the corridor briefly illuminated their latest arrival. Between that and the sheer cold of the place, Mogue knew that even sleep would not come easily here.

"Ah, a fresh one!"

"And young too. 'Mere, love, gis a kiss!"

"Here, see if he tastes as sweet as he looks!"

Through the murk, his eyes gradually adjusting, Mogue now thought he saw human shapes, the outline of an arm or a chained ankle; white, glassy eyes blinked hungrily at him like neglected jewels with the fascination of trapped animals, claw-like hands made swipes for him. They were so close he felt and smelled a putrid whir of breath crawl over his face. Were it not for his fetters, he might have leapt out of his skin. A hand closed over his wrist, and he blindly threw a fist into the dark; he felt it hit something soft and meaty, and heard a body crash to the slimed floor. A noise that could have easily been a sharp cough or hard chuckle echoed from elsewhere in the cell. It was a haven for vermin – human and rodent alike.

Finally, another voice broke through the gloom, one that rang clearer and more authoritatively despite the accent's coarseness. It also seemed to come right by Mogue's side. He felt the stale whiff of their breath brush his skin, and he lurched instinctively back.

"Leave him be, yis shower of cunts!!"

With that, the cacophony died away almost instantly. Mogue, still jolted, leaned against the frigid, clammy stone.

The voice spoke from the dark again – a dry, amused rasp. "Welcome, lad. No need to fret, now. You're not in hell, much as it may seem like it."

"I can't see your face."

"And a very good thing y'can't, too. Good thing I won't be shakin' yer hand, either. Lookit, don't mind them, young fella. We might be in refrac'try, but I daresay they're nothin' y'haven't met before." A note of amusement entered the voice. "Here, you're him, aren't ye? MacTíre's cub. The Wolf of Wexford's cub."

Mogue was too bewildered and strived to even feign surprise. "How do you know?"

"Dublin's small, laddy. Word gets 'round. Even in here. Besides, where the fuck else'd they send ye?"

"As you see me."

"I don't, but we've been expectin' ye, believe it nor not. Yer famous in these parts. I can see yer not in here for debt, either."

Mogue grimaced. He wasn't in the humour for this. "Really, how so?"

"I could embarrass yeh, but it's quite the rep ye have. Bin' growin' since ye burnt Tintern Abbey to the ground. That, and your name is on the lips of every wag in Dublin, it would seem. Not a man in this fuckin' kip doesn't know the name of Cap'n Joseph MacTíre. Yis're famous, like it or not."

"Not quite to the ground. Just made a nice bonfire of it."

The man in the shadows said nothing for a moment. "No doubt ye did. Tell ye, whenever I'd a chance, I'd look up how he was doin'. Hopin' I could work with him sometime. Name's Robert Buchanan, by the way. Rob, to me nearest and dearest. Tell me this...was MacTíre as ruthless in life as he was in the stories?"

"He wasn't the easiest to work with," Mogue replied. All he wished for now was for Rob to shut his trap and let him slumber.

"Ah man, really? He struck me as a fella with a nose for opportunity."

"He didn't 'specially care for workin' with people. Didn't tend to trust large groups."

"Mmm. Pity. Tha' grieves me full sore to hear, so it does. An' you?"

"What 'bout me?"

"You're locked up now and waitin' for the noose. Though, mind you, there's little worry of yeh bein' carted out to Stephens' fuckin' Green. Such are the enlightened times in which we live. No, ye'll be set to swing from that window they've out yonder, from the city crane. I know 'cos I'm the same. So, seems to me, maybe we can help each other out, so to speak."

"And how d'you think I could help you?" Mogue asked.

"Stick with me, you'll see. Be grand."

"I'd much prefer a concrete answer."

"Our fortunes are about to change," said Buchanan. "A change has come over this gaol. I've friends all over."

He was silent again, which Mogue took to mean he was appraising the cell and its denizens. "Not in here, y'realise."

"You sound like a man with no shortage of friends,' Mogue said with caution.

"You're not wrong there, but the question is, how many of them can really be trusted?"

"So, why me? We're only after meetin'."

"If even half of what's said about you and the road thief is true, I'd say we'd both do well to watch each other's backs. You're someone I'd much rather call a friend than a foe."

"We're both in chains in the hardest nick in Ireland. What makes you think we can be either help or hindrance to anyone?"

"Despair really doesn't become you, kid. There's always a chance to break loose."

"You'll be takin' your chances?"

"I will, yeh. And I've a feelin' in me waters you will, too."

"Aren't you optimistic."

"I've a nose for opportunity, fuck all else. And y'can never have too many irons in the fire, sure y'can't."

Mogue didn't move. "Somethin' else y'should prob'ly know 'bout MacTíre."

"Do tell."

"He showed me how to fight, true enough. But he also showed me how to lie in wait for the right moment to strike. They'll have doubled the guards here, seein' as I'm here now. We can't do very much without raising their suspicions. But we'll need to keep an eye out while we can."

"I sleep with one eye open."

"And I barely sleep at all." Though, at that moment, he would have welcomed sleep like a lover. "Let's see how this pans out. Escape just might be ours."

"Now you're talkin'." Buchanan's grin was palpable through the dark. "Hope y'fight as well as they say."

Mogue couldn't help but smile to himself. "Better."

"Good man yourself. Pleasure to finally make yer 'quaintance –" the voice paused. "What're y'rightly known as, lad?"

Mogue had no inclination to think of a pseudonym. "Trench," he finally murmured. "Mogue Trench."

He wasn't sure, but he sensed Buchanan grinning. "Well, Master Trench. Happy to know ye."

And so, the days rolled by in a blur of cold granite and broken voices. Mogue wept himself quietly to sleep the first night, as the others raved around him, not in lamentation of the hand he'd been dealt but only in remorse for losing both MacTíre and Gráinne. The thought that he had not been able to utter words of farewell to either of them hounded his every waking moment. He did not live in fear for his person; even without a blade to hand, his natural fighting instinct would see off any aggressor; in any case, his fellow prisoners were all similarly enchained. What was to become of him now, whether the gibbet or the slow decay of years incarcerated, or even the corrosive hold of madness that only isolation could induce, his mind dared not linger upon.

Despite the lack of windows, the cell was so cold that Mogue found himself firmly beyond the reach of sleep. Had his eyes been able to pierce the darkness, he might have seen his own breath condense and then evaporate against the bare walls. Food was scarce, and the cell was so cramped and crowded there was little he could do to even stand up and pace about to relieve his boredom. He'd sit back and try to numb out the pestilent smells and sounds of his fellow prisoners, ignoring Rob's incessant chatter, whose monologues ranged from their method of escaping this place to the varying degrees of evil of each turnkey who worked their cell block. Mogue gathered after a while that he seemed to be the closest to a leader this den of wretches had. The others didn't dare come near him out of fear of whatever Rob might do or say.

He sat next to him for days, unable to fully put a face to the voice that never seemed to be still. Often, he wondered if he imagined the coarse Dublin brogue that whispered to him in a series of oaths and half-deluded declarations, that it was an angel or a demon or some lethal figment conjured by a severely taxed mind. Only the foulness of the man's breath occasionally brushing his face told him the speaker in the dark was as flesh and blood as he. Mogue had no understanding of God or Satan; if either had sent an emissary to him, he'd have greeted both with equal confusion.

As many as fourteen prisoners were confined to a single cell together. *No different than a tenement*, he found himself thinking. There seemed to be a strict policy amongst the prison authorities that no hierarchy of malfeasance was to be observed here, no distinction as to the severity or quantity or even intent of a man's individual crimes. Those serving a few years' hard labour for picking pockets rubbed elbows with murderers condemned to wait the noose. The tried and untried, the innocent and the guilty. The soot-coloured uniforms of the turnkeys seemed to blend with the shadows, the jangle of the keys girdled at their belts the only signal of their approach.

Of all the rumours Mogue heard of Newgate, this circumstance was the one he somehow had had the most trouble believing. Only anarchy and infection could prevail in such an arrangement. Felons mingled freely, the rapists and the thieves, the madmen and highwaymen's apprentices would easily share a filthy floor with the most sordid of killers, as opposed to each being allocated their own cell. This dearth of space and ever-present crowdedness had naturally led to a hideous putrefaction within the prison, with the swift contagion of all manner of dreadful maladies. Often so many felons fell foul to such agues and fevers that it was not unusual to see their corpses carted from the prison yard, along with those recently cut down from the city crane, to be dumped *en masse* in the pauper's cemetery down at Bully's Acre, with neither ceremony nor blessing to mark their demise.

The days passed, but there was no telling of their coming or going. No book he had read in MacTíre's vast library (which, he imagined, had long since gone up in smoke) could have prepared him for this ordeal. There were nights he imagined the prison to be suspended in complete isolation from the rest of the known world, like a ship riding at anchor in some trackless sea; the darkness of the cell seemed absolute and without end. After four years, he had at last arrived back in his city, and yet he could not get reacquainted with it. Beyond the walls of Newgate, the city he had once called home was nearly within reach.

Rob seemed to be the only other prisoner capable of intelligent conversation and retaining cheerful spirits. If madness had taken him, too, it at least had not deprived him of the ability to joke and laugh. The darkness and his own growing deformity troubled him barely a jot. Nor did he care that Mogue rarely offered him a reply beyond a rudimentary ascension; Mogue learned he'd been a weaver by trade on the outside, the various cuts on his arms the result of many a nick from the measuring knife; he'd been sent to Newgate for knifing a man in a drunken fight on Henrietta Street.

Occasionally, he'd ask, with the air of a child inquiring about a god, about MacTíre and his exploits.

"Joseph MacTíre was a knave. He answered to no one. It was the one thing I both admired and despised about him."

That usually put an end to Rob's inquiries. Even on days or nights of merciful silence. But now he found himself dreaming, his dreams more vivid than they'd ever been in the cave or the forest. With no books to keep his mind engrossed, he found all the unmarshalled thoughts stirred by the tomes he'd devoured inflicting themselves upon him like demons. Newgate was built from stone and shadow, quite unlike those he had known in MacTíre's hideaway, for they had at least been punctuated by the glow of lamplight. Even in the rare hours when his cellmates had raved and whimpered and babbled themselves to sleep, strange visions paraded before his sun-starved eye: ghostly hordes of huntsmen giving chase to an eternally elusive wolf, his *gralloch*, freshly soaked with blood, and the moon, sharp as a vampire's fang and becalmed in the firmament, and all the dread carnivals of heaven, the wonderlands of hell.

In those moments, he truly wished he had been mauled to death along with MacTíre, or else struck down by some redcoat's bullet. For what else had he to wait for now, if not the gibbet?

Would he be sent off to the convict hulks? Shipped off with a few hundred other poor bastards to the penal colonies across the farthest ocean, for God knows how many years' imprisonment with hard labour, as the sun's rippling heat bit into his flesh on the frontier where they broke rocks above the swells where Cook first sighted his crimson comet, tasting the piquancy of sea salt on every shoreward breeze? Or would he be kept here, in this tomblike box until the reaper chose to visit him?

For all Rob's loquaciousness and voluble manner, Mogue noticed that the usual attacks he had expected from his fellow inmates never materialised. Rarely did he find himself cornered or raped by any of the faceless demons with whom he shared the fathomless depths of the cell. He began to gather that Rob held some sort of unspoken position of authority, at least within the cell block's flinty, stinking confines. He quickly realised he was better off listening to his ramblings if he were to survive this place. Rob had been a guest in Newgate for a good while, he gathered, and was therefore a handy guide that may usher him through this most unsavoury hell. He gave Mogue a full description of the prison as much as he were able, from the confines of their dungeon to the prisoners' yard and gatehouse just beyond. What was more, he knew its denizens with an encyclopaedic precision, it seemed – from the governors, the warders, their fellow inmates, the overseers and the board. He advised the lad on which turnkeys could be trusted and which could not; and on which of their fellow inmates should be given a wide berth. He was an exhaustive hoarder of detail, yet he was not miserly in sharing any of them.

For all his babblings, this did not surprise Mogue. The man had spent much of his days ensconced in his own private hell, with fuck-all else to do but observe everyone and anyone around him. The sheer wealth of intelligence he had amassed over the years was therefore incalculable.

Moreover, his speech seemed as prophetic as it was profane. Lines and passages from the Testaments spilled his lips as readily as oaths or stories, or the request for spare tobacco. Any religious understanding he possessed seemed restricted only to his ability to quote from scripture. He called for neither fire nor forgiveness. He did not damn his fellow inmates, nor seek to convert or salve them. If he did deign to preach, he did so with Mogue Trench as his unwilling congregation of one. What denomination he affiliated himself to, he never said. Rarely did he ever seem to pray for salvation, or that he would even find escape. Of the soul he had even less to say.

"God is a weaver, Mogue," he'd declare. "Sure, didn't he weave this very world from nothin'? Measured the cloth, cut and cleaved it unto his satisfaction, dyed it in all the colours of sin and saintliness. And aren't we just the rats who'd chew the fuckin' thing t'shreds?"

Despite grim pronouncements such as this, Rob seemed little perturbed by his current status. The grey slop they were made to eat, the weight of the horse-padlock holding his feet, and the near-endless dark and fetor of the dungeon produced little discernible effect on him. That the floor crawled with lice and that he seemed to be rotting away within his own flesh unnerved him barely a jot. That his own death would soon find him in this condemned hold or at the end of a noose was a matter of little import.

And evidently, he made many friends amongst their fellow prisoners and seemed to be held by most in high esteem. He had always been skilled at detachment, even here and now; Mogue noticed the cowed deference in which even the cruellest men here spoke to him and to the bald dwarf who never left his side. Though he barely stood to the shoulder of the lad, the urge to try and flee were it not for the chains was a powerful one. He seemed to have eyes narrow as a blade, yet his eternal squint seemed moulded into his features. His size made him dangerous; he could quickly dodge and weave his way through a skirmish, and with a swift flash of his knives, hamstringing men twice his size with kittenish agility. There was no hierarchy of knaves here; the debtors were thrown in with the thieves, those sentenced to death mingled with those condemned to see the years stretch out before them.

Mogue also noticed Rob was slipping more and more references into his monologues to their one day escaping from Newgate. At first, he paid them no heed, dismissing them as the delusions of a lifer, but soon he paid them greater heed. Rob tended to slip them in late after their food arrived, which was presumably long after dark, when the darkness around them thrummed with the snores and night-time mumblings of the others.

More and more, as he responded, he noticed Rob pausing and listening for a response from him whenever he embarked on one of his insane monologues. That the man in the shadows seemed to care what he thought and seemed eager for some measure of response from him beyond the usual monosyllabic grunts was not lost on Mogue. That Rob knew his command of the English language was far greater and more varied than many of the inchoate wretches with whom they were forced to share a cell was no secret.

More often than not, the man would comment on what he perceived to be Mogue's intellect, or 'smarts' as he put it. On occasion letters would be sent into the prison, and by the waxy glimmer of a candle, it was Mogue Trench to whom the task of interpreting them inevitably fell. Other times the turnkeys passed messages between cellblocks, scrawled morsels of intelligence passed between prisoners. These were written in a secretive language of their own, a code of stealth, one that the prisoners alone seemed to speak and be fluent in. Words were shorn of their original meaning and assigned others.

It was more than a mere lingo of solidarity amongst the condemned; it served a purpose of far greater, and quite surreptitous, use. The word 'catcher', he soon learned, meant 'chain', when uttered by one inmate to another. 'Grave', he eventually learned, though not without confusion, meant 'tunnel'. After a while he heard Rob mention the name 'Upton' with greater regularity – the name of the turnkey who oversaw their corridor.

Newgate was impregnable as any fortress; but, as any skilled besieger will attest, no fortress is ever without its holes, nor any suit of armour ever without its chinks. In this case, the chink in question was not a faulty lock or bolt whose mechanisms could be twisted and worked around; it was Upton, the squinty-eyed turnkey himself.

Upton, in his filthy scarlet coat, whose keys jingled from the ring slung to his leather belt, like a chapel bell calling the pious. He had popularity neither with the inmates nor amongst his fellow turnkeys. The least popular shifts were those that patrolled the lower corridors; Upton's fondness for whiskey and inability to control those whom he kept under guard ensured he was given the worst watch. Occasionally he entered the cell and the reek of whiskey off him was enough to contend with, and often enough even to drub any odour permeating the cell. Every day like clockwork, he'd open the cell and hand over the pewter-tinged plates piled with gruel. Rob was never short of a tired joke at his expense, which Upton usually failed to ignore. Because Rob was far off in the corner, he never needed to approach him. But between Rob and the cell door crouched Mogue Trench. Upton invariably had to pass quite close to him whenever he came and went. In the dim light of the corridor, MacTire's protégé noted his heavy coat, the askew outline of his tricorne, the shuffle of his movements and the presence of the turnkeys on his watch.

On the night when Roman Catholics celebrated the Assumption of Mary, many of the turnkeys had been permitted their obligations and allowed to leave. Upton was one of the few on night patrol, and he had double what he usually attended to. The cell block was never fully quiet, as was its wont. This was to their advantage, however. Few of the inmates seemed to have an idea of what was about to happen.

In the darkness of the cell, Mogue Trench crouched, half-listening to Rob recount some bizarre run-in he'd had with a thief-catcher named Ivory, waiting for the moment of reckoning to be upon them.

The door groaned open with its usual steely rattle and Upton entered, keys jingling loudly off their steel ring, and handed out the paltry rations. Mogue imagined it was close to nightfall, given his arrival. Rob's aimless blather petered off as the turnkey showed his face. The other prisoners were oddly quiet as the corridor's thin light spilled over them like a revelation. Mogue took a breath and waited.

"Evening, Upton," Rob grinned beside him. "Doin' yer rounds, yeh? Truly we know not the day nor the hour."

The turnkey did not respond, instead kneeling before Mogue to inspect his fetters, as he did with everyone. He placed his lantern by the open door. That was all the boy needed. The predictability of the routine was a greater ally than either of them had anticipated. Upton did not, of course, notice the boy's hand slide past his belt, and undo the key from its chain with a sharp flick of his wrist.

At that moment, as they had already agreed, Rob waited for the turnkey to kneel before him, and then got a hold of him while still manacled. Upton barely managed a shout of surprise before his neck was good and snapped, and his body slumped heavily on the stone like a gutted seal. He lay back, and Mogue saw the turnkey's jowly throat was parted by his own blade, his blood warming the floor like an oil slick.

By then, Mogue was already turning the key through his fetters. The manacles that encircled his wrists slid free, and the hour of liberty was upon him. The horse-padlock chaining him to the wall was heavy enough, but he eventually succeeded in cracking it open. Following this, he managed to wrench a weaker link in the fetters asunder, releasing himself. The chains gripping his ankles were far too thick to be unfastened, and so he removed his boots, tying the broken fetters by their ends to his limbs into what was left of his garters. The rest of his chains fell free, as did Rob's, and all of the others', and his blood was pumping freshly. He snatched Upton's lantern, and for the first time in months, they inched out of the cell door, throwing glances down the narrow vault, which, had it not been for the torches, would have been dark as ink.

The continuous dirge of the other prisoners' voices on their cell block muffled their footfalls. Robin had removed Upton's belt, and had slung it crudely athwart his torso like an officer's sash. They moved as a single entity, inching down the fetid passage. Mogue's hand instinctively ran to his hip before he remembered there was no knife-hilt there to draw.

"For, brethren, ye've been called unto liberty."

Rob spoke softly, his voice bouncing off the walls. The others seemed to lose their usual volubility. Mogue stood where he was, the lantern light quavering as Rob moved to the nearest cell door and unlocked it. He strode in, to a fusillade of roars and bellows, and moved around the room like a guard, undoing the locks.

"And to him was given the key to the bottomless pit."

In a matter of moments, scores of similarly bedraggled inmates surged out of the cell door and charged down the vault, too fast for Mogue to even take in individual faces. One or two tripped and hit the floor in the confusion. The noises to which his ear had become dulled now rippled and echoed ahead of them in full obscene crescendo as they spilled into the shadowy corridor and charged past them toward the warder's office, a torrent of haggard flesh and clanking leg-irons.

There were other noises too now; panicked calls and the frantic chiming of a bell. Rob watched after them, a smile warping his gnarled features, before charging forward, already ahead of everyone else.

As Mogue knew they would, the turnkeys on duty came racing down the tunnel to meet them, their bayonets already raised and primed, their lurid crimson coats giving them away. He wondered how truly equipped for this they were, for the hasty motion of their limbs told him they were taken quite off guard. There was no time to send more messages, no time to argue, no time to plead. There was no time to stand or present; this battle brooked no negotiation. Before a shot could be fired, the prisoners were on them like flies on a carcass. Rob was among them, his mangled fist writhing, slamming into belly and shoulder.

Blood fizzing, Mogue felt rapidly engulfed by the chaos, and the older man's relentless fury, buried deep in the last how-many-years he'd spent here, now seemed to surge through the narrow corridor like a burst dam and pervade everyone and everything. The impact of his fists seemed louder than any other noise there, even his own demonic roaring.

It had been ages since Mogue had struck or killed a man. He blindly threw a fist into a turnkey's face and felt it knock satisfyingly off bone. The man sprawled against the wall, already spitting blood over his lapel. Pain blossomed in his shoulder as a blade slashed across it; he barely reacted, instead knocking his attacker to the floor, hearing the growl in his own voice as though it were someone else's. Abandoning the lantern, he flung it aside, and as it smashed off the wall, the flaying light of newly ignited flames blasted through the vault. Mogue was already running, fighting to get to the drain opening, kicking and striking where he had to. The flames blazed over the coat of the fallen turnkey, licking through flesh and smouldering the corpse. Smoke roiled through the passage, as if exhaled from the craw of a dragon.

More turnkeys were racing down the vault, but they were too few to stem the inmates. They swarmed further ahead until the entire cellblock was a dizzying mess of thrashing limbs and ragged bellows and choking heat and bodies already on the floor. Fury thickened the air as well as smoke. The flames had caught more people, and they flailed as the heat tore them. Mogue kept the wall, eyes needled from the fumes, moving by inches. He saw Rob further up at the tunnel, having now gotten hold of a bayonet and pummelling a fallen turnkey's face with the stock, before rushing blindly past the others. There was another turnkey making for him, bayonet bristling.

"*Rob*, behind you!"

Somehow, he was heard above the commotion. Rob whirled around just in time to catch his attacker through the throat. He nodded to Mogue as he stepped over the body, racing alongside him down the passage toward the drain opening. Not caring who followed, they inched down the passage, and plunged in.

Mogue's feet and legs hit a freezing cascade of water, and, but for the lantern he held, his eyes would have hit nothing but pitch dark. Shining it down ahead of him, he saw he was in one of the tunnels that ran beneath the city, the walls, slick with damp, just narrow enough to walk through and the ceiling just low enough to brush his scalp. A second later, Rob and the others followed. The splashes they made were deafening; all around, the roar of rushing waters was a din of echoing, sluggish splendour.

"Ah, fuck me," Mogue heard Rob snarl nearby, his voice bouncing off the wall. "Words of his mouth are deep waters, wha'?"

"What is this?" Mogue spluttered back.

"The Bradogue. Runs right to the river. Let's get a fuckin' move on, shall we?"

Rob sloshed ahead and Mogue followed the noise he made, holding the lantern far ahead. Even in the light, the water seemed black as peat. He heard the others moving behind, all gagging to follow in some established direction. The water rushed in sludgy torrents around their thighs as they plodded through; evidently, it was a high tide. Grubby stone and brick were somewhere near, and he knew it was narrow. The darkness of the cell had prepared Mogue for this, but already the shivers were blossoming through his bones. His boots brushed over stray gravel and silt and ballast; he fought the rising urge to sputter.

The sweep of the current pushed them on. They all had to wade single file, burrowing through the slimy darkness that threatened to smother the lantern's feeble glow, their voices a morass of echoes ballooning and swollen and gurgled by the slats. The Liffey was not far. Mogue knew this because he could smell it, the sluiced shit and sewage clotting the air. The saltwater's scabrous whiff grew heavier as they sloshed downstream, toward the quays. No noise above could be heard.

His mind had settled on little else but where the sewage-clotted stream eventually met the river. Suds fizzed about them as if in a cauldron. Reeds brushed past with the hurtling tide. But now light could be seen, dim eddies of lamp-glow churning on the distant surface.

They had reached the culvert and the water's foaming spill, plunging loudly through the rusting gridirons from a hole in the wall of Ormond Quay. Mogue inched past the last of the brick wall, and just beyond he spied the rippling scud of the Liffey. It was a clear night, the moon looming luminous and full. It must have been weeks since he had last seen it, the buildings stark in its glare, the outlines heavy and marked, some blocking the light, the cobbles awash in its ghostly glaze. And just within Mogue's eyeline, Ormonde Bridge cut a black, arching swath through the light.

One by one, the former inmates of Newgate dived into the last high tide of the night, slipping through the bars, keeping close to the quay walls, and cradled by the foam. Mogue and Rob kept together; the city was quiet enough, for it was long after hours. Nonetheless, the caution of the newly escaped held them. The Charleys were on the prowl.

Still dripping wet, they hauled themselves up under the bridge and were finally able to breathe the city air again. Rob led him to Merchant's Quay and bade him walk south. On his heels, Mogue Trench followed his former cellmate through the warren of narrow streets, ducking and diving from where the Charleys' known positions were.

He followed through the tenement buildings, Rob's atrophied shape just ahead of him. The man walked as if he hadn't spent a good portion of the last few years bolted to a prison wall, silently, barely any urgency to his pace. Down odiferous and muddy alleys, under crooked archways, serenaded by the vague drunken singing of bowsies in the public-houses, the scorched pungency of hops from the brewery, foggy coronas of light encircling the lamps. They moved away from the river, over the cobbles, still drenched and letting the Liffey drip off them and dampen the flagstones, the gables clustered together like prisoners before a firing squad, and the church steeples making lofty skyward stabs. And through all of this, Rob moved without any noticeable trouble or confusion. Despite his stunted form, he almost seemed to glide, unhindered by the shadows or sharp corners or the smell of horse shite, his footing sure and steady.

And young Mogue Trench kept following. A heaviness had entered his eyes, the lateness of the hour taking its slow effect.

By the time it was discovered that a number of felons had escaped from Newgate through the sewers, the next shift was up. When it was revealed that the protégé of the recently killed notorious highwayman Joseph MacTíre was among them, bounties were immediately drawn up for his capture and arrest. By then, Mogue Trench had vanished into the city with his new companion, and the streets he had once known were now best avoided.

Chapter XIX
Her Dark Foundationſ

Dublin, 1791

By Mogue's reckoning, chaos was infinitely more preferable to tyranny. What had once been an unspoken inkling for him was rapidly becoming a firm conviction. In chaos, he'd come to believe, there was candour, possibility, fairness. Chaos permitted a man to act in accordance with his core nature, with his intuition and raw propensities. Mogue's loathing of all authority, fostered by MacTíre and now solidified by his time in Newgate, of priests, soldiers, guards, made him unable to see himself ever joining their ranks. He would much prefer to leave them their uniforms, their risible oaths, the arbitrary laws they were duty-bound to enforce, the despotic regimes to which they toadied and their willingness to be sent to their deaths at the uncaring whim of a king or general. Without such simulacra, such delusive semblances of identity, what were they? With chaos, however, everything was truly fair.

Yet he found himself unwilling to vanish off into Dublin's streets. Like as not, he had helped Rob, much and all as the man disgusted him. Whatever opportunity was presenting itself to him, he deemed it best to see where it was leading him.

Rob spoke no lie when he claimed to be a weaver. It transpired he had once been proprietor of a small tanner's workshop off New Row, although none of his labourers claimed affiliation with any of the city's guilds. The enterprise he had left to be managed by his old partner in crime, Alf Guerin. A rake of journeymen had been in his employ, and Guerin had kept the place up and running until the day of Rob's inevitable absconding. Even in Newgate, Rob had received regular intelligence on the various jobs he had a finger in. Few were skilled, and even fewer were of the Papist persuasion – though Rob cared little for the prayers a man uttered, and more for the prowess with which he wielded a fleshing blade.

He led Mogue down the leprous little boulevard, past beggars brawling and ranting in the portals, past journeymen weavers toiling away at Jacquard looms, mercers hawking velvets and silks from stalls, apprentice curriers hauling reeking hides into their workshops for tanning. The side-street the tanner was on was a slipshod row of gable-fronted houses banked roughly together, many of them elevated to four or five storeys, and all adjoined to a knackery and a wool warehouse. Rob's workshop squatted near the end, in a redbrick hulk whose patched windows seemed to scowl down like eyes blackened from a brawl. The caustic odours of lye, ordure and piss wafted foully from its door, hitting Mogue's unprepared nose like demons. He'd coughed gutturally at it at first, much to Rob's mirth. When he could finally stand to enter, he saw yellowed prints of King Billy adorning the inner walls; there was neither breath of air nor even ray of light from the dawn here. A charcoal fire burned at the rear, and the aroma of burnt carcasses pervaded the brazier, mingling with the acid.

Rob moved through this place with the same ease he had on clambering from the river. It was clear, from the raucous shouts and claps on the back he got from various passers-by, that he was king here. On entering the house, filled with four or five of his mates, all clad in the greasy aprons of their profession, boisterous greetings and calls met him.

His escape from Newgate was an occasion of rough celebration amongst his old mates – on entering the tannery, he was immediately handed a bottle of cheap brandy from which he swilled heartily before passing it around. They were a rough-looking crew, hands scarred and muscled from working the hides and skins, belts festooned with hooks, skivers, scrapers, and curved fleshing blades like instruments of war. Despite Rob's condition, none seemed apprehensive about approaching him with outstretched arms and welcoming him back.

When it became clear that the watchful young man accompanying him was in fact Joseph's MacTíre's protégé, the wags gathered around him in lurid fascination, before a barked growl from Rob, whose good cheer seemed to briefly desert him, sent them scurrying back to their stations.

As to who he was, Mogue was wary of saying much. The reward for his head seemed to swell daily. But he soon found himself at ease, skulling back the fiery waters of a whiskey jug Rob gave him, and recounting his choicest kills with the road thief to the others; clearly Rob had made it clear he was not to be touched. When he'd had his fill, Rob had approached him and handed him a freshly sharpened sleeker knife, beaming in the sunlight. He then indicated to a row of lethally stinking pelts that dangled from the rafters – fresh kills salted and ruby-red, stripped of hair and offal and innards; the raw stench of their guts wedged a nauseous lump in Mogue's craw. Nonetheless, he remembered a similar odour fuming off the corpses of men he'd killed with MacTíre, and he forced himself to keep staring at it.

He suddenly remembered the dagger Rob had handed him, and the avid eyes of everyone on him. He walked over to the nearest hide, angling the blade as best he could, began scraping the remnant meat off the hide with his customary methodical calm, his teeth baring. The others whooped as the corpse was thoroughly defleshed. The blade slid smoothly over the beast's ribs and back with a natural grace, and its flesh slid away as smoothly as bristles being shaved from a man's face.

To grip a blade once again, yet to use it for a trade other than crime, was a rare joy. It settled into his palm as naturally as a glove; his fingers closed around the hilt as if made for it. It was slender, sharp, and dripped with fresh flesh-morsels, a digit in his clenched fist as much as any of his fingers.

"We'd heard of yer skill with a blade," Rob had grinned. "Though yer sins be red as blood, wha'?"

Mogue kept his face unreadable as the rawhide was then rinsed down, limed and seasoned and plunged into the acidulous liquid with a savoury, vaporous hiss. He nodded to himself, refusing to blink, yet unwilling to cleanse his dagger. There was little butchery required of him, and yet the old fervid rush of heat was spilling through his bones once more, his mastery and inventiveness with a blade that never failed to keep him aright; how he welcomed it. It resurfaced burnished and crackling, a great husk of hardening, slowly simmering leather.

And so, all through the spring, summer and winter months, and well into the new year, Mogue Trench worked as a tanner, joining his mates at daybreak outside the fetid Dutch Billy with his blades sharpened, avid to burn for the next twelve hours in the trade of dead, priceless meat, direct from the slaughterhouses. Once he had specialised in butchering the flesh of men; now it was the beast's turn. It wasn't as profitable as his time with MacTíre, but food and warmth were guaranteed, as well as a chance for lively conversation once more. It didn't require much thought beyond what was needed in the immediate moment.

His hands might have been scorched raw from the acid, his sinews aching and flesh dampened with sweat, but there were shillings in his pocket and a satisfying sense of consummation of a job well done. For these reasons, he soon found he liked the work, the reek of the tannery to the daily film of sweat that drenched his brow. His skill with a knife stood him well; Rob barked his name once a fresh hide was taken from the mercer's cart. Whether it was stitching torn clothes their customers brought to the workshop or frizzing loose grain from the bowels – all of it gave him an itch in the teeth. He soon was unable to smell the reek of decaying animals and manure, the way it swirled out of the workshop and was hit by a hard easterly blowing fresh off the river.

All of this he came to associate with a growing sense of his own accomplishment, of his competence in applying his own particular talent to a different class of endeavour. And the working girls who sidled up from Fishamble and the Monto, who mingled amongst the workers and offered their wares, on the hunt for an easy payday. They seemed to like watching him work, especially, and Mogue prided himself on giving a good performance.

The acrid redolence of the place did not seem to faze them; in their line of work, far worse horrors were to be expected. To see his blade flash and scrape, his wrist moving swift as a striking snake, and the effusion of steam rising as a fresh skin was dunked in the acid. Under the girls' painted gaze, on the flint workfloor, Mogue helped drag a bull-hide up from the street, ignoring the weight as he drew out a flesher knife. The knife didn't come out 'til he was sure the thing was clean, de-haired. The steadiness of his hand combined with the fact that he kept his blades scrupulously sharp was quickly noted by his workmates, and by Rob especially. He sheared the stinking meat off the hide, helped see it stretched out until taut, doused it in lime and season, helped haul it into the acid cauldron. He rushed to help see the muscle and bowels and colons and anything else soft and meaty that couldn't be salvaged tossed into the offal pile. Once that was done, they delimed it with lye and gargle and readied to plunge it into the pit. It helped that the flesh was rarely ever tenderised when they did this. Some farmer would always buy it later for fertilizer. Mogue and the lads emerged from the Dutch Billy stinking, tired and sweaty, their pockets jangling with coin and in need of a decent shag, and the girls would inevitably be waiting.

"Sacrifice thereon thy burnt offerings!" Rob would cough and laugh over the steam's hiss. His habit of barking scriptural quotation without even an ounce of holiness soon became a means of measuring time.

The burning stench seemed to block out everything else; the steam bit the air and every nose in the room shrivelled. Sweat on his brow oozed; shillings rattled in his pocket. The hide hissed vaporously as it plunged into liquid. The way the acid was capable of eating through a fella's flesh if he wasn't careful. The weight and heft of the work tools; the shouts and the calls of the other men over the boiling of a skin. Parchment, vellum, were spat out of the workshop at animal speed. Soon, he knew the skilled hands from the seasonal jobbers; it changed with enough regularity that learning a man's name became less and less important. This suited him; his own name was best left unrevealed.

Despite this, he worried often of the Charleys venturing into the Liberties, that word of his presence there was rolling through the city. The Charleys that did venture always did so in numbers, brandishing their lanterns and pikes like glorified regimentals. They were only there to collect their weekly bribe off the gangs, and they were led by a louser patrolman named Paul Ivory, a silver-bearded Petty Constable who had his own version of justice. As long as Rob paid up, his skull remained uncracked and he was not carted back off to Newgate.

All of Rob's lads loathed him nonetheless; it was well known him and his boys fucked off across the river to the Smithfield cattle yards, to collect similar off their Papist rivals there, once he was done fleecing them. There was hardly anyone worked in the city's fetid heart who didn't owe the lantern-swinging bollix a bob. 'Thief-catcher', everyone called him. Mogue hated him on sight.

"See you've a new lad workin' for yeh, Rob," he'd smirk, once he saw Mogue among the usual rake of lads at the tanning vat.

"I do," Rob replied sullenly. "I often do."

The thief-catcher seemed to squint at the coins nestled in his palm, as if suspicious his requisite amount was no longer there. He was doing it deliberately; keep the younger lads on their toes.

"Much obliged, Rob, as always," he grinned, jangling the coins in his hand for effect. Of course, whatever he got off them that week, they managed to make back twice over on their nightly excursions. The Charleys were paid off with the spoils from the very firms they were often charged with investigating.

Soon, Mogue realized, he was oddly safe. Aside from their protection shillings, the Charleys rarely bothered with this part of the city, nor did they care to. That only a handful of Rob's employees were journeymen, there for a season and gone once the weather shifted, kept him on his toes. It suited him well that most didn't know him from Adam, or even cared – new faces meant new people to be suspicious of. New faces meant a potential thief-catcher infiltrating the tannery to claim the road thief's escaped protégé as his prize. But after a few months, he could relax. In cities, anonymity was as common as brick or mortar. In Wexford, he'd been Joseph MacTíre's protégé, son and heir to the roadside surveyor – in Dublin, he was just another bowsie.

That he was now part of a group, a guild of knifeworkers, as it were, was not lost on him. Here, he was in clear contradiction of every belief and dictum of self-interest MacTíre had schooled him in. But in Dublin, it did not pay to be a lone wolf, and he needed to know exactly who it was he and his new compatriots were aligned against. If pressed, Rob and the lads professed to be of the Protestant persuasion – but Mogue knew a man's stated affiliations, religious or otherwise, were almost always merely a prop he wielded, a camouflage of convenience he wore when trying to force the world to accommodate him and his fellows. In the evenings, when Rob hadn't sent him off on an errand, he stalked out sometimes as far as Faithful Place or the Monto, visiting the working girls there when he was able.

It soon became clear that the tannery served a darker purpose beyond the mere manufacture of leather aprons. Many of the waifs and strays Rob took under his seasonal employ were clearly street arabs and mayhem artists brought in for whatever reason; there was the core group he kept, a dubious elite of which Mogue was now an implicitly permanent member.

There was also Alf Guerin and his younger brother Ulick, and Paul Cobbe, a fierce-eyed Orangemen who didn't speak much but never ceased to smell of formaldehyde. All of them had murdered at least one man before the age of twenty; all of them knew the feeling of warm blood sprayed across their faces; all of them were never without a blade to hand. They were known to outsiders as the Liberty Boys. They'd a savagery he appreciated, and they felt happy to fight for what mattered to them.

It was Cobbe whose hatred for the Catholic Ormond lads across the river ran the deepest. Often enough, while they worked, he'd blather on about everything from the hell-born nature of papacy ("every man jack of 'em bound for the flames, by Jaysus") to the talk of the revolution in France, now set to see the entire world toppled by the rising precedence of democratic societies ("and may it bring the slanderous bastard on the banks of the Tiber with 'em").

Mogue never gave much thought to the former, and he found himself oddly intrigued by the latter, but held his peace nonetheless. He'd survived this long keeping his mouth shut, and despite Rob's generosity, he remained unsure as to whether the hazard man standing across from him with a skillet in hand felt the need to grab him and thrust his face into the scorching acid just beneath them and hold it there.

All the lads, he soon learned, shared his ability with knifework, and Rob had handpicked them for their reliability, their industriousness, and their keenness for keeping their acid-soured lips sealed. Were it not for Rob, many of them might well have died in the streets. All, Mogue later learned, earned a good deal extra than their journeymen colleagues for the extra jobs they did for Rob. Jobs Mogue soon found himself participating in as well, owing to his apprenticeship with the road thief of Wexford. Jobs he found himself looking forward to, once quitting time was upon him.

After work, under cover of night, when the tanning fires were doused and the city was quiet, bar the searing winds that cut inland from the bay, the four of them would venture out, and silently declare themselves kings. Many mistook them for the apprentice lads they were, and so paid them little heed. They prowled their way through the city like wolves on a delectable scent, never striking in the same place twice. The old thrill he'd felt stalking the forest land of Wexford was restored at last. They weren't alone, but Rob had his sights set above purse-cutting (though Mogue, ever handy with a blade, availed of their opportunity wherever he found it).

Dublin was hardly a city, he came to believe, but a festering patchwork of colonies, all at relentless and irresolvable war with each other, their borders as loose and ill-defined as they were present. If they were to venture north of the Liffey, to the butcher shops and cattle yards where the Ormond lads resided, they never did so alone and they were always armed to the teeth with their work-tools. The Ormond lads worked in the trade of dead meat also, but for eating rather than wearing. The weight and clink of the knives, resting reassuringly under their night-coats like talismans, was a good feeling on such excursions. Once the drovers had left, they broke the cattle loose from their holdings, sending them stampeding through the back and high streets as if on a run, destroying the silence of the night, their hooves clacking heavily off the damp, slippery cobblestones. The City Watchmen hadn't a clue how they did it.

And the fights they had. Street, alley, bridge, it mattered not where the blood splashed. It grieved Mogue more to lose his blade in a fight than any wound incurred or loss suffered. As in the forest, even the faintest whiff of blood seemed to blind Mogue to friend, foe, or even blameless bystander, for he became known to bellow with the ferocity of a berserker from some saga, lunging and thrusting at anyone who crossed his path, his blades striking like lightning in his hands, slicing through tendon and hamstring.

Once, after an especially heated mill, they dragged the bodies of several Ormond gets back to their fly-ridden abattoir, where they cut down the gutted pig and calf carcasses that hung skewered from the roof slat. He grabbed a steel meat hook, stuck it in the mouth of the nearest Ormond lad, as far back as his jaw, and sliced through it viciously, like a fisherman tearing a fresh catch from his bait. The screams over Smithfield that night ripped through the yards and, it was claimed, could be heard as far as the docks; the butchers were left to dangle from their own hooks, blood trickling from their torn lips and sprinkling the flagstones.

In the moments after a brawl, he could often enough be found stalking amongst the heaps of shattered limbs, the moans of the dying, the blood and guts splurged over the cobbles, drenched in blood, kicking aside corpses in an effort to find his blade, if he had lost it. The first time Mogue had seen the end of a fight, Rob had walked up to him, his own blades still unwashed. Mogue had been cursing under his breath: "Fuckin' Papist scum..."

"What's troublin' yeh, Trench?"

"Lost me fuckin' knife. It'll cost me a month in wages to see it replaced."

Rob pondered this, glancing around at the myriad corpses where they lay on the blood-slicked cobbles. "Ye'd do well to keep it closer next time."

"I'll need it by sunrise, Rob, that's me main problem."

Rob smirked at the lad's earnestness. "That ye will. I wouldn't worry too much, but. Plenty of blades back at the Billy, and you're welcome to yer share. The lads all agree you're better off as one of us. One of 'em just might give ye a lend of his. 'Til then, I'd say be glad we won this one."

That gave Mogue pause; his skill with a knife could be held as greater value than the mere shearing of animal hides. An unbidden memory of Newgate's clammy corridors and hellish cellar he shared with a cluster of the walking damned, all as mad as he and Rob and worse besides, the plan he had devised to escape, his unspoken acceptance into Rob's gang. In the battle there were more men amassed on the bridge than he had dared imagine, yet he had emerged neither killed nor wounded. Many now lay at his feet, and the odd satisfaction he felt at being the administer of so many deaths was consolation enough.

He had used his blade well, wading into the fray and slashing into the gullet of an opponent like a reaper threshing his way through a particularly overgrown pasture. He had neither backed down nor allowed himself to suffer the killing blow; for a long time, pride had been a singularly stellar emotion he felt he had little right to. But MacTíre had taught him well on many accounts. He had roared into the faces of men now faced with death: "Tell the devil I'm coming!"

"If it's rage ye prefer to live by, Trench," Rob said, his face a study of shrewdness, "then I'd say you're in the right place. After today, rumours of ye will spread and before ye know it, yer reputation'll precede ye where's ever ye go. That said, but, I also do be wonderin' if this is yer plan? Forch'nately for you, I think we're better off stickin' together, while yer still young. Wouldn't yeh agree?"

"I won't be young forever, Rob."

Rob leered at that. "No, yeh won't be. But while y'still are, 'mon down to Peg's with us. Tonight. I know a moll there I think y'might like."

"Who's that?"

"Maggie Drake, Princess of Vice and Queen of Songs."

*

By nightfall, Mogue, Rob and the others were bobbing and weaving their way to Leeson's flash house, known locally as Pimping Peg's, a late-night seraglio located at the end of Pitt Street. All four of them wore their best tins of fruit (all nicked, of course), and carried a bouquet of flowers each. No man could cross the doorway of Peg's without either, and yobbos like them were no different. Not the Monto, not Faithful Place, but sequestered off in one of the city's more respectable corners. Meaning there was less danger of the Charleys to come prowling. Nonetheless, the leather-bound Bible displayed in the vanilla-scented foyer was kept conspicuously open. At the opening section to the Song of Songs, Mogue could not help but notice with a grin.

Mogue knew the place, having seen numerous posters extolling its unique delights plastered across the city, but had never actually crossed its doors. The parlour walls were painted a shocking crimson, resembling freshly spilled blood. Once there, immersed in the fragrance of orange blossom and sandalwood, with a mug of porter frothing before him, he had been watchful at first. He did not know how long it had been since he had a woman. Observation made him suss out early enough that Rob was well-in with the establishment's madam; it took him a moment before he noticed one of the girls was staring at him.

Bordellos had a unique way of unifying people, he felt, of allowing possibilities to flourish that anywhere else might have been forbidden or, at the very least, discouraged. Ostensibly, Peg's catered to the wealthier end, but this was more of a technicality than anything else. If you had the cash and the manners, entry could readily be yours. How a man made his money, and the coarseness of his tongue, were of little concern to Peg. Clearly, Rob, as a businessman, knew this well.

In Peg's, a tacit understanding was shared by men who – in the diurnal hours when alleged normality reigned – would have no earthly reason to converse, but who were now in communion by the pleasures of the flesh, simply by dint of being in the same panelled parlour and sampling the same profane waters. Garrulous bucks in laced liveries rubbed elbows with bowsies just in from the docks, a lord lieutenant would share a dram of whiskey with a sailor freshly spewed off his ship, or a young redcoat on leave from one of the many garrisons dotted around the capital; oily aldermen and off-duty merchants were seen to trade good-natured barbs with blacksmith's apprentices and even their own footmen.

Many had arrived not by walking the streets, but via special tunnels dug directly under the streets from College Green or elsewhere; others simply showed up with their aides-de-camp, cash jingling in palm.

Regulars and newcomers alike were greeted just the same by the man at the door. There was no class, no colour, no creed to be excluded, as long as the shillings were to hand. All were fated to be fecked out of doors by four o'clock in the morning, in any case.

Meanwhile, the molls sashayed by, hips swivelling under their voluminous side hoops, taking men by the hands and leading them off to one of their private rooms. Mogue recognised many of them as the girls who often patrolled the weavers' quarter and under whose suggestive gaze he found himself working with greater finesse. These girls were handpicked by the madam, from the purlieus of Drury Lane, and were suited to nothing less than the appellation of 'lady'. These weren't the dead-eyed waifs whom Gráinne had peddled, nor were they the overpainted flaggers whom he sought out at Fishamble; all were noticeably free of the marks of pox or violence or rough luck. And not a one of them could boast a tan; they were kept indoors to maintain their ashy pallor.

The one staring at him right now was no different. Rob had told him about her, and the lads all sung her praises in lewd, profane elan. Besides her beauty, they spoke of her dark curls, the moon-pale hue of her complexion, the strange songs she'd sit and play and sing for the patrons, the way she could make a man's concerns vanish into ether with just a look or a single night in her bed.

He knew her the second he saw her. She was seated at the clavichord beneath the oily glow from the window, willowy fingers coaxing a stale polonaise from the keys, holding notes down repeatedly, sometimes hammering the pitch to cacophony or else pressing it back to dulcet accord. The Old Masters made paintings of women such as her. Hair dark as a raven's wing, she was all rouged and powdered and oval-lipped, enough to put any man's heart in hurdle. A savoury veil of ambrosia hovered over her. Red became her; her breasts fell heavily forward in her corset, and he noticed the chain of rosary beads slung about her throat like a knife wound; they rattled slightly to her every legato and keystroke.

Yet she did not seem to be looking with an eye to gaining a patron (in Leeson's, there were no customers, only patrons), though there was no shortage of leering men and cackling girls who ambled through the place's doors and who relished her song. Nor did anyone dare to approach her, he noticed.

On the way there, the lads had spoken of her sloe eyes; more specifically, the white fleck that danced behind plumose lashes. But when she'd looked up and fixed Mogue with a look of sidelong concernment, continuing to play through her piece without skipping a beat, Mogue saw nothing of the lightness they described. The sight of him alone made her frown, as if she smelt the blood and leather and acid off him all the way across the room. Yet, all the while, her eyes did not leave him, and he felt no fear under her gaze. He felt himself harden, like the hilt of his scalping-blade.

Mogue threw his shoulders back and sipped his porter, forcing himself to stare back. She finished the polonaise and started up something decidedly more sombre, a Haydn adagio. The ribald saloon songs would commence later, when the night had grown seamy; for now, the aesthetics of the ballroom prevailed. But never in his life had Mogue heard what he was hearing now. Her hands seemed to glide in silken alchemy across the keys, weaving magic into every note, her grace surreptitious as a thief's. To be caressed by such hands was worth more than his pockets ever carried. He could not think of a better overture. He barely realized his mouth was agape when she took his hand and led him upstairs.

The next few pieces played were for him and him alone. She led him up the stairs like a prima donna making her grand exit. There was a performance to her every move, he sensed, but he knew not when the time for applause was near. Though she was not the madam, the entire house seemed built to be her stage, for her every overture and finale. The hem of her dress barely brushed the floorboards as she led him to the back room. As he opened the door to her dark bedchamber, his eyes needed a moment to adjust to the light thrown by the meagre lantern.

"I see," he murmured.

A sharp aroma of ambrosia hit him. Once the door was shut, the noises from downstairs were drowned out, the hollering of the patrons, the salacious tones of the clavichord as bawdier songs were started up. But Mogue's eye was drawn to something else. The room was crawling with rosary beads. They hung from the ornate posts of the damask-draped bed, slung over the divan, coiled around the girandoles she had placed there, framed the lone looking-glass, bunched and glistening, ruddy as redcurrant berries. He knew there were many more, placed in the corners and concealed in her patch box, just out of the reach of the candle-glow. He smirked as she shut the door and crossed the floor to him.

"I'd no idea Peg's girls were so devout."

"Hardly. I just enjoy collecting them. If all goes well tonight, I may procure more."

These were the first words she addressed to him and him alone. It was only then he saw she was barefoot, and as she pressed against him and their lips at last met, he finally returned her embrace.

"Is it true what they say about you?" she'd asked as he moved down and kissed her neck. The softness of her was thrilling, like a bewitchment; so rarely did he encounter it. "You're really him, aren't you? The road thief's boy?"

Somehow, he couldn't find an answer; not even a trite or pitiful one. Boasting had never come easily to him; he feared if he did speak, she'd vanish. Instead, he moved to unbuckle his belt, but she got there first. The fingers that worked through Haydn and Mozart now reached up to undo the buttons on his tunic with the same measure of precision, before running through his hair. She drew his tunic expertly off and he stood bare before her, shaking in the crimson dark.

"Well?"

It was only then did Mogue Trench feel the cold bite of the blade pressed against his gullet. Her face was now close to his, eyes suddenly level, and unreadable as two pools of ink.

"Are you, or are you not him?"

"I…" Mogue gasped. "I…was. I am no longer. Did I wrong you ever?"

"You've wronged many, but not me, boy," was her reply.

"Then what do you want from me?"

"You pay for my services, and I pay for your arrest. Thousand guineas. As the law currently has it. And that's only if you're taken alive, of course. Tempting figure, wouldn't you agree?"

He didn't quite know how she did it, for she barely moved; but he distinctly felt the knife-edge bite down a hair sharper.

"Now, from what I've heard, you were MacTíre's protégé and heir. Always quick for a fight. How true is that?"

He glanced down at his chest. Even in the low light, the patchwork of scars and stab wounds he had accumulated over the years were visible on his torso.

"Some of these are recent, girl. Some were inflicted upon me by MacTíre himself. But make no mistake – before him, I was no one. I came from nowhere, from nothing. And I, who am native to nowhere, chose naught but this life. I was born and I am as I have become. I fought only when necessary once. Avoided a fight if I could. But now, without him, I am nothing once more. But somehow, men were sent into the forest all on my account. Many more refused, convinced they would be next under my blade. There are no more wolves in Ireland, but thanks to me, people could not believe it. I was once the nightmare they warned their children about, until I wasn't. I escaped with my life, whilst MacTíre was left to die like a rabid cur in the forest. Many thought he was a demon; turns out he was a man like any other. He certainly bled like any other. Whatever legends you've heard, let me assure you…the reality is far worse. And I am alive for a reason. And could be worth far more to you free than enchained."

Their eyes remained locked. As he waited for her reply, lines from Milton came to him:

"Yet beauty, though injurious, hath strange power..."

She did not remove the blade as she spoke. "Do not believe you are safe. They hunt for you still, even if they know not where to begin. We all heard about the escape from Newgate. It surprised no one. The price on your head remains. So, I should ask...what's to stop me from turning you in for that bounty? A girl must eat, after all."

Mogue did his best not to swallow. Yet even here, with the prospect of death once more upon him, the wheels of his mind began to turn with ever greater velocity. "Turn me in, and you'll lose one of your best customers."

The blade remained at his throat, but he sensed a flicker of curiosity cross her face.

"Keep me as your secret," he went on, "and you needn't ever worry about a slow night or going hungry. The cash is good as far as I'm concerned. I'm willing to spend more'n this place than anywhere else. Any grief you get, some gurrier wanders in and tries hurtin' you or any of the others, I'll see they don't again. Ask any of the lads, or else just listen to the rumours. I'm quite nifty with a blade."

She was wavering, he could see. Likelihood was, she'd little need for protection, not if she was one of Peg's girls. In her young life, she'd heard all manner of shite and bollocks off the men she serviced. No doubt she'd had to draw her blade on a fair few of them; no doubt it was deserved every time. She was no slouch with a blade either, he sensed. So he was surprised when she warily lowered it. He made no move to approach or flee. She was searching his face, smoking out any lie or artifice written there. She'd be as versed in those as she was in music, he reckoned.

She put the knife away, placing it on the dresser, and turned back to him, looking at his chest now.

When she reached tentatively out to touch his scars, tracing over their crude outlines with her fingertip, he made no move to stop her.

"Like what you see?"

"How is it you have so many?"

"We all have scars. These are mine."

His tongue twined with hers; her breasts rose against him. He inhaled her, her scent flooding through him like an opiate of perfume and clean, fresh sweat. Her hands now slid up to her bodice and he couldn't help but watch hungrily as she undid the strings, and soon her clothes lay crumpled at their feet. Under her skirt, fine hair covered her legs and the soft, wet cave between her legs he knelt to explore, the hot saltiness of it spicing his tongue. She squirmed softly against him in the dark and let small gasps of pleasure as his caresses grew more ardent. Her hands tore through his hair, and he found he enjoyed even the pain of that, even the sting of tears it brought to his eyes.

Hardly a word was spoken afterward. She lay in his arms, and they cradled each other's slumber. Mogue had expected her to get up and leave, but she stayed instead, continuing to touch at his scars. Down below, the raucous roars of the bucks shouted up; yet beyond the window, the city was still.

"You're here because of him," she said, finally.

"Who?" he responded, his voice hoarse.

"Rob. He threaten you, or was it of yer own accord?"

She kissed his neck before awaiting a reply, and he was too lulled by the feeling of it to speak for a moment. She continued, "If he or any of his lads come here, there's always a new recruit. His reasons for bein' with them are never good. Many like you have passed through this place. Many more will again." She touched his temple, where the scar tissue of an old knife fight with the road thief had lingered.

Mogue said, "And could I not say the same about you?" Her eyes narrowed questioningly, but he pressed on. "Does anyone ever go into whoring of their own accord? We're all thieves here. You're as doomed to infamy as much as I. You've to make a living as much as I. Tell us, what song was it you were playing earlier? I liked it."

"Wasn't a song. It was a sonata. By Haydn."

"Who's that?"

"Perhaps if you come back another night, I'll tell you."

Chapter XX
Tannery Boy
Dublin

And so, the upstairs room of the bordello on Pitt Street became a regular and welcome haven for Mogue Trench. Beyond the stinking vats of the tan yard, it was a welcome thing to look forward to, the parlour's dim glow and notes from Maggie's clavichord falling languidly like leaves in a soft breeze, calming the drunken storm of cackling and hooting that raged and buffeted all around her.

For the music never stopped with Maggie Drake. It was both her solace and means of maintaining sanity. She performed in true style, indifferent to the candlelight and ribald shouts for something a little bawdier. But these were few and far between. Discretion, after all, was a principal attraction of Peg's, as much as the music and pleasurable company. Whatever wanton lives Mogue and the other patrons lived outside of Peg's, they left it at the door.

Hunched over the glossy pianoforte, face flushed with gargle and an exhilarated trance, the strings tweaked to clarity; she played and sang the unfinished oratorio like a card hand, melodic emulation, phrases of gloom hammering in slow movement, steeling the spine to satisfaction. And when she finished, and led the sullen tannery boy upstairs, when her legs were drawn tight around him, the applause she could have garnered would have been rapturous.

He was all hers and she all his, as long as the cash was right. She was kept now; his as long as he could afford her, or the one grew bored of the other. He did not expect he would anytime soon. Nor was there a fear of her walking out in the streets; she had no need for it. He'd leave her in the morning with a kiss and promise to have some new trinket for her by dusk. His blades clinked at his belt like armament as he trawled the streets. He had something like purpose again, someone to whom he wanted to give attention, the thought of whom carried him like a current through the working day and who, when he wasn't at Peg's, he could visit in his dreams. A woman to fight and kill and steal for, who made this cesspit of a city worth making a home in.

Flames smouldered his mind; they both knew what they were doing as he climbed atop her. She had little curiosity for his life as Joseph MacTíre's ward. Such things neither seemed to impress nor excite her, and so he did little enough boasting on that account. In the hour before dawn, he'd leave her to sleep, and he'd quietly sharpen his knives by the window, watching dawn crawl over the city beyond the sashes. He'd then leave, making for the tannery, his hands scrubbed and itching for work, and his head clear from the warm, dreamless sleep his orgasm never failed to induce.

Of course, he wasn't able to see her every night. On the nights he couldn't, he'd venture south of the Liffey and into the labyrinthine night-town hell, where the city's rags and bones gathered furtively under the hallowed, piss-damp walls of the cathedral in a perpetual witching hour. It was there, in the sloping lounger's paradise of the wine cellars that he met 'Grace', one of the molls who worked the quays. It was here he couldn't say who he was, and to his relief he found no one cared to know. The lamp-flow and river mist conspired to hide and warp every face there. He'd no worry for the pickpockets, sharing much of their stealth.

The girls there were scarred, frightened; many stared right through him as they lay together. He could have told them he was MacTíre's protégé; he could have claimed to be the Anti-Christ himself, come to collect their grim-coated souls. He suspected the reaction would have been the same, either way.

It was known that Constable Ivory and several of his cronies would amble up here after dark, ostensibly on police business. Being that far past the river held greater danger than Pitt Street. Neither Ivory for any of his Charleys dared venture out toward Peg's; there was far more satisfaction (and considerably less scandal) to be had in menacing the working girls north of the river beat.

Once they were seen striding up the lane, greatcoats flapping starkly in the glow like wings, the ponderous thump of their boots knocking off the cobbles, as urgent whispers of, "Here's Ivory. Run!" slithered through the night air. Brazzers and gougers alike scattered if and where they could – it was either run or take a beating. Fair means or foul meant fuck-all after dark.

Doors were kicked open and molls yanked from their beds by the hair. A truncheon glistened in the dark; the after-hours bellows and cries in the streets were legendary. Anyone who hit back was given a swift lesson in defence – the blows came down like hail on granite. It was doubtful any names were ever taken.

Ivory's lads were mostly joyless, punitive men sent up from the marshlands of nowhere, fueled by malice and an unholy loathing for Dublin's dirt. They held their vocation for roughing up half-starved drunks and urchins paramount; some even called it the Lord's work. If there were thugs in need of a hiding, there were decent skins on the steps of the main drag who felt their skulls crack under a nightstick's blunt swing.

The first few times it happened to Mogue, he marveled at the ease with which they left, their victims left lying and groaning like ragdolls. Then he saw Grace's face in smithereens that one night, fresh bruises glowering through the dark, her ribs broken as she tried to resume their transaction. She'd lost two teeth, and the sound of her quietly weeping as she fell asleep in his arms put him in mind for revenge.

Ofttimes he and Rob's boys stalked out as far as the Liffey and the docks, keeping close to the shadows, eyes peeled for any ships that had made berth that day along the reeking quaysides. There was never any shortage of loot to be had. They'd board surreptitiously, confident the vessel's crew had departed onto the town, and always ready to slit a watchman's throat, should they be discovered. Anything was fair game. There were ships from all over, and if they were lucky enough to survive the storms of Dublin Bay, you could be sure there were pickings galore. Anything Mogue Trench could lay his hands on, he took.

Rob kept a small skiff aground at the marshy flats off Usher's Island. At the rising of the dusk tides, his apprentices sallied upstream, under Marrows Bridge, scudding with rapids and dodging algae-smeared cutwaters, 'til the first shadows of the masts fell over them. They'd crawl up the heavy anchor chains, stealthy as rats; Cobbe usually kept a lookout. Mogue taught the others his trick of smearing his face in ash, imitating a skull and thus eliminating the necessity for cowls. On such excursions, they rarely wore boots, but went barefoot, so as not to give themselves away.

For Dublin was a city much given to thievery. Not for nothing were visitors told to gird their pockets on entering. Dublin: a city of workhorses and shit-speckled cobbles, the winter moon a fanged Peeping Tom. The Angelus clangs echoed adagio from St Patrick's, its operatic air heard from stable lane to quayside, the oil-smeared lamps and tavern sign, signalling a feral grin to the girls in doorways. Mogue's own tempest was in major and minor: hailstones gushed in slow harmony, sucks of sepia breath scraped the lung, an opium fantasia drew out the blade of borrowed time, patient tide.

Peg's remained closed during daytime hours, a shutter of black steel hinged firmly on varnished oak. The muse was having one of her off days, and there he was, humbled and raw, trying to face the music. Even a dram of cheap port would do him for the night, when Maggie had other clients to see. On such nights, with neither a fight nor a robbery to partake in he was unable to sleep without the aid of a whiskey bottle. Immune to the stink of self, with pockets emptied to sombre depths, he took to playing chess with his soul on such nights, lingering with far more care over the white pieces, and hastily putting forward the black. From this he took some solace.

But it was in the robbing of homes that Mogue found the most solace. Rarely had he broken into fine homes with MacTíre, but his natural acrobatic skills, alongside his knifework, were put to good use. They scaled the walls of the finer houses of the city and slipped through the backdoors. Noiselessly they crossed the landings, filling their pockets with whatever portable articles were near, and always with their boots off, treading with such stealth that the floorboards made nary a creak under their weight. The only noise that could be determined were those of the house's inhabitants, adrift in sleep and undisturbed. They forced back locks with their blades, which they honed to work as easily as keys. Papist or Protestant, it mattered little what they rifled through and took. Coin, chain-pockets, tankards, goblets, dishes, silver belt and shoe buckles – no article was too cumbersome. If ever he found a set of rosary beads, Mogue pocketed them immediately – a gift for Maggie was never unwelcome. And the lads had an ability to ensure they did not clatter in the canvas bag they carried. Mogue enjoyed these jobs the most, as they afforded him the opportunity to swipe more books and documents, anything to feed his famished mind.

The easiest of these operations, he soon discovered, could be carried out during wintertime, at the peak of the season, when hordes of young ladies and gentlemen of fashion perambulated up to the capital intent on carousing up at Dublin Castle or the Powerscourt townhouse with the sublime aim of surrendering themselves to all manner of pleasures their tenants could only dream of. Often during the daytime he saw them, lolling about Stephen's Green or near Anne's Church, in their white wigs and gowns of muslin and silk, brandishing silvertops and fluttering parasols against the sun. At night, he'd see more than several of the men, who presumably had shirked their attendance with some fumbling excuse or another, sauntering up toward Pitt Street, on a scuttered beeline for Peg's, their brocaded coats already stained with whiskey and sweat.

He gave them little thought except when and how they might be fleeced.

Of such people MacTíre would have dearly loved to rid the world. At night, Mogue knew the men who had evaded the temptations of Peg's lounged over their hands of faro at the gaming tables, the women awaited a dance in the cavernous ballroom, and Mogue Trench and his comrades slipped in the back, gliding lightly as ghosts through the mansion's backrooms, unheeded by host, guest, or guard. Their takings on such nights were ever plentiful, and always went well on the nether market.

On one such occasion, he had crept past a large room wherein several dozen bewigged ponces were sat. At the far end, a sextet was moving through a concerto by Bach, though he knew not what it was or even what they were doing. Yet Mogue found himself briefly halting in his tracks. The varnished sheen of the cello and violins, not to mention the strange, hypnotic hauteur of the notes being coaxed from the two harpsichords, and the stately, cavernous quiet of the audience seated the room in which the recital was held, put him in mind of a place where monks might convene for prayer and absolution.

For now, no psaltery, no trumpet, no zither, no rampage nor riot had a place there; no organ pipes trumpeted their parched tones. But once the cellos were plucked, the overture rose like smoke to the choir balcony and he imagined that a deaf god, eyes etched from lidless marble and earlobes of granite, would swagger to the rite and ritual of percussion. It was then that his ears were filled with nothing save the dismal throb of his own heartbeat. Was it a hymn to love, or the failure of it? He could not tell. The maestro was bowing to the wave of polite applause that now broke over him. Mogue Trench had stalked off down the corridor, suddenly mindful again of where he was. Never before had he heard that sound.

And his wonderment was indeed short-lived. During the interval, he imagined the overly mannered smiles were exchanged under sweat-damp wigs over glasses of shared Bordeaux.

Appearances were everything in places such as this. The cerebral glamour of the townhouse upheld a palatial silence that even Mogue knew better than to break. He prayed with a vehemence for the cultured talk to be drowned out by curses, blistering vows, cross-haired slurs on nation and name, and for the earnest veneer of civility to combust with rapid spontaneity, a cloud of ash sliding down every throat.

If Rob gave him a day off and he was at a loose end, he'd amble off toward Capel Street or College Green, and lose himself among the crowds. Often, with an instinct he wasn't sure was rooted in madness or curiosity, he'd steal out back to Newgate to watch the public hangings from above its grim entrance. Each time he shuffled away from that place while the body swung, grimly glad he had been spared such a fate.

He kept his head down out of habit, but soon realised there was little need for it. In Dublin, he was just another wag, on his way to somewhere. The city was no Nineveh, he knew, but it was big enough to hide in, especially if no one truly cared to know who you were. Interest in MacTíre's vanished ward soon faded, though the offer for his capture remained. He knew this, for few paid any mind to the young man in the sodden greatcoat, weaving his way through the streets, like a ship navigating shoals. In any case, the city was a hotbed of endless distraction for any man seeking to enkindle his mind or satisfy his loins. The library of Alexandria and Temple of Venus alike could share the same street address.

The streets wound and unwound dimly before him, the townhouse roofs seeming to soar like treetops over a forest path. Beggars and baronets alike shared the narrow warrens; citadels wrought from stone and granite crowded the docks of the gull-troubled Liffey, dwarfing the ships. These hulking colossi rose to such majestic heights, as if fashioned by the hands of a god; Customs House, with columns and domes looming in limestone defiance against the grey sky, seemed to Mogue's eye as splendorous as a Babylonian ziggurat or the pyramids at Giza.

But splendour, of course, inevitably stalked Dublin hand in hand with squalor. Dublin was never to be entirely civilized, Mogue sensed, yet this was no lamentable thing. There was life undeniable in every sharp corner and not even the most elevated cathedral or townhouse seemed free of the feverish and volatile churn of humanity roiling at their doorways. That she could be engulfed by flood, flame, famine, or fever at any given time only made her all the more precious to walk about and witness. The roiling stink of horse manure and rotgut whiskey and still-warm porter vomited over the cobbles converged with the sweet musks and attars oozing from the perfumers' shop. The clatter of dray and curricle-wheel and pot-pan vied with the hawkers and the street balladeers' tuneless puling and the jarveys whipping them out of the way as they trundled past, and all for dubious supremacy of the streets. Mogue was certain he had passed Mister Grattan himself one morning on College Green, striding briskly up the steps of the Parliament Building, his sable cloak brushing off the grime-heavy cobbles. He knew, on some fine level of abstraction, that compared to London, Paris, or Rome, Dublin was hardly a jewel in the Empire's circlet, her grandeur too stunted by far.

But the anonymity it bestowed on him was like being granted access to Paradise; rarely had he ever known such relief. Letting its noise swallow him, elicited oddly a calm in his blood he had only previously felt in the silence of MacTíre's hideaway. The daily storm and stress of Dublin, the millions of lives of book-standers, redcoats, navvies, coal-porters, councilmen, vendors, all on the way to somewhere, all in retreat from elsewhere.

He eyed the offerings that stood in tantalising display in the windows of China shops, chandlers, drapers, hosiers, jewellers, apothecaries, watchmakers, smiths in silver and gold, even the cattle-markets and their constant reek of blood, chophouses, all establishments of varying eminence; it mattered not that he could scarcely afford their wares. Simply stopping and surveying these menageries for a moment or two, noting down the contours of their craftsmanship and calculating when best to rob such an establishment, was priceless enough.

Often enough, he passed with a smirk by some of the finer houses he'd had a hand robbing. Trade was booming across all fronts by then. The deluge of gilt-covered tomes, newspapers, and pamphlets weighing down the shelves of booksellers all across the city was overwhelming. Always he sought out the shop off Grafton where Byrne, the sedition-minded sympathiser, plied his wares. The roughness of Mogue's appearance did not seem to see him turned away.

Men met there in the mornings, on the main coffee room on the first floor. Men of fashion, fortune, and condition, he saw, always sat in heated discussion over copious cups of coffee. As in the brothels, Mogue found no man was unwelcome, provided he paid his due. The debate was never ending; scores of aspiring poets and rhetoricians, dandies and revolutionaries, students of law and politics pored over the latest gazette reportage whilst dealing out an energised hand of cards and relighting pipes. They sampled the black, mud-like concoction Byrne served them from his cauldron like clovers plucked from the lotus tree.

News foreign and domestic was their preferred mode of discussion; they fed off these as much as the caffeinated loam in their cup. But no subject was too sacrosanct, no theory or incident off limits. Their discussion was sprinkled with quotes from Boethius, ostentatiously delivered in the original Latin and with the dramatic flare of an actor (a profession many of them, he noted, held in no large esteem). No doubt most deemed themselves as latter-day Plutarchs or Ciceros or Mirandolas; some clearly believed they inhabited a higher sphere of comprehension, untethered to the fog and over-trod filth of Dublin. Many still clung to quixotic notions regarding liberty and truth and justice. Notions of which Mogue had long since dispelled himself. It amazed him that men years older than he could still afford to be so full of shite.

Discerning the posers and prigs from the true-hearted nonetheless proved difficult, for they all spoke with the brash confidence of the cosmopolite. Conversation was the currency; as long as coffee could be brought, discussions would often enough escalate into virulent arguments. Losers and winners alike would challenge one another to a duel. Their bottomless pretensions to radicalism or to the cold glare of reason was undermined by their quickness of temper or a compulsive inability to admit to ever being in error.

Whatever their views, Mogue would have been happy to join them; but his natural reticence, and his lingering worry over being discovered kept his lips watchfully sealed. Was all MacTíre taught him for nothing? What good was his ability to read, to traverse the writings of so many august scribes, if he could not discuss them? But what words had he to say, really? To many of these pipe-smoking bucks, the life he'd lived was no doubt as fantastical and alien as a passage from Baron Munchausen. Instead, he sat where he was and sipped at his coffee, with the air of an audience. Some inner sense told him he truly belonged to this discussion, or what it might result in.

To Mogue's confusion, many uproariously called for the abolition of the very class to which they belonged, the perks of which enabled them to sit over a coffee all the livelong day at their arguments. If men lived in prosperity, he noted, it seemed they were little satisfied by it. A life of leisure merely increased a man's desire for action. The endless parade of engagements and balls could weary a man starved of adventure – restlessness across all classes seemed to scorch the air. From the chambers of Parliament to every dram-shop cellar to kerbstone, an efflorescence of insurrectionary fervour was spreading. Yet he doubted many of these pampered, chinless bucks had ever lifted a weapon in their lives, save to pink an innocent passer-by.

Genius and treason were also forged in such fiery discussions. Times were changing, it was becoming clear. It wasn't just Byrne's, but countless coffee houses citywide, that were packed with students, angry young men incited by the writings of Voltaire, Diderot, Locke, who argued without relent. Religion held no sway for them; the secular illumination of reason was their new god. And yet all this talk of enlightenment did little to burn away the myriad corners of shadow pervading the city.

God no longer held the interest of educated men, if ever he had before; the state of one's soul mattered little when it came to changing the state of a nation, or, for that, matter, an empire. Many hoped to see the weight of English influence dislodged at last.

And all the while, Mogue Trench sat and listened.

Chapter XXI
Dayſ of Ardour
Dublin, Onwardſ to 1798

After the battle of Ormonde Bridge, Mogue wandered off into the streets for a while, not caring about the blood on his shirttails. It was the city wanted Ivory dead, he decided, and so the city had set him alight. He could neither fight nor bribe his way out of being burnt alive; every skull he'd ever cracked, every moll he'd ever menaced, every penny of extortion cash he'd collected; all of it was kindling. He'd been stacking up that fuel for years; a single spark would have been enough.

By rights, Mogue knew it should have been him who lit the flame.

Yet that was that, also. There'd be another Ivory soon enough; his kind tended to sprout up with great rapidity, to the bloody bidding of others. It was force people feared, he realised; chaos only erupted when the threat of a baton breaking one's face in two no longer carried effectiveness. This morning had been proof of that.

After watching the flames smoulder out and seeing the body dumped in the Liffey, Mogue limped off towards College Green. News of the battle and the involvement of the Charleys must have already spread citywide – he couldn't tell if martial law was in place or not. Perhaps not, for the streets were as filled as they'd been that morning. Hawkers shouting and carriages clacking, as every morning could be. The seagulls were still squawking strong. The sun blazed down like an indictment; he had to shield his eyes.

He cared little now for getting arrested, even given the state he was in. The blood would wash off naturally, he kept telling himself. It always did.

Mogue decided against heading up to Grace and telling her his promise to her was settled. She'd find out eventually, in any case. Nor was he in the humour for heading over to Maggie, either. He wanted only solitude while he could get it. His vision blurred from red to black, like a magician's trick. As he moved back up College Green, more and more people showed themselves. Clearly the battle was of little consequence, even a stone's throw from the bridge.

Already, he imagined the bodies were being hauled off across the river to the Acre for mass dumping, to be interred in quicklime and oblivion. It'd be ages before they were done and dusted. The ones that weren't fished out of the Liffey would be left to drift downriver with the coal boats. It wouldn't matter which side they had fought for; they'd all be toppled upon each other from the carts. There'd be no memorial mass for any of them, Mogue was certain of it. Just as there hadn't been one for MacTíre. Just as there'd never be.

He was jolted from his thoughts by the sound of a man bellowing. He looked at the tall, greatcoated figure who stood at the foot of the statue of King Billy, flanked by two others dressed in dyed green tunics. All three wore scarlet Phrygian caps. His voice carried high through the square, over the hawkers and seagulls. A ragtag crowd were listening to him; most paid him no mind and carried on.

"The British government seeks to keep you at its mercy, now and forever! I share these streets with the very best of citizens, who know not themselves what they are! Centuries of wrong must not go unavenged, brethren! Which hand holds the olive branch, and which the dagger? Such a question must not even be considered. United Irish! There is courage in you, if only you would see it. They fear you, and so they should! They slander you, ridicule you, but know this: 'tis your very duty as Irish citizens to stand up against them! In the very shadow of the Parliament where they convene to quibble over the question of your liberty..."

The speaker was haggard and sallow of face; the scars on his hands told Mogue he was some class of labourer. He held his hand forward to shield his eyes from the sun's lazy glare. Every word spat from his steely mouth seemed to sizzle and convulse on the air. He carried on his oration as if preaching to thousands.

"Fuck off out of it, Tandy, yer past it!"

An off-duty jarvey shouted back. "Let the man speak, by Jaysus!"

"A notion of treason now, Tandy, that the fuckin' way of it?"

The man called Tandy ignored these shouts. He reminded Mogue of a preacher sprung from the Old Testament's more wrathful passages, crazed with revelation. The street was his pulpit, and like as not, he'd command its attention.

"They say I lack reason, that I have lost my mind completely! But I ask you, what is reasonable in allowing one's country to be subjugated to a foreign power? They will tell you we are prospering under the Empire. How are we prospering when men and women are daily left to starve in the streets? I ask you, fellow citizens, where lies the reason in allowing this to continue? Papist, Protestant, we are all children of Erin, ultimately. Be ye hoors for the Ascendancy? Be it known, then, division is the devil's stratagem, for he sows amongst all who would be united!"

It was precisely the sort of thing MacTíre would have scoffed at, and no different to what the bucks often fulminated about in Byrne's, but Mogue Trench could not deny the effectiveness of Tandy's delivery, nor his ability to brush off the hostility of his audience.

More were coming to listen to him. Mogue stayed where he was and watched for a while, impressed by how the man called Tandy was pelted with both horse shite and insults, yet did not cease in his execrations. He had as much support as scorn. He did not dodge when rotten fruit was chucked or even when his cap was knocked off. Mogue expected the Charleys to be on him any second now, but then he remembered most were still down at the bridge, searching for their dead and rounding up survivors for Newgate.

"Ireland is a prosperous nation, yet I guarantee many of your pockets this very instant are empty. Poverty unites, citizens, though it be used to divide ye!"

"He's fuckin' cracked, this fella."

"Ah, stop."

Mogue thought of Maggie, heard her singing at the base of his skull. He wanted to hear her really singing, and then head upstairs to her room for a while, watch her undress and then have her fall asleep in his arms. There were some hours yet before she started work, but he had little enough to pay her the night. Rob's tannery had shut down for the day, allowing it hadn't been raided yet. There was still dried blood crusting his face and coat, but blood had never bothered Maggie. A part of her seemed to like him visiting her while still trailing gore, though he doubted she'd ever admit it.

Finally, he moved on, not in especial direction, letting the sun burn slowly over him and Napper Tandy's thunderous voice boring through his ears.

*

And so it went.

The next few years were mad. Mogue Trench remained in trade, kept his head down, worked away in the tannery and hid out in Byrne's during the day and Pitt Street by night. Maggie received him with songs and warmth, and he fell asleep to her softly singing a ballad. They'd fuck and sleep and awake to the sound of the other girls waking and chucking their fellas out. After a day of silence, working the hides, only to Maggie Drake did he feel he could speak with anything like candour or plainness. He knew this, for she preferred he refer to her as a 'moll' in place of 'whore'. When he asked her if she was ashamed of her profession, she replied, "Not at all. But the word just likes me."

Maggie never chucked him out. A kiss goodbye was her preferred farewell gesture. He got what he paid for.

If she wanted to know anything of his life, she always seemed to know the right time to ask. She saw nothing romantic about him, nothing poetic or glamorous. His 'legend', whatever it was, was fading fast, but Maggie never cared much for such things, he came to learn with considerable relief. MacTíre was just another absurdity, she'd decided. His protégé would soon understand that, too. As history unfolded, his name and exploits would not be recorded, not even as a joke. The world was neither better nor worse for his death.

Such thoughts he kept under lock and key; Maggie need not know of them. They were not her concern, nor should they be. Braggadocio never impressed her, so there was little need to play any kind of role whenever he visited her. He knew she found him slightly absurd; the potential legend now reduced to tannery work, and he dependent on her for emotional upkeep. He told her his memories of his time with MacTíre were vague; he barely recalled how the knife felt when he held it, less so the faces of the men he'd killed. In truth, the less she knew, the better. Why subject her to pains he alone needed to be privy to? She was familiar enough with them already.

Yet this too was a lie. Shame stalked him like the wolves that Ireland no longer had. Grief had a way of ensuring ghosts remained alive. He had fought and killed but did so for no higher cause than his own survival. Often enough, he heard men say on their deathbeds that they had no regrets, but never once did he believe it. How could anyone truly live any kind of life devoid of regrets?

And yet he desired not general forgiveness nor a need to enter a state of penitence. He kept robbing houses with the Guerin lads and Cobbe, always finding more trinkets for her. They did so with such stealth, he found no joy, no excitement in it anymore. Rarely did he pay the newspapers any mind. They printed only lies, and sellable lies at that – why trust them at all? he eventually decided.

He found he was bored of it now, in the way only seasoned veterans of any profession were. The Charleys left the tannery alone for the most part. There were too few of them, and too much hostility for them to make any kind of effective arrest. The people of the Liberties tended to band together to protect their own; a Charley's truncheon was little against their solidarity.

Though he'd no true concept of home, Dublin slowly became one to him – albeit a home where Joseph MacTíre was long dead, and the hours seemed to be ticking down to some class of uprising. He stopped going to the executions for a while, though morbidity drew him back time and again to see the bodies swing before Newgate's doors. There were nights, when he was gripped by a feverishness that lack of sleep tended to bring, when he desired to quit the city, and ride back out to Wexford, visit the forest where the only family he had known was killed. He even thought of perhaps visiting Tintern, or the alehouse Gráinne had run, showing his face and relishing their fearful recognition. MacTíre did not even have the dignity of a grave; it was widely rumoured his body was burnt.

As the years crept by, he felt the legend of Joseph MacTíre slowly vanish from history. There was no romance or glamour about him, more an embarrassed silence. In time, Mogue's association with the road thief became less and less of a point of interest until it vanished entirely from all conversation. His workmates no longer asked wild questions; even Rob quite forgot his original fascination.

Yet Mogue had no desire to see the man commemorated, either. Not that he felt penitence for his criminal life – for without it, would he have learned the beauty of language and of bloodshed? There was no grand battle, no epic fight worthy of Miltonic stanzas – in short, nothing worthy of who he had been. Had he truly been a legend, why, then, was his legacy so short-lived? What had it all been for?

Certainly, the rumour that Joseph MacTíre transformed himself into a wolf was one of the more amusing stories about him. He was nothing that ordinary people needed or wanted in a hero. What else had he been if not one more knave awaiting the noose? There would have been no trial for him, just execution. He'd evinced brutality, rage, bloodlust, crime, representing nothing to which any man of decency ought to aspire. He had spoken like the brute he was (though he was known to have robbed books at every chance). He'd held no attraction for women, not even as a roguish outlaw. He'd fought neither for the cause of rebel or redcoat. He had no cause to speak of, save his own rage, his own desire to see the world in flames. Only those who lived and died for a cause beyond themselves were immortalised in the songs. For nation, for liberty, for the shite the over-indulged bucks above in Byrne's were never done blathering on about – all things Joseph MacTíre would readily have sneered at.

In other circumstances, he could have been the subject of a great rebel ballad, an outlaw hero who stole from the rich for the poor to be sated – though Mogue could see his former master's scarred lip twisting into a smirk at such an outcome. The man had died like the beast the world had believed him to be – before it lost all memory of him. Nor had there been any final words between them, not a goodbye or a good luck. MacTíre was the subject of a barrack-room melodrama or a lurid street ballad, at best; in fact, he was a monster best forgotten.

Mogue soon took to wandering Bully's Acre after dark, usually after watching a hanging. Some of the tombs there, he knew, went as far back as the founding of Dublin, to when Vikings first edged their ships upriver. The mass graves there, piled high with the anonymous damned, the extinct generations, the countless, nameless dead upon whom he trod, those who were not granted life as he had been. Was it merited, his survival? Why had he been pardoned the fate of so many? His own ingenuity? The workings of some higher being who wished to see him outlive all else?

It was only when he took up prize-fighting that he sensed such notions dispel, if only momentarily. The old excitement burned through him, now untethered to the worry of being arrested.

And a decent crowd could always be got for a decent bout. In the pit, for as many rounds as Mogue was able, it was only him and the other fella, locked in a vulcanised tournament of Olympian brawling, blood smoked in resilience, hissing flame through their teeth. No one else existed, not even the punters who formed a bellowing ring around them, cheering and dishing out wagers. He kept his eye fixed on his opponent, flashed a crimson grin at him as they circled each other in a murderous trance, until the distance was closed and the brawling kicked off. In the twenty or so seconds before the punches were thrown, he would know how the fight would finish up. Pinned against the ropes in the sixth round, only the clenched torrent of his fists helped him endure every minute before the bell clanged, ending the butchery. He needed just one sign, just one unwitting giveaway of fear or frailty. A downward averting of the eyes. Lips pressed tightly together. A sharp, sudden blink. A slight bobbing of the head. Even a crick of the neck. These were all signals for which he kept his eyes peeled, a chink in the pugilist amour he had only twenty seconds to detect before the bell sounded.

Mogue had not expected to live past fifteen; now he was throwing stiff jabs and wild body shots in the faces of men twice his age and bearing. The punters' roars, engulfing and porter-fuelled, faded to a murmur in his ears, both by now swollen to cauliflower-like abnormalities. He could not see their faces, their bloodthirst and admiration, the bookies and the slum socialites, the wealthier bastards who mixed with the lower orders like naturalists observing predators, all their palms itching with prospective cash.

If they were booing him or cheering his name, he could no longer tell after a while. The only sound he cared to hear was his fist's meaty crunch cannonading through a fella's solar plexus, or shattering his jaw beyond repair. He would stand over his opponent, torso glazed in sweat until he was sure the man was out. He threw his head back and spewed up his rage. He couldn't think of a finer way to stave off the ghostliness of his thoughts. He bared his teeth and spat gristle, savouring the taste of his own blood.

He bobbed hungrily, left shoulder hunched at his jaw, firing parries and power shots before meting out a stinging left hook to finish the job. Left hooks curved under jaws, swiping uppercuts ripped already-fermenting scars freshly open, and bruises the colour of burnt wine shelled eyelids. Nobody expected to see the way his fist would whirl, the way he would dodge and land blows with the roughest of stealth, the way he would tire his opponent with nimble curves of legwork, the way he would dance the brutal tango of a prize-fighter.

As he prowled across the ring, bobbing, weaving, his name was chanted and bellowed, ricocheting off the walls in crescendo. For Mogue, every bruise and cut became yet another blunted emblem of pride. The gong sounded, the body collapsed to the ground, the man milled into a coma. He made a point of letting the blood dry on his knuckles. Only then would Rob approach laughing and slap him on the back, overjoyed at the fresh revenue.

"Jacob didn't wrestle the angel, lads. He fought it bare-knuckle, wha'!" he'd shout. It became a welcome substitute for stabbing lads on bridges. His natural stealth served him well. With his guard up, a bout could last from dawn 'til dusk.

In the dread month of February, when Dublin was smothered in snow, Astley's Amphitheatre thrummed with the heat of nearly a thousand punters clustered ringside, already brimful with porter and rotgut whiskey, thunderously chanting the name of Daniel Mendoza, the English champion pugilist. The sweat oozed from Mogue's brow as he took his place, Rob beside him.

"Greatest Jew-man ever to have lived!" the latter bellowed jovially, nodding up at the gracile, sable-haired mauler with the scornfully knitted brow, who paced about his corner like a caged beast.

"Here, wasn't Christ himself a Jew-man?" Mogue shouted back, barely hiding a smirk.

"Wha'? Fuck off outta tha'. *So fight I, not as one that beateth the air*! Up Mendoza! The Lightnin' of Israel strikes fuckin' fast!"

The Lightning of Israel, Mogue thought. Mendoza's nickname. *Nearly as good as the Wolf of Wexford. Nearly.*

Only the hangings outside Newgate attracted this much of a crowd. The auditorium seemed to shudder with the din. Mendoza's opponent, a lanky middleweight named Fitzgerald who, according to the handbill, was also a butcher and a foot taller than the Hebrew contender, adopted a brawler's stance and tried apeing his opponent's fretful pace. Mendoza stared him down, despite having to look up, murderous intent electrifying his movements.

Glancing around, Mogue hadn't been able to make out any faces through the haze, though it was rumoured the Duke of Leinster himself was in attendance. Nor could he even hear any individual voices; they all melted into a single, savage choir howling for blood. At last, to a frenzied volley of applause, Mendoza and his opponent stepped into the ring. The former waved impishly at the crowd before adopting a fighting stance. The Lightning of Israel's eyebrows creased into a mercenary furrow; his punches seemed to erupt from thin air as he began circling his opponent.

In a way, it wasn't him or his opponent's name that brought the punters in, but the sight and smell of blood – and perhaps only that. Allegiances could easily shift to whoever hit the hardest and fastest. Either way, Mendoza would give them a fight to remember, just as he always did. Mogue envisioned himself adopting a slugger's stance in the opposite corner, raising his fists and striking at the Jew-man with viper-like stealth. He would have no need for blades; Mendoza was an opponent not easily beaten and therefore worthy of his fists.

The fight was long but never dull. Each round finished only when one of the gladiators hit the floor. It ended when Mendoza, breathless, half-stupefied and his knuckles crusted in blood, finally caught his opponent square in the jaw by way of a thunderous left; the man crashed to the wooden floor, his mauled ribs cracked beyond repair.

Afterward, Mogue and Rob collected their winnings; odds had been in the Lightning of Israel's favour, as they'd known it would be. They retired to Pitt Street and got roaring drunk on the proceeds; Maggie woke up pleasantly sore and forty crowns richer the next morning.

And so the years passed. Mogue boxed, collected winnings, returned whenever he was able. His fights were in high demand; they called him the Liberties Wolfhound. Yet he kept to himself. From all people, he felt at a cold remove. He was too close to things in the city to ever return to the forest. There would always be another fight, another job. Whenever he saw trees or the ferny canal bank, unshaven with yellowed reeds, or inhaled a mouthful of river air on his nightly strolls, he imagined the banks of the river that spilled through Tintern, saw the moon hanging fang-like above the abbey's battlements, saw MacTíre's dangerous smile as he took aim with his weapon. He decided ultimately against ever going back, for what good would it do? The forest had nothing but ghosts now; it was best to leave them be. By and by, Maggie asked him about it often, about the crimes he'd committed, his learning to read in the cave, the men killed and the intoxicating rage of MacTíre. A part of her wondered if he regretted the killings. He always said no. In survival, as she knew well, morality was not so easy to uphold.

The years did not pass peaceably. The entire realm now smouldered with a new ardour for radical insurrection. The daily fulminations in Byrne's now took on a determined, more seditious air. The revolution in Paris reigned over every conversation. Some were horrified, others invigorated by the toppling of the French crown. Some of the bucks had only recently returned from Paris and claimed to have witnessed King Louis' beheading. Many both feared and hoped for a French invasion. Others claimed to have fought in the colonies, and so knew in what uncharted direction the political winds blew.

Yet it was somehow unimaginable that a rebel army would conquer, let alone march on the city. Skirmishes and battles in the country between Defenders and loyalists were read with the distracted curiosity of the untouched. The spectacles of shootings, burnings, cattle houghings, and the seizures of caches of weaponry were dismissed as primitive peasant antics at first. It was a distant thing, a storm on the horizon, one likely to wear itself out before it made landfall. Mogue Trench placed little stock in such a thought.

The man called Tandy led a small army of pikers in a night-time parade honouring the storming of the Bastille. Pamphlets penned by the man known as Wolfe Tone, espousing the wild French principles of liberty, equality, and fraternity, and calling Catholics into the fold, were circulated from Byrne's before being systematically banned. Mogue remembered their meetings in Back Lane, urging the need for Ireland to be reborn as a republic. The shock at this 'Back Lane Parliament', that no distinction lay between men of opposing faiths if they fell under the appellation of Irish, was unprecedented. The sovereignty of Grattan's parliament deemed itself under threat; debates raged daily in the chambers. The Catholic Committee were doing their best, but the House of Commons vetoed their every move for papal citizenship. Diehards and dissidents spat murderous invective from the upper tiers; Sir Vesey Colclough died, or so the *Freeman* reported.

The shadow of war spread across the realm. Houses were burned and their occupants arrested *en masse*. The United Irishmen found themselves outlawed, just as they reinvented themselves as a military outfit; soon anyone even suspected of membership was subject to arrest. The gaols overflowed with alleged rebels-in-waiting; Newgate's loathsome cells were fit to bursting. Corpses swung from its scaffold like menagerie apes; Mogue could not help but think that the government were hoping for widespread rebellion to erupt throughout Ireland.

The following year the Orange Order, with the aid of the Yeomanry, began setting houses alight. Protestant clergymen enjoined their flocks to drub any Papist scum they should come across. Wanton debasement of civilians was rampant. Wolfe Tone fled to Philadelphia and soon reached out to Paris, hoping to enlist French aid in the fight against the Crown; and indeed, French warships were eventually sighted in the foggy harbour of Bantry Bay, just off Cork. Dublin's streets remained restless and abuzz with activity of lord and labourer alike. It was only after the French vessels were dispersed by inclement winds that this hope, too, died down.

The true horror of it was slower in arriving, however. A rebellion was soon planned in full effect. General Lake, dragooner-in-chief, was put in charge of Irish military affairs, after his predecessor Abercromby resigned in disgust over the soldiery's overall conduct. Far from being cowed, many Irish were quite happy to take up pikes. A second French landing was deemed imminent. In Dublin, the militiamen and local yeos were billeted freely, more or less the new lords of the streets, their blood-toned uniforms and sabres ever at the ready as they lounged at their stations. Paul Cobbe took up their oath as a freeman and was soon wearing the uniform, carrying out the pitchcappings with ferocious glee. As regular troops were moved off, the guardhouses were often attended by the strangulated screams of men being pitchcapped.

The militiamen took great pleasure in this, whipping the poor bastards first before forcing a cap besmeared with pitch over their skull. They were seen wandering the streets, these pitch men; their flesh and hair ripped clean from their skulls, blinded and blistered, from where the cap had been wrenched off. Many died in the streets, howling blindly for mercy.

Even then, many clung to the belief that there was no more danger of a rebellion, that the spark of widespread insurrection would be doused long before it could be lit.

The spring of the year 1798 was scorching. By then, it was not the laws of men that governed, but the draconian rule of soldiers and the hanging judges that prevailed across the land. Restraint was scarce. After Bantry, rebellion was soon bound to happen, with or without French aid.

On the night of Lord Fitzgerald's arrest, Mogue Trench had been walking down Bridge Street. Martial law would soon be in effect; anyone of a peaceable disposition was confined to their homes.

Because he was used to walking at night, it took a moment before the sheer, numbing silence of the surrounding lanes and alleys to become clear to him. Only in the very early mornings had Mogue known the streets to be as deserted as they were now. The quays, the lanes; no footfall or dray-wheel to be heard. He remembered stopping in his stride, having forgotten where he was headed. The air was closer than it usually was; a feint whiff of smoke was on it; he had to remind himself the sun was blazing down.

He heard the footsteps, the frenzied voices. He barely the saw the scabrous crimson blur of the uniforms as they hurtled from every available alleyway. He neither sensed nor saw the rifle stock as it cracked horribly against his jaw. He certainly didn't see the cobbles as he crumbled against them, nor the sudden darkening of the sky.

All he heard was Maggie's voice, working her way through an aria.

*

Those who were brought before the presence of Chief Justice John Toler, the 1st Lord of Norbury, in his capacity as magistrate, could not easily forget him, and thoroughly could not help but loathe him. The imperious drill of his eye, his ruddy hatchet face glowering at the defendant as they made their claim, his voice clear with actorly pretensions – his courtroom tended to be packed to bursting, given his ententainment value. Loathed as he was by most Dubliners, none denied he knew how to give a hearty performance from the bench. His name invited much cheerful invective, for Norbury was an inveterate and enthusiastic member of that dubiously esteemed class known as the 'hanging judges'. Men hung in their droves at his whim, though it was well known he sentenced lads to death for far more miniscule crimes – shearing sheep, or sleeping rough. With Lord Norbury, it was said with a bitter grin, all life hung in the balance.

Of course, Mogue Trench knew his name as well as any – much of his comrades among the Liberty Boys had fallen foul of Norbury's desultory whim. He was still groggy from the hit he had taken, and so his perception of his surroundings was clouded. On seeing the judge, however, he fancied the man had been imbibing – the drunkard's ruddy exuberance blazed clear beneath his wig.

"And this reprobate who stands before me – what is he charged with?"

"Conspiracy to commit treasonous acts against the realm, your worship," replied the nearest Charley.

"Yet another dissident? Tell me, why can't these miscreants be more imaginative in their nefariousness, pray?"

The Charley seemed at a loss as to how to respond. Before he could, however, Norbury continued, his reptilian gaze trained on Mogue.

"You, boy – plead you guilty to these charges? I see by your jib your allegiance falls with the United Irishmen."

Mogue kept his silence – while he knew few enough judges, instinct told him no response would fall in his favour. Whatever it was he stood accused of, he was in the dock at last – and for a crime, a feeling in his waters told him, he hadn't committed. But Norbury required an answer.

"Sir…I am but a tailor –"

"Lies and more damned lies! Wilt thou ever be a foul-mouth'd and calumnious knave?"

The spittle from Norbury's mouth splashed just short of the bench. "As of today, we are under martial law, unless the news has yet to reach you. With that in mind, what exactly were you doing on Bridge Street?

Many arrests have been made of this day. What did you think your being out of doors would incur?"

"I merely thought it was a day like any other, sir."

"News of a mass uprising against His Majesty's rule have been widespread for months. Can you claim any ignorance of this?"

"If it please your worship, I was aware of it, but I deemed it to be merely the usual to-and-fro of gossip-mongers –"

"You are not only a slipshod rebel, but a poor excuse for a liar. Truly, and I must address the entire court as much as yourself, master miscreant, Milton would have it better than I:

Wolves shall succeed for teachers, grievous wolves,
Who all the holy mysteries of Heaven
To their own vile advantages shall turn
Of lucre and ambition, and the truth
With superstitions and traditions taint,
Left only in those written records pure,
Thought not but by the spirit understood –"

"Sacred." Mogue Trench's voice cut through his oration like a blade.

For a brief moment, silence reigned in the court. Norbury's face was a study of imperium in shock, though whether from the interruption, the contradiction, or that it came from a member of the lower orders, it was difficult to say. He angled his bifocals, his voice dangerously low.

"Beg pardon?"

"Sir, you were in error when you quoted Milton there. You said 'all the holy mysteries of heaven'. You should have said 'all the *sacred* mysteries of heaven'.

"Do you presume to challenge me, young sir?"

"No, your worship – it's just you misquoted Milton. I know the piece – Paradise Lost, Book 12, lines 509-14. Remarkable poem, your worship will surely agree."

"Hang him."

The galleries erupted; even some of the bailiffs present, Mogue saw, exchanged dubious glances.

"Hang this rapscallion from the neck 'til he is dead! Must I do all things myself?"

The rebellion in Ireland was underway soon enough. Men were hanged with indiscriminate regularity; Norbury presided over most of their cases. Guilty or innocent, many of those who fell under his gavel were seen to weep, plead, bargain, even soil themselves when the sentence was passed. But everyone present in Norbury's court that day in March 1798, agreed it was an entertaining trial, and Norbury's aplomb was in its usual steady supply. None quite forgot, however, the calmness which attended the young defendant as he was hauled from the dock and led to the antechambers, a look of strange beatification marking his features as the door shut behind him. There was no outcry, no feverish protestations of innocence, no pleading.

Epilogue
Dublin, 1798

Alone, crammed in his cell, Mogue Trench expected no visitors, and received none. He did, however, receive regular updates on the goings-on in the outside world courtesy of Quigley, one of the young turnkeys who brought him his bread and water. In the months between his sentence and hanging, rebellion had indeed broken out. The fighting was at its fiercest in Wexford, apparently, with battles between rebels and redcoats an almost daily occurrence. Battles increased with the months; martial law was imposed upon Dublin with immediate effect. Of all the crimes Mogue Trench could claim to be guilty, it was the one he did not commit that sent him to Newgate, and to his death. It was an irony Joseph MacTíre would have appreciated.

He thought not of Maggie, nor Rob, nor even Grace. There was no one to miss anymore, nobody to hanker for. He was alone at last, in this dank grotto of damp and filth, only his gnarled thoughts and the reek of his own piss and shite for company.

He awoke in the dark and struggled to remember his dreams. In the cell, he was brought back to the forest with MacTíre, his blades at the ready. The forest didn't wait for him, ready to shelter him in the expanse of its pinery. 'Twas a lawless tapestry of branches and leaning trees; its overhead foliage so thick that not a shaving of light cut through. It was nothing like Dublin, and Mogue knew not if this was pleasing. Dublin's light was the brassy amber glow of streetlamps, but at least it was light. In the forest, shadows leapt and stacked upon one another, and were it not for his timepiece, Mogue would never have known when to sleep or rise.

For all his literacy, he couldn't imagine a poet waxing lyrical about its tousled mud passages, its grottos teeming with insects, the long curtains of shadow thrown by its fallen trees. It didn't care about travellers, or even the small army of lumberjacks who invaded every six months armed with axes and rusty saws. No roads ran through it, not even dirt tracks paved by hikers or keen nature aficionados. It hadn't been tamed into a nature trail or a bird sanctuary; he hoped it remained wildly tangled, a green beast with a boggy stomach, a leaved cathedral with pillars and minarets of oak and evergreen. It was said that even the redcoats let it be.

There was no way of knowing day or night. The trees were bleached white and gnarled. They were trimmed by encroaching autumn, like javelins. Leaves guttered on branches, mauled by a sharp wind. It was an autumn that burned slowly, simmering the summer's tail-end, its invasion a slow parade of greying skies and ever more feverish rain. The floor of the place may well have been a museum piece for the kaleidoscope of dirty colour. Instead of his cell, he lay on a bed of soil, the insects mistaken him for a corpse. The soil was kicked up and bumpy, like dark pixels. It looked scorched. There was no birdsong, no dark rustling of coppice, no wolves to range its intricacies, even the wind seemed to hold its breath. Not a tinge of life could be detected. But he could smell a sour tang of smoke.

Mogue was fond of the silence, normally. But as he stood and the cold stone of the cell snaked up through his limbs, he sensed the deadly weight closing in — a daunting, incalculable calm. The forest was an immense edifice, its brick-and-mortar shade and hush. A metallic torch was slung from his belt, and he thrust its glare about him, momentarily breaking up the shade. He had always been reluctant to move, to flout the calm. Only tiny thickets offered an escape.

But as the months leading to his execution ticked down, he struggled to remember his dreams. Some jungle impulse, long buried, had revealed itself in that forest and had never left him since MacTíre's death. It wasn't fear, as such – more stealth. If he lay on his back, and ignored the dank flint kissing his ribs, he soon found he could imagine the sky, far above the city and the morass of treetops that snarled his thoughts.

There was no question of him being moved to a new cell. Of his own death, he worried little. Its very inevitability was almost a consolation, and there was a sort of peace in knowing exactly how one's demise would come about.

Soon enough, he would hang, regardless of culpability. Soon enough, he would join the legions of condemned, guilty and innocent alike, who were dragged into the square before a mob of serfs howling mockery and execration like blighted fruit, a cordon of Charleys keeping them separate, who climbed the scaffold and were finally left to swing. He had seen enough of the hangings beyond the walls of Newgate to know that many people had the stomach for it – craved the spectacle, in fact. For every man who was violently sick at the sight of a corpse jerking violently before calming, there were a hundred more who cheered at the sight. There was no right or wrong in either reaction, Mogue reasoned. Every man had his limits. He knew his own extended far beyond the sight of a carcass left to rot.

And through all of this, not once he did he find himself wishing to escape, nor fretting over fanciful notions of it, nor even of being released at the final moment. The machine of justice must keep inexorably turning, and whatever fuel was necessary to see that process through, so be it. The law needed its victims as much he and MacTíre had once needed theirs. It slaked that need with the blood of condemned men, the truth and severity of their crimes be damned.

He had never wanted to encounter predators, but whenever he did, he vowed to be ready, whether the moment required him to fight or flee. Now the law itself was a predator, a wolf demanding eternal satisfaction for its bloated cravings. His own mouth was shut, but behind it his jaws were flexed. The sharp rustling of leaves, as his boots kicked them up, didn't provoke anything. He let out a breath, realising he'd no clue where he was going, to what trackless void the law intended on sending him to.

What an ignominious end to be faced with! His ears were pricked for the chime of church bells. But the cell walls sanctioned no sound. The months of silence and virtually no contact from the outside world soon made him doubt he was anywhere near the high road, or even within reach of the city. Allowing that he was still in Ireland, and he was almost positive he was, he imagined he was out in the central plain. He could be imprisoned on some farmer's land, and therefore a trespasser and likely to be shot if discovered. No witnesses or defenders would see him cut down. His mind was a flat calm of thoughtlessness one hour, a storm of questions the next. Would he be dragged from this place, or carried on someone's shoulders?

He had some meagre blessings to count – he was alive, able to walk, as well as see and hear everything. Despite the shadows, a new clarity seeped over him, not just in his sight, but also in his gut. His mouth tasted salty, and because he often woke in a foetal position, his posture was badly curved. These were the facts he could confront, the facts didn't frighten him, much as the forest had never frightened him.

The thought of Joseph's exact whereabouts was one he could never quite withstand. Did the road thief survive the bullets, or the mauling that took him? Mogue tried pushing such infectious thoughts of shallow graves and his friend's open-eyed corpse from his mind; yet for all the years that had passed, these were the thoughts he'd never been able to evict.

He did not remember if MacTíre had yearned for salvation; there was plenty he could be accused of, yet he had moved like a man unfreighted by guilt. He was rightly suspected of the worst crimes in the land. Assault and battery were his gifts, murder even more so. Mogue often mistook himself as the impotent, awkward lackey next to the road thief's full-blooded stature. Perhaps he was simply better at keeping his crimes under wraps; MacTíre flaunted his without shame or remorse.

Mogue received but one visitor, and this the day before his hanging. He did not expect her, though on learning her name, he was not surprised. He had been thinking of Maggie, for the first time in a long while. He had not heard from her, not even a letter. And why should he? It was probably assumed he were dead, if thoughts of him crossed anyone's mind at all since his arrest. Was she alive, still? Did she carry on servicing wealthy miscreants who darkened Peg's door? Such thoughts reigned supreme. So much so, that he did not hear the footsteps advancing down the corridor, only the harsh clank of the key rattling in the lock. It was almost as loud as the cell door groaning open for the first time in months, before a woman's voice, icy and authoritative, came to him in the echoey dark.

"Leave us."

He heard her enter, though the darkness ensured he could not quite see her as she approached, the hem of her skirt brushing off the rough, cold stone. The turnkey had handed her a torch, and Mogue found himself blinking painfully before the dim light revealed a well-kept lady, swathed in a black round gown, and she seemingly unmoved by the filth of the cell or the bedraggled sight of the prisoner before her, who sat slouched against the wall to which he was shackled.

Under her arm she carried a large leather-bound sketchpad. She placed the torch to one side, the pool of light flickering over her features. Mogue, a bearded scarecrow by now, could not read her and found he didn't much care to. Whatever the nature of this visit, instinct told him it wasn't friendly.

"Don't be alarmed. Know you me?" she inquired. She placed the torch into a nearby sconce on the wall opposite him; it seemed to flicker in mid-air.

He did not respond, merely gawked at her. Though he was enchained, she sat opposite him at a good distance, placing the pad on her lap. Her dark eyes scanned his face, caked in the cell's accumulated filth, as if memorising it. As if he were a strange and curious specimen, the last of a species verging on extinction. A predator humanity simply could not abide to let live. Carefully, slowly, almost as if by magic, she produced a small charcoal pencil, and rolled back her sleeves.

"Most men in your position know me eventually. And, because of me, the world eventually knows them. I am Elizabeth Sugrue, of Roscommon. Tell me, have you any remorse?"

The charcoal scratched along the parchment, her hand moving in deft, seasoned strokes. They were strong hands, he could see, sinewy yet manicured. She gazed at him over the rim of the pad every so often, noting the haggardness of his features: his eyes' bloodshot glare, the matted twist of his beard, his shoulders' swarthy crouch.

"Remorse for what?" Mogue's voice, after months of not speaking, was little more than a dry croak in his ears. He sat up a little straighter, inclining against the wall, the shackles that held him clanking from the movement, as if in protest.

She ceased her etching and eyed him. "Your part in the rebellion. Treason against your King and so forth."

"'Fraid I don't know what you mean."

The woman called Sugrue looked down and resumed sketching, her hands moving assuredly. "The rebellion was over before it began, really," she said, after a time. She sounded weary, as if she'd explained this many times over. "Its leaders have been rounded up; just like you, they have faced Toler's gavel. I've drawn many of them already. You've missed the worst of it. The battles, the burnings. It surprises me not a whit they allowed you to rot so ignominiously here. I was determined to see you rendered, nonetheless."

"Why?"

One hand reached out to smooth her skirt, eyes never faltering from the pad. "'Tis a small pastime of mine, albeit one I've come to make a good living off. If you're anything like the others, you'll go to your death with little fuss. It's one of the better qualities the Irish can boast – a ready acceptance of doom."

"This..." Mogue broke off, frowning at his sudden lack of eloquence. He found himself avoiding eye contact he as murmured, "This is...habitual for you?"

She nodded, a frown gathering on her brow. "More than habitual – I make a decent wage from it. Death is profitable – as I'm sure you'll agree. People adore seeing the likenesses of those they hate and fear rendered by mine own hand. Right now, you can count yourself amongst that exalted class."

"And you do this without regret?" His attention was now drawn to the sketch she drew. He suspected he would not see it, even on its completion. He cared not; MacTíre had seen his own warped likeness often enough on posters calling for his death. Mogue imagined the

Sugrue woman drew him instead as a beast, a reprobate worthy of the death awaiting him.

"None whatsoever. There is profit to be reaped, even from a man's doom. One needed merely have the stomach for it."

"Which, fortunately, you have."

A querulous sigh followed this. "It isn't quite the same as offering absolution, I grant you, but there is much to be read from a man's face in his last few hours on this earth. Be assured, when you and those men are left to swing, your deaths shall usher in a new epoch for this place. 'Tis on everyone's tongue; the fever of galvanised insurgency may well be struck into the hearts of many. Many more than who probably cared to take up arms before. Once they watch you die, do not mistake their cheers for rejoicement."

All of this was spoken with an indifference that perturbed him; Sugrue's eyes gave nothing away. Not concern, pity, nor even an attempt at reassurance; though he'd have spat in her face if she had offered such. Her voice was low, tinged with forewarning and a hint of some deadly truth only she perhaps could disclose. "From the ashes of your death, a new flame shall spring. It will give no brightness, though. Only fury. Fury and blood and what's more –"

He cut her off, the base of his skull now resting against the stone. "Save your breath. Sermons are no use here. Not within these four walls. The suffering they have contained – I doubt you could even comprehend it." He imagined she was taken aback by his interruption. The conceit of her bearing told him she was used to holding court. He heard the scuffing cease for a moment. When she spoke again, he knew a blistering glare crossed her features and her lips were set indignantly tight.

"Young Man, I have hung men in your position. Many of them were kept in this very cell before God called them. They were so wretched, many were desperate to believe my sex would somehow soften the severity of the act. They were, of course, all mistaken. I know not what you imagine awaits you tomorrow, but it will certainly not be what you expect. Death is your companion; your entire incorrigible life has seen to that. Always by your side, always ready to take your victims and those who would hunt you. But now, it finally intends to greet you, with no fanfare. You'll slip from this life into the next in a matter of seconds. If you've never known fear or doom, you will know them now."

"I've been doomed for years."

The ghost of a smile crossed her features as she leaned forward. "I can imagine. Though you do me a fine service in keeping still."

"Have I any other choice?"

Her smile widened; it was not completely glacial. "I've often wondered if good and evil are inscribed in the faces of all men. Do you pray for salvation?"

"I pray for fuck-all."

"I suspected so. You've led a full life of iniquity, I'm well aware. A noose is the best destination for men such as you."

He eyed her dully. He shifted his back a little, letting the stone press against his ribs. She carried on sketching a while longer; the expression of concentration she wore told him not to interrupt. But a strange curiosity for something she said now had him. "What of the rebellion? What happened?" he asked in a low voice.

"Routed. At Vinegar Hill, in Wexford. As many suspected it would be. The ones that weren't killed will be hung for treason, like you. The rest will be shipped off to the colonies, I expect. Eternity awaits you."

"And I hope to embrace it."

She carried on drawing, closing one eye and then the other. The soft scuff of the nib was oddly soothing, to the point of being soporific. Mogue Trench found himself drifting into sleep. When he awoke, he was alone once more in the cell.

He never saw the sketch that Elizabeth Sugrue drew of him.

*

Dublin remained quiet in October of 1798, not from peace but from the qualmish calm that follows the cessation of prolonged violence. For many, the rebellion remained too fresh in people's minds to even be spoken of. The countryside was neither asleep nor awake. Many feared stepping out of doors, and resentment pervaded the air like gunsmoke.

After everything that occurred that summer, Mogue was amazed the city itself was no longer burning. Many of the rebels who conspired to see Ireland liberated against the full weight of the redcoat army had long since surrendered to the flame or the noose. Ireland would be unyoked from the King's rule, they sword; and they swore too that they would perish in their attempts to see her delivered. The nobility of the cause far outweighed the bitterness of the terms. Of course, chances of their success had been bleak from the start. The failure they had reaped was now felt everywhere.

It was an outcome Joseph MacTíre would readily have smirked at.

Hardly a patch of Ireland was unscathed by blood and rapine. Corpses lay buried or abandoned where flowers were noted to grow. There were rumours of small pockets of resistance remaining, rebels on the run in Wicklow and Wexford, and across the midlands, marching on foot through rocky *bóithrín* and crouching at the heel of every hill, hoping to ambush Crown forces and torching barns. Smoke rings drifted and stretched over dew-rinsed hectares. Gunfire spurted from behind tufts of furze; some said martyrdom was too good for them.

Mogue Trench stood beneath the noose and knew he was no martyr, despite what the Sugrue woman may have told him. All the eddies and maelstroms of the crucible of his past, he knew, had been distilled to this very moment. Just as all the truculent palaver of freedom in the coffeehouses had led to the man called Wolfe Tone scuttled in the bay. If Mogue Trench held firm to anything now, it was to the notion that a different kind of freedom awaited him – a freedom attainable only by death, the freedom from existence, from its sundry burdens, its very impermanence. What awaited him after the noose concerned him little; only that he was at liberty from life at last.

He would be hung, his body left to swing over the city walls with the sinking of the sun. Were MacTíre here, he perhaps would be scheming an escape; would perhaps have absconded from the grimy prison walls long before now. He did not wish to be saved; many in the crowd noted his sheer indifference to where he was. He no longer had the capacity for tears, for screams, for a rousing farewell speech to be put forever on the record. The future held no place for him. When the noose stretched, his spirit would have long since hurdled over the walls.

Rob was somewhere in the crowd, though Mogue could not see him. Maggie and a few of the molls perhaps, clad in their finest. No one knew his face. He was just one rebel, doomed to a noose. There was little point he felt in correcting the record or imagining how else it could have gone.

The noose would be tightened, the trap door would empty beneath him, his neck would snap. Some in the crowd would look away, others would cheer. He'd dance his final dance by the greying light.

> *Besides what the grim wolf with privy paw*
> *Daily devours apace and nothing said;*
> *But that two-handed engine at the door*
> *Stands ready to smite once, and smite no more.*

Milton's words were with him. In the quiet of the gallows yard, Mogue Trench looked up as the noose was tightened and saw the sky, already set to darken, as the thunk of the hangman's boots approached behind him. He took a final breath and waited to fall into eternity.

"Farewell, old friend," he murmured. "Farewell forever."

Deireadh

Author'ſ Afterword

'Pray you, no more of this, 'tis like the howling of Irish wolves against the moon.'
Shakespeare, *As You Like It*, Act V, Scene II

It never fails to fascinate me how divergent a final book can be from the initial idea from which it originated. For me, it's one of the more enjoyable aspects of the writing life, watching an idea steadily grow and emerge into something greater. Having spent much of 2020 and '21 researching and working on *A Land Without Wolves* – lockdown and strenuous quarantine measures afforded me a rare opportunity to write with greater abandon than ever before – it would be remiss of me to say that it emerged fully formed.

If it began anywhere, it was on the Hook Peninsula, in the southern tip of Wexford. As a child and a teenager, during the height of the Celtic Tiger years, I spent my summers on that sea-lashed headland, strolling its various shingled beaches and letting my imagination run wild. It was and remains a beguiling place, with sun-drenched fields and dotted by a plethora of medieval ruins, once-proud abbeys and long-abandoned drystone cottages. Salty breezes kept me alert, shadows lengthened in the evening as the sun slowly sank out of sight. Perhaps it was my imagination, but I sensed a change in the place after dark. There was a tranquility, undeniably, but an eeriness as well. The continual flash of the Hook Lighthouse, allegedly the oldest lighthouse in Europe, stabbing through the dark, swift as a bird of prey, was an unnerving sight. Not too far from where I stayed was Loftus Hall, the Georgian mansion reputedly haunted by the devil himself; a bit further up the coast was Baginbun, the landing site of Norman invaders in the 1200s.

Above all, the most compelling place to venture into was Tintern Forest, a great tangled woodland which straddles the Bannow river as it tapers inland, and which also makes several appearances in *A Land Without Wolves*. Exploring its many winding overgrown trails, I was both intrigued and frightened by how beautifully untamed it was. On a summer's day, rays of sunlight pierced luminously down through the ivy, lending the place an enchantingly lush atmosphere. But after dark, especially on moonless evenings, regardless of the season, it became a haunted, primeval boscage straight from Poe or Hawthorne, aswarm with evil spirits and phantasmagoria. A cold, forbidding darkness seemed to emanate from its eldritch bed of soil and mulch and moss; leaves ceased to rustle, no birds could be heard chirping, and even the scurry and scamper of animals seemed to fall quiet. A menace seemed to take possession of oak and chestnut, luring unsuspecting hikers away from the path.

To say that the place ignited my young mind would be an understatement. There was an abandoned gardener's lodge that I imagined to be a witch's hut; hidden on the far bank, easily missed unless one stared directly at it, was the grim ruin of what had once been a limestone mill. The weathered turrets and tower of nearby Tintern Abbey only added to the place's eeriness. At the river mouth, a battlemented stone bridge served as a reminder that Tintern had a military purpose as much as a religious one. A storm of images rioted in my head, all vying to be put into words. One kept burning in my mind whilst all others eventually smoked themselves out – a highwayman, under cover of darkness, lying in wait for his prey under the bridge, his flintlock primed and hatred flaring in his eyes. I had no idea who he was and why he felt the need to do what he was about to do, only that he refused to be evicted from my mind. And, unusually, he did not wear a mask – instead, his features were smeared in ash, crudely imitating a skull.

A Land Without Wolves began, innocuously enough, as a college assignment. In 2013, when I was an English Lit. student in IADT, during a creative writing elective overseen by the poet Katie O'Donovan, we were assigned a short story set in an historical era. The idea of a lone highwayman stalking Tintern Forest re-surfaced like a phantom, and so I began crafting a tale around this figure, lying in wait for his intended target whilst musing on his past and what horrors drove him to lead the life he did. The suggestion that we needed to know more about this man, what drove him to live as he did, and perhaps even offer him a chance at salvation, did not occur to me at first. Rather than forget about it, I kept tinkering around with the story, adding more and more detail that better reflected the era in which this man lived.

It wasn't until I was encouraged by my editors at Temple Dark Books to expand the story into a fully realised novel that I must give him his due. I named him MacTíre, which derives from the Irish for wolf (literally 'son of the country'), due to his zealously friendless nature. I made his story begin in the late 1780s, a full decade before the 1798 rebellion erupted, when the French Revolution was still an ominously simmering rumour, and he found himself bearing witness to a nation on the brink of irreparable change.

The challenges in writing historical fiction are manifold. One gains a sense of duty in staying true to the facts, of setting a story within a long-vanished time and place, and of rendering same with as much accuracy as one can muster. The historical context of 1798 was overwhelming: various Redcoat regiments, the names of various towns and battles that took place before, during and after the insurrection, the names of its primary players. This was long before the smaller details were taken into account: the smell of gunsmoke, the manner in which people spoke to one another, the reality of the Irish landscape.

Hand in hand with all this was the need to tell a rollicking good story populated with compelling characters. I've always had a casual interest in history, though historical fiction was never too prominent on my cultural radar. Writing a full-length novel set in pre-Famine Ireland, therefore, presented a unique array of challenges. Research was crucial if the world that Joseph MacTíre and Mogue Trench inhabited was to be believably rendered on the page. Before I could begin the story aproper, I thought it best to engorge myself on as much historical detail as possible. In addition, I was painfully aware that, at some point, my fictional characters would have to interact with some very real world figures who were by the crucible of 1790s Ireland. Napper

Tandy, John Tohler, and Elizabeth Sugrue are among the few with whom my protagonists find themselves crossing paths.

Much like today, the late 18th century, in both Ireland and across the wider world, was a time of both great progress and grinding poverty. The philosophies of Voltaire, Rousseau, and Montesquieu were beginning to bear radical and often violent fruit. In Ireland, tensions between a Protestant and Presbyterian gentry and a predominantly Catholic underclass would be briefly assuaged by the formation of the United Irishmen in Belfast. Such tensions, however, were not mere disagreements on matters of faith; the warring gangs the Liberty Boys (Protestant weavers from the Liberties) and the Ormond Boys (comprised of Catholic butchers from Smithfield) frequently fought pitched battles on the city's relatively few bridges over their religious affiliations. At the same time, giants of Irish letters such as Swift, Berkeley, Goldsmith, Sterne, Hutcheson, and Burke were at the forefront of popular debate and the nascent marketplace of ideas.

Whilst greater parliamentary independence had been gained thanks to the efforts of Henry Grattan from 1782 onwards, Dublin, the alleged second city of the British Empire after London, remained riven by extreme poverty, gang warfare, exploitation of the lower orders and a colonial administrative chokehold represented by British rule and military presence. Still to come was the Reign of Terror, and the months of galvanised insurgency that would eventually be known as the 1798 Rebellion.

1798 was a brutal and bloody conflict that seems to have been, like many Irish wars, sanitized and glorified to the extent of its darker ramifications being ignored. This means good people on both sides of the conflict are taken by it. No one is ever fully a hero or a villain, no matter how laudatory or corrosive their ideals. Which brought me back to Joseph MacTíre, *A Land Without Wolves'* criminal protagonist.

As I delved deeper into his story, he began to warp and change by the paragraph. He became more than just a black-hearted outlaw; he was cunning, embittered, sarcastic, haunted by execrable traumas to which not even I, as his creator, was fully privy. Nor was he above sharing a joke, and he harboured a love of books that, in the predominantly illiterate society of 18th century Ireland, would have marked him as eccentric at best, and suspicious at worst. I realised he had a deep affinity for the writings of John Milton. The English laureate's sympathetic portrayal of Lucifer, the established corrupter of mankind, showcases how darkness and light, whilst always concurrent with one another, can take many guises and meaning. Like Lucifer, MacTíre inhabits a paradise, albeit one that is perpetually threatened by violence and murderous vendettas which he is ultimately powerless to transcend. The name Lucifer originally meant 'bringer of light', and I have spoken of the Age of Enlightenment's influence on this book.

Alongside the adolescent appeal of being a lone wolf, I've come to view Joseph as a deconstruction of the archetypal highwayman as represented by Dick Turpin and Joseph Wild, and Alfred Noyes' classic poem 'The Highwayman'; as well as of the classic Irish figure of the raparee, who had a distinctly political hue to their crimes. If MacTíre represents anything it is the dark side of freedom, one that ensures you have no allies due to being so solitary in your mission for independence. Mogue comes to realize that declaring war on the entire world out of a misguided (if understandable) sense of revenge isn't the best way to go. I could go with that lens. Eschewing any romantic notions of the criminal figure, I tried to get to the heart of such a man, one who operated cloaked in the shroud of his own self-made myth: a myth that ultimately saw him cut off from rejoining society. For indeed, what can a man's individual freedom measure against those of his fellow citizens?

I began working on it in earnest in a rented rain-lashed cottage on the island of Inishbofin, and immediately found myself confounded by yet another issue: that of getting the novel's narrative voice just right. As a 21st century man writing about the lives of ordinary people from several centuries ago, it felt inappropriate to write in a style that was too contemporaneous. The novel, I had to keep reminding myself, was then only in its infancy. Nonetheless, I read 18th century classics such as Henry Fielding's *Tom Jones*, Samuel Richardson's *Pamela*, Defoe's *Robinson Crusoe*, as well as the memoirs of brothel keeper Margaret Leeson and the boxing champion Daniel Mendoza, to give the background as true an atmosphere as possible. Writing this book was a seemingly endless exercise in grappling with the boundaries of one's knowledge and understanding; it is my hope that most of those boundaries were successfully crossed.

Now that it is finally finished, and the relief of seeing it finished has passed, the grappling I must now do is with its shortcomings, and where it will go. I hope whoever picks it up will get some measure of enjoyment or insight from it, and perhaps even sees the things it was written towards. With a sense of inevitability and no shortage of heavy-heartedness, I must say goodbye to my old friend, the wolfish, ash-smeared highwayman who kept a solitary vigil in the forest of my head throughout the years, see him swagger off into the wider world and hopefully make his impact on whomever he encounters. Such is the way of these pursuits; I hope there's something in these pages that will stay with you.

Daniel Wade, 2021

Gloffary of Termf

Here you will find a select list of colloquialisms and Irish (Gaelic) words, phrases, and salutations featured in the book

blather – meaningless talk

bocage – pastureland divided into small, hedged fields interspersed with groves of trees

Buachaillí Bána – The Whiteboys; an agitator group set up to protect the interests of rural Irish tenants

Cá as duit? – Where do you come from?

cailín – literally 'girl'

Cá raibh tú? - Where were you/where have you been?

Céad míle failte (duit) – A hundred thousand welcomes (to you)

céilí (also céilidh) – traditional Irish social gathering, focusing on music and dance

cottier – a cottage-dweller

charley – colloquial nickname for a patrol member of the Dublin Police (founded 1786)

Dutch Billy – a distinctive type of gable-fronted house dating from the late 17th and early 18th centuries, commonly attributed to Huguenot and Quaker labourers

gargle – an alcoholic drink

gralloch – a hunting blade used specifically for the evisceration of captured animals, chiefly deer

Is mise Ifreann. Anois, beidh aithne agat ormsa – I am Hell itself. Now you shall know me.

jarvey – driver of a horse-drawn carriage

leitheoir – a bookworm (a reader)

meirleach - rebel

milleadh – impairment, ruination, destruction

misneach – courage

moll – a prostitute

plámás – Flattery; manipulation

redcoat – derogatory name for a rank-and-file member of the British Army

ropairí – robbers, scoundrels

Samhain – traditional festival in Gaelic Ireland marking the end of harvest season and the beginning of winter, usually held on the first day of November

Sassenach (var. *Sasanagh*) – derogatory term for an English person; derived from the Middle Irish word for 'Saxon'

sibín – an illicit bar or club where alcohol is sold without a license

Sluagh (na marbh) – literally 'fairy host' or 'host of the dead', a spectral procession or army that appears in the sky

spailpín – an agrarian labourer who roamed the countryside in search of seasonal work

Tá dreach cíocras fola ar gach rud ann – All things appear bloody (lit. *there is an air of blood(iness) upon everything*)

taibshe – an apparition, a spectre

Further notes

The song sung by Redmond MacTíre at the close of Chapter IV is the traditional rebel ballad '*Éamonn an Chnoic*' ('Ned of the Hill'). Ned was an Irish highwayman active in the late 16th and early 17th centuries.

One of the earliest texts Mogue stammers his way through in Chapter XIV is Act I, Scene II of Shakespeare's *King Lear*.

MacTíre's drunken recitation of lines from *Winter*, from James Thomson's *The Seasons* would surely have us all ready for sleep in that flame-crackled cave.

Thank you for reading A Land Without Wolves
Joseph MacTíre would have found the thought amusing indeed.

Printed in Great Britain
by Amazon